The Day She Can't Forget

Meg Carter worked as a journalist for twenty years before turning her hand to fiction. Her features have appeared in many newspapers, magazines and online with contributions to titles including *You* magazine, *Independent*, *Guardian*, *Financial Times*, and *Radio Times*. She is on the advisory committee of Women in Journalism. Meg recently relocated from west London to Bath, where she now lives with her husband and teenage son. *The Lies We Tell* is her first novel.

Also by Meg Carter

The Lies We Tell
The Day She Can't Forget

THE DAY SHE CAN'T FORGET

MEG CARTER

CANELO

First published in the the United Kingdom in 2016 by Canelo

This edition published in the United Kingdom in 2020 by Canelo

Canelo Digital Publishing Limited
31 Helen Road
Oxford OX2 0DF
United Kingdom

Copyright © Meg Carter, 2016

The moral right of Meg Carter to be identified as the creator of this work
has been asserted in accordance with the Copyright, Designs and Patents
Act, 1988.

All rights reserved. No part of this publication may be reproduced or
transmitted in any form or by any means, electronic or mechanical,
including photocopy, recording, or any information storage and retrieval
system, without permission in writing from the publisher.

A CIP catalogue record for this book is available from the British Library.

Print ISBN 978 1 80032 094 9
Ebook ISBN 978 1 911420 47 7

This book is a work of fiction. Names, characters, businesses, organizations,
places and events are either the product of the author's imagination or are
used fictitiously. Any resemblance to actual persons, living or dead, events
or locales is entirely coincidental.

Look for more great books at www.canelo.co

Printed and bound in Great Britain by Clays Ltd, Elcograf S.p.A.

For Martin and Tom

Chapter 1

A road appears through the shifting whiteness. Along it walks a woman.

She is beyond cold. Coatless and sodden, hobbled by city shoes, she staggers forward. Her nostrils flare. Her mind struggles to focus. She doesn't stop to think why she has no coat, or what brought her here, stumbling along this tarmac lifeline, in an ice-bound landscape, however long ago. Yet two things are certain. She must keep walking: left then right, repeat. And she must not turn back.

A tree looms to her left, cresting a brittle verge. The image distracts her; obliterates, for a beat, the approaching pulse of an engine. Almost too late, she decodes the jarring squeak of tyres on snow. A shape emerges, tentatively feeling its way through the fog. It is a white Ford.

Panicking, the woman lurches to a halt, as the car pulls over a short distance away. It waits beside a group of sheep standing by the roadside like an ancient stone circle. No longer lulled by her footsteps and their rhythmic swing, the woman's throat constricts.

Who is this? she wonders, bleakly.

Is it him?

'Excuse me.' The driver of the Fiesta winds down the window and leans out. Her breath hangs heavy in the air. 'Do you need any help?'

'What is it, Mummy?'

The walker looks up. No, it's not him. She is OK. As the child in the back of the car leans forwards for a better view, though, her heart quakes. Where have you been, Baby Boy? Because they are the same age, this child before her and her own. Though the face gazing at her is pale, not golden, with clumsy freckles and copper hair.

No, not Matty.

'Who's the lady? Why's she got blood on her face?'

'That's enough, Billy,' says the driver, calmly, releasing her seat belt. 'Sit tight, OK?'

The door opens and out climbs a slender, auburn-haired woman with a round face. She looks to be in her mid-thirties. A rainbow-knit hooded cardigan hangs loosely over her nurse's uniform. Thick black tights tuck into purple quilted boots that have a dark red stain on the left toe. Spilled wine, perhaps, the walker thinks – I should know. The car door slams shut. Tugging the cardigan tight around her, the driver seems momentarily unsure what to do. After weighing up possible threats, she takes a tentative step forwards.

'My name is Jean,' the driver tries again. Her voice has an unfamiliar burr, Scottish. 'Can I help you?'

The walker struggles to find some words, any words, or an appropriate response. For she has now glimpsed her reflection in the window. Her pale face, smeared with red. Dark flecks in her hair, too. Where have I come from? she wonders, dropping her hand and seeing the red streaks across her right fist.

What. Have. I. Done?

'I think you'd better come with me,' Jean coaxes, reaching out her hand. At the stranger's touch, the walker registers her own skin, cod-cold beneath the damp sleeve of her ripped shirt. She shivers softly as Jean's fingers close around her wrist. 'We can't have you wandering around like this, can we?'

Jean scans the walker's face for any sign of injury but apparently finds none. Despite the scarlet criss-crossing her ashen cheeks. The clots stubbornly lodged in the fine hairs just above her temple. The splash of something on her left shoe, which makes Jean glance down, self-consciously, at her own.

'Been in the wars, too, haven't we. Mmm?' Jean punctuates her words with a reassuring smile as she steers the walker around the front of the car, pausing only once to shoot a warning glance at Billy, who is sitting in his car seat wide-eyed with excitement. Silently, she implores her son to hold his tongue. Then, carefully, she helps the stranger climb into the front passenger seat of the Fiesta.

After helping her with her seatbelt, Jean walks around to the driver's door.

'You're in luck, you know,' she says, lightly, as she carefully executes a perfect U-turn. 'The nearest A&E is only a few miles from here, it won't take long. And you—' Shooting a glance in the rear-view mirror, Jean catches her son's eye. 'You have the perfect excuse to be late for school.'

'Hey!' the boy cries, happily drumming his heels on the back of his mother's seat. 'A real life emergency! If only we had a siren…'

With her eyes fixed on the icy road, Jean reaches forward and twiddles a knob on the dashboard. A sudden burst of rap music makes the other woman flinch. The volume drops as the dial is hastily retuned. As the car pulls away, the stranger's body softens.

Three pips sound and the local DJ starts reading the headlines. Fragments of news from the real world herald the beginnings of a subtle thaw. Stories about falling oil prices. The refugee crisis. The Scottish Government's concern about Britain leaving the EU. A boy missing in Kent. Mid-way through the details, the driver taps the dashboard and the radio falls silent.

The fog is thinning. A T-junction has appeared by the dry stone wall now looming ahead, where they will turn left onto the B-road to the nearest town. The road is clear, apart from pocks of ice and clumps of frozen earth. But the stranger sees none of this, because her eyes are closed.

Jean risks a cautious sideways glance at the passenger beside her, her gaze drawn by something shiny in the woman's hand. It is a chain, stubbornly gripped between her frayed fingers, and from it hangs a silver charm in the shape of a tiny piano.

Chapter 2

Kensington, September 1974

'Over there, Dad! On the left – there's a white Fiesta about to pull out,' cries Alma. Infuriated as she always is by the slowness of her father's reactions, she leans forward to poke her head between the two front seats, then jabs an urgent finger at the gap in the parked cars a short distance ahead.

'White Fiesta?' mutters the Reverend Dean. A pearl of sweat courses the contour of his cheek before dispersing into his salt and pepper beard. Adjusting his black-framed spectacles, he peers once more along the closely-packed cars parked along either side of the street. 'Where?'

'Beneath the sycamore, Gordon,' sighs Alma's mother, Angela. 'Do get a move on, dear, or someone else will get it.'

The car nudges forwards into the empty space. Sinking back into her seat, Alma watches her father's hands clench the steering wheel so tightly the white leather of his driving gloves shines, taut. She scowls.

It has been a tiresome drive into London – far slower than any of them expected, with many ill-tempered drivers stubbornly refusing to give way. She could just as easily have carried a couple of cases up by train – and would have preferred to, only he wouldn't hear of it. Doing the right thing matters most. And if Reverend

Dean's only daughter had travelled alone, what might other people think?

So they drove. But the closer they got, the slower they progressed and her father's mood began to sour. The obvious explanation was bad traffic and the late summer heat. But there was another, his daughter knew. Because for all his grand ambitions, there was one thing that Reverend Dean loathed more than anything – more than blue jeans, garlic, even Tony Benn – and that was change.

A flurry of activity on the pavement draws Alma's attention, as students hurriedly converge on the building ahead. Laden with boxes of books, bags of clothes and armfuls of bedding, they then disappear in an ant-like stream into the building which will be their – and now her – home for the next nine months.

Over the lintel above the main front door hangs a sign welcoming all first year music students. *Freshers '74*, it says, humorously replacing the 'e's with treble clefs. *Quickstep This Way!* Alma eyes the plaque on the wall below bearing the building's name, Engel House. The name sounds elite but fusty, just like her impressions of The Conservatoire when she had first auditioned.

And judging by the assortment of bluestockings before her, she grimaces, the traditional element remains strong.

Yet this privately-run music academy – discreetly tucked away along a south Kensington backstreet – was not the Deans' preferred place of further education for their only daughter. Despite being the best musician in years at Burford High, the girls school Alma attended on a church scholarship, both the Royal Academy and the Royal College had turned her down.

The place in front of her is third best, then. But given that most of the classical performers it turns out will earn a respectable living, it's good enough.

Alma exhales, slowly, and thinks back to when imagining being grown up meant playing in a small chamber ensemble. It was a dream her father was only too happy to indulge. Having bought her a toy piano for her fifth birthday and private tuition before her sixth, he watched his little angel's rapid progress through grades one to eight with swelling pride.

By the time Alma turned ten, she was regularly called on to perform to family, friends and visiting parishioners. She did what was expected, always. But then, around her thirteenth birthday, something changed. Tired of daily practice, she started to rail against the twice-weekly private tuition and the impromptu home concerts, and buck against the never-ending rounds of rehearsals and performances. However, when Burford's third formers chose their O-level options a few months later her future suddenly fell into dreary focus.

The simple fact of the matter was that Alma wasn't much good at anything else. And with little else to set her apart from the less academic girls in her class, chances were she'd end up sleep-walking into secretarial college. Only then did she understand that buried in her music lay the keys to her escape.

As Reverend Dean kills the engine Alma flings open the door and clambers out onto the pavement.

Tilting her face, her gaze roams across the rooftops of the densely-packed townhouses, beyond which, barely glimpsed through the trees, she can just make out a chapel spire and gothic arches. This will do, Alma thinks, letting slip a secret smile at her first taste of the city. Its baked concrete and petrol fumes catch in her throat; the smell of hope. This place promises the perfect antidote to the church-fete, small-town tedium that has defined the boundaries of her life so far. Her salvation.

'Darling,' urges Angela Dean, warily eying the white van roughly parked with two wheels on the kerb a short distance away. 'Kung Fu Fighting' blares through its open window. 'Don't you think someone should keep an eye on the car?'

Alma tries not to laugh at how out of place her mother now seems. So small and awkward in this alien city, far from the South Downs hamlet where she was raised. A closed society where the parishioners are as upright as they are well-heeled and where the local vicar's wife is universally known and respected; her opinion valued, her ministrations to her local community welcomed.

Like her husband, Angela Dean takes pride in doing the right thing, like preparing care parcels for the less fortunate. As a homemaker, she takes pleasure in simple cooking – milk puddings, boiled vegetables, basic stews. Hers is a world in which everything has its place and everyone knows theirs – the complete antithesis, then, to London. To Alma's mother, this alien city with its loose morals, its high rate of crime and now its terrorist threat feels like a jungle.

It's only been two months since the IRA bomb blast at the Tower of London, and everyone has been on edge for weeks in anticipation of another attack. Which almost led to an eleventh-hour change of plan. Thank God, then, for Reverend Dean's blind ambition for his only child. Her father's vanity had narrowly outweighed his wife's anxiety. Without it, Alma would still be at home, her future hobbled. For what I am about to receive may the Lord make me truly thankful, she murmurs, softly.

'You take the navy suitcase and I'll start bringing in some of the heavier boxes,' her father declares, clicking open their car's boot. 'What floor did they say your room is on?'

Reaching into the back pocket of her cotton skirt, Alma tugs free the confirmation letter from the admissions secretary. 'Third.'

'Come along, dear,' he motions to his wife. 'You can bring the potted fern.'

Alma's room would be a spacious bedsit for one, were it not for the two single beds positioned on either side of the large bay window. To the left is a small kitchenette – more an alcove, really. To the right, a wooden door opens into a tiny bathroom that smells of bleach. Beside each bed stands a narrow, white-washed cupboard. Yet with the lower sash of the bay window thrown open, the room's tired furnishings and modest dimensions seem light and airy.

'Hope you don't mind, but I've already taken the one on the left,' announces a slender stranger. Her hooded eyes, sculpted cheeks and bobbed hair, the colour of burnished copper, remind Alma of Faye Dunaway. The girl pauses in the open doorway, as if unsure, before making her entrance. Stepping forward, she introduces herself as Alma's new roommate. Her name is Viola.

Alma straightens her cheesecloth shirt and tucks its hem back into her waistband.

Tall and slim, Viola has a boyish air. But the sharp tilt of her chin and the angularity of her shoulders are confounded by what she is wearing. Her sundress is ankle length and halter-necked with a vibrant pattern of blues and greens. There is a natural, peacock elegance to the way she moves. She has the air of someone who's never bothered to compete, because she knows she's already won.

'The kettle's just boiled,' Viola beams, turning towards Reverend Dean. 'Would you like a cup of tea?'

Viola had arrived only an hour before, she explains as she unwraps porcelain cups and a matching teapot from cocoons of newspaper. Her family are based north of Edinburgh, though thanks to her father's job – something important in finance – they lived for three years in Hong Kong. Her mother is a painter. Her older brother has just left Cambridge, where he read law.

All of this Alma takes in silently as the tea brews, busying herself with opening bags and boxes, though for now she is blind to the contents. Surrounded by small talk in which she plays no part, she feels diminished and infuriatingly child-like. She glances down to check her watch, wishing her parents would leave.

Her attention is snagged by a page of newspaper loosely crumpled on the floor. *County Orchestra Takes Top Honours in Vienna*, the headline reads. But it is to the accompanying picture that Alma's gaze is drawn. The familiar face with its aquiline nose, pale eyes and high forehead topped by a crown of receding silver hair. His expression, staring directly into the camera as if challenging the photographer, makes her shudder.

Sharing the plaudits at the 1974 European Music Festival, reads the caption, *was Burford High School's former head of music, Leonard Parmenter.*

Bending down to adjust the strap of her sandal, Alma deftly crumples the paper into a tight wad then kicks it out of sight beneath the bed. Only when she straightens up does she notice that Viola is watching. Alma holds the other girl's gaze until she looks away.

'So you travelled down from Scotland alone, then?' enquires her father. Perched on the edge of his daughter's bed, he takes a sip of tea.

'I did, but I'm used to that,' Viola demurs. 'I went to boarding school on the south coast, not far from Brighton.'

'St Jude's?' Reverend Dean ventures, carefully placing his cup and saucer on the floor. 'Such a wonderful reputation for its music. We had hoped Alma might…' He hesitates, steeples his fingers, then slowly shakes his head. 'But no, it was not to be.'

Alma frowns.

At Burford, ever since she could remember, she had always been the best.

As a result of her third year epiphany, she practised her music with near religious zeal and even mentored a group of enthusiastic first years. Then, a few months before her A-levels, she led the county orchestra at the grand final of the prestigious European inter-schools youth competition. Yet the rigorous selection process for music college with its assessments and auditions had proven sobering. It wasn't enough to excel at piano: applicants were also expected to be able to demonstrate both vocal skills and theoretical abilities. The first refusal had knocked her confidence, making the second almost inevitable. Only by her third audition, for the lesser-known Conservatoire, did Alma's spirits rally sufficiently to secure a place.

'Take good care,' Angela Dean whispers in her daughter's ear as they embrace. 'And remember to be careful about who you go out with, where you go. Stay central, where there are crowds.'

Avoid Kilburn, Van Morrison, Guinness, books by James Joyce, poetry by Yeats, any West End play by Wilde or, for that matter, George Bernard bloody Shaw, she might as well have added, Alma fumes. As if boycotting all things Irish would make any difference to what was going on in the world. As if, just for one moment, the woman really cares.

True, her parents have made sacrifices to get her to this point. But when did they ever stop to listen to what she said or wanted? And why had they never tried to understand who she is; her hopes and dreams and fears, not theirs?

The stultifying nature of their relationship made Leonard Parmenter's interest in Alma appealing at first. But she doubts she can ever forgive her parents for what happened next. How, when she told them what he did in Vienna, they'd disbelieved her – for fear of the mess that the truth might unleash.

Not so long ago, Alma yearned for a way to patch the snags and dropped stitches in her relationship with her mother and father. But their stubborn refusal to believe her soon made her question why she should even try.

Carefully, Reverend Dean eases each finger back into his driving gloves then turns towards his daughter. Seeing him hesitate, undecided whether to hug her or shake her hand, makes Alma almost choke with rage. But by the time she is monitoring her parents' retreat from the open window, she is calm. As they climb into the car, they do not look up and she doesn't care.

Alma reaches back to release the plaits that have neatly secured her hair since she started school. She shakes her blonde mane free. Then she hears it. Someone singing.

She turns back slowly to face the room.

'Oh you pretty things,' repeats Viola who, having discreetly retreated into the kitchenette while the good-byes were made, is now standing in the narrow doorway. 'Don't you know you're driving your mothers and fathers insane?' Her gaze is steady. 'Gotta make way for the Mother Superior.'

Alma smiles, coolly. 'Isn't it homo superior?'

'Not in my book,' Viola sighs, extracting a silver hip flask from a secret pocket by her thigh, in the right side of her dress. '*Nil carborundum illegitimi*, as my beloved father would say,' she declares, tipping generous splashes of whisky into two of her finest porcelain teacups. 'Now come on, girl, buck up.' With a broad grin, she holds one out towards her new roommate. 'Onwards and upwards, as they say.'

'Well, I'll drink to that,' says Alma, boldly accepting the cup. She has drunk little until now, save for the glass of Harvey's Bristol Cream she was allowed last Christmas.

Now I am in London, I will live life in colour, not in black and white, she silently pledges then blinks, vigorously, as the whisky catches her throat. Her eyes widen in surprise as deep inside her something stirs, like a tiny bird unfurling its wings.

Chapter 3

Scotland, February 2016

The patient opens her eyes and blinks.

Colour, shape and definition come gradually as she adjusts to the world in which she finds herself. A primrose cell crowned by white ceiling tiles. Strip lighting that dazzles. To the left of her bed, there is a vase of unopened daffodils beside a jug of drinking water. To her right, a wipe-down plastic armchair. The smell of antiseptic; safe, but nullifying. The drive to the hospital with Jean now a waking dream.

As she rolls onto her side, the mattress protector squeaks. She stares at the sleet-flecked window. Through the pane, distant mountains loom against a leaden sky.

'Welcome back.'

Startled, the patient recoils. Willing her thumping heart to slow, she turns her head towards the open doorway where a nurse stands. He is in his mid-twenties, dressed in scrubs with cropped beach-blonde hair. Kind eyes, though, she thinks. Moving towards the bed, he reaches up to check a monitor attached to a saline drip. Only then does she register the tube connected to the back of her right hand.

'Well you've had a good sleep, I must say,' he soothes. 'Feel better for it, though, don't you?'

'Yes.' The hoarse croak of her voice is unexpected.

Her body tenses with a sudden terror.

Someone strokes her hand. It is the nurse. And as the patient's fear subsides she gazes at her left arm resting limply on the bed. The bruising around her wrist. The scratches above it. How grey the skin on the inside of her arm looks; skin into which the man now inserts a needle. She tries to object but her mouth seems so small – even just to say no – as the mist thickens. When she wakes it is almost dark.

Her chest is tight. She feels breathless. For she has been dreaming. A terrible dream in which she was trapped inside a strange house with a crenellated façade and a clock tower with a round, Play School window. She was there to visit someone, though she can't recall who. Waiting in a tiny sitting room as her host prepared tea to pass the time. But when she went into the kitchen to offer help what she saw there was – what, exactly? She can't remember. But whatever it was, was unspeakable.

She'd fled into the tiny downstairs bathroom where, balanced on the edge of an old enamel bath, she'd tried to force the window. But the wood was too warped to budge. So she'd dropped to her knees, cowering in the corner on the dusty floor as she'd fought against a welling tide of panic. Gulping back sobs as a fist hammered against the door. Staring in horror at her bloodied hands. Knowing the rusty old hinges would not hold for long.

She rolls onto her side, ignoring the creak of the plastic mattress. The backs of her knees and the small of her back are slick with sweat. The muscles in her legs shake like she's been running. It's only dream, she thinks. Just a bad dream. She must pull herself together. That's what she'd tell Matty.

'How long have I been here?' she wonders out loud. 'Where am I?'

'Belleview.'

The reply comes from a white-coated figure who stands at the window, adjusting the blinds. A doctor, she guesses. He has thick, dark hair, swept back and streaked with silver. 'That's in Fort William,' he adds, turning towards her, and as he speaks an unseasonal golf resort tan is accentuated by the gleam of his teeth. 'You were brought in two days ago. Not to worry if it's still a bit of a blur – it's often like that when we've taken a bit of a tumble.' He pauses, as if for effect. 'I'm Dr Prentiss.'

She is fine apart from minor cuts and bruising. Mild hypothermia, but no evidence of anything else... untoward. The blood remains a bit of a mystery because it was canine, not human, he gently explains. The bump on her head is the most likely cause of her memory loss. She will remain under observation for a day or two and the head trauma specialist will need to check her, just to be sure. But the scan she had earlier is encouraging.

'The police are waiting to speak to you, too, if you're feeling up to it,' Dr Prentiss concludes, moving towards the door. 'They want to do a media appeal – which can help get things sorted when someone's picked up with a dicky memory and no ID.' He smiles. 'In the meantime, buzz a nurse if you need anything.'

Alone once more, she turns towards the flowers. Daffodils with heads still barely opened and petals that are dull and paper-dry. Refocusing on the base of the vase where the water has turned soupy, she notices the silver necklace coiled snake-like by its side. Her hand hovers above it for a moment before she hooks it over her forefinger then holds it up for a closer view. The links of the chain are fine, the detailing on the silver grand piano intricate. Who does it belong to?

For no apparent reason, she starts to cry.

–

The local TV reporter is a sharp-faced brunette whose bitten fingernails belie her brassy confidence.

She arrives at tea time, shooting her own footage on a hand-held digital camera, quizzing her subject with brisk efficiency under the watchful eye of the constable appointed as her minder. The pair are quite at ease discussing the case and its scant details across the foot of the patient's bed. Like I'm not even here, the patient notes, though she is too tired to find this irritating. Too distracted, too, by what the hours ahead might bring.

What effect the TV appeal will have. Who might come.

When the reporter is done, the patient looks towards the window. Snow is falling once more. The flakes are tight and grey. More like ash than the soft and billowy eider flakes of childhood. Closing her eyes she sleeps and as she does she finds a younger version of herself walking on ice. Tentatively pushing forwards, her left foot an inch or two away from her, shifting her balance slightly before pushing forwards on her right. Just like Matty all those years later, the Christmas she took him to the rink at Somerset House.

That's it. Good girl. Left then right, left then—

With a rasp, the skates slowly scored the frozen surface and for a moment she felt her fear subside enough to steal a quick glance downwards. Her own feet, tightly encased in pristine white leather with scarlet laces tied into a double bow, seemed to have taken on a life of their own.

Got you!

The arm around her waist suddenly braced to absorb her weight as her legs shot in either direction and her body began to buckle. Then, before she could fall, she was scooped up into the air and spun around until she started to squeal.

Stop it, she pleaded. Y*ou're making me dizzy. Daddy, please, no!*

The world sharpened as her father gently lowered her back down onto the ice and she found her bearings staring at his feet. He was wearing thick rubber Wellingtons, large and dependable boots with reinforced toes on which she never tired of balancing as he tried to walk. His broad face creased into a grin. His cheek was still flecked with paint from the canvas he'd been working on earlier. His chin, decisively pointed, was the most visible Hamilton family trait she'd inherited. His pale blue eyes danced as he smiled.

Taking her mittened hand in his, Dad gently tugged her back the way they had come; towards the bank and then on to home.

Time to get going. Letting slip an earthy chuckle, he swung her up into his arms once more. *And I've cooked our favourite for lunch.*

Shepherd's pie? Please say it's shepherd's pie. Daddy? It is, isn't it? Tell me it is!

Hoisting her up onto his back, he carried her up the snowy bank to where a wooden bench stood on a patch of level ground. Beneath it sat a plastic bag containing extra jumpers and scarves and a pair of bright red children's Wellies. He lowered her down gently onto the bench. As he unlaced her ice skates, his fingers quickly tickled each foot before boots were slipped back on.

Come on, Zeb – let's go...

'Elizabeth.'

Picking up the plastic bag, Dad slipped her skates inside before setting off at a slow stride towards the line of trees. Eager not to be left behind she hurried after him, stumbling every now and then on the uneven ground that lurked beneath the snow, rubbing her nose which had started to run. Just by the gate she caught him up. Then they walked, hand in hand, along the path towards home.

'Elizabeth?'

Home.

Doctor Prentiss clears his throat before trying once more.

'Elizabeth! I've good news.'

She turns towards the voice, blinded for a moment by the sunshine cutting through the window. For it is morning now and temporarily, it seems the snow cloud has lifted. As her eyes refocus she sees him standing at the foot of her bed, clutching a manila folder with writing on the front she can't make out.

A name, but whose?

'It is Elizabeth, isn't it?' he presses on gently. 'Elizabeth Hamilton?'

No. Not Elizabeth. Or Liza. Lis. Lizzy. Beth.

'It's Zeb.' Not a question, but a statement of fact. Like Matty, never Matthew.

'I'm sorry?'

'Zeb. Not Elizabeth. My name is Zeb.'

'Ah. Right. Zeb. Good, very good.' He pauses for a moment, thoughtfully pinching the bridge of his nose between forefinger and thumb. In that instant she remembers who he reminds her of. Dad. 'Can you remember anything else?'

'Bits and pieces.' Zeb frowns. 'Playing in the snow. Shepherd's pie. My dad.'

She hesitates, uncertain for a moment whether she's thought or spoken this. Grimacing at the sudden, fleeting image of the draughty toilet with its broken window. Approaching footsteps. Glass jam jars on a kitchen counter. The fear which almost undid her. Biting her lip, Zeb says no more.

'An encouraging sign,' he declares. 'And a good start, too, which we can build on with a bit of extra help. It seems the police have had a positive response to the media appeal. A friend of yours from London – a Mrs Christine Allitt, your neighbour – gave the police your name and they've just advised me she's on her way. She's most concerned, it seems – positively insisted she had to come, in fact. Which will certainly help.'

Zeb sinks back against the pillow. London. Yes, that feels right. Maresfield House, that's the name of it. A Victorian building converted into flats. But Mrs Allitt the name means nothing. Her mouth is sticky, ash-dry.

'But how will I what if I don't…?'

–

Mrs Allitt is in her mid-sixties with smoky hair that might once have been auburn. Her face is round with cheeks so uniformly paled by powder that every nuance that might otherwise have added warmth or depth has been obliterated. Short and stout, she wears a mustard-coloured roll neck – to conceal a double chin, perhaps, Zeb thinks. Her skirt is made from a thick plaid of interlocking browns and greens.

But it is the woman's eyes that draw Zeb's attention as she takes a seat at her bedside. Deep-set like currants, just a bit too far apart.

'Miss Hamilton—' the policeman from yesterday begins. 'I'm PC Heath and this is Mrs Allitt – she lives in the flat next to yours on Bridge Street, Camden. And she has very kindly offered to come and see you today in the hope we can help… clear things up.'

Reaching for his notepad, he leans forward. There's something about the way he's sitting – even the toes of his regulation police boots are spotless and meticulously aligned. Disorientated, Zeb wonders for a moment if she is dreaming.

'As I was saying,' he continues. 'Mrs Allitt lives in the same building as you and has done for – how many years did you say, Mrs Allitt?'

'Call me Christine,' says the woman, lowering her voice as she turns towards the policeman, conspiratorially. Like two adults discussing grown-up things they hope I won't understand, Zeb thinks. 'Twenty-five years – that's how long I've lived at Maresfield House.' Turning back towards the bed the woman modifies her voice to a tone more appropriate for a young child or someone who is hard of hearing. 'Though you and I have been on and off neighbours, dear. You've lived there almost a year – this time round.'

Zeb stares at the overnight bag on the floor by the woman's feet, willing herself to remember. Adjusting her gaze, her attention is snagged by the woman's right hand which rests on the patent leather handbag cradled in her lap. The silver Celtic ring jammed onto Christine's stubby forefinger does looks familiar. But how can she be sure? Zeb's eyes narrow. Did PC Heath really need this stranger to travel all this way to identify her? How can he know the woman is telling the truth? Though somewhere, deep down inside her, she senses something *has* happened between the two of them… which she can't quite recall. Unsettled by a sudden and inexplicable stirring of anger, she looks away.

Gently, PC Heath probes further. 'What do you remember?'

The woman in 3a. Mrs Allitt. The carpeted stairs leading upwards from the communal hallway where the day's post is always left in neat piles on the old oak dresser standing against the wall, its carved hoof-like feet askew against the cracked black and white tiled floor.

Zeb meets his gaze. 'Maresfield House.'

The door to the woman's flat, chipped and cracked; the smell of boiled vegetables emanating from somewhere behind it. Zeb knows she has never seen her neighbour's door anything other than sealed or ajar as the woman peers over the thick metal chain, her pale hand clutching the edge of the door.

'Your flat?'

Up the first flight of stairs. Past her neighbour's door. Right along the landing.

'Yes, 3b.'

The policeman says nothing, waiting for her to carry on. Mrs Allitt, however, cannot resist. '3b. That's right – that's your flat. Opposite mine. I keep an eye on the place when you and Matty are away. Feed your cat, Norton. A silver tabby, remember?'

The woman is leaning forward, both hands now clutching the looped strap of her bag from which the plastic ring of a security tag still dangles. Their eyes meet and Zeb stares, hard, until the other woman looks away.

There is something about her neighbour, a certain shifti-ness, that makes her uncomfortable but she'll be damned if she shows it. So, instead, she turns to the window where rods of sunlight now dart through breaks in the cloud.

Eager to return to the landing on the first floor of Maresfield House, Zeb shuts her eyes. She nudges open her front door and peeps inside. Sees her hand reach into her handbag, the one Dad bought her last Christmas, and pull out her keys. Stares for a moment at the chrome letter Z dangling from the keyring then unlocks the door and pushes it open with her knee. Because her arms are full of flowers.

No, that's not right. A wreath.

Looking down at her feet she registers black patent court shoes. The matching tights, opaque. Her scarf and overcoat, her pencil skirt and V-neck jumper beneath. All in black.

Zeb's eyes snap open.

'Don't worry, you're doing really well,' PC Heath soothes, handing her a box of tissues.

'Sorry. It's just it's all a bit muddled…' Zeb mumbles, wiping her eyes.

'As it would be after what you've been through,' Mrs Allitt chips in, steepling her fingers. 'Don't underestimate how stressful the last few weeks have been for you, Eliza-beth.'

With a brisk click the woman releases the catch on her handbag and reaches inside. After a moment or two she tugs out a plastic bag of salted liquorice. She rips off a corner, carefully selects a sweet, then offers Zeb the bag.

'I found them in the shop at the airport,' she purrs, clearly pleased with herself. 'Your favourite.'

Zeb reaches into the bag and pops a sweet into her mouth, but the pungent ammonium chloride kick makes her almost retch. Quickly, she spits the liquorice into a tissue and reaches for the glass of water standing on the bedside table.

Do I really like these? Has the woman done this on purpose?

'Sorry,' she says, regaining her composure. 'I've not had much of an appetite these past few days.'

With a brief nod, the older woman folds down the top of the bag then places the sweets next to the vase of wilting flowers. 'Save them for Matty,' she says with a smile that fails to make it to her eyes. She reaches into her handbag once more she pulls out a set of house keys. 'And while I remember, you'd better keep these. They're the ones you asked me to look after. Don't worry about Norton – I've a spare set, just in case.'

The keys dance for a moment before Mrs Allitt lowers her hand. Zeb rubs her eyes. What if I'm wrong? She's brought my things from home, after all. Come all this way to see me. Her face burns. The policeman clears his throat and the two women look towards him, expectantly.

'I'm sorry, but we really must move on,' he says. 'Now Miss Hamilton, think back. Can you remember anything about coming to Scotland?'

Zeb fixes her gaze on the wall above the door opposite and tries to think. But all she can remember is arriving back in the house that morning. Alone – Matty was with Richard, again. Because she'd had so much on her plate. Too much. And he had loved that, hadn't he? Any excuse to steal some extra time with her son. Richard and his fiancée, Helene, who'd wasted no time positioning herself as Matty's *other mummy*.

He'd told her to take as long as she needed to sort herself out, the patronising shit. *Helene and I will always be here to pick up any slack.* Even though he was Matty's father she'd been expected to be grateful.

'Miss Hamilton?'

Opening her eyes Zeb finds an intangible urgency now pumping in her veins. Like the feeling you get when you've left home but can't remember shutting the bedroom window, or locking the front door. She thinks of Matty. Of the boxes of stuff on her sitting room floor that need sorting. What is she doing here, wasting time? Her memory is a bit patchy, that's all, but it will come back – Dr Prentiss said so.

Home, she now thinks. I should be at home.

Taking a deep breath, Zeb wills them not to press her for too much detail as her mind scrambles to concoct a suitable story.

'I came here for a short break just a few days ago. It's been a tough few weeks,' she freestyles, latching on to Mrs Allitt's earlier comment. 'I really needed to get away. But then while I was out I slipped and banged my head and came to all muddled and confused.' Lies, a voice inside her chides. Every single word, and you know it. Zeb won't falter, though. Now she even manages to force a smile. 'But now I'm starting to remember I'm beginning to feel much… better. Which is why I'd like to leave now. To go home.'

Chapter 4

'Penny for them!'

Seated on the edge of the bathtub brushing her hair with long, firm strokes – twenty-five on the left side of her head, twenty-five on the right, then the same again at the front and back – Alma is frowning at her reflection in the mirror. Putting down her brush, she turns towards the doorway where Viola is standing with her arms folded. Though dressed in black – a ribbed jumper over a pair of charcoal-coloured drainpipes – somehow she manages to look glamorous, not plain.

'Sorry?'

Viola smiles. 'I said, penny for them. What's up? You seem miles away.'

Alma shrugs. 'Well don't take this the wrong way but…'

Her friend's face darkens. 'You're not in the mood?'

'Not really. Look, I'm sorry. It's just I've had period pain all day and, well—' Alma waves a hand towards what she is wearing – her performance outfit, comprising a high-necked black satin shirt, an A-line skirt cut from burgundy cord, black tights and matching court shoes '—I'm not exactly dressed for the part. You don't get much opportunity to eat out and visit clubs where my parents live.'

It's late afternoon on the second Thursday of term and Viola is determined that Alma should join her for a night out on the town to celebrate her twentieth birthday.

With compulsory lessons in theory, harmony and music history as well as one-to-one instrument tuition concentrated over just two days each week, the students are expected to spend the rest of their time perfecting their primary instrument. As practice is banned in the halls of residence, Alma and the other girls spend much of their time in The Conservatoire's main building, drifting between the canteen, bar and common room while waiting for a turn in one of the handful of tiny rehearsal rooms.

Not tonight, though. Viola has bought tickets to see *The Towering Inferno* at the Empire in Leicester Square and booked a table at her favourite Chinese restaurant in Soho to introduce her new friend to the delights of Peking duck and jasmine tea. Later, she hopes to take them to a bar with live music her older brother has recommended, in the heart of Soho.

Initially, Alma was excited. Until Viola let slip she'd invited someone from Imperial College to join them. He is an engineering student called Geoff who the pair met the previous weekend in the neighbouring college's student union bar, which has a reputation for rowdiness thanks to Imperial's almost exclusively male studentship. He bears a passing resemblance to Phil Lynott and, even better, he's in a band. But none of this is a compelling enough reason to convince Alma to play gooseberry.

Despite Viola's nonchalance, Geoff's persistence in phoning her daily over the days since they met makes it only too clear where his interests lie. And who can blame him? Alma thinks as she tugs her brush through stubborn knots of tangled hair. Her roommate is – she ponders what exactly for a moment or two before she has it – compelling.

Beautiful and self-assured, Viola is different to the other girls, most of whom have taken time out between school and college to single-mindedly develop their music skills – touring with local and national youth orchestras, or tutoring younger children. Instead, Alma's roommate spent six months working as an au pair in St Moritz, then another six travelling around the US. Moreover, for all her attempts to affect an attitude of languid disdain towards her music, Viola is a musical all-rounder, able to play piano, violin and flute with equal brilliance. She is also blessed with a powerful singing voice.

While Alma, at just eighteen, is the year's youngest student, Viola is the oldest. No wonder her new friend seems to live life on a different plane. Yet the common ground between them – a sense of otherness, perhaps – has quickly been acknowledged.

Unable to play most contemporary performers' records back home without upsetting her father, Alma is hungry to embrace the city's soundscape and the release it offers from the stifling confines of the vicarage. Heavy metal music blares from the open windows of Gabor House, the nearby Imperial College hall where Geoff lives. Then there is the darker, harsher style of the underground New York bands whose imports are all the rage on the record stalls of Portobello Road. Joni Mitchell. Some soulful Tamla Motown tracks.

Richer, deeper musical influences seem to seep from the corners of this new world. Everywhere apart from within the hallowed confines of The Conservatoire, whose great and good pride themselves on the purity of its focus – a goal every student is expected to pursue. And everyone she's encountered so far seems more than willing to conform. With one exception.

Viola has come to London with one ambition: to compose and perform her own music. Her aim is to deepen her musical education on her own terms at her parents' expense, she confided over vodka and blackcurrant that first night in halls. So from the outset she's merely gone through the motions, doing just enough to keep the teachers happy while scanning the latest ads for musicians wanted in the *NME*. Not that she'd admitted this to her family or any of her tutors.

How about you? her roommate demanded later on that first day, pinioning Alma with a quizzical stare. *What do you want to do – you know, with all of this?*

Her tongue loosened by the unfamiliar collision of mixers and spirits, Alma laughed. For she'd not thought about her studies like this. Beyond getting here she'd not had much of a plan. A chance to wipe the slate clean; perhaps to start again? But no, that wasn't right. Bad stuff had happened, and would happen again. What was important was how you dealt with it. To not let it define you. That's what Jean-Claude had said.

I'm not sure – not yet, Alma had replied. *Find out how to be me, I guess.*

'Can't decide what to wear?' Alma shrugs. Viola pulls her roommate to her feet. 'Well if you're looking for style advice you're looking at the right person.'

Half an hour later, with only a bath towel wrapped around her, Alma steps over the tangle of Viola's clothes the pair have strewn across the floor. Hanging over her arm is the winning combination: a plum–coloured cock-tail dress – a perfect match for the high–heeled sandals Alma wore for her final prize giving, and a nearly new men's jacket; no tights.

Taking a seat at the dressing table, she pulls her hair back from her face then stares at her roommate in the mirror. Freshly showered and wearing only a calf-length satin dressing gown with a multi-coloured dragon motif, Viola seems oblivious to the fact that the fabric now gapes open almost to her navel as she casually flicks through a dog-eared magazine.

Could I ever get away with it? Alma wonders, quickly finding herself transfixed by the unbroken sweep of Viola's tan. The upward slope of her nipples. The shallow scoop of her tiny breasts.

Look like… be like… that?

'Have you ever cut hair?' she blurts, awkwardly.

'Often,' Viola replies, meeting her gaze. 'Why?'

Staring at the thick blonde mane that almost reaches her waist, tears begin to well in Alma's eyes. It has taken her years to grow and she loves it. Used to, at least. But that was before those few days in Vienna. 'Please. Cut mine.'

Casually retying the gown around her, Viola rises to her feet. 'OK. A shorter style always suits a heart-shaped face. But your hair – it's beautifully thick. Are you sure?'

Alma nods and Viola takes up position behind her, staring at her face intently as she raises a handful of hair and scrutinises the effect as she slowly moves it up and down. Their eyes meet and they stare at each other for a moment. Is this a good idea? Alma wonders. She won't make me look monstrous, will she? But that's ridiculous. As if someone like me could pose any kind of threat to someone like her.

'Don't look so worried,' her roommate chuckles. 'Really, I have done this before.'

At the first snip Alma shudders. Not at the sound of the scissors, but at the memory triggered by a stranger's touch. The stubbiness of his fingers as he ran them through her hair. His quickening breath. The warmth of his lap. He shouldn't have done it, taken advantage like that. A man in his position of responsibility. Chairman of an educational trust, for goodness sake.

Call me Uncle Leonard, he said that first time.

It began when she was little, playing sardines amidst the bushes and trees in her parents' back garden. Spinning her round and around until she laughed so much, begging him to stop, that tears ran down her face. Slipping her sweets when no one was watching. Sherbet Fountains, acrid and sweet. Dib Dabs. One time he even bought her sugar cigarettes tasting of banana.

Just for fun, he whispered, every time. *Our little secret – just for fun*.

Leonard Parmenter, former head of music at Alma's old school and patron of the county orchestra, had touched her many times since. But Vienna was different.

It happened on the night they got through the semi-finals of the European inter-schools youth orchestra competition. She'd returned to her room early with a headache; he'd knocked on the door to check she was all right. He seemed louder and more animated than usual, she remembered thinking as they exchanged pleasantries in the open doorway. Then suddenly, with some weak excuse or other, he'd breached the divide. Stepped into her room, and closed the door.

With the lock secured, Leonard Parmenter sat down on the side of her bed and tugged her onto his lap. Before she knew it he was playing with her hair, his hot breath thick against her neck. Slipping his hands down, then lower. Running the tip of his forefinger around the edge of her pants. Holding her firmly so she couldn't clamber off. Gambling that the shock of it would buy her acquiescence. Which it did – even while he wiped himself down with her towel afterwards, the one she'd brought from home.

Once he'd left it took what felt like hours to rub away his touch beneath a scalding shower. The humiliation at the thought of how frightened and confused she'd been. He was her father's age and she had struggled to resist his benevolent interest. Afterwards, however, she felt tainted. Dirty. Because the dawning realisation of what he had always wanted made her feel complicit.

She got dressed and crept out into the corridor in search of her friends. But all the rooms allocated to the young musicians were empty. Fearful of bumping into him if she went back downstairs, Alma made her way back along the corridor towards her room. Before she could reach it, however, a figure appeared at the far end of the landing.

He was a flautist from one of the French orchestras. Two years her senior. Dark-eyed and strikingly handsome. He spoke little English but when he saw she was upset his concern was genuine. If anyone had taken advantage it was her, not him. When she invited herself inside, asked for a drink, accepted his offer to share a joint. And as she leaned towards him, willing him to kiss her, she knew that now she was in control.

The time and place were of her choosing, no one else's. If Uncle Leonard pushed things further, well, he'd find he was bloody well too late.

It hurt, though the French flautist had been gentle. And still, months after that night, her conscience pricked at the memory of it – not the blood on the sheets, but the look on his face. His expression of... reproach. For she had duped him, they'd both known that. And she had laughed. As she did again the following day when their eyes locked across a crowded stage at the awards presentation.

Her orchestra came second – to St Jude's; his third. And that was it: she never saw Jean-Claude again.

Though Alma tried to tell her parents about Uncle Leonard when she got back home, they wouldn't listen. He had already phoned to let them know how badly she'd behaved. How stubborn and surly she'd grown. How rude she was when he'd chastised her. That a number of the girls had been gossiping about Alma engaging in heavy petting with a young French musician.

The shame of it, they said.

Now, looking back, Alma can only marvel at her parents' unassailable belief in the goodness of their friend. How their blind faith in him served only to stoke a growing despair in the waywardness of their only child. The thought of his fat, stubby fingers inside her. How brazenly he'd lied. The injustice of it. All of this had marked her, deeply. Even so, she'd never allowed it to make her cry. Until now. And as the tears finally spill, hot and fast, she is conscious only of the sound of Viola's scissors.

'Christ, I'm so sorry, but I thought you wanted—'

Alma's eyes snap open. The first thing she sees is her roommate's expression: she looks anxious. 'Don't worry,' she interrupts. 'That's not why I... Really, it's something else.'

Her voice falters. Because she has a fringe — just a wispy one, and as she turns her head she notices the layers Viola has cut into the side to give it shape. Her face looks different. The new style accentuates the roundness of her pale grey eyes, making her cheeks look more sculpted, softening her chin. Shaking her head from left to right, Alma takes pleasure in the novelty of how freely she now moves.

Emboldened, she starts to tell Viola about Leonard. Just a few, brief facts at first. Then as she sees how closely the other girl is listening, outraged on her behalf, more detail tumbles forth. Like how soon after, Leonard moved to Bristol — a precautionary measure. How he kept a low profile for a while until, buoyed by the realisation that she must have said nothing, he sent a good luck card which arrived the week before Alma left for London.

Wishing you all the best, my dear. She can still see the handwriting; his old-fashioned, curling hand. *I look forward to treating you when I'm next in town very soon.*

The message, which she ripped into confetti, cast a pall over her final days at home and the excitement she might otherwise have felt at her imminent escape. Now, though, as she stares at the coil of hair dangling from Viola's hand as if weighing up the old life it embodies, something inside her shifts. Besides, even if Leonard does come, chances are he won't even recognise her now.

'No one's going to treat me like he did,' Alma concludes, lightly. 'Ever.'

'Too right,' Viola exclaims. 'Us girls have got to stick together in the face of creatures like that. Fuck Leonard, that's what I say, and all dirty old sods like him. Now come on, you. Let's get gorgeous, hit the town and have some fun.'

Chapter 5

Scotland, February 2016

Zeb stood on the doorstep, waiting. Wondering if, having knocked twice already, she should try again. Because she had come to see someone and it was important.

With a shiver, she braced against the quickening wind. Fought, too, the temptation to once more glance up at the front of the house and its curious tower with the Cyclops eye. She cast a quick glance back down the hill from where she'd come, towards the village with its street lights just flickering into life. Up here on the hillside, with its craggy skyline, night already seemed to have fallen. Then, as she was convincing herself to return the following morning, a figure appeared spotlit in the doorway.

The woman stood with hands on hips. A good ten to fifteen years older than Zeb, her face was half-cupped by a loose tendril of grey hair which had slipped free from an otherwise meticulous bun. Her floral housecoat was made from some kind of wipe-down plastic. An old pair of sheepskin slippers were perched on her feet. But though she stared at the visitor intently, her expression was not unfriendly.

Lost your way, mmm? the woman offered, not unkindly. *It's not unusual*, she nodded, pre-empting Zeb's answer. *We're a satellite navigation black spot, according to my son.*

Mrs Duffy? I'm looking for... your lodger.

Zeb wakes in an instant.

Her heart is galloping.

Disoriented, her eyes dart around the room to make sure, registering with relief this time the full-blown daffodils, the plastic armchair, the curtained window and the half-light battling to poke through.

It is morning and this is the hospital, she tells herself. I am in Belleview. Somewhere near Fort William. Safe and well. Even if my head is pounding. Even if, try as I might, I can't place the setting for the doorstep scene that is already fading, fast.

She rubs her eyes as she struggles to remember, desperate for a clear outline of the image already fading in her head. But now the fog is regathering, pushing her further from the truth that lies just beyond.

Scotland, it looked like Scotland, she thinks. But as she battles to recapture the views from the hillside, she fears with a sense of dread that she can't be sure she was ever on that doorstep. Somehow she knows it was her. That she was there. And that she was lured there, so far from home, by something momentous. Something that led to her wandering, cold and frightened, along that icy road before she met Jean.

Zeb considers this for a moment. Stares into the blackness. Feels her fledgling resolve start to liquefy. Because not knowing what happened to her during those lost hours is dreadful. Once more, her body starts to shake as she stares at the white plastic control panel on the mattress beside her. The rubber cable connected to it loops twice around the metal bed frame before plunging out of sight behind the pillow towards the floor.

It would be so easy, she thinks. To call for help. Only she knows she shouldn't. Mustn't. That by admitting her fear and confusion about what may or may not have happened, what is real and what is not, she will be forced to stay. *If I can just keep it quiet I'll be discharged a little later today,* she decides. *It is a dream, that's all. Something formed in my subconscious from strands of stories I've read and films I've seen. Unrelated to whatever happened. Nothing to do with me.*

Rolling onto her side, Zeb reaches for her watch on the bedside cabinet. Mrs Allitt brought it, she remembers, along with the bag of things from home that now sits on the floor. The familiar sight of both is reassuring.

Not long now, she thinks, *and I'll be on my way. Back to Matty.*

–

'Hello.'

'Richard? It's me.' Zeb tightens her grip on the phone. The hospital corridor is busy and she has to block her free ear with her left hand to dull the prattle of voices.

'I can't take your call right now. But leave a brief message after the tone and I'll call you back as soon as I can.'

Irritated at being confounded – still – by her ex-husband's halting telephone manner, Zeb frowns. *Where is he?* she wonders, checking her watch. It's just before twelve. A meeting, perhaps. Though he rarely leaves his corner office on the ninth floor of the DeHaan building at Heron Quays – unless on official business with one of his company's dockland neighbours, of course. A client meeting. Or out for an early lunch with Helene.

Her mood darkens at the thought of the soon-to-be second Mrs Richard Latham, a twenty-nine-year-old lawyer with a double first from Cambridge – and the four-storey house in Bayswater they've recently moved into. But then there's a tone, and silence to be filled, so she starts to speak.

'Richard. It's Zeb. On – um, Thursday. I'm fine, now, and on my way back home. From Scotland...' She grimaces. Too much detail, as always. Get to the point, for God's sake. 'Anyway, I'm just calling to speak to Matty.' To see how you are, Baby Boy. What you've been up to. Whether you've missed me. When you're coming home. She lets slip an involuntary sigh. 'Call me later when you get this, OK? But on my home number as I've a problem with my mobile—'

Her phone had been in her bag – the one Dad gave her last Christmas – which she lost a few days ago, somewhere in Scotland. Along with her purse, all her cards, keys, coat and God knows what else. She can't think how she would have coped if Christine hadn't brought her overnight bag. Or the cash Zeb had left in her flat on the table by the front door, which was more than enough to keep her going until her new bank cards came through.

'—I'll be back there in a couple of hours, OK?'

Replacing the handset Zeb exhales, slowly.

She is still dressed in her hospital gown, though over this she wears a zip-up hooded sweatshirt and a pair of sheepskin slippers from London. She could have changed sooner, she thinks, staring for a moment at her right wrist which is still encircled by a white plastic hospital ID wrist-band, but somehow that would have felt like tempting fate.

Glancing along the corridor, Zeb sees Dr Prentiss, flanked by a huddle of junior doctors, emerge from the ward two down from hers. They are coming her way, which means she won't have to wait for too much longer.

Home, she tells herself, lightly. I'm going home.

Though as she says it, all she can think of is the three bedroom semi in Chiswick which she, Richard and Matty shared up until a year ago.

Glumly, she shakes her head. In recent months she's moved back into the small two-bedroom flat her dad bought years ago and had let her stay in when she first arrived in London. Zeb frowns. After meeting Richard, she never dreamed she'd have to live there again.

No wonder the word 'home' feels so hollow.

—

'Nice top.'

Zeb's fingers freeze around the cotton-covered button she is trying to ease through its corresponding hole. As she looks up, the face peering around the door – yet another nurse – creases into a warm smile that seems more than merely professional. And then she recognises her – the woman who'd picked her up and brought her to safety. Billy's mum.

'Sorry, I didn't mean to take you by surprise,' Jean continues. 'It's just I've not been in for a couple of days. I thought I'd pop over and see how you were doing.'

'That's really good of you.' As Zeb's hand relaxes, the button slides into position. Straightening her blouse, she rises to her feet. 'I was hoping to see you before I left. I well, I wanted to say… thanks.'

Jean waves her hand dismissively. 'Really – anyone would've done the same.'

The shoes she is wearing have thick rubber soles and the dark leather uppers are stained with tidemarks of salt from the slushy pavements outside. *Steaming*, Zeb thinks. That's what Dad always recommended for cleaning stained shoes. A good steam then a firm rub with a wire brush.

'Though you had luck on your side,' Jean continues, her eyes skimming the clothes and other bits and pieces Mrs Allitt had brought with her, which now lay across Zeb's bed. 'Billy and I had spent the night at my mother's – we don't normally come that way. So. You're away today, then?'

'Yes,' Zeb replies with greater certainty than she feels. Finally, she has a clear image in her mind of where she lives, the photography museum where she works as education officer, the view from the window opposite her desk. Yet still has little idea of what occurred between arriving in Scotland and waking in hospital.

Dr Prentiss had begrudgingly discharged her at lunchtime. Now she's gambling on the fog still obscuring her view lifting, soon. But what if it doesn't? The thought is frightening, but now she's feeling stronger she'll just have to deal with it. For Matty's sake.

'And you're OK, now?' Simple words, almost innocent, though Jean's stare feels forensic.

'Fine, thanks,' Zeb mumbles, noting another lie. Something bad did happen; something worse might still.

'I can remember most of what happened, now, and hour by hour more bits and pieces come back.' She takes a deep breath before continuing as she focused on the script she's spent much of the previous night writing.

'I came for a long weekend, you see. I hired a car at the station and found a place to stay in a village not far from where you found me, but while I was out walking the weather took a turn for the worse and I had a fall. When I came to it was snowing and I couldn't find my coat or bag. And it was so hard to see I couldn't tell which way to go...'

A thought stops Zeb in her tracks. There was blood on her when she was found: dog's blood. And she's been struggling to account for it. But maybe Jean won't remember because this particular detail has not been released to the press.

'So I picked a direction and started to walk,' she presses on, scooping up the rest of her belongings then stuffing them into her case and clicking it shut. Zeb conjures a laugh but the sound is tinny. 'Anyway, you know the rest.'

Jean stares at her for a few seconds that seem never-ending until, abruptly, she rises to her feet. 'Mystery solved then,' she declares brightly. 'Well you've certainly had a time of it, I must say. But at least you're on your way home now.'

'Yes,' Zeb laughs, hoping the other woman can't see the tell-tale flush of deceit now branding her cheeks. 'It's certainly a relief.'

'Quite. Well. Good luck then. And have a safe trip.' Jean takes a couple of steps towards the door then turns. 'Oh, I almost forgot.' She fumbles in the pocket of her nurse's uniform then pulls out a piece of folded A4 which she holds out towards Zeb with a fleeting smile.

The makeshift card flaps open, revealing a message carefully printed in multi-coloured crayon. DEAR PIANO GIRL GET WELL SOON! it reads in big bold red capitals. LOVE BILLY. But as she closes the card to admire the drawing on its front, Zeb's legs almost buckle.

The picture is of a blue-faced woman with pale eyes and matted hair walking coatless and barefoot along a white road. A short distance behind is a tall, grey house with snow-topped battlements and, to one side, a clock tower with a round window. Standing between the two is a giant blunt-nosed dog with yellow eyes.

Reaching for the glass on the bedside table, Zeb drains its contents, trying to erase from her mind the memory of dog's paws clawing at a kitchen door.

But all she can now hear is the click as the catch slipped – before the creature, hackles bristling, skittered towards her across the floor. The rumbling crescendo from its growl. The way it paused before it leaped, weighing her up with a mathematical eye.

Zeb shakes. Jean doesn't seem to notice.

'That's Billy for you,' the other woman chuckles. 'Obsessed with animals. Can't draw a picture without putting one in. It's the dog that lives in the big house just up the road from where we found you. It really is a beautiful spot with stunning views of the mountains on a clear day – you should come back sometime and see it at its best.'

Pressing her fingernails into the soft flesh of each palm, Zeb's fear subsides as she focuses not on past but present and self-inflicted pain. Calm yourself, girl, a voice inside her soothes. Jean knows nothing; how could she? She forces her face into a smile.

'Tell him I love it,' Zeb lies.

Chapter 6

Weaving left then right between the crowded tables, Alma makes her way back towards the backlit bar where Viola is seated on a high stool.

It is almost midnight, and they are in the public bar of a private members club called Number Nineteen, which occupies four floors of a Georgian townhouse on Soho Square. From the outside, darkened windows make the building look empty. Inside, the bar is thick with cigarette smoke and raucous chatter. An acoustic session by an Irish youth with a mournful voice has just finished but, though it's late, none of the clientele are showing any inclination to leave yet.

'We were about to give up on you,' Viola cries, playfully brushing a stranger's arm off her shoulders.

Resuming her seat, Alma reaches for what's left of her third glass of sparkling perry. 'Sorry,' she says, raising her voice to be heard above the roar of voices. 'There was quite a queue.'

'Here you are, one for the road!' declares a lanky figure wearing a black long-sleeved shirt, skin-tight trousers and leather boots. Stepping over his donkey jacket, which he's left slumped on the floor, Geoff hands each girl a fresh drink.

43

Alma grins her thanks. Though Viola is old enough to drink here, she is not. But with her roommate's admirer buying, no one seems to notice let alone care.

With his angular jawline and dark, expressive eyes Geoff is, as Viola hinted, extremely good looking. More importantly, he is quick-witted and considerate and has been suitably attentive towards Alma despite the palpable attraction he feels for her glamorous roommate. He has just been telling them about the band he's in; he's the drummer; they will be placing an announcement for a singer in *NME* soon. Viola is now intent on persuading him to delay the ad and let her audition first. It's all far more exciting than his engineering degree.

Alma takes a large sip from her glass then looks away as Geoff turns to whisper something in Viola's ear.

Low ceilings, dimmed lighting and casual formality make the place thrilling for being precisely the kind of place Alma knows her parents would hate. These people are without a doubt a most curious assortment, she reckons, surveying the room once more. A group too eclectic for either the post-theatre or the after-work office crowd.

In every direction, groups of men in dark suits are interspersed with heavily made-up young girls in high heels and low-cut dresses. Girls not much older than her. There are a handful of older women with powdered faces and back-brushed hair, too. And at a table in the far corner, two West Indian men in black roll-necks and cord trousers.

Alma's gaze lingers on a figure standing at the bar a few feet away. A young blonde woman – girl, rather, for she looks barely old enough to have left school – with stiff, lacquered hair teased into a Sixties-style beehive.

She is wearing a glittering green dress and high-heeled silver sandals. Yet though she is enviably slender, something waif-like about her makes the elegant clothes she is wearing seem borrowed. Alma's attention slips to the ring on the third finger of the woman's left hand – prominent on the band encircling it is a cluster of emerald stones set within a halo of diamonds. As Alma stares, the woman-child steps into the crowd and starts making her way towards the rear door. With the film companies that line nearby Wardour Street so close, Alma wonders with a shiver of excitement whether perhaps some of these people are actors or directors.

'Hey, you! I said, will you be all right here for a minute? We won't be long.' Viola is now on her feet, leaning into Geoff whose eyes are shining.

'Sure,' Alma nods.

The pair retreat hand in hand through the throng, edging their way towards the end of the bar then out of view through the doorway at the end leading to the public toilets. As the door swings too, Alma sees the couple slip together into the Gents. She smiles to herself as she toys with her drink.

'Mind yourself!' someone close by suddenly exclaims.

Too slow to take evasive action, Alma watches helplessly as her glass is knocked from her hand by a short blond man carrying a metal tray of freshly-poured beers. As the drink clatters to the floor, sparkling wine drenches her right arm and thigh.

'Idiot!' the voice beside her continues. 'Hey, Brian. Any chance of a towel down this end?'

The barman, a balled fist of a man in tight black trousers and a crisp white shirt, turns their way. His shaved head and close-set eyes give him an air of calculated menace. Yet when he recognises the tall stranger now standing by Alma's side, his face is transformed by a broad smile.

'Here,' the man called Brian calls, tossing a clean beer towel in the dark-haired man's direction. 'Better not let the old man see you're here, though,' he warns the stranger now dabbing her sleeve. 'He's in, you know. They've just gone upstairs.' He winks. 'Him and the child bride.'

The dark-haired stranger hands Alma the towel.

He is a man not much older than her, with dark, unruly hair and pale eyes, she notes as she pats her leg dry. Unlike the rest of the bar's clientele, he is dressed in jeans and a Rolling Stones' T-shirt. A camera is looped over his shoulder, and a faded army jacket is hanging from his hand. With his high cheekbones and the dimple in his chin, he is striking. And in this light, Alma can't help but notice, his eyes look cornflower blue. As their eyes lock, her cheeks burn.

'Can I get you another?'

Alma feels tongue-tied. 'Sorry?' she mumbles, at last.

'Another. Drink.'

'Sure. Yes. Thanks.'

'Same again for the lady here, and a quick pint for me. I guess you heard what happened?'

The barman shrugs. 'I've been working since three.'

'Another bomb. At some members' club off Piccadilly. Heath was just round the corner, only he said he didn't think it was intended for him, according to the Nine O'Clock News. Three staff were injured. West of Regent Street's pretty much gridlocked.'

Alma's eyes widen.

It is a little over a year since a bomb exploded in a snack bar at Euston Station, and in the previous few months

46

there has been an attack on Parliament and a blast at the Tower of London. Another IRA attack – it has to be, though she can't bring herself to say it. She checks her watch. She wonders for a moment what her parents are doing; whether they are still awake. But of course they will be – her mother, certainly, unsettled by the news. She should call them to let them know she is OK.

'Christ.' The barman shakes his head then, with a frown, casts a glance towards the bar's rear exit. 'Only—'

'Yes, Brian, I heard you,' the man beside her sighs. Reaching into the back pocket of his jeans, he tugs free a folded brown envelope. 'Can you give Phil this? I just got paid for a commission for *The Post* which means I've got him the rent I owe. Plus whatever the drinks are, of course.'

'Sure.'

The barman holds a fresh drink out, which the stranger now takes and hands to Alma. 'Sorry about the spill.'

'Thanks,' Alma smiles, raising her glass in a silent toast.

The man grins. 'My sort-of-stepdad owns this place.'

'Sort of?'

'My mother's ex,' he sighs. 'It's a long story. Enough to say we don't exactly see eye to eye.'

'Yet you get on well enough to be his tenant.'

The man laughs. 'Well yes, you've got me there. There is indeed a certain irony to that. But needs must. One day, soon, when I can support myself through my photography, I'll be able to afford to have principles. Until then…' He shrugs. 'So tell me, what brings you this way?'

Alma shrugs. 'I'm a music student. I'm here tonight with my roommate and her friend.' She casts a quick glance around the bar which is slowly beginning to empty. 'They won't be long.'

The stranger pulls a packet of cigarettes from his trouser pocket then holds it out, watches as Alma takes one, carefully lights a match then offers it cupped in his hands. 'So where are you from then, with a voice like that?'

'Hampshire.'

His eyes widen in mock surprise. 'Never been. Should I?'

'Well that depends.' She laughs, tentatively.

'On what?'

'Whether you like cricket, ponies, homemade cream teas, Jane Austen.'

A sudden image of the handsome stranger before her dressed in casual slacks and a tweed jacket, walking along the local high street on a Saturday afternoon, makes laughter bubble in her throat. She wonders what he'd look like in smarter clothes; how his hair looked fresh from the shower.

Alma uncrosses then recrosses her legs.

'And do you?'

'No, not really,' she stammers. 'Well, not enough to stay.'

The rectory. Burford Girls School. Holidays in Dawlish. Dreams of the big city. Escape. She can't stop herself, the words come so fast. And although she realises she is tipsy, she can sense his interest. The encouraging roll of his eyes. The flirtatious twitch of his lips. The brush of skin on skin as just for a moment, as he reaches for his glass, his fingers flicker across her hand.

'So you ran away to an exclusive music academy in Kensington,' the man murmurs, shifting position on his stool. Though his leg doesn't quite touch hers, Alma can feel the warmth radiating from his thigh. The pure physicality of it is thrilling.

48

She pulls back. 'Now you're making fun—'

'No, it was just an observation. What do you play?'

She takes another sip of her drink. 'Piano.' For the first time Alma notices an upright piano pushed against the back wall.

Her companion nods. 'Of course. You must be good – to get into music school, I mean.' He smiles. 'It must be fun to be able to devote yourself to something like that. Something you really want to do.'

'I suppose so. I mean, I thought it would be but I'm not sure I'd call it fun now.'

He puts down his glass. 'Why, what changed?'

'I guess I did. I don't know—' she replies, caught off guard. '—Thought it would be different, but The Con—music college feels like being back at school.'

'You want more.' Dropping his voice, he leans forward in his seat.

'Yes, I suppose I do.'

'Action. Adventure. Romance?'

She looks up sharply. Is he teasing? 'No,' she retorts, shifting position in her seat. 'Just a bit of reality will do.'

His face darkens. 'It's over-rated.'

'So how long has your sort-of-stepdad owned this place?'

'A year or two – he won it in a game of poker. His day job is running a property company – buying and renting out flats, that kind of thing.' He hands her the book of matches he used to light her cigarettes. On one side is the name of a pub in east London, The Bricklayers Arms, on Rivington Street. 'He owns this one, too – my flat's on the floor above.'

'And what about your real dad?'

'He's dead.'

Alma bites her lip. 'Sorry.'

He shrugs. 'Don't be. It happened a long time ago. I barely remember him.'

'That's tough.'

'It was for a while, but we got through it.'

'We?'

'Mum and me.' He nods towards the distant barman. 'And Brian over there – my sort-of-stepbrother...'

'Your sort-of-stepdad's son?'

'That's the one. He might not look like much but he's heir to the empire.' He shakes his head. 'Not that I'm bitter, or anything. I wouldn't want it, anyway. It's just... well, his old man's a bully. The only reason Brian works here is that he's got nowhere else to go. His dad traded in my mum for a younger model, did I mention that? And now she's pregnant.' He finishes his drink. 'Sorry. I mean, Christ. Why the hell did I tell you all that?'

Alma grins. 'Maybe I've got a sympathetic face?'

'Hey,' a low voice hisses.

The barman, who has appeared once more at their end of the bar, is repeatedly nodding his head towards the main exit beyond which a wide staircase leads down one floor to street level. A squat figure in a dark suit is talking animatedly with one of the two West Indians – a man in a brown two-piece suit – who, having left his companion seated at their table, is now standing with arms crossed in the open doorway.

Brian narrows his eyes, conspiratorially. 'Your cue to leave, I think.'

'Sorry, sorry!' Viola declares, reappearing at the same moment arm in arm with Geoff by her side. 'I bet you were about to give up on us, weren't you? Only, really, there was such a queue! And now I've lost my lighter.'

Waving the unlit cigarette she is holding in one hand, she reaches with the other for the book of matches still sitting on the bar and hands it to her escort. 'Any chance you could oblige?'

'Actually, we've just been talking,' Alma starts to explain as Geoff lights a match and leans forward. But when she turns around to introduce her friends the stranger has gone.

Chapter 7

Closing her eyes, Zeb fights a pulsing wave of nausea that's over almost as soon as it's begun. She is standing on the kerb just outside Maresfield House in Camden Town while the cab driver extracts her bag from the back seat. Her head is spinning.

Perhaps Dr Prentiss was right. Maybe she should have stayed in hospital a few days longer. But she'd been so keen to get back to London. So sure, too, that being back home would fill in the remaining blanks in her memory. Because she'd decided she would be fine, for Matty's sake. That was how she'd found the strength to not let them see how she was really feeling. Vulnerable. Exposed.

As the moment passes, leaving her abruptly aware of a brisk wind that nips to the bone, Zeb shudders.

Staring up at the cracked stone steps leading to the front door, Zeb sees the white plastic numbers – a four and a three, the bottom half of which has long been missing. The ground floor flat in this three-storey townhouse with its mismatched bricks is owned by the assistant manager of the NatWest on the High Street. The top floor, with its windows shrouded by net curtains, belongs to an itinerant IT consultant called Neil. But she is drawn to the slatted blinds of the two-bedroom flat on the floor in between. The place she calls home.

'Don't forget this, luv.'

The taxi driver, a man of rugby dimensions with a grey crew cut, holds out her bag. A sudden smile reveals a cracked front tooth hanging at an odd angle from his upper gum like a stalactite.

Zeb rethreads her woollen scarf beneath her upturned collar. Pulling two twenties from her bag to cover the fare from the airport, she tells him to keep the change. Stepping towards the front door, she scans the three buzzers on the entry system fixed to the wall on her right. The middle one boasts a neatly typed label detailing only her initial and surname.

Best not to advertise you're a single girl living alone, Dad had said; a warning issued the day she moved in on a lead-skied afternoon not unlike this one. He'd driven up specially despite the fact she'd been living in London almost three years by then, working her way through an array of pointless jobs. Phone canvasser for a market research business. Office manager for an independent travel firm. PA to the director of a graphic design company – until it went bust.

Zeb shakes her head. All those months struggling to find a niche, having dropped out of art school. Because she'd never been good enough – not to make a career out of it. Then, finally – thankfully – Dad stepped in.

He got back in touch with an old contact who'd told him about a position that might suit, as an education assistant at a central London photographers' gallery. The job involved helping to organise public talks, workshops and kids' courses. Then, worried by the number of house shares she'd tried that had never quite worked out, he set about finding her somewhere stable to live.

He remortgaged his own place then spruced up a small flat he'd rented out for years.

It was Dad who helped her settle down. And she had, for a while, until at a sponsors' event at DeHaans she met Richard and everything changed. Thank God Dad had kept the place on after the two of them moved in together and then had Matty. With a turn of the key the front door swings open.

The communal hallway is exactly as she remembers. The post stacked in neat piles on the tatty dresser to her right. The cracked, black and white tiled floor in need of a proper clean, as ever. The stairs ahead dimly illuminated by what daylight makes it through the whorled glass of the first floor landing window. Tightening her grip on her bag, Zeb climbs the stairs slowly, savouring the familiarity. Catching her breath on the landing on the first floor.

The final approach to her flat is reassuring.

To her left is Mrs Allitt's front door, its windowless façade punctuated by the tiny peephole's all-seeing eye. To her right is her own, which she now turns towards with keys out-held, unsure for a moment which of the three locks to try first. She takes her time, trying each key methodically before the catches are finally released. As she steps inside her flat she registers the sound of movement just behind her neighbour's front door.

Inside her flat, as the door clicks to behind her, Zeb lets her bag drop to the floor.

She is home.

Oblivious to disarray within – airing cupboard doors that hang open, towels spilled across the floor – she hurries past the bathroom with its free-standing bath and sunflower head shower. Ignoring her bedroom – where, opposite the wrought iron bedstead draped in its Indian throws, the drawers in the junk shop dresser gape open-mouthed – and Matty's too, she bursts into the sitting room where boxes of half-sorted papers sit spread across the floor.

Am I always this messy? she wonders.

In the kitchenette at the flat's rear she fills a kettle then leans against the kitchen counter as she waits for the water to boil. The window looks down onto the communal yard at the building's rear where the flats' residents keep their bins. Aside from a pile of refuse sacks filled with rubble, the space is empty. Like the flat. And as hope turns to lead her mood darkens. Zeb rubs her eyes.

A calendar hangs on the wall before her and as she stares at it she slowly counts off the days in her head. It was Monday the 7th she was found, which makes today Thursday the 10th. The corresponding square is empty. But two squares along, she has written: MATTY BACK FROM PORTUGAL. Next Tuesday she has a meeting with a solicitor but apart from that entry, there is nothing else. Switching her attention back to Sunday, where the 'a' of Matty is a tiny heart, Zeb recalls how at first she'd objected to Richard's determination to take their son on a half-term break overseas but then reluctantly agreed.

Of course. That's why her ex had not answered his phone earlier. Her heart sinks.

Zeb reaches for the large conch sitting on the windowsill and weighs it in her hand. The solid coolness of the shell against her palm is reassuring; the contrast between the coarse grain of its outer shell and the slick pinkness within; exquisite. A memento from the Andaman Sea, she knows, savouring the memory; the fact that this she can recall.

She bought it on holiday one year from a small boy on the beach in Khao Lak, an hour's drive north of Phuket. The trip was a long-haul adventure in between jobs, one she'd paid for with the money one of Dad's distant relations had left her in a trust for her twenty-first. He'd expected her to use it as a down payment on her first flat but she'd more than blown it travelling. Worse: the trip had left her badly in debt. The reason she'd worked so hard during the following months was to clear her credit card.

Dad must have guessed the truth, of course. But instead of having a go at her he'd turned a blind eye – reasoning, perhaps, her guilt was punishment enough.

My little nomad, he sometimes calls her.

In the fridge Zeb finds an unopened carton of milk. Poking her nose inside, she recoils. Straightening up, she fills the kettle, deciding she'll drink it black.

As the water boils, Zeb stares at the cork board on the wall beside her, hung with photos, doodles by Matty, postcards, Post-its and – jutting out from behind – a black-rimmed card. As she waits for the tea, she sees a photo of a pretty dark-haired woman with her hand on her hip. It's Sam Gardner, her best friend and Matty's godmother, she knows as, without trying, the woman's mobile phone number plays out inside her skull. Spotting a familiar figure to Sam's left, Zeb tugs the picture free and stares at herself, closely.

She is a slim woman in her late thirties. Medium-built with dark-blonde hair cut into a shoulder-length bob. Cinnamon eyes, full lips and a determined chin. But it isn't Zeb's own face that draws her attention; it's how she's dressed. A man's jacket thrown over an antique lace shirt, a denim skirt with a frayed hem and tan suede boots.

Glancing down at the shapeless slacks and nylon blouse she is wearing – the things her neighbourly Samaritan brought her to wear home – Zeb frowns. Shapeless, baggy and smelling of moth balls, she notes, wondering for the first time if the clothes she is now wearing are really hers.

Elsewhere among the rag-tag mosaic of her life is a faded Polaroid of a child standing barefoot on the steel-capped toes of a large pair of Wellington boots. Dressed in a pale cotton sundress, her head is thrown back in laughter at some long-forgotten joke as she clings to a man's waist looking up towards a beloved face unseen. Zeb's eyes burn. But before she can process further she is distracted by the sound of voices from the landing.

Slipping off her boots, Zeb pads into the hallway then edges towards the front door peephole to squint through the monocle of glass. On the other side of the landing stands Mrs Allitt, dressed in a calf-length tartan skirt and matching cape. Her cheeks are pale and powdery, like before. Though now, a pair of thick-rimmed bifocals accentuates the intensity of her watery eyes as she puts out three supermarket bags of glass, cardboard and plastic intended for recycling.

A man Zeb does not recognise arrives on the landing from the floor above and the two exchange polite nods. Thick-set beneath his overcoat, he is of medium height with a heavily lined face and chestnut hair so dense in colour it must be dyed. As she straightens up as he passes, Mrs Allitt's eyes dart beadily towards her neighbour's door.

Self-consciously, Zeb stumbles a step back.

Can she hear me, she wonders, willing her heart to slow and the pounding of blood in her ears to cease.

The landing is silent.

Zeb creeps back towards the peephole and leans towards it, focusing one eye. As her neighbour's face suddenly looms towards hers, she bites her hand to smother her cry. With only a few inches of wood between them, Zeb's breath comes in low, shallow rasps as her neighbour taps a silvered knuckle on the door.

'Anyone at home. Elizabeth? I know you're back – I wondered if there was anything you needed? If I could be of any help? Whether you'd like to pop over now – for a cup of tea?'

Zeb hesitates. If she answers too soon, her neighbour will know she's been hovering by the door, spying. Not replying at all will seem odd. But her indecision is soon outweighed by curiosity, piqued by this woman's peculiar interest in her welfare, and a sudden and desperate loathing for her empty flat.

She thinks of the milk gone sour in her fridge. Of the craving she now has for company. The unease she has felt these past few days from being able to see only the dark shapes that loom around the edges of her consciousness, and no more.

'That would be lovely,' Zeb calls out brightly. 'Thanks.'

–

'How do you like your tea?'

Zeb's body tenses. Because the woman's words, called from the kitchen separated by a beaded curtain from the room in which she now sits, are like an echo. She's done this before – and recently, too – though not in this house but another, somewhere else. And that time the person doing the calling was a man.

Her jaw clenches at the sudden image in her mind's eye of a man-child, overweight in his stained sweatpant bottoms as he hurried down the stairs and past the open doorway opposite where she was sitting. Beneath the dark sweatshirt he was wearing, the bulbous bulge of his belly. Hanging idle, his spade-like hands. The intimidating bulk of him. All this confounded by a bud-smooth face.

How do you like you tea, he'd asked her. *Loose or bagged?*

It was in Scotland.

At that house with the peculiar, round window.

Miss Duffy had let her in but then asked her to wait while she popped out for more fresh milk from the Co-op.

Zeb sat in the sitting room, perched on the tatty sofa as the man, Mrs Duffy's son, matched chipped saucers to glue-veined cups in the kitchen. Outside it was getting dark. Staring down at the carpet, she shivered – not from cold but the unmistakeable traces of another resident. Dog hair crests the tatty shag pile in surf-like peaks. From somewhere close-by comes a scuffling sound. Ever since she was a child she'd been scared of dogs. And this one was huge. A mastiff.

Thank God that Mrs Duffy had chained the creature up in the back yard before she'd come in. Even so, its close proximity weakened her resolve.

Actually, it's getting late, she'd called out, stumbling to her feet. She would return in the morning, in daylight. When the woman would be there and, ideally, alone. *Really*, she'd added. *I should be getting back.*

Someone coughs.

'I said, your tea – how do you take it?' Standing in the beaded doorway, Mrs Allitt is holding a Chinese lacquered tray with bamboo handles.

Stumbling to her feet, Zeb moves towards her hostess and takes the tray of tea things. It didn't happen, she tries to reassure herself, struggling not to think of the heavy thumps on the bathroom door. 'A little milk would be lovely, thanks. And thanks for coming to the hospital, too. All that way, it was really kind.'

Seated on the sofa once more, her cup of tea positioned on the coffee table before her, Zeb smiles, noticing her neighbour's expression has grown expectant.

'Really, you must let me give you something towards the cost of the ticket.'

'I knew you'd see me right,' her neighbour nods. 'I'll fish out the receipt when we've had our tea. Now I know I have some nice nibbles somewhere – bear with me, I'll just go and check.'

With the heating on full blast, the room feels airless and oppressive. Though this flat is a mirror image of her own with an identical layout, the space feels smaller. The hallway is cramped – the width halved by the piles of fading newspapers meticulously banked against the wall from floor to waist level on either side.

In the sitting room, dark oak cupboards line the entire breadth and length of one wall. Along the opposite wall is a ramshackle line of grey filing cabinets. On top of these sit rows of cardboard boxes stamped with an assortment of food and supermarket brands; each crammed with neatly bound bundles of A4 paper stacked upright to make the most of the space available.

Shifting position to turn her gaze behind her, Zeb registers the dusty green velvet curtains that reach from ceiling to floor around each window. The ancient leather stool like an elephant's foot. A shape like a tailor's dummy in the far corner, concealed beneath a dirty dust sheet. The glass bell jar beside it containing a glass-eyed red squirrel posed awkwardly, mid-clamber, on a dusty branch.

A sudden image of outsized hands filling a tiny teapot makes Zeb's insides lurch. Spilling her tea, she quickly replaces her cup on its saucer.

Zeb stares at the brown liquid as it begins to pool on the wooden table. With nothing to blot it, she turns instead to move a nearby assortment of buff-coloured folders, blank sheets of A4 and newspaper cuttings out of harm's way. It looks like Mrs Allitt is compiling some sort of scrapbook, she thinks, using her sleeve to blot the spill.

Leaning forward, Zeb flips open the folder closest to her. Inside, a collection of official-looking letters – which she is about to put down when she registers the name on the uppermost sheet, a bank statement. It's addressed to Stan Williams, the tenant in the ground floor flat. Curious, Zeb scans the sheets behind it, which include a response from the local council about his application for a refund on his resident's parking permit. A postcard from his friend in Paris. A letter from the oncology department at the Royal Free detailing the time and date scheduled for a number of tests and scans.

What's Mrs Allitt doing with all this?

Zeb snaps shut the folder and slides it away but as she does she dislodges another which now tumbles off the table and onto the floor. Hastily retrieving it, she is about to replace the set of papers beneath the first when she sees something sticking out from one side. A newspaper cutting about a coatless woman wandering dazed and confused along a secluded Highlands road.

With a sharp intake of breath Zeb snatches back her hand. But her gaze remains fixed on the image of her own face, staring blankly from her hospital bed. Quickly, she flicks through the other sheets inside the second folder. The selection of newspaper cuttings it contains count back the past few days. Beside a grainy shot of herself sitting up in bed is a close-up image of the silver chain and its piano charm, suspended from PC Heath's forefinger and thumb. *Piano Girl*, the caption reads.

Me, this file is about me, she realises, her anger rising.

Turning over another piece of newsprint Zeb is surprised to find a proof of purchase from a recent book order she must have made on Amazon and a subscription renewal reminder, also addressed to her, for *Hello!* Though old and creased, both look like they have been carefully flattened out.

She sees a handwritten letter at the back, dated two weeks earlier. *Dear Elizabeth*, it begins, *I am so very sorry to have upset you yesterday by coming unannounced*. Scanning to the bottom she sees it is signed with a name she doesn't recognise: Cynthia Purnell. But before she can read any further Mrs Allitt is standing beside her, glaring.

'Nosy,' the old woman observes, tartly.

'Sorry—' Zeb begins, struggling to her feet, but then it strikes her: she's not the one who should be apologising '—but that letter, and others in there, no doubt, belong to me. What do you think you're—'

'A letter? Addressed to you?' Mrs Allitt cuts in, crisply, as she reaches for the large knife resting beside a Victoria sponge which has appeared on the coffee table beside two mismatched side plates. 'Well I don't know how that could possibly have happened. I'm ever so sorry, really I am, I must have picked it up without noticing in a pile of post for me.'

With the knife clasped tightly in her right hand, the older woman reaches with her left for the top plate.

'What, and opened it too?' Zeb is astounded by her neighbour's nerve.

'Why yes, I must have – by mistake, of course. Care for a slice?'

Zeb hesitates, her attention flitting between the steel glinting in the other woman's hand and the lack of any awkwardness or embarrassment on her face. A moment later, the cake is cut and the sugary knife replaced on the far side of the table, once more out of reach. Wearing an expression of pained innocence, Mrs Allitt places Zeb's plate on the table then takes a seat at the far end of the sofa.

Zeb wonders if the message is from a friend of Dad's. The older woman leans forward. Reaching towards a soup bowl piled with Turkish Delight at the far end of the table, she selects a fleshy sweet then quickly pops it into her mouth. The intimate smell of the bowl now looming towards her is so intense Zeb fears she will retch.

'I was terribly sorry to hear about your father, you know,' her neighbour commiserates. The woman's lips are sticky with icing sugar, her voice is soft. 'I mean to say, sixty-four seems so young nowadays. You know, to die. Of a heart attack.'

Zeb buckles as the truth clicks into focus. The reason for the black-edged card pinned to her kitchen wall. The sombre outfit she was wearing the morning she recalled returning to the flat while still in hospital. Why her flat had become a temporary staging post for Dad's stuff. Her eyes fill with tears.

'May I use your loo?' she gasps, stumbling to her feet.

'Of course, dear,' the older woman nods, licking her fingers. 'It's the last door on the right. Just like in your flat, but without the designer touches.'

In the bathroom doorway Zeb falters. A large Victorian cistern is suspended from the wall just below the ceiling in front of her, an ancient wooden-seated toilet lurking on the floor beneath. Her mouth is alive with the sudden scorch of vomit. She gasps for breath.

Fearful she will faint if she doesn't get some fresh air, fast, she races to the front door where she wrestles for a moment with the bolt and chain before tumbling out onto the landing and finally back inside her own flat.

Why did you go so soon, Daddy? a child-like voice inside her wails.

Hurrying into the kitchen, Zeb searches a number of cupboards before finding what she's looking for: a selection of spirits including a set of miniature whiskies and an unopened bottle of cherry liqueur, tucked away from view behind a box of cornflakes. As her fingers close around a half-drunk bottle of vodka she fleetingly recalls a decision she made not so long ago to cut back on her drinking. But the thought is gone as soon as it registers.

With a shaking hand, Zeb tips more than a double shot into an oversized tumbler, downs it in one then pours herself another. The moment feels as unreal as her neighbour's words.

How could I forget?

Swaying slightly, she retraces her steps back down the corridor, bottle and glass now in hand, to secure the front door chain. For now, at least, I'm safe from the old bitch with a spare key, Zeb thinks as she retreats into Matty's bedroom and carefully places the vodka beside her son's night light on the bedside table. She's certainly no friend.

Without bothering to get undressed, she slips under Matty's duvet. Hugging herself tight, she buries her face in his pillow. The smell of Matty's sheets, the ones with the rocket man motif, is reassuring. But as Zeb reaches for the bottle and swallows three more mouthfuls she starts to sob.

'Don't be gone, Dad,' she begs. 'Tell me anything, just don't be gone.'

Chapter 8

Soho, October 1974

A shard of light suddenly reflected from one of the top floor windows of the buildings opposite makes Alma blink. Above her head, the morning-after sky beams cobalt. With its scant heat, the brightness of the low-hung sun feels like a cheap con.

She is sitting on a wooden bench in Soho Square, facing Number Nineteen. It is early – she has skipped the breakfast rehearsal she should be doing before the start of her daily classes. But she has had to, to retrieve the purse she left on the bar while drinking with Viola and Geoff the previous evening. The purse contains her room key. If she's lost it, the porter at Engel House will go insane. Her only chance is to ask the barman who lent her his towel. But with the building's windows still darkened and its door locked, all she can do is wait.

Alma breathes out, slowly. It's only just gone nine but already it's been a difficult morning. She slept fitfully then woke early with a thumping headache. She discovered her purse was missing in the refectory as she reached the front of the queue to pay for breakfast, and had to put everything back. And then there was another special delivery.

It had begun with a bouquet, a spray of roses with petals the colour of clotted cream wrapped in tissue paper and secured with a pink ribbon.

Definitely for Alma – the label said so, though there was no message either attached or slipped inside. The other girls on her corridor teased her mercilessly about her secret admirer. Speculated wildly about his identity. Competed madly to nominate the most eligible contenders amongst the slender contingent of male associates and faculty staff. All of which would have been funny, if Alma hadn't been struck by a hideous thought.

What if this was some kind of peace token from Leonard?

Then, this morning, she found in her pigeonhole chocolates gift-wrapped in silver paper. The box had been delivered to the porter's office while she'd been out on the town with Viola and Geoff the previous night, by hand. The satin-covered box inside was embossed with a line drawing of the Leaning Tower of Pisa. And this time there was a message.

To the girl with the laugh in her eyes, the card read. *From the man with a child in his heart.*

The oblique reference to Alma Cogan – the girl with the laugh in her voice – had made Alma feel sick. Though her famous namesake had long been her mother's favourite singer, she had warmed neither to the name nor to the style of music. Both were so old-fashioned. Uncommon enough, too, as a name for most people to make some comment or other. Which was why, when she was little, she dreamed of changing her name to something simpler. Like Anna, or Mary.

Rereading the message, however, caused Alma a curious conflict of emotions.

The persistence of her father's friend is sickening; his intentions shockingly outrageous. Yet with its light dusting of chocolate, the card smells almost sweet. As does the revelation that her admirer comes from outside the student body. He is a grown-up. And though she hates herself for it, the secret knowledge of this is exciting and naughty. She hates him, bitterly. But something about being sought out by him makes her feel special.

A vigorous flapping sound from the tiled roof of the timbered hut before her makes Alma look up. At the building's highest point, the bungled courtship dance of a ragged pair of pigeons looks more like an assault. She's always loathed birds, pigeons especially. Shifting position on the bench, she stares at the patch of green at the centre of the square and the folly that marks its central point.

It is a Tudor-style construction with wooden arches that sweep abruptly downwards. A wooden door is visible on the near side at ground level, the building's narrowest point, behind which a single flight of stairs leads to the only room on the timbered, upper floor. The building has intrigued Alma since her first visit to the square. And reminded her, too, of the colour plate where the collection of fairy tales she received one Christmas as a child would always fall open. The picture is an illustration of the witch's house in *Hansel and Gretel*.

Where's that book now, she wonders?

In the cardboard box of childish bits and pieces her mother has stowed beneath her bed back home, she guesses, as she readies the place for the decorators she's booked to turn it into the new guest room.

A car roars into the square with its stereo blaring. From inside, David Essex promises anyone who cares to listen that he's 'Gonna Make You a Star'.

The car traverses three sides of the scrap of green in search of a parking space to park. Eventually the driver gives up, and pulls to a halt on the pavement. As a short compact figure in dark trousers and a black leather jacket climbs out, Alma's spirits rally.

It is the barman, she is sure of it.

A moment later, the man is standing at the main front door fumbling with a bunch of keys. Stumbling to her feet, she hurries towards him.

'Excuse me.'

The barman glances over his shoulder without turning around but says nothing.

'It's Brian, isn't it?'

His eyes narrow. 'So?'

'I was here. Last night, with some friends. And I think I left my purse on the bar upstairs.'

The man nods. 'Your purse.'

'Yes, did you see it – you know, later, when you were clearing up?'

Turning back towards the door he finally chooses the right keys then nudges it open with his foot, but waits a beat before stepping inside. 'Might have.'

Alma takes a step forward. 'Oh that's great,' she exclaims. 'It's not so much the money, it's the keys that are inside. If I could come up—'

'Wait here.' With a heavy thud the door swings shut.

Sinking down onto the top step, Alma hugs her knees.

Not only is she uncertain the barman will find her purse, but even if he does she's left unsure by his manner if he'll even return. Craving a cigarette, Alma paws inside her coat pocket but the only thing she pulls free is Leonard's card. With a scowl, the tears it into two, then four, and then again and scatters what's left.

A black cab turns onto the square from Frith Street and pulls in a short distance away. In the back, obscured from view, a man and woman are shouting. It takes a moment or two for the argument to subside and when it does, a thick-set man wearing a sheepskin coat steps out onto the kerb then swiftly slams to the door. With his companion still sealed inside, the taxi pulls away.

Too late, Alma registers that the man is striding towards where she now sits.

'Can I help you?' He has stopped on the second to last step and though he's standing below her the bulk of him now looms above. A crumpled pinstriped suit is visible beneath his coat. There is a scuff on the left toe of his otherwise immaculate buckled slip-on shoes. His silver hair is straggly and combed-over.

The man crosses his arms.

'No, that's all right,' Alma mumbles. 'I'm just—'

He leans towards her to better make his point. 'Only this is private property.'

'Oh, right.' His stale cigar breath makes Alma gasp.

'If you want to sit down there's a bench over there, in the public square.'

Alma nods, enthusiastically, as she tries not to show she is intimidated. 'Yes, of course. Only—'

'Next to the bin.'

'I'm sorry?'

'The bin,' the man repeats. As he points to the remnants of Leonard's message, a clump of hair from his comb-over slips loose. 'That was you, wasn't it? Littering up my bit of the street.'

'It was,' she cries, hurriedly bending forward to make amends. 'But really, I wasn't going to—'

The man steps past her, so close Alma can feel the heat of him, and by the time she is on her feet cupping the torn card in her hands he has extracted a large bunch of keys from his inside pocket. A second later he has disappeared inside. Is this Number Nineteen's owner, Alma wonders? The sort-of-stepdad described by the man who came to her aid last night in the bar? She thinks of her rescuer for a moment.

Where did he go to, she wonders. Perhaps she could ask his sort-of-stepbrother.

Assuming the barman ever comes back.

Retracing her steps back down onto the pavement, Alma decides to wait by the nearest lamp post a short distance away. Thinking back to the night before, she tries to imagine what might have happened if the stranger had not left before she had a chance to introduce him to Viola. At least then she'd have learned his name. She idly wonders if he comes to this place often.

'You're in luck.'

Alma looks up. The barman is standing once more in the open doorway. In his hand is her purse.

'I didn't check, but it feels quite full,' he adds with a lopsided grin, dipping his hand as if loaded down by its weight. 'Fingers crossed the keys are still in there.'

'That's brilliant,' Alma gushes, quickly unzipping the pouch inside and finding her keys still there. 'Really. I mean, thanks.'

With a curt nod, Brian turns back towards the open doorway. A moment later the door will be closed and Alma's chance will have gone. Dare she ask him for his stepbrother's name and, maybe, even his phone number?

Viola would, Alma is sure of it. Though whatever her roommate would do is irrelevant, of course. Alma isn't her. They may share some common ground but they are not the same.

Convention and upbringing bind Alma to all received expectations, dictating her every move, and making her miserable with the sudden knowledge that she does not have the courage to ask for anything. And even if by some miracle she remembered the name of the pub on the book of matches he showed her, the one he lived above, she would never be the first to call. Because you don't, do you? Just in case the other person says no.

So much for women's lib, she thinks, glumly. For it's not as simple as just being strong enough to be your true self. Viola has read all the right books and taken out a subscription to *Spare Rib* but it's not adherence to the latest fashionable thinking that enables her to get what she wants, it's the innate poise and self-confidence that come with money and class. Her sense of prerogative.

'Thanks then, and see you later,' Alma calls out to Brian as he steps into the shadows.

The barman turns back towards her then winks. 'Not unless I see you first.'

Chapter 9

Camden, February 2016

Mrs Duffy? I'm looking for your lodger – I wonder, is she in?

The older woman took a step back into the house, bracing her arm against the half-open door. Her eyes narrowed. *No.*

I don't suppose you know how long…? Zeb hoped her smile looked reassuring.

Half-turning her head back into the house as if out of fear of being overheard, Mrs Duffy frowned. *I don't suppose I do.*

Zeb took a tentative step forward. Clearly a different tack was needed. *She got in touch after my dad died a few weeks ago. They are – were – old friends, you see. And I've come all the way from London,* she offered, half-raising her arms with palms up-raised. Like a criminal eager to prove their innocence.

Mrs Duffy's face softened. *I suppose you could wait inside,* she offered. *Come on in, then. Quickly, now – best not let all the warm air out. Have a seat in the lounge while I make some tea. She won't be long.*

The corridor towards the kitchen was stone-flagged, shadowed and draughty. Though it was equally unwelcoming, Zeb stepped into the dimly-lit oak-furnished lounge and took a seat in the leather armchair standing beside a three-bar gas fire.

Warming her hands, Zeb took in the room's finer details. Its vague smell of heather. The ticking of an unseen clock close by, providing a welcome pulse. To her left stood a faded three-piece suite with lace-trimmed covers. On an old oak bureau stood a selection of bottles including Gordon's gin and Croft sweet sherry. Her eyes lingered for a moment on the half-drunk bottle of Drambuie.

Someone – Mrs Duffy, probably – had positioned some well-thumbed magazines on the footstool. *Birdwatch. The Puzzler. Woman's Realm.* Lined along the windowsill above was a mismatched collection of Toby jugs. An asthma inhaler lies on a three-legged occasional table beside a pile of unpaid bills.

We're all out of milk. Standing in the open doorway, Mrs Duffy greeted Zeb's glance with an anxious frown. *You caught me just on my way to the shops, see. But if you don't mind waiting… Davy?* she barked in a raised voice intended to carry up the stairs. *I'm just popping out to get some milk. Be on your best behaviour, now, we have a guest.*

Once the woman had gone, Zeb sank back into her seat. She fished in her bag for her mobile, to check for messages. With the old stone walls there was no network coverage so, instead, she pulled from her bag the envelope she received two days earlier, containing the silver chain with the charm in the shape of a tiny grand piano. Zeb scrutinised it once more for any meaning. But there was nothing. The postmark was blurred and there was no clue as to who sent it or why.

She tipped the necklace into the palm of her hands and held it up to the light, as a low whistle announced the kettle boiling.

Zeb stepped towards the mirror above the mantelpiece and stood for a moment, holding the chain against her throat to gauge the effect. She secured the clasp and let the charm drop softly against her skin. Should she turn off that kettle, she wondered, briefly, until with a volley of heavy footfalls on the stairs, a broad-shouldered figure thundered past the open door.

As soon as the whistling stopped, she heard the brisk snap of a bolt being released then the click of claws clattering across a stone flagged floor.

Zeb hovered uneasily in the sitting room doorway. Though the hall was in darkness, the distant kitchen at its end emitted a welcoming glow.

Anything I can do? she called.

It's a'right, because I've instructions written out. His voice was breathy, and higher in tone than the size of him would otherwise suggest; childlike. *You've gotta choose, though. Loose tea or bagged?*

–

Zeb wakes in an instant. Disoriented, her eyes scan the room just to make sure, registering the stacked plastic boxes of Brio, Lego, and all things Action Man. Afternoon daylight poking through the gully between the hastily-drawn curtains. She glances at the bedside clock. It's almost one.

I am at home – in Matty's room in Camden, she tells herself.

I. Am. Safe.

Even so, she is shaking. The recurring scene is unnerving. She is sure now that it must have happened, and some time in the last two weeks. Yet she still cannot recall the events that led her there or, indeed, what happened next.

Zeb pulls on her clothes and pads to the kitchen to make herself a strong black coffee. As she waits for the water to boil, she stares once more at the calendar pinned to the wall. If Jean picked her up on Monday 7th, did she visit Mrs Duffy some time during the weekend before? She wonders how long she was in Scotland. Rubbing her eyes, hard, she tries to remember where else she might have gone; how long she might have stayed.

On a copy of the previous weekend's *Observer* there are some sheets of scrap paper. She takes a pen from the pot on the windowsill and begins to list the past fortnight in reverse, day by day. Starting at the top, Thursday, she writes *TODAY – At home*. Then, on the day before – *Discharged/Arrived home*. Then on Monday – *Picked up by Jean*.

Zeb glances back towards the calendar. The only entries marked on the previous week are *Pay Credit Card* and a dental appointment on the morning of Wednesday 3rd. She runs the tip of her tongue across the front of her teeth. If she kept that appointment, that left four days unaccounted for. She stares for a moment at the sheet she's marked up, then draws a circle to highlight Thursday 4th to Sunday 6th.

How would you travel to Scotland? she asks herself. Would you go by train, or would you fly?

Idly turning over the piece of paper, Zeb sees on its reverse a list of train times she must have printed from a website. It's part of the Euston to Fort William timetable, and one train on the Wednesday evening has been marked with a handwritten star. Her mood lightens. *So she took the overnight sleeper.*

Zeb turns back to her notes and fills this in. But as hard as she tries, even after two mugs of coffee, she can't fill in any more gaps. Again, her head is aching. Too much caffeine on an empty stomach, perhaps. She pours herself a bowl of cereal, but without fresh milk can barely eat it dry. She starts to write herself a shopping list. This will be why Dr Prentiss advised against her leaving hospital so soon, she knows as, soothed by practicalities, her head starts to clear and the fear begins to ebb.

Best not to rush it, he said. *And once back home take it easy. Recent memories are a bit like naughty errant children – they will come back, just give them time.*

Exhaling slowly, she thinks of something else Dr Prentiss told her. How a combination of shock and physical trauma will often result in short- to mid-term memory loss. *Think of it like a bookcase*, he said, *with our oldest, longest laid down memories on the bottom shelf rising towards our latest, freshest memories on the top shelf. Your memory books on the top shelf have toppled over. The good news is, they're not lost – you just need to straighten them up. Try to relax and distract yourself and it will soon come back.*

Opening the cupboard to return the cornflakes, Zeb stares at the half-drunk bottles of alcohol, then carefully lines them up on the kitchen counter. Methodically, she tips the remnants of each down the sink, along with what's left of the vodka from Matty's room, then fills an empty carrier bag with bottles to put out later for recycling. Beneath the sink stands an empty pickle jar which she opens. The vinegar smell stirs another memory.

Leaning against the kitchen door jamb of that house in Scotland, she'd watched him.

A baby-faced figure, barefooted in tracksuit bottoms, with an old T-shirt beneath a padded, multi-pocketed fisherman's vest. Between dampened lips, only just visible, the kitten tip of his tongue. As he measured out the correct quantity of loose leaf Earl Grey his concentration was total.

But then, feeling awkward, she began to scan the debris across the kitchen worktop. To the right, plastic cable binders were piled in a neat pyramid next to a glass bottle of what looked like water. Beside this was wadded gauze, a roll of duct tape and an outsized glass syringe. Just tiny details, yet they made the scene feel… wrong.

There was a scuffling sound from just outside the back door followed by a low, warning growl. Which is when, as she turned towards the unseen creature's location, the collection of screw-topped preserving jars lined up along the window ledge came into view. In each, a dull indeterminate mass was visible suspended in some kind of viscous liquid. Pickled vegetables, she assumed, before recognising in the nearest the pearl eyes and snub nose of a tiny squirrel.

She stumbled back from the doorway. The man-child looked up. As their eyes locked, his face no longer seemed soft and boyish.

May I use your bathroom?

She tried to sound offhand, even though, in that instant, she felt acutely conscious of the ring of light in which they stood. Of the pulsing darkness closing in. The oppressive heat of the wood burning stove. The dog's squall.

Slipping his hand into the hip pocket of his gilet, he pulled free a large Stanley knife and as he delicately positioned it on the worktop, his lips twisted into a cunning smile. In a blink Zeb was in the bathroom, crouched on an old Victorian toilet seat, fumbling urgently with the catch of an ancient window as soon as she'd bolted the door.

To open that sash was all she wanted, all she'd ever wanted. As if her entire life had been spent working up to that moment. And as the memory of it sharpens, her eyes fill with tears. Her mouth fills with a rank, foul taste; the smack of fear.

–

'Yes?'

Zeb is blind-sided by Richard's father's clipped, staccato delivery, when he answers her phone call a short while later. She is in the sitting room, cross-legged on the floor beside her fourth mug of black coffee.

Skittering across the room, she comes to focus on what's left of a bottle of gin standing on the book shelf behind the TV and feels the stirring of conflicting emotions: longing, regret. Silently she curses. Why does the old sod, a retired naval officer who's not averse to a mid-morning tipple, always make her feel like a naughty child?

'Hugh? It's Zeb,' she enunciates, praying the man won't notice her voice is slightly slurred. Can he tell?

A furtive glance towards the kitchen doorway at the clock above the cooker confirms it's just gone one. Not that early, really, she thinks, lamenting her decision not to call later once her head was clear; dismissing her idea that maybe a short, sharp mouthful of gin might help. The sun would be well over the yardarm, if it weren't so cloudy.

If the pair of them were at sea. Which they are not.

She clears her throat. 'May I speak to Richard, please?'

'What? No, of course not.'

The harshness of his retort is unexpected. For though neither of Richard's parents had ever warmed to her and had only come to tolerate her after the arrival of their beloved first grandchild, they were polite. At first she'd put the distance down to the time it had taken for Richard and her to marry. But latterly she'd come to realise nothing would ever be enough to win their approval. She isn't good enough for their precious son, that's all. Worse, that it wouldn't last had always been a foregone conclusion – for them, at least.

Since she and Matty moved out of Richard's place the previous summer his parents had been more than accommodating, of course. Positively eager, in fact, to provide childcare with next to no notice when something came up. Zeb knows she should be grateful for this yet, instead, feels anything but. Not just because of how their unconcealed hunger for their grandson grates but how, despite the split, she's come to be more dependent on them, not less.

It's about the support network Richard can draw on, too. Aside from Hugh and Jennifer, his two sisters and an older cousin still live in and around the Holland Park family home where he grew up. Yet who does she have? The only child of a single parent, and now... not even that.

Zeb's eyes burn. Dammit, she thinks. If only I could just hang up.

'I'm sorry, but—'

'Richard is still in Spain, Elizabeth. With Matthew.'

Of course, they are staying at his colleague Anthony's place in Valderrama, Zeb remembers, banishing her tears with her hand. She first went there with Richard soon after they got together at work. His work – as the temp she was, in theory, only passing through. Can it really be ten years ago? Though she'd been there a few times after she had Matty. The apartment is in a purpose-built block close to the golf course. A pretty dull set up, really, though Matty adores the water park.

As Zeb struggles to remember what day it is and when exactly her son should be back, Hugh exhales loudly – as if paving the way for some portentous announcement.

'The three of them—' he declares, pointedly '—are back late tomorrow evening. Matthew will be back with you in two days' time, as agreed.'

So he's out there with Helene. Zeb tightens her grip on the phone. Hugh has mentioned it on purpose, she senses. But she will not take the bait. 'Sorry,' she mumbles, feebly. 'I thought it was today.'

'Well you're mistaken. You could try the mobile, if it's an emergency.' Richard's mobile. Of course. Only he recently got a new one and she doesn't know the number without checking on her own phone which was in the bag she lost in Scotland. The bag her father got her. 'No, no, it doesn't matter. I can wait.'

Hastily returning the phone to its cradle, Zeb sinks back into the sofa.

She and Richard have informally agreed joint custody. Yet Matty and she have spent a growing amount of time apart in recent months because of her work commitments. All she's trying to do is earn a living, though her job is not the only reason her son spends more time with his father, of course. Though hungry for detail of recent events, she'd rather banish from her mind altogether the thought of something from a few months before, something which she has no trouble remembering at all: her ex's concerns about her drinking. It had got embarrassingly out of hand since autumn, when he and Helene announced their engagement. And then again, more recently, when Dad died.

Forcing her breathing to slow, Zeb modulates her outward breath to fully empty her lungs then waits before gradually inhaling. Does this make me a bad mother – unreliable, incapable? No, it does not. And I will remind Richard of this, she pledges, just as soon as they return.

She waits for the pulse of outrage to subside. She knows she mustn't allow him to make her feel like this. How Richard behaves is his own business. But how I deal with this is down to me. She stares at the gin, weighing up the pros and then the cons. But she's got the next eighteen hours to get through. The world really does feel so overwhelming right now. Meanwhile she feels, well, just all hulled out.

Zeb crosses the room and reaches for the bottle.

–

Zeb fumbles for the strip of painkillers she keeps in her bedside drawer. It is well past four now, and she has fallen asleep once more in Matty's room.

Groggily, she makes her way to the bathroom where, next to an open packet of Nurofen on the windowsill, she is brought to a halt by a half-empty bottle of aftershave. The make Dad uses. Her heart trips as she wonders, briefly, when he left it here. Until she remembers: she

82

was the one who'd brought it back. From the cottage in Woodleigh, the small Wiltshire village where he lives. Lived. The day she visited for the first time after his death.

Zeb picks up the aftershave and unscrews the cap. As she breathes in the familiar smell of fresh-dug earth and mountain pine, the intimacy of it makes her chest tighten.

So it is real, she thinks as she screws the cap back on the bottle. He is gone. Dead. The starkest of words with more than enough weight to upend her world. Trying to be practical, she swallows the tablets with a handful of water. But her ability to erase Dad's dying from her mind, albeit temporarily, is unnerving. The mind can play tricks sometimes, she reasons. Close down for self-protection by shutting things out. A subconscious defence mechanism. Even so, being unable to remember Dad's death seems like the ultimate betrayal.

Slumping down onto the side of the bath, Zeb buries her head in her hands as she remembers the policewoman who came to the flat.

The first thing she'd done was invite her to take a seat – as clear a sign as any that bad news was to come. Dad was found too late by a neighbour who'd been invited to lunch, she'd been told. Lying on his side on the floor in the office upstairs. Though the front door was found ajar, there was no evidence of any break-in. Nothing obvious missing. No signs of any struggle – no cuts, or bruises. Just enough evidence to suggest an acute myocardial infarction – not a term she'd encountered before, but one she'll now struggle to forget. A by-product, most likely, the post mortem suggested, of undiagnosed high blood pressure.

Orphaned: that was how Zeb felt when she first heard the news, and now feels all over again. Which is perfectly understandable, the bereavement counsellor told

83

her. Because ever since she can remember, Dad has been – was – there for her. Always and without fail. Just him. For she'd had no mum – at least, not one she'd been old enough to remember.

Zeb's eyes fill with tears. How she wishes she had known him back when he was an ambitious young photographer whose portfolio was starting to attract positive attention. Around the time she was born, a number of his pictures had been chosen for inclusion in a best of young British talent exhibition in New York – an endorsement that finally offered him a long-hoped for staff position on Fleet Street. Yet he'd traded in all this and more – prospects, independence, freedom – after a woman she never knew died from complications during her birth. Which left Dad to be her everything. Her comforter and rock.

If only he could tell her now what she should do, how she should feel, she thinks, drying her face on her sleeve. But the harder she craves this, the more clearly she hears Richard's voice.

You've had it tough, her ex told her, by phone, the evening before Dad's funeral. *But you're a parent yourself now, with responsibilities. Like being there for your son when he needs you and showing him the difference between right and wrong. It's about actions, not words. And that's why the best thing right now is for Matty to be with Helene and me.*

Zeb grimaces. How she still hates her ex for saying that; the timing of it, too. Yet didn't he have a point? As she had struggled to cope in the weeks and months following their split, the firm hold she'd had on life as she once knew it started to unravel.

It was Christmas 2014 when she first suspected he was seeing someone else. His coltishness after the DeHaan

Christmas party was an early indicator. His work shirt reeked of the cloying sweetness of the perfume she later learned Helene used.

Within a few short months she'd taken Matty with her back to the flat in Camden – though her son had spent more time at his place than hers during that first summer. Then, before she could see it coming, Richard was talking about having him most weeknights during term for 'stability'. Starting tutoring. And changing schools. Having parents who lived just around the corner meant there would always be someone on hand when he had to work late, he explained. Or when he was out for dinner. Or at the theatre, with Helene.

Just how things got so bad so fast during those difficult first few months remains obscured by an alcoholic haze. But the fact of it was that as Zeb's drinking began to escalate it became harder to get Matty to school on time with all the right bits and pieces. To remind him to keep up with his music practice. To remember what to put on the weekly online shopping order. And while her boss was understanding at first, she lived in fear of the inevitable day when her colleagues would decide she'd worn their patience too thin.

Reluctant to confide any of this in her best friend Sam, it had been Dad she'd relied on to be there for her, stand by her, help her get back on her feet, again. Encourage her to enrol at a gym close to work where she could go to work out most lunchtimes. Urge her to self-impose a new rule not to drink between Monday and Friday, unless invited out on a weeknight to meet friends and even then, when she did drink, to cut her wine with soda.

Do it for you, he said. *But most of all, do it for Matty.*

Powered by a sudden primal longing for her son, Zeb hurries back into the sitting room. She picks up the cordless phone, punches in a number then holds it tight against her ear.

'Hello?'

The youngest of four sisters, Samantha Gardner is fiercely loyal to those she cares about. Independent-minded, too, having scandalised both family and friends by choosing to live not in Manchester, where she'd grown up, but down south, in London, where she moved after art college. After a decade trying to make it as a magazine photographer, Sam turned her back on publishing to become a curator at the gallery where Zeb now works.

'Hey you,' Zeb presses on, wandering back into the kitchen. 'It's me.'

A sharp intake of breath is followed by a brief silence. When eventually the other woman does speak her voice is tight. 'You've got a nerve.'

'I know, I'm sorry. I've been away for a few days. In Scotland, it's a long story – one for another time, preferably involving a bottle of wine, maybe even two – but I was just wondering, now I'm back, you know, how things are?'

'Fucking hell, Zeb.'

'Sorry?'

'It's a bit late for that, don't you think?'

'What?' Struggling to decode the other woman's voice, Zeb tightens her grip on the phone.

'Sorry.'

'Oh, sorry. No, I mean...' What is Sam going on about? Zeb wonders. What does her friend think she's done? But once more she can't remember. 'Look. Sam. I don't know how to say this, but... I had a bit of an accident. Up in Scotland. I banged my head. I've been in hospital, actually. I mean, I'm home now, but I'm still finding it quite difficult to remember—'

'How… convenient.'

'No, it's not.' Zeb struggles in vain to swallow a sob. 'It's not at all. In fact it's turning into a bit of a nightmare—'

'So you really don't remember what happened at William's party?' Sam interrupts. Her voice is cold. Incredulous.

'No… I—'

'Don't remember leaving with Marcus? Right.'

'Marcus…'

'My boyfriend? Or rather, my ex?'

Zeb's eyes widen. Marcus Palmer. Estate agent and keen golfer. Yes, the pair had met at a French jive dance class. A short man, almost handsome, with deep-set eyes that made him look shifty. Older than Dad… would have been. An unlikely pairing. And certainly not her type. 'No, I think you've got that wrong—'

'Really.'

'Yes, really. I've had a tough few weeks—' Zeb begins, desperately threading together the fragments of her recent past '—what with Dad's death, the funeral and everything. Then the accident.' She remembers Marcus following her out of William's kitchen after something the host's boyfriend said about absentee mothers had made her upset. He'd put his arm around her, tried to persuade her not to leave, then having failed in his mission, insisted on driving her back to her flat. 'It was nothing, honestly. He was just trying to help. I think you may have got… the wrong end of the stick.'

Sam sighs. 'His words exactly.'

'Maybe because it's true?' Zeb's says, hopefully. It is true, she knows it. 'Look, I'm sorry if you two are going through a difficult patch. But there's nothing going on, I promise. And I'm sorry if anything I did made things worse. It's just, well, I've missed you, OK? And at this particular moment, well—' she sniffs. 'I suppose it would just be nice to see a friendly face.'

There's silence once more at the other end of the line and for a moment Zeb fears Sam might have put down the phone, but she is wrong.

'OK,' the other woman sighs. 'To tell you the truth, I'm rather enjoying all the effort he's going to to win me back. Look, if you're free later come to mine for dinner. Best not to go anywhere too central, not close to work – you're the last person Kirsty will want to see after what happened. I mean really, Zeb, walking out like that, the day before the Young Blood launch event you'd been organising. You left everyone in the lurch—'

'Oh Sam,' Zeb sighs, struggling to understand what her friend has just said. So she quit her job, and recently, too, though she can't recall the precise details. But Sam has agreed to see her, at least. Once they meet and talk more, surely things will start falling into place. 'To tell the truth, I'm really not feeling up to going out. But I'm not feeling up to a night in alone, either. Christ, Sam, I'm so sorry—'

'Zeb?'

With the heel of her free palm she rubs her eyes. 'Still here.'

'Let's hook up Saturday evening – I'll come to you.' A steeliness in Sam's voice signals that she'll not be argued with. 'I'll bring dinner, too. I think we've both got some explaining to do.'

Zeb readjusts her grip on the phone.

Looking up, she stares at the blown-up print of a black and white on the wall opposite, a photo Dad took on his twenty-first birthday. It is of an old Routemaster London bus in the rain. He gave it to her when she too reached that age – a gesture that still moves her deeply. *Am I going mad, Dad?* Zeb wonders, meeting the dull gaze of the West African driver. She considers the struggle it has become to stay strong enough to care for herself and his beloved grandson. *Dad, how did things end up like this?*

Zeb thinks for a moment about the meeting she has next Tuesday with a solicitor. That will be a meeting with her dad's solicitor, of course. How did she not guess? And what the hell will she need? Papers, his papers, most of which are still sitting in the upstairs office at the house in Woodleigh – not a trip she fancies taking with Matty in tow. For it is her role now to get things in order. His affairs. Her life. She checks her watch. With nothing better to do, maybe she'll go tomorrow.

'Hello?'

'Sorry, Sam,' Zeb answers quickly, returning her attention to the call. 'That would be lovely. Saturday night, any time after seven.'

Chapter 10

Kensington Gardens, November 1974

'It's called Round Pond, did you know?'

'Sorry?'

Viola waves a gloved hand at the dull expanse of water spread out before them like a slate tarpaulin. With a shiver, she raises the collar of her winter coat – a vintage pea-green, knee-length number she'd bought the previous week from Portobello Market – and tucks the fur trim more snugly around her throat.

'This, the ornamental lake.'

'Oh,' Alma responds, though she's not really listening. There is something about this place, its dull flatness, that oppresses her.

They are by the boating lake in Kensington Gardens, near the large wooden box used to store rented deckchairs. Its padlock is broken, its door ajar. A short distance beyond, a figure in a woolly hat and donkey jacket squats on his haunches as he adjusts the rudder of a model yacht. The only other living person in sight.

Alma pans the entire skyline. In the distance, towering concrete marks the office blocks at Marble Arch. Straight ahead, behind the branches of the line of trees criss-crossing the sky like Japanese script, the tower of the Old

Admiralty Building on Horse Guards Parade, just visible. Behind that, Big Ben. Above hang dull, swollen clouds.

A lash of wind takes her by surprise. The grey November morning is too chill to wake the dozens of swans that nest here. But all Alma has on her mind is the looming presence of Leonard Parmenter, and the fear he will always be there.

A week earlier, on her mother's insistence, Alma had made her first trip back home for the weekend. It had been a disaster. During Saturday lunch, Angela Dean had let her know that a few close friends would be joining her at the vicarage a little later for an informal tea. Alma was lying on her bed, reading, when she heard the echo of his laughter from the downstairs hallway.

Knowing that at any moment she'd be summoned to join them, she quickly dimmed the lamp and drew the curtains. *A migraine*, she whispered miserably from beneath the covers. *I've had an aspirin. All I can do now is ride it out.* It was the flimsiest of excuses, but her mother had believed her, and after she'd fussed about the dangers of reading in poor light she'd left her to it, muttering something about an eye test as the bedroom door swung to.

Thankfully Leonard did not stay long that day. But when her mother came back upstairs to check on her a little later, she pressed a sealed envelope into Alma's hand containing ten one pound notes and a postcard featuring a colour photo of Big Ben.

Please accept this token of my appreciation in the spirit in which it is intended, he had written. *You have been much in my thoughts these past few months since Vienna and I pray that I have been in yours, too. Let me know when I can see you, Alma, dearest. Always, your Uncle L.*

Horrified, Alma stared at the pound notes, wondering what to do.

The money felt like some kind of payment, and that made her feel dirty. Even so, this unexpected windfall would more than cover the costs of a nice slap-up meal for her and Viola, with change to spare. Conflicted, she crumpled the card and tucked it down into the bottom of her overnight bag before carefully folding the cash and stuffing that into her pocket.

But in the days that followed Alma found the ten pounds impossible to spend.

She sighs, her breath misting the air. She wanted to have confided all this in Viola, but her friend has grown increasingly preoccupied in recent weeks by a plan she's hatched with Geoff to start a new group together with a faster, harder-edged musical style inspired by The Velvet Underground. The pair have even begun sleeping over at a flat in Lancaster Gate owned by Viola's older brother, which she is allowed to use now and then when he's away.

Today has been the first time they've spoken, properly, in what seems like a lifetime, Alma thinks, folding her arms to hug her body more tightly through the coarse woven fabric of her winter coat, then waiting for her roommate to process the latest details of her predicament and give her assessment.

'Alma.'

'What?'

'This can't go on. You've had a face like a wet weekend for days. So what are you going to do?'

Alma narrows her eyes. 'Do?'

'Yes, do.'

'What do you mean?'

'Come on, Alma. It's really quite simple.' Viola stamps her feet to keep warm. 'You've got a decision to make. He's a creep, right? You don't want him around. So tell him. And if he keeps coming back, tell someone else. Whoever runs that music council he's involved with. Fight back. Get him in trouble with his boss. Or believe you're powerless and get on with that, living life at his beck and call. Either way, make a choice. Us girls don't have to stand for any of that kind of shit any more. Haven't you read *The Female Eunuch*?'

Alma's fists clench. Because of course she has – well, flicked through it.

'So what are you saying, Viola?' she cries, with more anger than she realises has been building inside her, for weeks. 'That I'm naïve? That I'm some kind of sad type for being hurt and upset? That it would be wrong if, some day, I meet someone – a proper man, my own age, like that man I met at Number Nineteen with you and Geoff, someone interesting – who'll look after me, settle down and have children?'

'Of course not,' Viola groans, extracting a pack of cigarettes from her coat pocket. 'What I am saying is the world won't stop turning, so whether you like it or not, you've got to move on.'

Alma leans towards the lit match Viola proffers in her cupped, gloved hand. Recognising the cardboard book of matches her friend is clutching makes her think, just for a moment: what if? But it is pointless, she knows, and the memory is swiftly crowded out by other thoughts.

Alma inhales and for a second or two her head swims and her temper lessens.

What happened with Leonard isn't her fault. Nor is she to blame for the fact that he took advantage of her. She's not the one who was blind, careless and naïve: her parents were. They should have been the ones to guard her, not pave his way to her door. She should have been protected. She was only a child. And in the kind of situation she'd found herself in, how the hell can a child be the one to take control? But she is an adult now. And maybe an adult can.

Alma turns towards Viola.

'So what would you do?'

'Oh that's not fair,' her friend exclaims. 'I mean, it's irrelevant. I'm not you and I'm not in your situation, am I?' She lets slip a laugh. 'We're very different, you and I.' Alma opens her mouth, about to object. 'Don't deny it. I can see as clear as day from the look on your face what you think about me and Geoff. But you're entitled to your opinion. My point is simply this: you've got to do what you've got to do. It doesn't matter what other people might say. Only you know what's right for you.'

And she is right, Alma knows. Though she has been shocked by some of the details Viola has shared about her sex life with Geoff, she also knows that other people's opinions shouldn't matter. Because she's hated her parents' fixation with how things might look; their willingness to kowtow to expectation and do the right thing. And yet here Alma is passing judgment on her friend. Still bound by convention, maybe she is more like her mother and father than she'd like to think.

'But you didn't answer,' Alma presses on, taking a final drag on her cigarette then flicking the butt across the ground. 'My question – about what you would do if you were me. And not just about Leonard.'

'Really?'

Alma nods.

'Hell, you're honest and brave and beautiful,' Viola declares. 'You need to start putting yourself first and live a little. You need to ditch the creep and bury the past. How you deal with what's happened is down to you and only you. Take control of it. Do what suits you, not what pleases everyone else.' She grins. 'You need to find someone you want to be with who turns you on. I mean, it's 1974, for Christ's sake, Alma. Us girls have got to stand up for what we want. No one saves us but ourselves.'

–

'Hey, Alma, you've got a visitor.'

Both girls turn as one towards Trish, the girl from the room opposite theirs. She is standing by the pigeonholes outside the porter's office holding a mug of tea as Alma and Viola burst through the main door of Engel House, flushed and freezing from their walk, a short while later.

With raised eyebrows, Viola opens her mouth to speak but the other girl gets there first.

'It's your uncle,' Trish continues, dropping her voice to a conspiratorial whisper. 'I hope everything's OK.'

Uncle? The word makes Alma freeze.

'Uncle,' Viola echoes, straining for Alma's nearest hand. For a moment, their fingers interlace. 'I take it—'

'No,' Alma whispers, tightly. 'I don't.'

Her roommate nods. 'OK. So. What shall we do?'

Alma pulls out the slim wad of folded notes she's been carrying with her for the past couple of weeks. And as she stares at them and an idea starts to forms a weight begins to lift. 'Here,' she says, shrugging off her coat. 'Take this for me, I'll be up in a minute.'

Viola hesitates.

'Go on,' Alma urges. 'You've got to change, haven't you?'

'Sorry?' Her roommate looks even more confused.

'For the tarts and vicars Christmas party Geoff's taking you to later – at the student union bar on Malet Street. Isn't he picking you up in half an hour?'

Viola checks her watch. 'Shit.'

'So go on. Get gorgeous.'

Her roommate smiles. 'I will. And you—'

'I'll be OK. Where is he?' she adds, turning back to Trish.

'The TV room.'

Alma nods then makes her way towards what was once a drawing room and is now the communal TV viewing area where, after signing in, all visitors are asked to wait.

Leonard Parmenter is standing by the open fireplace with his back to her as she enters the room. Still dressed in his outdoor coat with his gloved hands interlinked behind his back, he is slowly moving his weight from one foot to the other and then back again. Her eyes range across the sofas and straight-backed armchairs pulled into clumsy clusters. They appear to be alone.

'Hello,' she calls out in a measured tone.

'Alma!' he exclaims, turning around. 'You look… different.'

'Oh this,' she demurs, raising a hand to her hair. She'd almost forgotten. 'Well yes, I guess I am.'

'I thought I'd treat us to tea. At the Savoy!' Leonard beams, unperturbed. He takes a step forward as if intending to embrace her, but she takes a purposeful side-step, neatly avoiding his touch.

'No thank you,' she says, battling hard to dismiss the memory of herself seated on his lap. The sensation of his

96

bloated fingers in her hair; pawing her body. The sound like a low groan as he held her firm. The sourness of his breath. Don't give into it, she orders herself. Don't. Let. Him. Win. Then suddenly the tension welling inside her releases. No. She will not let him win, she decides, raising her head as she gathers herself up to her full height. And she will do so by embracing not cowering from this moment.

Alma's lips twitch as she fights a triumphant smile. The wrongness of what he did is her power.

'On me, I said,' he declares. 'Now run along and get your coat, there's a good girl.'

'I said, no thank you,' Alma repeats, firmly.

Leonard frowns.

'But there is one thing you can do for me,' she adds, evenly, holding the pound notes neatly folded in her hand out towards him. 'You can take this back. Then you can leave me be.'

'Why Alma—' he objects.

'I said, you can take this back.'

'Alma?'

'Please. Hold out your hand.'

To her surprise, he does just that. And then, to her amazement, before he can take them she opens her hand and lets the notes float to the floor.

'Alma!' he chides. His voice now has a menacing edge.

'But I will hold on to this.' Alma holds up the Big Ben postcard around which the notes had been wrapped. She has carefully flattened out the card and now disdainfully holds it up between a finger and thumb, like the dirty secret it stands for. 'In case you have any more ideas about lying about me to my mother and father.'

Leonard lets slip a laugh. 'They won't believe you.'

'Probably not,' she agrees. 'But your boss might be interested. Donald Pietersen, the regional director of music?'

Leonards' lips purse. Then, taking her by surprise, he makes a grab for Alma's hand and grips it so tight it makes her wince. 'I'll have that, shall I?' he mutters, coldly.

'No, I'll be having it,' another voice interjects. Its owner, a tall man in a sombre black suit, clerical shirt and dog collar, steps between them from a pair of high-backed armchairs immediately to their left where he must have been sitting. Beneath the pair of thick-rimmed Mary Whitehouse spectacles he is wearing, the face reminds her of someone. Though his thick dark hair is all slicked back. And his dress is… unexpected. Biting her lip, she tries not to laugh.

'Is this gentleman bothering you, Alma?'

'Reverend,' she gasps, doing her best not to grin. For the false teeth she can now see he is wearing have totally changed the shape of his mouth. And as he speaks, carefully enunciating the tip of each word with his tongue, all she can think of is that 'Vicar of Belching by the Sea' played by Dick Emery.

'My child,' Geoff nods, reverentially, before snatching the postcard and dangling it high above Leonard's head 'And you—' he says, firmly jabbing the older man's chest with the forefinger of his free hand. '—explain yourself, why don't you?'

Struggling for breath, Leonard is now highly agitated by his apparent inability to muster an answer.

'Well then,' Geoff continues, coolly. 'If you can't explain yourself to me, maybe you can to your superiors. Who will be hearing from me, you can rest assured. I've met people like you before, you know, Mr—'

'Parmenter,' Alma offers, helpfully.

'Indeed. And I can tell you, Mr Parmenter, that you are all the same – tawdry and squalid. An absolute shower. So go on. Please leave, now. You will be hearing from my superiors in due course.'

As Leonard scuttles from the room Alma stares for a moment wide-eyed at her saviour.

'Geoff—' she begins until he holds up a finger, urging her to wait for the main front door to swing to with a decisive thud. At which point Alma collapses onto the nearest sofa in fits of hysterics. 'Thank you,' she gasps. 'Oh Geoff, that was simply priceless. An absolute shower… Who do you think you are, Leslie Phillips?'

'Actually, I'd been planning to do a bit of a Terry Thomas. But once I got going, it took on a bit of a life of its own,' Geoff grins, removing his glasses and ruffling his hair. 'I'll tell you what, though. This bloody outfit's going to require a few modifications if it's going to last me the evening.'

Chapter 11

Zeb peers through the rain-streaked window at the outskirts of the village where she grew up, with its rows of tightly-curtained houses, their faces dimly glowing. She has come to collect the rest of her father's papers and check the house which, she has decided, will be far quicker and easier to do alone, ahead of Matty's return the following morning.

Slowing to a crawl, she passes the bus shelter from which she used to depart each morning for secondary school. The pub where she had a Saturday job for a while waiting on tables. The green which, she can see from the beams cast by her headlights, is half-submerged by standing water. And beyond that the right-hand turn, just after the empty building which was once the village primary school; the way to Dad's.

A short distance ahead she turns onto the track that leads to her father's house.

As Zeb parks on the muddy verge opposite the last in a row of semi-detached cottages, a silver SUV that's shadowed her since she left the A-road pulls up a short distance behind her. One of Dad's neighbours, she guesses, though the driver makes no attempt to leave the car. Buttoning her coat to the neck, Zeb hurries along the rutted track that leads to the boarded-up cricket pavilion, swings a sharp right half-way along, then follows the narrow footpath that leads to Dad's front door. The Friday traffic was far worse than she'd expected and now it is getting late, almost six, which means she'll have to get her skates on. But goodness, she can't help thinking. Was the place always as dark as this?

Number 2, Rose Cottages is the right-hand half of an estate worker's house built by a local landowner in Victorian times. With its latticed windows and gabled front it would be the mirror image of number one, its left-hand neighbour, were it not for the colour of its front door – dark green not pale blue – and its plain, not floral, curtains.

Light cheers the interior of just one half and it is to this side of the house that Zeb now turns. Fat wet drops of rain break across her back. Though before she can get to the front door, Dad's neighbour – Joyce, a retired teacher in her early seventies – appears in the open doorway.

'I do wish you'd told me you were coming. Given me a chance to tidy up,' the woman exclaims, brushing the dog hair from her navy Guernsey downwards onto her crumpled, brown trousers. 'Only the place is pretty much as it was found, you know, after your father…'

Zeb forces a smile. 'Honestly, it's not a problem, Mrs Cunningham. I just came on a whim to collect a few bits. Don't worry, I've got a key. I just wanted to let you know it was me so you wouldn't worry – you know, seeing the lights on next door.'

'Goodness, Elizabeth, you're getting soaked – please, come inside!' Joyce frowns. 'Join me for some supper, I've enough to share.'

'Really, I'm fine,' Zeb lies, trying to ignore the pulse of warmth through the open doorway. The honeyed smell of just-baked bread. *Pointless* on the kitchen TV. 'I'm not staying long. But maybe a little later, before I go, for a cup of tea?'

'Well that would be lovely,' Joyce replies, turning to a pile of envelopes slipped between two pots of herbs that stand behind her. 'While I remember, you'd better take this post – just bills, I'm afraid. Oh, and so you know, the chain's across the front door.'

As Joyce had hinted, the kitchen is a mess.

Cupboard doors yawn wide, their contents roughly strewn across the kitchen counter beneath. A number of drawers have been left open, too, and an assortment of instruction booklets and receipts for different household gadgets lie scattered on the floor. It's the same in the sitting room, where cushions have been upended, bookshelves rifled and DVD boxes opened. Like the place has been burgled.

It must have been the police, Zeb reasons, grimly, straightening the sofa then perching awkwardly on its edge. Even so, they could have shown some respect.

Turning towards the mantelpiece – a slab of reclaimed timber set into the plaster surround of a tiled fireplace containing a modern gas fire – her eyes range left to right along the assortment of postcards and snapshots it bears, some framed, others not. Propped right in the centre is the photograph Dad took of her on the afternoon of her graduation. As Zeb stares at this she hears his voice.

Work here, with me, he'd urged. *I could train you up and you could easily take over the business.*

They were in the car driving Bristol-wards that golden July morning on their way to Zeb's certificate ceremony.

He was wearing the suit he usually reserved for weddings. A tiny fleck of white tissue clung to the place on his left cheek where he'd nicked himself shaving. She was seated, stiff-backed and stony-faced, on the front seat by his side. Anger, so intense its aftertaste still lingered, from the argument they'd had at breakfast.

But you just don't understand, she'd snapped. *That's your dream. I've my own life to lead. I just want to be me.*

Dad had been vehemently opposed to her decision to move to the city from the quiet of the countryside she'd grown up in and then returned to at the end of her studies, albeit briefly. Why was he so opposed to her moving to London? He'd grown up in the place, after all. Something happened, she now recalls him saying once. It was the nearest he ever came to providing an explanation for why, when she was three, he'd abruptly packed their bags, left the city where he was born – in a two-up, two-down in Clapton – and started again as a local photographer in a small village near Wells.

Something bad happened, Dad had once said. *The final straw.*

Now, though, all Zeb can feel is shame for how casually she'd dismissed his feelings. How stubbornly she'd refused the urge to place her arm around him to reassure him that everything would be OK. Because that day in the car she'd done neither, opting instead to sit in stubborn silence staring into the middle distance, head turned away. For Wendy, the smiling woman in the next picture – Dad's partner of almost ten years – had been diagnosed with breast cancer not long before, which was the reason why she hadn't come with them that day.

Wendy. Like a mum but not quite the same – though not for want of trying, Zeb thinks, guiltily. The woman, who had married her dad around the time she'd started school, and died when the cancer returned, not long before Zeb moved into Maresfield House. And in the main she had been a good stepmum.

Yet Zeb had sensed the incompleteness of their relationship from an early age. Now, looking back, she wonders how much this – despite Wendy's obvious affection for her – has contributed to a certain restlessness. A lingering feeling that a fundamental part of her life, critical to the framework of her very being, was missing. The vague sense of loss this brought had cast a shadow across her otherwise untroubled childhood, a subtle patina.

Beside the graduation day picture is another snapshot of her taken on the morning of her first day in senior school. Dressed in regulation pale blue and grey, she stands glowering beneath a pudding bowl haircut between Dad and Wendy. He is wearing a leather jacket and *Top Gun* shades – a look they'd both ribbed him for, mercilessly. The three of them are outside the corner shop in the village where she grew up. It's sunny and the trees are budding. Was it Easter? She can't recall.

The remaining line of pictures distracts her with other memories. Wendy's valiant attempts to encourage her to ride her bike unaided. Her failed attempts to teach her tennis. The two of them with hair freshly styled, faces made up and nails painted after a girls' trip to a local beauty salon. Though they'd not told Dad, of course: the excursion had been Wendy's idea to mark the start of her first period.

Zeb picks up the final image in which the three of them sit behind a giant ice-cream cocktail adorned with paper parasol and sizzling sparkler, mugging for the camera, unbothered by the scarlet sheen branding their faces and shoulders.

They'd been on holiday, staying in a beachside hotel in a small fishing village somewhere in the Algarve. Mid-August – a mad time for any English man or woman to venture far beneath a scorching Mediterranean sun, especially in the days before Factor 40. She can still see the shopkeeper's face when they bought all that Greek yoghurt. *Not just the perfect breakfast*, Wendy declared, knowledgeably, punctuating her observation with her snort of laughter. *But the best sunburn cure in the world, ever!*

Familiar stories from a shared past now help Zeb forget the fear of her lost days in Scotland. These people, this place, they shaped who she is. As she thinks of how little she'd seen him in those last few months, tears prick her eyes. Just every few Sundays for lunch at his. Dinner in a restaurant when he was up in town. Though he was here, always here on call to listen or advise.

How casually she takes him – took him, rather – for granted.

Retracing her steps back into the kitchen, Zeb is relieved to see the pilot light still flickering in the boiler. She fires up the heating then opens the hanging cupboards in search of something to drink. There is tinned soup, cream of tomato, which she heats on the hob then pours into a mug.

At least it was quick, she thinks. Better that way than to die of some dreadful, lingering disease.

Back in the sitting room, Zeb sifts through the letters Joyce gave her. Junk mail. Notifications of bank changes. A couple of unpaid bills. It starts to rain again and the wind shakes the windows. From the garden next door comes the sound of Mrs Cunningham gathering in her dogs. Putting out her recycling. Securing the lid of an old metal bin.

Dad's side of the house feels too quiet.

Zeb turns on the TV and flicks through the channels, but nothing engages her. She crosses the room to stand at the window that looks out across the common. The silver BMW is now parked outside the house next door and the outline of its driver, who is slumped in his seat reading the paper and smoking, is illuminated by the dashboard's gentle glow. Noting the main road is still busy she decides to wait another half hour before leaving, to be doubly sure of missing the rush hour traffic, even though it's already gone seven.

The flickering screen behind her is mirrored in the window and as she watches, the reflected body of a woman washes up on a tropical beach. Death even in paradise, she thinks, drawing the curtains. Turning the set to mute, she wraps her coat around her then stretches out on the sofa and slips into an erratic doze.

By the time Zeb wakes a little later the room is warmer. But now it's too late to sort Dad's papers and she feels too weary to drive home. The sofa is uncomfortable. She moves to the armchair but its back is too straight. She goes into the kitchen and double-bolts the back door, then makes a tour of all ground floor windows, checking the locks and drawing the curtains. Only then does she turn towards the stairs.

Zeb stops on the first floor landing. She is opposite Dad's bedroom and his next door office, the place where he was found. Taking a deep breath, she steps past both closed doors towards the back of the house and the room above the kitchen which she will forever think of as hers. Opening her bedroom door, she sniffs the air. It's still there, the vague funk that's always tinged this particular corner of the house, due to a damp spot halfway up the bricked-in chimney. The familiarity of it is reassuring.

Crossing the room in darkness, Zeb peers out towards the close-packed, towering leylandii wall dividing the grounds of the luxury bungalow at the rear with its tennis court and ha-ha from Dad's pocket handkerchief of a garden. Though she doesn't really need to, she draws the curtains.

Her old bed is made up but the eiderdown is thin, so Zeb reaches up to the top shelf of the old oak wardrobe to pull down two spare pillows and an armful of extra blankets. She eases the mattress off the frame and onto the floor where it neatly fills in the gully between bed and window. She then heaps the extra covers on top, taking her time arranging pillows and cushions.

I did just this the day Dad told me about my mum, she remembers, dimming the light.

–

It happened on the evening of her seventh birthday, after the swimming party she'd had at the local open air pool. The other girls had gone home and Wendy was clearing up after tea when Dad popped his head round the door of the sitting room, where Zeb was carefully arranging her new collection of animal Wade Whimsies, to tell her to go upstairs for her bath.

No, she'd snapped, her lungs ragged from too much swimming; bloated with cake, and beyond tired.

Do as your father says, Wendy chided, appearing unannounced in the open doorway.

Don't want to. Shan't. Won't, Zeb cried. *Especially not for you.*

As their eyes locked, Zeb churned with a profound and all-encompassing surge of anger. Resentment for the woman who'd wandered uninvited into her home just a few months earlier, with her unwanted life lessons drawn from her childhood in Singapore and her unasked-for attempts to buy Zeb's affection with porcelain figures. Cooking them strange food she'd never heard of, and from scratch. Dividing Dad's attention. And now, telling her what to do like she thought she was her mum.

Wendy's eyes narrowed.

Oh for Jesus effin' Christ's sake! Zeb cried.

Excitement eclipsed anger as the words somehow just slipped from her childish lips and she savoured the sound of the expletive she'd often thought but never before dared say. She wondered for a moment if now she was a bad person – like Jennifer Cox, the teenage girl next door whom she'd heard shouting this when caught shoplifting in WH Smiths. Dad took a step towards her then stopped, his jaw tensed. After a controlled exhalation of breath, he directed an instructive nod at Wendy which made her immediately leave the room.

What is it, Zeb? he asked, taking a seat on the sofa then patting the cushion at his side. *Don't you like our new friend?* Zeb was too confused to answer. Because she'd expected him to be cross. So all she could do now was stand her ground with arms tightly folded, scowling fiercely.

You need a bath because you smell of chlorine, and to rinse your hair.

Dad paused, weighing up the gamble he was about to make. He patted the cushion once more and this time she perched beside him, though with head bowed. *And you will apologise to Wendy, for me. Because I like her, Zeb, a lot. And I want her to stay. You are everything to me, but you must understand – it's been difficult doing it all on my own these last few years.*

Zeb looked up, quickly. Challenging him to meet her gaze. Because he was wrong. *You're not alone – you've got me.*

That's not what I mean. As he placed an arm around her shoulders he kissed the top of her head, softly. *Don't you think Wendy would be nice to have as an almost-mum?*

What about my real mum?

It was the first and only time the question that had been – and forever would be – locked inside her heart was aired. Looking back, she can still remember it so vividly, down to the tiniest detail. How the sun had stencilled the pattern from her sandal onto her left foot. The way his arm around her shoulder made her feel she could conquer anything, even Jonny Lidster – the boy in her class at school who always teased her so.

The tang on his breath from the can of beer he'd been drinking.

The way his body warmed her own.

Won't she mind? Zeb stuttered. *What will she say? Because everyone has a real mum, somewhere – Sara said so.*

Dad's arm tensed. A moment before, it had buoyed her up. Now it was a weight pressing her down.

You're right. Everybody does have a mum. And you did, too. But sadly your mum can't come and see you, he sighed, squeezing her tightly. *Because, my little love, she died when you were born.*

Zeb's eyes widened, as anger and frustration faded to a distant memory. For Dad had not said anything about her mum before, ever. At least not directly. Just: *She loves you very much.* Or: *If she could be here she'd be so proud.* Now, as she tried to process what he'd just said, all she could focus on was the smell of Sandwich Spread from the gobbet she'd spilled down her front at tea. Though the gloop had been quickly wiped clean, a greasy stain marked the chest of her party dress. It smelled like sick.

Her lips quivered.

I'm sorry I couldn't tell you before, Zeb, but it was too hard. You were too young. But you're getting to be such a big girl now. Smart, too – everyone says so. Especially Wendy. Having her around these past few months has made things a lot easier for me, you know. It's not about replacing your mum – no one ever could. But wouldn't it be good to have someone other than me to, well, talk to as you get bigger? About feelings and so on.

She looked up, hopefully. *About my real mum?*

Dad's mouth twitched into a kind-of-smile, though it didn't reach his eyes. *Perhaps. And other stuff, too.*

Was she… pretty?

Dad looked baffled for a moment, then nodded. *Your mother? Yes, very.*

And clever?

He squeezed her knee. *Yes, clever too. Just like you. We loved each other… very much. And we so wanted to be together. But it wasn't meant to be. It happens like that sometimes – complications when a woman has a difficult birth. Now come on, champ,* he pressed on, lightly. *How about that bath?*

No, she snapped, wriggling free of his embrace.

Zeb—

But now she was scrambling up the stairs. Burning her knee on the carpet as she slipped where the top step met the landing. Scuttling towards the rear of the house, to the room at the back Dad always called the guest room, though visitors rarely came to stay. Slamming the only door in the house with a functioning lock and key behind her, securing her sanctuary.

Because Wendy was no one, she knew as she hurled herself into the darkest corner to one side of the bedroom window; buried her head beneath folded arms. Rocked her body, to and fro. Because her mum was dead.

Disorientated, Zeb gasps for breath as her head rings with the old, familiar chant.

Dead because of me.

–

Zeb wakes bewildered to find herself in her old childhood bed as an adult; at home, but homeless without Dad. Even so, waking dreams from her childhood have out-played the lingering fear about what happened in Scotland, trumping it with familiarity, reassurance and grief.

She rolls onto her back. Her neck is cricked and her mouth dust-dry. It's morning – early, judging by the half-light. The house is still. Yet though alone, she knows she has slept well and finds herself calmer than she's been in weeks; reassured, too, by being closer to a familiar past. Though she struggled to believe it age seven when life was so much more black and white, no one could – or ever did – blame her for what happened to her mother.

Running the shower as hot as she can bear, Zeb scrubs herself until her skin feels raw. Then, once she has dressed in yesterday's clothes, she sets about tidying the house in readiness for the estate agents she must soon approach for a valuation, meticulously checking cupboards and desk drawers in the downstairs dining room which also doubled as an office.

An hour later, a pile of Dad's things sits neatly piled by the back door. Beside a boxed set of family photo albums and an ancient family Bible is the metal filing box he used to store the financial paperwork. As Zeb stares at it, she realises that these remnants of his life are also future foundation for her own. With his solicitor, she will formulate a plan for selling the place. Schedule a weekend to return and sort through everything. Find somewhere to put what she wants to keep in storage, in the hope that, one day, she and Matty will have a bigger place to live – maybe with the proceeds of the sale. Even though tomorrow's uncertainties feel too raw to address, life will move forward.

Zeb picks up her car keys then puts them down again. There is still one thing she has to do.

Upstairs on the landing she hesitates passing the closed door of the room where he was found. Her heart is racing. Though the thought of what she might find is dreadful, she knows she must go inside to prove there is nothing to see. Which is almost, somehow, worse.

The door swings open. Inside the room, the Indian rug stretches diagonally across the wooden floor as it has always done, its fabric flush against the board. The weave is un-snagged, the pattern unmarked. But this is where he was found, she thinks. On the floor. Almost dead, but not quite.

How long had he been lying here, in need of help? Alone.

Zeb shakes her head, willing herself to be strong. For there is no visible evidence of the end of a life so recently played out here. Only in her imagination.

She straightens the curtains then takes in the sole picture standing, framed, on the sill. It is of her, as a baby, at her christening. She slips it into her pocket.

On the far side stand floor-to-ceiling shelves containing box after box of Dad's archived photos. For now, she decides, they'll be safest left there. Everything, it seems, is in its rightful place – including the pile of books stacked on their sides on the floor beside Dad's bed. A Webster's biographical dictionary beneath a battered-looking thesaurus and, sandwiched between them, a cookery book with a cream-coloured spine which makes her pause.

Curious, Zeb thinks, pulling *100 Amazing Tastes of the Sea* free. Because unlike her, Dad hated fish.

As soon as she weighs the recipe book in her hand she knows there's something odd about it. It isn't as heavy as it should be. And it doesn't open because its pages seem to have become stuck together. Holding it up, Zeb gives it a shake. It's hollow, she realises as something inside shifts. The cover appears to be a lid and when she peers at the side she sees a tiny keyhole.

Still clutching the secret safe, she retraces her steps back downstairs and finds a screwdriver.

Seated on the bottom stair, Zeb carefully inserts the tip beneath one side of the lid and prises it open. Inside is a tiny glass phial containing a gold lock of baby hair – hers, she guesses; the pair of amber earrings Dad gave Wendy the Christmas before she died; and a brown envelope worn furry with a split along one side. The envelope's flap is folded inside rather than stuck down.

Hello stranger, the handwritten letter begins. *How have you been?*

> *Better than me, I hope. Life here is very different,*
> *as I'm sure you can imagine. But we are surviving,*
> *just, and counting the days until we see you again.*
> *I hoped you would make it up last weekend but*
> *I know you've been busy. How did the exhibition*

opening go, by the way? How I wish could have been there.

We've been spending a lot of my time reading and listening to music.

There's a pretty good library here, but having no instrument has been a challenge. Do you think it's possible to lose dexterity in your fingers by not playing? I hope not but just in case, there's an exercise I've taught myself from an article I read. You put your hands on a table as if you were resting your finger on keys, then 'play' 1-3-5-2-4 over and then over.

You should try it if ever you have some spare months to kill.

Sorry, I must be strong. And knowing you're still on my side keeps me going – along with the review coming up in a few months' time. Anyway, there's not much else to say, sadly, as nothing much else has happened. But come and see me soon, please. I'm not sure you realise quite how lonely it is here. Whatever's happened, remember, nothing will change the way I feel about you.

Yours, truly & forever,

Always,

A

x

Zeb ponders the intriguing initial but it means nothing to her. The writer's petulant tone gives her the air of a jilted lover. A teenage crush perhaps, though with no date to indicate when the letter was written, it's hard to say. She refolds the letter and slips it back inside the envelope. If this was important enough for Dad to hide then she should look after it, too, she thinks, adding it to the collection of things to drive back to London.

Though the rain has stopped as she loads the remaining boxes of papers into the boot of her car, she is too preoccupied by thoughts of her imminent reunion with Matty to notice. Which is why the four-by-four she saw last night, a silver BMW still parked a short distance away with its driver hunched down in in the front seat with his head bowed as if sleeping, barely merits her attention.

Chapter 12

Shoreditch, March 1975

Stepping over the smouldering cigarette butt Viola has just let slip, Alma moves towards the tin map on the wall detailing the geographical vagaries of Old Street station. Tunnels, stale-smelling and dimly-lit, stretch away from them in all directions. Any of the main exits will bring them back to the surface into open air, but only one will do so the right side of the busy roundabout.

'Second on the left should do it,' Viola finally declares. 'Come on.'

'This clothes shop had better bloody well be worth it,' Alma mutters, darkly. 'These heels won't stand traipsing around in circles a second time.'

They could have travelled by tube as far as Moorgate; it would have been closer. But neither has had the stomach for it since the crash there which killed so many just a few weeks earlier. Though no one has yet discovered the cause, speculation about terrorist involvement is rife. So though neither would ever admit to believing any old rubbish about plots or curses, they'd silently risen as one to disembark as the train slowed to a halt one stop earlier than was required.

The two girls leave the ticketing area and turn along a grimy passage. This leads into a wider, tile-hung walkway at the end of which they face two choices. To their right is a gentle slope, to their left a set of steep steps. They choose the latter and quickly emerge at street level on the right side of the busy City Road. The sky is bright with the kind of spring sunshine that makes the world seem good once more.

A lonely Christmas back home with her parents now seems long ago. As does her mother's revelation during their last Sunday night phone call that she's finally redecorated Alma's bedroom. And that she had also let slip that Leonard has moved to Germany to take up an honorary position at the Hochschule für Musik, in Dresden. Not a place Alma plans to visit in a hurry, ever.

Grabbing hold of her friend's hand, Viola bustles her along the side of the main road for a short distance then tugs her down a narrow alley between two boarded up buildings. Alma's ankles, already stiff from compensating for the new boots her friend encouraged to buy the previous weekend from a stall in Camden Market, bow as she struggles to keep up.

Entirely in shadow, the alley has a lingering, vegetable smell which makes both girls' pace quicken until they burst into sunshine once more.

They stop to catch their breath by a barber's, the first shop in a parade of shuttered stores and narrow offices that veers off to their right. Alma frowns. Unfamiliar with this part of London, she is finding it difficult to get her bearings and wishes she'd brought her A-to-Z.

'Which way now?'

'Down the road then right at The Weaver's Arms,' Viola replies. 'Another five minutes at most.'

Alma groans. And then again more loudly when, a minute later, the heel of her left boot snaps.

Gripping onto a window ledge, she examines the damage. But with the plastic heel dangling from the upper by a thread, there is no way she can walk in it now. Cupping her hands around her eyes she leans into the window of what looks like a saloon bar of a pub. But the glass, distorting like smeared bi-focals, makes the interior impossible to see.

'Come on,' calls Viola, already striding ahead having spotted an entrance just around the corner. 'We'll have a drink, fix your boot, then be on our way.'

They buy two Cokes then choose an empty table by the window. An elderly man with a tangle of white hair is playing the slot machine. On the other side of the bar, two men nursing empty pint glasses talk at each other quickly in broad Irish accents.

Crossing her legs, Alma slips off the broken boot, taking care not to let her unsheathed foot touch the sticky floor. With its stale odour, the brown carpet is a pungent testament to the clumsiness of the establishment's clientele.

'Wait here,' Viola instructs. 'I'll ask if the barman's got any Sellotape or glue.'

Leaning closer to the window, Alma attempts to decode the blurred shapes passing outside.

The first is a taxi, that's easy. And next a cyclist. Two women – they are chattering loudly, which is a bit of a cheat. Then a man on foot – she can just make out jeans, a white T-shirt; his thick dark hair. This figure quickly steps out of range only to reappear in the pub doorway. He begins making his way towards the bar but then, noticing Alma, seems to think again. A moment later he is walking towards her.

'Hi.'

He stands next to her, waiting for Alma to look up. But she resists, irritated by the unwelcome intrusion. Searching for Viola, her throat knots in anger when she sees how quickly her roommate has fallen into deep conversation with the man behind the bar. Then, when it becomes clear that the stranger isn't giving up so easily, she slowly puts down her glass and offers up a blank stare.

'Can I buy you another?'

'No thanks,' she answers. 'We're just about to leave.'

'We?'

The man makes a show of glancing around the almost empty room before fixing his gaze on Viola, now seated at the bar. He pulls up a stool. 'Your friend doesn't look like she's about to go anywhere.' Alma frowns, because he's right. 'Go on, let me buy you another,' he presses on. 'Was that Coke you were drinking?'

Alma turns back towards the bar to see Viola throw her a merry wave without pausing her conversation. Defeated, she sighs. 'OK'.

What is it about some men that makes them so confident they will not be refused, she wonders, as the stranger make his way to the bar. He seems supremely comfortable in himself; master of the moment, as he exchanges pleasantries with Viola. As Alma watches, something he says makes her roommate look at her then laugh.

'So tell me,' the man begins, pouring her drink a few minutes later. 'Do you come here often?'

Alma takes a lengthy gulp from her glass. Something about him seems familiar. But though she is sure they've met before, she can't place him. Whoever he is, he is extremely good-looking. Her mood softens. 'No, why?'

'Only your friend says it's one of your favourite pubs.'

'Sorry?'

'She says you've often talked about it.'

'What?'

He laughs, holding up a book of matches Viola has left next to her sunglasses on the table. On one side is the name of the pub they are now in. The Bricklayers Arms on Rivington Street. Then, as Alma remembers the handsome stranger who came to her aid that night in the bar in Soho Square, her eyes widen. A sudden reminder of the days she spent wondering about him on and off. Embarrassed, she coughs then covers her mouth with her hands in a vain attempt to divert attention from her burning cheeks. Alma flicks open the book of matches. Only three have been used. Did Viola have this the whole time? Or has it been lying somewhere in their room for weeks, unnoticed and overlooked? 'I only came in because I broke my heel,' she mumbles.

'And you were passing.'

'Yes, just passing.'

'That's not what your friend says.'

Alma shifts in her seat.

The man grins. 'I think you wish you'd worn those lace-up plimsolls you almost put on this morning but then decided not to. You're annoyed you didn't bring that A-to-Z, so you could have found that shop you're looking for more quickly. You pray your friend would stop being so… just like she always is – at the bar. And, I think, Alma, that you'd rather I would just piss off and leave you alone.'

'No!' she objects, uncertain if he is serious or teasing. The last thing she wants is for him to leave her be.

He laughs, going into his back pocket for a pouch of tobacco which he then unfolds onto the table. Tongue-tied, she watches in silence as he rolls himself a cigarette. She passes him the matches, which he accepts, then wrestles with for a second or two while Alma turns to the bar where Viola is still sitting, looking away. When she turns back the man is taking his first drag on the roll-up. Then he holds out his hand.

'Sorry, maybe we should start again,' he offers, contritely. 'I'm—'

'Pete,' Alma blurts. 'I know.'

They both laugh.

'So. How are you doing?' he asks, ignoring the opportunity she's given him to make more fun.

'OK.'

'And your music?'

'Fine. Yes, good.'

Touched he's remembered, Alma smiles as she tells him about the past month or two. The mid-year music theory exams she is currently cramming for. A piano recital she attended at the Wigmore Hall the night before. And as she speaks, Pete listens with the attentiveness she remembers from their first meeting. He seems genuinely interested in her, how she's coping, what she is going to do next – almost as if it matters to him.

Switching his attention to her socked foot, Pete offers to fix the broken heel. He is sure he had some gaffer tape in the studio flat where he lives, just upstairs. Maybe, even, some heavy duty glue. If Viola doesn't mind waiting they could go up and see.

Pete's place is up a narrow set of stairs behind the bar. It's a single open-plan room of the same proportions as the public bar two floors below but the ceiling is high and the walls painted white which makes the space feel even bigger.

An old brass bedstead has been artfully pulled away from the wall to make the most of the view through a wide bay window. On the other side of the room is a tattered brown leather sofa and, behind that, camera paraphernalia, a mountain of photos and film on an old trestle table.

Alma finds herself staring at a small, open-plan kitchenette. To its left, a boxed out area separated by a pair of wooden, slatted doors must be the bathroom.

'What you see is what you get,' he declares, sweeping an arm across his domain. 'So, what do you think?'

'Very… homely.'

Alma takes a seat on the sofa, which is lower than she expected. Adjusting her position, she turns towards the wall behind and notices a large frame standing against it on the floor. Inside is a black and white photographic print of a Brixton-bound number thirteen Routemaster. Its driver, an elderly Jamaican, has two enamelled badges clearly visible on the left breast of his meticulously pressed black tunic and matching cap. Its sole passenger, an elderly white woman whose wrinkled face is encircled by a fluffy woollen balaclava, is seated on the top deck directly above the driver. With identical blank stares, both are looking straight ahead.

It is an arresting image, Alma decides, made all the more compelling by its simplicity and depth.

'I love that photo,' she exclaims. 'Where did you get it?'

'That one?' Pete follows her gaze. 'I took it. I'm glad you like it.'

Though impressed, Alma is unsure how best to show it. 'Got any others?'

'Plenty.' Placing her boot on one end of the table, Pete squats down on his haunches to pull a large box from beneath. Removing its lid, he plunges his hands inside to sift through its contents. 'Right then, let's see what we've got in here.'

Alma takes in the finer details of the rest of the room. The pull-down blackout blinds on the curtain-less windows. A crowded garment rail acting as wardrobe. Photography, cookery and travel books piled on top of an ancient sailor's trunk. A sheepskin off-cut providing a bedside rug. The mantelpiece of the fireplace opposite is part of an old railway sleeper. And in the hearth, two empty red wine bottles with a half-burned candle wedged into their necks.

'Here, remember this?'

Still crouched on the floor, Pete holds out a black and white ten-by-eight of a young woman leaning against a lamp post on the corner of a street beside a city square. It looks like late autumn, with sun shining through the empty branches of the trees in the foreground like shafts of smoke. The jacket the woman is wearing is ill-fitting though stylish; her short bobbed hair dishevelled. The way the light catches her skin makes the side of her face, just visible, seem translucent.

'Goodness!' she exclaims. 'That looks like me. In Soho Square.'

Pete nods. 'I was going to come over and say hello, but then Brian turned up. And then his dad. I thought maybe I'd run into you again inside.'

Unnerved, Alma shakes her head. 'We've not been back.'

'You were beautiful that day,' Pete murmurs, turning his attention back to her boot, which he is still holding. 'Still are. So listen, here's an idea. Once I've got this fixed, before you and your friend head off, shall we fix a date to meet?'

Chapter 13

Camden, February 2016

'Mummy!' Matty cries, hurling himself into her arms before the door is fully open. 'I got you a surprise, a present. You're going to like it, it's a—'

'Don't spoil it,' Richard interjects, placing his son's travel bag on the floor beneath the radiator.

Zeb's ex looks tired even though his face is lightly tanned, she notices, smug with the hope that he has discovered that solo parenting is harder than it looks. Though with Helene there too, he'd not really taken their son to Valderrama for a week on his own, had he?

'Oh it's so good to see you, pumpkin,' she cries, burying her face into her son's neck; joyously drinking in the warmth and softness of his skin, his sweet and milky smell. 'Was it sunny? How was flying? Did you have fun?'

'It was sooo good,' her son declares, wriggling free. 'I swam every day and learned to butterfly,' he grins, swinging both arms around in their sockets to show how. He starts to force-gasp. 'And proper breathing, like this—'

'He can swim a whole width underwater, too, can't you now, champ?' Richard chuckles, ruffling the child's hair. 'Helene taught him. You should see the pair of them, really, it's like they both have webbed feet.'

Zeb bites her lip. It is typical of him to spoil the moment by being brusque and dismissive, but the insensitivity of this last observation is impressive – even for him.

As Richard wrestles to undo the knotted laces of Matty's Kickers, she stares down in anger at the bald patch on the top of his head. Registers with loathing the sharp creases pressed into each sleeve of the Lacoste shirt he wears tucked into a pair of mustard-coloured chinos.

What is it about men of a certain age and income and inappropriately-coloured casual trousers? she thinks. Wonders, too, and not for the first time: what did I ever see in him? This was the first question Dad asked when she told him they planned to marry, too – concerned, perhaps, by the twelve year age difference.

Richard was never the father figure Sam once suggested he was, that much was for sure. At first she'd found the assuredness that came with his age and responsibilities at work made him seem dependable. But then, as he grew frustrated – by what he saw as her childish emotional over-dependence on her father, her over-protectiveness of their son – she came to see him as he really was: bombastic and condescending. And her dad had never been like that. 'Good for you!' Zeb exclaims as her son hurries past her towards his bedroom. 'And thank you for dropping him off.' She motions towards the open front door. 'I'm sure you've got lots of unpacking to do so I won't keep you…'

Richard jiggles his car keys. 'Oh, Helene takes care of all of that.'

Taking a step forward, Zeb drops her voice. 'Well isn't that nice of her?'

Her ex, ignoring this last comment, steps out onto the landing then pauses. 'I almost forgot,' Richard exclaims.

'Matty's got a party this afternoon – at Kirsty's, from three to five. But it's all sorted because Fred's mum said she'd pick him up and drop him off as you're on their way. We got him a present to take so don't worry about that – it's in his bag.'

Something else Helene probably sorted, Zeb thinks, grimly. 'Oh, right. Thanks,' she mutters.

How dare he make arrangements for Matty to be out again so soon after dropping him back? She is desperate to spend time with him. The morning is brightening; she could have taken him to the park. But she is being selfish. Of course Matty would want to go to Kirsty's party. She remembers Kirsty's mum mentioning something a while back about booking a party entertainer who did tricks dressed up as a mad scientist. She'll just have to wait: after all, there's plenty of time.

Looking up, Zeb notices Richard staring at her, intently.

'Are you all right?' he asks. 'Only, you look really pale.'

'Fine, why?' Probing for evidence I'm struggling to cope, more like, she thinks. Being unreasonable. Irrational. Working too late. Drinking too much. Any reason for Matty to spend more time with them.

'No reason,' he shrugs. 'Just asking.'

'Sorry. I'm just a bit tired,' she smiles, relieved by the sudden realisation that he must have missed what coverage there was of the media appeal while she was in hospital. 'But thank you so much for asking.'

As soon as he is gone and the door is closed, Zeb's spirits surge. 'Matty?' she calls, spinning around on her heels. 'Come into the kitchen and I'll make you a hot chocolate with marshmallows. I want to hear all about what you got up to. And what's this about a surprise?'

The repeated buzzing of the doorbell wakes Zeb some time around three.

After tidying the flat in readiness for Sam's arrival she has drifted off, lying on the sofa. A simple and mundane task, completing the housework felt like a minor triumph – a barely perceptible regaining of control. I can make this work – my new life here, on my own with Matty, she has decided. I will show the world that I am strong. A good mother. Now, rolling onto her side, she frowns. It's too early to be Fred's mum dropping Matty back off.

By the time she gets to the door the entry phone has fallen silent. Lifting the handset, all she can hear is the irregular pulse of traffic. The caller has gone.

Day is fading, drained of light by dark, low-hanging clouds. A silver saloon is parked outside the house opposite – she can just make out the blunt profile of the driver, who appears to be smoking a cigarette, and a wisp of white that curls from the exhaust. A taxi perhaps. Otherwise the pavements and road, flanked on either side by cars packed nose to tail, are empty.

She stares at the rug which half covers a red wine stain on the carpet beneath, a distant echo of the Christmas party Zeb hosted just a few months earlier. How recently the natural rhythms of her life had seemed so normal, ordered and predictable, when everything now feels like it is spiralling wildly out of control.

Salt it thoroughly, Dad would have advised. *Left to dry properly, the wine is less likely to stain.*

With just enough time before Matty's return and Sam's arrival, Zeb runs herself a bath.

Gingerly, with arms braced against the enamel, she lowers herself into the water. Though the heat makes her body stiffen, the intensity of it is irresistible. She dips beneath the filmy surface, shakes her head then pulls herself up. She feels purged.

As her body grows used to the temperature, she settles back, allowing her arms and knees to float. A collection of bath toys have been left beside the tap at her feet: the stackable multi-coloured cups Matty was given as a toddler and still loves makes her smile. There is a rubber shark with a hollow stomach that lets you squirt water, and a bizarrely aquatic Action Man complete with hand grenade, belt pack and flippers grafted onto his feet. The mirrored doors of the cabinet that hangs on the wall above the sink are milky white.

Zeb pats her sweating face dry with Matty's Pooh Bear flannel.

Without warning, a stuttering thud-thud from the corridor makes her brace. Barely daring to breathe, Zeb turns towards the door and hears a distant whirring from the kitchen marking the washing machine's movement towards its final spin. Her shoulders start to relax, but before she can lean her head back against the bath she hears something else just outside the bathroom door. The unmistakable tread of footsteps.

Zeb realises with a clench of fear that she has left the bathroom door ajar. The horror of being confined within her own flat, naked, with an unseen intruder, is overwhelming.

She quickly decides she must do two things. Cover herself. Secure the door. Though not necessarily in that order, she thinks as she slides across the tiles, flicks the lock, then wrestles jeans over her still damp body. She fumbles with the clasps on her bra then quickly discards it, slipping back on her long-sleeved T-shirt.

Crouched like a sprinter at the foot of the door, Zeb waits for the heaving in her chest to subside so she can listen, her instinct to run made pointless by the knowledge there is no place to hide. The footsteps approach, draw level, slow, then stop. Is it her imagination or can she hear the breathing as whoever it is leans in towards the door?

An abrupt rattle as the doorknob receives a single, sharp turn. Then there is nothing. Just silence, she thinks, slowly dropping to her knees and laying her head against the floor to peer at the corridor beneath the bathroom door.

Through the narrow gap, Zeb can just make out the hallway outside is in darkness. The strip of carpet, illuminated by spindles of light from the bathroom, is empty. She slowly stands, her ears straining for any evidence of movement outside. But now, it seems, even the washing machine is still.

Zeb tries to think what's best to do. Whether to risk a peek into the hall. Whether to force the window, somehow.

Instinctively, she brushes the front right pocket of her jeans with her hand but remembers leaving her new mobile on the table in the sitting room. Gazing upwards, as if seeking divine inspiration, she sees the ceiling is obscured by a thick halo of steam.

Pull yourself together, girl, she tells herself. Be practical.

Beside the laundry bin is a wicker basket containing a selection of shampoos, conditioners, body lotions and a can of hairspray. The latter has got to sting, surely, if sprayed into your face full blast, she thinks, slipping it into her back pocket. In the far corner propped against the wall behind the loo, she spots the long arm-hook Dad bought her – though she's never used it – to open the kitchen Velux. Weighing it in her hand, Zeb notices with satisfaction the rigidity of the stick's aluminium shaft.

Gripping the pole tightly, she extends her free hand towards the lock.

As the bathroom door swings open Zeb can see only a sharp shaft of sun from the glass panel above her front door. And it is into this spotlight that, before she has taken more than a couple of strides, a broad-shouldered figure suddenly steps. It is a man, she knows, even though his face is obscured. Stumbling back inside the bathroom, she slams home the bolt on the inside of the door.

Three elements are burned into her mind's eye. His outline with its thick-necked bullet head and close-cropped hair. His long overcoat, still buttoned. And the fact that he is wearing gloves.

Heavy steps approach the door and a hand worries the handle, loosening paint dust from around the frame.

Thinking fast, Zeb shoves the old chest she uses for storing sheets and towels against the door. There is a fire escape a short drop beneath the sealed window. She remembers how Dad secured the sash when she'd moved in – another security measure, she recalls now with an acid smile. Maybe if she broke a pane of glass she could clamber through the window, but would there be time?

The door frame shakes as the intruder pounds the door.

Once. Twice. Three times.

Just like before, Zeb realises, as her waking dream once more nudges reality.

The world had seemed to slow as she jiggled the catch, forcing it one way and then the other, in her desperate attempt to open the sash. And as it began to give, oblivious to the dank smell, and the catacomb tangle of cobwebs obscuring her escape, she'd grown almost hopeful. Until, after easing, briefly, it snapped off in her hand.

Pinioned beneath a naked light bulb, silent and unmoving, Zeb had desperately scanned the confines of the room only to find she was out of options. Luck, too. The only choice was to go back the way she'd come in. Somehow front it out. String him along. Then, as soon as the opportunity arose, make a dash for the front door.

Clinging to the cracked porcelain, she caught her reflection in the mirror. Her hair was lank. Her cheeks flushed and sweaty. Then, driven by the sound of his approach, she tugged the ancient chain that hung down from the water cistern.

Twisting the cold tap, she cupped her hands beneath the icy trickle to splash her face. Wiping her cheeks with her sleeve, she straightened up. The footsteps stopped just outside the door.

You a'right in there? Staccato words fired into the wood-work like bullets.

His fist shook the doorknob.

Zeb released the bolt.

Just as she does now.

Take anything, she rehearses, as her hand hovers at the door. Whatever you want. I won't say anything. Just take it, and go. Leave me alone, please. I didn't see you properly. I won't tell anyone you were here...

But now the flat seems silent.

Zeb turns her head instinctively to press her ear against the wood.

Any minute now, she thinks as blood pounds her temples, this door will give. As she swallows back a dry sob, her mouth fills with the taste of metal. Her eyes feel hot and dry. As she blinks she hears a muffled voice.

'No sign of it,' she clearly hears him say. Is he speaking on the phone? And then, at the sound of a familiar, approaching clatter, there is a sharp intake of breath. 'Not now. There's someone coming.'

A series of clunks: the sound of a shopping bag on wheels being slowly bumped up the building's communal stairs. The front door is open, she realises with a surge of hope, and now she can hear a woman humming. Then, a minute later, a familiar voice echoes from the landing.

'Hello?' a woman calls. 'Is there anybody there?'

Zeb springs towards the bathroom door, trembling.

'Christine?'

–

The locksmith beams as he hands Zeb a new set of keys.

'All done!' he declares. 'The bronze one is for the Banham. The silver Yale is for the five-lever mortice. Then you've got new top and bottom bolts. Plus all your rooms now have window locks – even the window in the bathroom which doesn't open. You should do something about that, you know; it could be a useful alternative exit in—'

'In case of fire. Yes, I know.' That's what Dad had long told her, because the narrow, steel grating walkway that clings to the building's rear runs right past that window – though she'd never got around to doing anything about it, of course. Zeb forces a smile, though she needn't have bothered, for the locksmith now has his back towards her, as he puts his tools away.

Straightening up, the man hesitates in the open doorway.

'Thanks,' she adds. 'I mean, for coming so quickly.'

'All part of the service,' he winks. The locksmith hands her a business card from his back trouser pocket. 'Recommend us to a friend and you'll get ten per cent off next time.' Zeb frowns. 'Sorry love, you know what I mean.'

'Well let's hope there isn't a next time,' trills Mrs Allitt, who is watching from her open doorway. 'Elizabeth – I'm so sorry,' she gushes once the locksmith has gone. 'Honestly, I don't know what to say. Are you sure you don't both want to sleep here tonight, with me?'

'No, really thanks. We'll be OK,' Zeb answers, her mind now solely set on retreating back behind her own front door with Matty, with whom she's made a great deal of effort to downplay the break-in. It was a silly mistake, she told him. Nothing to worry about at all. Just like she told the junior policewoman who, with time to kill before a bigger crime was committed, seemed to have come round simply to go through the motions. With no signs of forced entry, might Zeb have left the key in the front door, providing irresistible opportunity to the next passing opportunist? It was certainly a possibility, her neighbour had quickly chipped in.

Elizabeth's not quite been herself recently, the woman had confided before Zeb could object. *First Richard leaving, then her poor dear father dying suddenly… so difficult for anyone to think straight when they're going through that much stress.*

The idea that this was no more than a simple blunder had been further reinforced by Zeb's rueful admission that nothing of value seemed to have been taken. What's left of the pile of banknotes her neighbour brought to her in hospital still sits on the bedroom dresser beside her car keys and her mobile phone.

'Come on, Mummy – per-lease!' Matty calls from the sitting room where he is lying on the sofa wrapped in a snuggle sack watching TV. '*Mike the Knight*'s about to start.'

'Not *Mike the Knight*!' cries Sam, suddenly appearing at the top of the stairs. 'Hold on, hun, he's my Number One favourite.' Adjusting her grip on some plastic shopping bags, she drops her voice. 'Sorry I didn't buzz, only the guy from the ground floor flat was just leaving and he let me in.'

'Goodbye,' Zeb says firmly, tightening her grip on the spare set of keys she now has no intention of leaving with her neighbour. 'Sam,' she smiles, reaching for the bags, which are heavier than they look. 'What perfect timing.'

It's raining outside, and watery beads glint like silver in her friend's hair, which tonight she is wearing swept back off her face and loosely secured against the back of her head with what looks like a pair of lacquered chopsticks. Her coat, which is knee-length and inappropriately woollen, is sodden so Zeb hangs it in the hall by the radiator, beside which Sam leans the daypack she's also been carrying.

'A few overnight things – just in case,' Sam grins. 'You look great, by the way. If a little pale. Like the necklace, too. Is it new?'

As Zeb's fingers brush the silver chain around her neck she has a nagging sense of unease. She'd forgotten she had it on, and is unsure why she's still wearing it. But, she also hopes, if the piano charm is against her skin long enough maybe through some kind of osmosis she'll understand the secret of it. And when the mists finally clear, she senses, maybe she'll find it has something to do with Dad.

'You know something funny?' Zeb murmurs, as her friend hurries past her into the sitting room in search of her godson. 'I'm not quite sure.'

In the kitchen a short while later they unpack the provisions Sam has brought. Breadsticks and a selection of dips. Fresh pasta and Arrabbiata sauce in a plastic tub. A bag of mixed salad. Ready-made dressing. A tarte au citron. Two bottles of Pinot Grigio – the sight of which make Sam blush. 'I know, I did remember you were clinging onto the wagon but I thought – well, under the circumstances – you might need to make an exception…'

How long has it – had it – been, Zeb wonders, trying not to think of the wine at Dad's and the empty bottle of vodka in the recycling bin, since she'd tried to cut back? She forces a laugh as she takes the bottles from her friend.

'Expecting visitors, were you?'

Sam chuckles. 'Well, we could always invite the Grantham Menace to join us, if you're desperate for company. The old bag from over the landing. Your nosy-neighbour – what's her name?'

Zeb frowns. 'Mrs Allitt.'

'That's the one.' Sam grimaces as she wrestles with the cork. 'Although I prefer the nickname you came up with for her—'

'—because she's always banging on about going to the same primary school as Margaret Thatcher!' The memory of it raises Zeb's spirits. 'No, she will not be joining us tonight.'

'Christ, this one's tough,' Sam exclaims, putting down the first wine bottle.

'Here, let me,' Zeb quickly counters, offering the second bottle before her friend has a chance to split the cork. A moment later, with an expert twist of her wrist, the wine is open. She fills two of the fine-cut wine-glasses Dad gave her as a moving-in present then hands one to her friend. 'Thanks!' Zeb raises her drink in a toast, relishing the wave of confidence and hope that comes with the first mouthful. She'll stop again tomorrow. 'For coming over. For bringing food. For helping me remember.' She drops her voice so as not to be overheard by Matty, who's now in bed. 'Fuck it, for being a friend!'

'Now, now – don't get all mushy on me,' Sam counters, briskly. 'Not yet, at least. First things first, let's eat.'

Sam reads Matty his bedtime stories while supper is cooking, then they retreat with a bowl of snacks into the sitting room which is now lit by candles. The curtains are open and the windows streaked with rain but the bleakness of the world outside serves only to make the flat's interior more comforting. Slipping off her shoes, Sam takes a seat one end of the sofa with her feet tucked beneath her. She looks cosy, childlike, Zeb thinks, though her face is shadowed by a mixture of guilt and concern.

'How was Spain?' Sam asks.

'Helene went with them, though of course he didn't mention that beforehand.'

'Oh.'

Sam sits in silence for a moment, lost in thought, then sips more wine. 'So go on, tell me,' she says at last, changing the subject. 'Where have you been? What's going on?'

She listens carefully as Zeb fills in the gaps, relating the facts – or at least as much as she can recall – about what happened in Scotland in between mouthfuls of food and sips of wine. But Zeb is getting weary and has to reluctantly admit that she still can't remember what happened in the hours immediately before she was picked up by Jean.

'I mean, goodness, and please don't take this the wrong way, Zeb—' Sam drains her glass. 'But anything could have happened.'

Zeb nods, thinking of the man in Mrs Duffy's kitchen. Tears well up and she feels Sam's arm around her shoulders, holding tight. Unable to speak at first, she simply squeezes her friend's hand. 'You're right,' she stutters. 'Something did happen… only I'm still not quite sure what.'

'Come on,' her friend soothes. 'Let's talk about something else. Like work – it's been crazy since you left. Natalie will be back full-time from Easter, now the doctors have finally given her the all-clear. Oh, and the council are still considering the stage two development plan, which means there's now no time to complete work on the extension before the autumn. So it will be winter in a Portakabin for the education department and marketing. All good fun.'

'About that—' Wiping her eyes on her sleeve, Zeb picks up a breadstick and dips it in the hummus. 'I'm still a bit sketchy on some of what's gone on in recent weeks.' She offers Sam a tentative smile. 'You're going to have to fill me in. You mentioned I walked out… when was that, exactly?'

'I'm not surprised you've blocked that out,' her friend snorts. 'It was quite a scene. Now, let me see.' She leans back in her seat and munches thoughtfully.

'It was a fortnight ago. You'd just got back to work after, you know, the funeral. But I could tell you weren't right. You seemed so distracted. Then, at William's leaving do, it all seemed to come to a head. We'd all had quite a lot to drink, and you started talking about some friend of your dad's you'd never heard of turning up at the funeral unannounced and sending flowers. You even had the card from the wreath in your purse. You went on and on about it, about wanting to track them down. An ex-lover, perhaps—'

Zeb sighs, remembering the card. It was attached to a mystery wreath: the only one without a sender's name. The only hint was a tiny sticker securing the cellophane with the name of a local Scottish florist. She'd put both in the purse that disappeared when she lost her bag.

Her friend presses on.

'—only you'd just had time off on compassionate leave and Kirsty point blank refused to give you any more. You got quite cross about it. Just as we were about to move on to the club, you just let rip. Told her to stick it. I can't remember what else, we were all a bit taken aback, not to mention pretty drunk. Then Marcus tried to calm you down, but you weren't having any of it.'

Awkwardly dropping her gaze, Sam stares at her meticulous fingernails, freshly painted in a seashell pink, as she toys with the base of her wine glass.

'Next morning, when heads cleared, you not only didn't show up to work but also couriered over the proofs for the Bert Hardy exhibition catalogue, unedited. According to Marcus, the last thing you said before disappearing on your lost weekend was that you were going to find an old friend of your dad's. In Scotland.'

Chapter 14

Kings Cross, March 1975

'Close your eyes and take my hand,' says Pete, guiding Alma onto the narrow landing at the top of the final set of steps. Her heart is pounding from their steep ascent. 'Slowly, slowly,' he murmurs, urging her forward step by step. 'And whatever you do, don't look until I say.'

It had taken him a week to phone her after their encounter in Rivington Street; the conversation had been brief. He'd like to see her again and yes, she would like to see him, too. But rather than meet one night at a bar or restaurant he proposed they should rendezvous one evening outside the Kings Cross Cinema on Pentonville Road.

The suggestion left Alma mystified, because when she'd asked he'd insisted that no, they'd not be seeing a film. There was something special he wanted to show her, he insisted, though even when pressed he wouldn't say what.

Pleased that he'd called and intrigued by his evasiveness, Alma was happy to play along – allowing herself to be led through the lanes of traffic that filled the wide roads near Kings Cross Station. It was just past six and already dark, but the day had been fine and she was wearing only a light jacket and thin-soled shoes as the weather was unseasonably mild.

A few paces on, outside the monolithic façade of St Pancras Chambers, he stopped, turned towards her and instructed her to shut her eyes. Once the Midland Grand Hotel, the building had fallen into disrepair and had been turned into British Rail offices. Alma hesitated until he leaned towards her – not to kiss her, as she'd secretly wanted – but to whisper something in her ear.

Trust me, he breathed.

And she did – well, almost – peeking only every now and then as he led her towards what looked like some kind of service entrance at the far end of the gothic façade. Here they stopped momentarily as he tried the door then let slip a quick laugh as it swung ajar. He had arranged this with a friend who worked in one of the offices upstairs, he explained. A friend who owed him a favour – and this was a good one; the kind of thing money can't buy. Which she can see too as she stands by Pete's side at the building's peak, a narrow maintenance walkway skirting the inside of the upper level of the clock tower.

Alma's stomach lurches at the dizzying perspective this vantage point gives over the southward sweep of London. In the foreground she can make out the interlocking grid of streets and garden squares of Bloomsbury and, beyond that, the canyon of Oxford Street and then, further away, Soho. Shaftesbury Avenue. The Strand. Visible to the left is the necklace of street lights lining the Embankment and St Paul's distant dome. To the right, she imagines – for, in truth, she cannot quite see – Westminster and Big Ben.

'My god, Pete,' she murmurs, enthralled. 'It feels just like we're on top of the world.'

'Not a great place to be if you suffer from vertigo, of course,' he smiles. He rubs the pane of glass with the edge of his sleeve. 'But yes, I know exactly what you mean. It makes you feel tiny, doesn't it, looking down on the world from up here. Then again from this perspective, you almost feel like you could fold up the city below and tuck it in your pocket... Fancy some of this, by the way?'

'Got a couple of glasses in there, too, have you?' Alma grins as Pete pulls a bottle of red wine and a Swiss army penknife from his coat pocket. Accepting the opened bottle, she takes a deep mouthful before passing it back.

'To you,' he smiles, raising the bottle. 'To me. To all this.'

They stay another ten minutes or so, enough time to drink their fill of the view and almost half of the wine.

She tells him about The Conservatoire and her growing disillusionment with the course. Her teachers' obsession with received notions of what is and is not correct musical interpretation. How liberating it would be to play something spontaneously. How Viola is on the verge of dropping out altogether as Geoff's band is building quite a following. How she, meanwhile, is earning beer money lunchtimes and some evenings playing the original compositions of a frustrated third-year composer – another of her disenfranchised fellow students, whose real passion is jazz.

Alma half expects Pete to tease her for the high hopes she had for student life. Yet instead he seems to understand as, with a sweep of his hand towards the north, he tells her about growing up in a modest terrace in Hackney where money was tight and tempers short as his father worked all hours to build his own business. How he'd struggled at school – smarter than his contemporaries, and not sporty enough to fit in. How he'd spent his formative years whiling away hours in the local library, dreaming of escape as he pored over ancient maps and photographic plates in reference books about Kalahari bushmen; Genghis Khan's legacy; the fledgling Israeli state.

Determined to make his own way without anyone else's help, when he left school, Pete first joined a local newspaper as an apprentice typesetter – an occupation he reluctantly pursued until a lower paid job came up as general dogsbody for a north London photographic agency. The experience was an eye-opener, providing a rough and ready introduction to the basics of professional photography and the magical chemistry of film processing.

Around the time Alma arrived in London, Pete handed his notice at the agency to try his hand as a freelancer. She imagines how, able to fulfil his dreams, life felt rich with possibilities he determined not to waste.

He is, she decides, draining her last mouthful of wine, quite unlike anyone she has ever met – or, indeed, will ever meet. With an inner strength and surface stillness that is totally and utterly compelling. And as they make their way back down the flights of stairs towards ground level, Alma finds herself overwhelmed by a pressing need to show him how touched she feels by the experience they've just shared.

At ground level they slip back outside then onto the street to walk silently towards Euston. On a wooden bench in the scrub-like hinterland between the station entrance and the Euston Road they sit, side by side, sharing a large portion of fish and chips. It is almost nine when they have finished and he offers to walk her towards home – south to Oxford Street and the nearest stop for buses going her way. Alma finds herself affected and amused in equal measure.

'Actually,' she grins, taking his hand. 'I was wondering if we might go back to yours.'

–

Alma wakes to the sound of Pete busying himself in the kitchenette whisking eggs, slicing bread. She breathes in air infused with coffee, with creamy top notes from butter softly melting in the pan. Rolling onto her front, she slips his pillow onto hers then props herself on top to watch.

Dressed only in yesterday's jeans, his feet are bare. But though his face still looks crumpled from sleep, the attention he is paying to every detail of his preparations is intense.

'Hello,' she calls, hungry for his attention.

'French toast, all right?' he grins. 'Freshly squeezed orange, or just coffee?'

'No kippers? Smoked salmon?' Alma teases, for she has discovered fish is one of his pet hates. 'Never mind!' She kicks her legs free from the cotton sheet knotted around them. With the windows thrown open to release the steam from the pans, a pulse of early morning air makes her naked skin tingle. She sighs. 'I've must say, Pete, your hotel offers the best room service in town.'

'And from where I'm standing,' he quickly counters, 'I'd say I've got the best view.'

Alma lets the sheet slip onto the floor. 'Really? How about now?'

'Don't go there,' he begs. 'These eggs are almost done.'

Rolling onto her back, Alma slowly runs the palm of her hand across the flatness of her belly, just above her pubic hairline. 'Or now?'

Quickly removing the pan from the stove, Pete snatches the Polaroid camera sitting on the kitchen worktop. With just a couple of strides he is standing over her, taking a picture.

'Definitely now,' he chuckles, relishing the look of shock on her face the instant before she springs towards him, her right hand grasping at where the photographic paper will soon appear at the camera's base. 'Oh no you don't,' he teases, ripping the picture free then holding it beyond her reach as the image slowly forms. 'You're going to have to be a good girl if you're going to convince me you should have this.'

'Bully,' Alma pouts, half-heartedly, as she heads towards the bathroom to shower.

'Naughty,' Pete calls with a grin, 'but nice.'

Once the water is warm enough, Alma washes. Slipping out the cap Viola had helped her get from Marie Stopes, she rinses it under the running water. *Better safe than sorry*, her friend had winked, taking her by the hand as they'd walked back down the clinic's front steps. *And I should know.*

It had happened the spring before she started at The Conservatoire. Viola had fallen pregnant following an encounter with the eldest son of one of her father's friends. It had taken her almost three months to realise it but when she had, thankfully, he'd known just what to do and had made all the arrangements. He waited outside for her, in the car, during the procedure. Which had hurt like hell at the time. After, for the first few hours, she'd bled like mad. But then it was over, done.

Not something you'd wish on your worst enemy, Viola had shuddered. *Let alone your best friend.*

Alma had commiserated, hoping sympathy would mask not just her shock but also her disapproval. For how could it be right, whatever the circumstances, to wilfully kill an unborn child, so tiny and defenceless? If the unforeseen were to happen, well, you'd just get on with it and cope as best you could. And one day she will have one, she thinks, but when the time is right.

Dressed in Pete's shirt from the day before, Alma eats breakfast perched on the edge of the bed by his side, with her plate balanced across her thighs. The French toast is creamy and rich and all the better for being made by him.

Pete has cooked Alma many meals in the weeks since that first date, and each time he's done so she's been impressed by the novelty not just of a man who cooks but one who takes pleasure in doing so.

He has challenged her palate, too, with their first dates following an eclectic itinerary of intimate restaurants where the food was as unfamiliar as their locations. Bengali down Brick Lane. Turkish on Newington Green. French Algerian in Kentish Town. Which is why Alma thought he was joking when over a home-cooked coq au vin he'd ruefully admitted to never having travelled beyond the south coast of England.

But as they have got to know each other better she has come to understand the pleasure he takes in exploring the unknown. The kick he gets from hunting down unusual ingredients. His hunger for life. How different he is to anyone she's ever met before, she thinks, watching him wipe the buttery juices from the plate with his final corner of bread.

'You look happy.' He puts her empty plate on his then places both on the floor.

'Because I am,' she smiles, curling up against his chest. Positioned like this, his heart pounds against her ear.

'Good.' He places his arm around her shoulder. 'Not like before.'

'Before?' she murmurs.

'You know, before – when we first met?' Alma frowns, unsure what he meant. 'With your ex?'

Her chest tightens. 'Sorry?'

'Nothing. Only, I just wondered if he made you happy.'

Leonard, he must mean Leonard, Alma thinks, wondering what little detail she's inadvertently let slip about her recent past. Because how can Leonard be an ex when they never went out, not in the normal way?

Pete's expression, though serious, is hard to read. What does he want her to say, she wonders. How else should – could – she answer? She is fearful of saying the wrong thing. With Viola spending more and more time with Geoff and her parents distracted by their own affairs, her world's axis is tilting towards Pete. And that feels tantalising and exciting.

Don't blow this, cautions a voice insider her. Not now, just as life is opening up before you like a treasure map.

'It's complicated.'

'Is it? Sorry. It's just I…' He looks away. 'Forget it, it doesn't matter.'

Alma touches his arm. Maybe she should try to explain. Then again, maybe not. The thought that he might think she'd let it happen, been complicit, was just too awful. And even if he didn't, it would surely make him see her in a different, darker light. Besides, he should respect her privacy. Everyone is entitled to their secrets. Now, surely, with Leonard Parmenter finally gone she's entitled to start again with a fresh slate?

What a curious contradiction Pete is, she thinks. So self-assured and single-minded, yet at times tentative and insecure.

'Hey, you,' she murmurs.

'Forget it,' he quickly shoots back. Shifting position suddenly, he looks about to pull himself to his feet.

'No,' Alma declares, firmly enclosing his hand in hers.

Pete turns towards her.

'My ex? He didn't make me happy,' she begins. 'It was nothing. Nothing at all, compared to being with you. But it was complicated. And one day I'll explain, I promise. Not now, though. Now's about more important things. You make me happy – happier than I ever thought I could be. And I hope I make you happy too. What's most important is us, and staying us.'

'You're right.' He nods. 'Best not to tempt fate.'

Chapter 15

Zeb's gaze drifts beyond Sam's shoulder. The darkness outside has turned the windowpane into a mirror and the sight of the pair of them, alone in the spotlit flat, makes her feel vulnerable. She crosses the room to draw the curtains. On the street below a silver taxi waits with its engine running. Distracted, she shakes her head. So she'd set out to see a friend of Dad's, someone in Scotland. But she can't think who that would be.

When she was little she'd wanted to go to Scotland but for some reason Dad would never take her. *Too much history*, apparently, though what he meant by this he wouldn't say. So she had to settle on north Wales, instead, with its slick slate roofs and purple skies.

West is almost as good as north of the border but with sea you can actually swim in, he'd smiled.

That first year they'd bought a rubber dinghy. Drifted in soft summer rain off a sandy beach opposite a small town called Aber-something where the abrupt realisation that a nearby sandbank was in fact a giant basking shark left a tearful Zeb begging her father to paddle them straight back to shore.

Keep paddling. Faster, Daddy, faster. Please! Don't stop.

'So did you find them, your dad's friend?'

With a weary smile, Zeb turns back towards her friend. 'I don't think so,' she says. 'To be honest, I'm not—'

'Maybe something will turn up through the solicitor.'

'Sorry?'

'Whoever's handling his affairs. You know, the will? I guess that will take the pressure off you having to find another job for a little while. Give you some space to get things together for you and Matty, too, as soon as he's back from Richard's.' Sam raises her hand to her mouth as she sees Zeb frown. 'Oh God, there I go again. Sorry, I really shouldn't have said that—'

'No, you shouldn't.'

You shouldn't have mentioned anything to do with what Dad may or may not have left me, she thinks, crossly. Because it is way too soon and none of your business. Sam's expression takes the edge off her anger. Reluctant to say something she will regret, Zeb bites her lip. Because she's only trying to help, of course. To make her feel better. The same reason she brought the wine. Which is ironic, really, because in the end it never does.

'I'm sorry. It's just still so… raw. Was there anything else – you know, that I said, before I left for Scotland?'

'Nothing I can think of, no.' Sam frowns. 'What about you, what can you remember?'

Zeb sighs. 'That's the thing. Nothing. Until I was found in the middle of nowhere by a local woman taking her son to school.' Her friend's eyes widen. 'Although images of certain scenes keep coming back to me – like flashbacks to a film I've seen.'

'What kind of things?'

'Waiting in a strange house while someone made tea.' Zeb shudders as another memory surfaces.

Angel. The man called it Angel. A strange name for a dog. Especially for a beast that size. Some kind of mastiff, short-haired and that shade of grey that's more like smoky blue. It yapped like a puppy when its master opened the kitchen door but when it sensed her presence, it snarled. Faster than a toddler throwing a tantrum, the creature's demeanour transformed as muscles tensed and nostrils flared. Then as its eyes locked onto hers, its vocal chords began to thrum.

The dog had taunted her in her weakness, challenging her to move away. Which was when her attention was drawn to the counter opposite and a large kitchen knife at rest on its wooden chopping block.

Her hand starts to shake. With a swift gulp, she finishes her wine.

'Zeb?'

'Don't worry, I'm OK.' Unless you're not, a voice inside her cautions. Take it easy. Don't tempt fate. She shakes her head. 'Actually, I'm not. Mrs Duffy who owned the house left me alone with her son while she popped out for some milk. Only her son was… odd. Eccentric, to put it mildly. And how he behaved, the way he looked at me, was frightening.' She puts down her glass. 'I hid in the downstairs loo. He was banging on the door.' Her fists clench. 'It was awful, there was no place to hide…'

'Go on,' Sam urges.

Zeb remembers how the steel tip scored the empty air as she waved the blade. Like the mark of Zorro, she thinks. She closes her eyes.

'I decided to bluff my way out. So I opened the door. Only by then he'd let the dog in. It was a huge creature, standing between me and the front door.' Her face tenses.

'The son was in the sitting room by that point, so I couldn't get my coat or bag. I ran into the kitchen to find the back door.' Now, her whole body clenches. 'But it was fast, bounding towards me along the corridor. Too fast for me to shut it out. And when it stopped, just a foot from where I stood, the sound it was making from the back of its throat...'

Angel, he'd cried, dropping to his knees in the pool of blood. *My Angel*.

'What happened next?'

'I... I don't know.' Because there is nothing. Just blackness where whatever happened next has been self-redacted.

Sam slips her arm around her shoulders. 'Sssh,' she soothes. 'Don't beat yourself up. I'm sure it will come back, in time.'

'But that's not the point,' Zeb mumbles, tears now burning her cheeks. 'I don't think I want to know.'

'Hey, this is pretty.' In a desperate attempt to change the subject, Sam has reached for the chain around her friend's neck. Now she is lifting the silver piano with the tip of her forefinger.

Piano girl, Zeb thinks, suddenly seeing herself inside her neighbour's flat. That's what the newspaper cutting I saw at Mrs Allitt's called me. And then, in the same moment, she sees the handwritten letter. *Dear Elizabeth...* it began. *I am so very sorry to have upset you yesterday by coming unannounced*. To the funeral. The woman came unannounced to the funeral, for the letter was dated the day after.

Now she remembers, though the name still means nothing to her. Cynthia Purnell. Is that who she'd gone to Scotland to see?

Hurriedly, she explains this to her friend.

'You're kidding!' Sam yelps when Zeb is done.

'She had a whole folder on me, actually. Including a letter I didn't recognise sent by an old friend of Dad's, I think.' Zeb's voice trails away. 'Only I can't remember the name.'

'Well you must get it back, all of it,' Sam declares with such force that Zeb can't help but smile. How she values her friend's fierce sense of justice. 'I mean, the stuff she's stolen – it belongs to you. Demand she returns it and if she won't, take it somehow. Maybe I could try. You could distract her on the landing while I nip round behind her. Maybe we could pretend your cat slipped inside and we could ask ourselves in to find him.'

'Well that's certainly an idea.' Zeb smiles, stretching for the remaining bottle of wine and pouring another glass.

–

'Sorry, did I wake you?' Sam is standing in the doorway of the sitting room where Zeb has spent the night, holding two mugs of tea. 'Though I can't believe you slept at all in here. Honestly, I thought you said you'd snuggle up with Matty so I could have your bed. I'd have caught a cab home if I'd known.'

Zeb yawns. 'It's fine. I was going to share with him, but he was restless and I thought we'd both be better off if I camped out in here.' Shifting position, she pulls herself upright, swings her feet down, then pats the cushion. Sam takes up position cross-legged beside her.

'He's up, you know,' her friend says. 'In your room, watching TV. I got him some warm milk while the kettle boiled, I hope that's OK.'

'I'm sorry if he woke you—'

'Well I'll have to start getting used to it some time, won't I? I mean, if me and Marcus… You know?'

'You're not!'

Sam grins. 'No, but we have talked about it. I just hope if and when we do he or she turns out as good as Matty.'

'Trust me, he has his moments,' Zeb chuckles, indulgently.

'I know, they all do. But you know what I mean. How's school going? I know you said he's been having an up and down time recently; are things OK now?'

'Bloody Richard,' Zeb replies, her mood darkening. 'He wants to hire a tutor, you know. Already. For the exams to get into St Paul's. Which is ridiculous, of course, because Matty's only one term into Year 3. But according to the font of all knowledge it pays to start early, even though he's at prep school. I mean honestly, Sam, what the hell does he think he pays school fees for?'

'Of course Matty will get into somewhere good in a couple of years' time,' Sam soothes. 'He is my godson, after all!'

'But it's too soon to start cramming,' Zeb objects, her throat tightening. 'And on top of that, Richard's signed him up for one-on-one music tuition – just in case, he says. He's even bought a piano…' Her eyes fill at the thought of the soon-to-be second Mrs Latham, Helene, who plays the cello. And sings in a choir, too. 'I mean honestly, Sam, how the fuck can I compete?'

Am I a bad mother? Zeb wonders. And if I am, is that my fault?

How do you become a good one if you never had a mother of your own to learn from? Another advantage Helene was born with, she notes, recalling how on the one occasion the two women had met her ex's new partner had let slip that she and her own mother were so close they were *just like best friends*. Is that normal? Is she somehow diminished for having missed out? Though when she considers all the girl friends she's had over the years who've talked of rowing like cat and dog with their mothers, she guesses Helene's experience must be an exception.

Zeb sniffs. What is growing up if it isn't growing apart and then away?

'You don't have to compete with Helene because you're Matty's mum,' Sam replies, taking Zeb's hand and squeezing it, firmly. 'It's been a shit few months but things will settle down. It will get better – everything will be OK.'

'Aside from Dad, of course. Walking out of my job. Drinking too much. Oh, and losing access to my son—'

'That's not going to happen. Obviously, you can't change what's happened with your dad, but everything else is within your control. You can get things back on track, I know you can. Don't give up, for Christ's sake – and I don't just mean on Matty, I mean on you. You're better than all this. You're a great mum. A good friend. You've got to believe in yourself. You can get through this, you are strong.'

Strong like Dad, Zeb thinks. He coped and so can – will – I. For Matty's sake, and my own. She wonders briefly what her mum would have done. With no memory of her let alone a clear image to play with, it's impossible to say. Wendy, then. But as she tries to think she sees herself not by her stepmother's side but in Mrs Allitt's flat, flicking through the stolen letters which she knows she must now get back. A distant church bell chimes nine o'clock, which gives Zeb an idea.

'Do you fancy taking Matty to the park in a bit?' she asks, suddenly. Because it is Sunday. And in an hour or so her neighbour will go out to the shops, as she always does.

Sam nods. 'Of course.'

–

Sam and Matty leave for the park after breakfast, letting themselves out while Zeb washes the dishes. True to form, Mrs Allitt goes out on the hour. Even allowing her neighbour a ten minute start, Zeb reckons she has an hour clear to get in and out of her flat – more than enough time to find what she needs, she reassures herself, as she stands at her front door watching through the peephole as the woman departs.

A sailor's chest sits against the wall by which Zeb now stands. Its lid is closed, with an earthenware pottery bowl on top. She sifts through the bric-a-brac it holds and gathers up an assortment of keys. There's one for her car. Dad's house keys, which she quickly lets slip back as if for fear her skin might burn. And a Yale and a Chubb attached to a silver Celtic cross which she stares at for a couple of seconds, buoyed by a fleeting surge of triumph.

This is the spare set of keys Mrs Allitt offered in exchange for her own – a symbolic gesture of neighbourly trust that the other woman has clearly broken.

Stuffing her own keys into the pocket of her jeans, Zeb slips out onto the landing. At her neighbour's front door she pauses to check for the sound of one of the other residents' imminent approach. But the building is still; the only sound the muffled pulse of distant traffic. She slips the Yale into the lock and gives it a turn. The mechanism won't give so she pulls it free, rubs it on her trouser leg, then tries again. Wrestles with it for a moment. Removes it once more. Tries the Chubb next, but the damn thing won't even turn.

Clearly it's pointless. Neither key works. Perhaps someone else in the house has a spare set, but what excuse would persuade anyone to give them to her?

Exasperated by the opportunity lost, she retreats into her own flat where she slams the useless set into the kitchen bin then leans with arms outstretched against the kitchen worktop.

A familiar sound comes from her bedroom. A slow, rhythmic tap-tapping, which makes her hurry along the corridor and into her room where through the open blind she sees Norton, the silver tabby, sitting on the sill outside the window. Zeb loosens the catch and gives the sash a firm upward shove. The window opens easily and she opens her arms to gather up the cat, which often comes and goes using the fire escape at the rear of the building, to bring him inside. But as she leans out, something catches her eye.

Further along the metal walkway that extends from one side of her building to the other, just outside her bedroom window, a net curtain is softly flapping in and out of her neighbour's bedroom window.

Norton leaps from Zeb's arms, thudding onto the floor with a trademark throaty exclamation that is half burp, half purr. As she gives him a rub, she feels the rounded fullness of his belly. Locked inside somewhere, probably, she frowns, realising this is the first she's seen of the animal since her return. Someone's been feeding him, too – Mrs Allitt, probably. In fact she wouldn't put it past the woman to have lured him into her flat then kept him there until he slipped out through the open window.

The cat starts to mewl, demanding attention. But now Zeb is fixated on an idea starting to form. Mrs Allitt took her basket on wheels which surely means she'll be out a little while. She should do it now, she knows. Scramble out onto the fire escape, climb in through the open window, find the letter then leave, fast, and who would ever know? Eager to quell any second thoughts, Zeb pulls on a pair of trainers, slips into a hoody left hanging on the hook behind the bedroom door then clambers through the window.

Though the rain has eased, the metal walkway beneath her feet is slick with water. Cautiously, she positions her back against the brickwork then side-steps towards the window of the next door flat. The fire escape is narrower than she expected. Rickety, too, as with her left arm stretched out to one side she feels her way along, her fingertips skimming the cracked brickwork until she finds herself gripping the edge of the window frame. A moment later she is peering into a bedroom window the lower sash of which has been left half-raised.

Her neighbour's flat is in darkness, silent and empty, and the opportunity this presents is too good to miss. Despite this Zeb hesitates. What if someone sees me? Surely, if I wait for the woman's return and demand her folder as I initially intended, she won't refuse? But a stab of anger at the sudden thought of the peculiar clothes her neighbour brought to the hospital strengthens her resolve. Zeb stares across the empty room towards the corridor and sitting room beyond. The interior is in darkness, quiet and still.

With a deep breath she braces her arms against the lower sash to open it wide enough then climbs inside. Facing her is a large mahogany wardrobe and beside this a matching chest of drawers. On an old-fashioned dressing table by its side an assortment of cheap cosmetics, bottles of scent and a large canister of hairspray are neatly arranged before an oval-shaped mirror. Catching sight of her reflection, wild-haired and pale-faced, she hurries out into the hall and almost collides with a tower of papers bound with string.

She creeps around other obstacles now blocking her way – an assortment of cardboard boxes of varying sizes containing a selection of tinned fruit, a bulging pile of plastic carrier bags holding what looks like charity shop donations – until she is back in her neighbour's sitting room. But today the coffee table is empty. Apart from the buff-coloured envelope on the far side which she drops as soon as it is in her hand, realising it is bulging with at least a dozen twenty-pound notes.

Replacing the money, Zeb notices a business card that's slipped onto the floor printed with the name Brian Jackson – a property consultant with a Marbella office address. Uncertain whether or not it fell out of the envelope, she decides it's best to leave it on the rug. She scans the room once more. All she can hear is the blood now pounding against the inside of her skull.

What am I doing? I should not be doing this. Because it's wrong.

But then she forces herself to remember. To think about the letter from the stranger at Dad's funeral. Her letter. The letter she must now find.

Remembering the line of filing cabinets in the hallway, she retraces her steps back through the sitting room door. And there she sees them, lining almost the entire walls of the darkened hallway. Archiving the details of God only knows what. Which end to start at, she wonders, briefly, until she notices that each drawer has been carefully labelled.

The woman is meticulous, if nothing else, Zeb smiles, relieved. Her filing system even appears to be alphabetical. It takes only a couple of seconds to locate the drawer for H, tug it open and peer inside. A plastic tag, the third one in, is clearly marked with her own name. She pulls out the hanging file. Inside is a buff-coloured folder filled with her papers. With no time to spare, she stuffs this under her sweatshirt, securing it firmly beneath the belted waistband of her jeans. A distant slam signals the closing of the downstairs front door. Turning back towards the bedroom, she almost trips over a parcel the size of a shoebox, wrapped in brown paper and left standing upright on the floor. Noticing it bears her name, she takes this too.

Zeb clambers out then drops onto the metal walkway. Straightening up, she tugs down the sash with her free hand but there's no time to close it as the landing light flickers on in the communal hallway. As Mrs Allitt unlocks her front door, Zeb flattens her back against the brickwork. If her neighbour comes into the bedroom now, sees the window open, glances outside, she will surely be discovered. But no, the woman must have gone straight into the kitchen.

As Mrs Allitt unpacks her shopping, Zeb side-steps towards her open window. Then, hurriedly tossing the parcel and papers onto her bedroom floor, she clambers inside. Only with the sash firmly secured and blind redrawn does she start to take stock, considering with a mix of hilarity and relief the narrow escape she's just had, before turning her head towards the spoils. Seconds later she is opening the folder and staring once more at the handwritten letter.

Dear Elizabeth, it begins.

> *I am so very sorry to have upset you yesterday by coming unannounced to your father's funeral. It was not my intention to cause you any more heartache than you must surely be feeling at so difficult a time, and I regret now my decision to come in person rather than simply conveying my sympathies with flowers. But there was a reason I came — a pressing one, which is why I am writing now. To be blunt, I need to reach your mother. As will now be clear from this approach, I have not seen or heard from her in years. But it has become important that she and I now speak. I would therefore very much appreciate it if you could help by putting us back in touch. My address and phone number are detailed below.*
>
> *With gratitude,*
> *Cynthia Purnell*

Bemused, Zeb reads the letter again. So this is an old friend not of Dad's but of her mum's; so old a friend — so distant, too — that she does not know the woman died almost three decades ago. She shakes her head, battling to remember just what passed between them at Dad's funeral. Zeb thinks for a moment of the tall, ashen-faced woman with pale eyes and white cropped hair who'd seemed swamped by the grey overcoat and black trouser suit she was wearing. How she'd reached out for her hand and how when she clasped it her grip was weak, her wrist thin and brittle.

Elizabeth, she'd rasped. *Please. We need to speak.*

They were in the atrium outside the chapel at the crematorium, just after, looking at all the flowers. Zeb had just spotted the mystery floral tribute with its cryptic message and was holding the card in her hand.

Never forgotten, forever forgiven, the message had read.

Signed with a single letter: *A*.

Zeb turns her attention to the parcel which Mrs Allitt also intercepted, though unlike the folder of correspondence it does not appear to have been opened. Tearing apart one end, she pulls out a shoe box. Intrigued by what might lie inside, she carefully removes the lid. Inside there is a poetry anthology; a first edition collection by Stevie Smith. Audio cassettes – three C90s featuring home recordings of piano concertos recorded some time during 1973 and 1974, according to the spidery writing along their spines. A small toy rabbit. A brightly-beaded purse. A tortoiseshell hair brush and matching comb which, when she peers more closely, holds a handful of fine silk strands of baby-blonde hair. Relics from a distant childhood which feels almost familiar.

Turning her attention to a handful of photos of people she doesn't recognise in wing collars and flares, Zeb stares at a colour print of a young couple standing in the garden of a country pub, squinting into the sun.

The woman, a strawberry blonde with a fashionably short bob, is dressed in kitten heels, three-quarter-length skinny jeans and a halter-neck sun top. The man, in crepe-soled shoes, denim flares and a pristine white T-shirt, looks like a younger Dad – though the image is blurred, and from an era earlier than the one depicted in pictures she's familiar with from his house. He has a moustache, too, and curly hair like a young Kevin Keegan. Her gaze lingers for a beat on his hand, softly resting on the young woman's swollen belly.

How different the world was in the early Seventies, Zeb muses. A clash of gaudy tank tops and wing collars. Industrial action and power cuts. Glam rock and the IRA. Her father with his high hopes and a full head of curly hair. How young he looked, and hopeful, too. Pete the photographer struggling towards his big break.

Turning her attention back to the box and its contents, the last picture – a faded Polaroid of a child in its embroidered christening gown – makes Zeb pause.

Only just a toddler, the subject is of indeterminate gender. But that grumpy pout seems familiar. *A face like a festering storm.* That's how Dad described a similar picture he'd once taken of her. A picture quite like this – though the one she grew up with sits in pride of place on the mantelpiece in Dad's home. Zeb has paid little if any attention to that snapshot in years.

But now, spotting it amongst the papers she brought back from Dad's, she can only see the similarities. This a bona fide carbon copy, she thinks. Was whoever sent this at my christening?

As she pulls the last few bits and pieces from the box, a postcard drops to the floor. She picks it up. The card bears a pen and ink drawing of a Dickensian shop front, its window crammed with musical instruments. A name – The Bass Clef – is clearly visible in gold lettering above the front door. Printed along the bottom across the cobbled street is the shop's address: 15 Church Street, Fort William. Zeb shuts her eyes, this time to think.

Fort William, again. Where she was taken to hospital.

Glancing back at the postcard, Zeb sees a message written on the back. *Just a few things from your mother that she feels rightfully belong to you*, someone has written. *To find out more you can reach me at the shop. Ask for Anna.*

But now all Zeb can see is one word. Not felt, *feels*.

Your mother feels. Like the feeling is still...

Present.

She frowns. Because her mother is dead. She, Zeb, is the sole survivor. And on this single and unassailable fact rests her childhood, her relationship with Dad, the rest of the world, everything. It's sad, but simple. Unassailable. Mum died to give me life. What else is there to know?

Only the lifetime of gaps still to fill, she thinks, her mind suddenly racing. Everything about the woman I never knew which Dad seemed so reluctant to share. For he'd rarely talked of her when Zeb was young except to say how they'd fallen in love too young to know better. How not long after, she'd fallen pregnant. Too soon. And then, little more than a child herself, she was gone.

Zeb can still see Dad's face when he told her. The way his eyes seemed clouded. How while relating the tragedy, his sadness had seemed boundless. The weight of it had smothered all of the answers Zeb had not dared to ask for yet deeply craved.

Am I like her?

How did you meet?

Did she have family?

Did she look like me?

What were her parents like?

Have I got cousins?

Why didn't you tell me before?

And now here I am, she thinks, over thirty years later – a mother myself, wrestling with the same unanswered questions.

She impulsively dials the music shop's number but it is Sunday and all she hears is an answerphone. Hurriedly hanging up, she carefully redials a couple of times to scrutinise the recorded voice. It is a woman, though she does not sound Scottish. Her accent is… neutral. By the third listen Zeb wonders whether to leave a message and, if so, what she should say. But then, after a short tone, it is too late and she is being recorded.

Hurriedly, she asks whether someone can pass on her name and number to Anna, then quickly hangs up.

Stumbling into the kitchen, Zeb upends what's left of last night's second bottle of wine into yesterday's wine glass – just to steady her nerves. After a couple of sips she glances up at the clock on the kitchen wall above the cooker. As her attention is snagged by the faltering stagger of its second hand she senses an uneasy tremor of déjà vu. And then she knows. She has done this before, too. Standing here, against the counter, though then she was dressed in black. Holding the card from those flowers.

It was just past eleven three weeks ago when she first considered the insane possibility that perhaps her mum wasn't dead. With normal thought processes suspended, all she had felt was numb. Like her very existence had been frozen while, fast and ever faster, the world spun away. And as it did she'd felt nothing – neither anger nor upset, neither bafflement nor hurt. As if her emotions had been cauterised.

So, unable to digest the immensity of it or its meaning, she'd sat here with the unimaginable possibility that everything she'd believed and taken for granted, forever, had been built on shifting sand.

That life as she'd known and lived and loved up to this point had been based on a lie.

Chapter 16

Buckinghamshire, February 1975

They drive north out of London into open country where shabby fields cower beneath a concrete sky. Winter has returned, leaching the landscape of colour, and snow flits like ash against the shades of grey.

'Take my coat,' Pete offers. 'It's on the back seat.'

Wrapping the extra layer around her shoulders over the coat she is already wearing, Alma can't help but marvel at how, though poised for rebirth, the world outside feels like a terminal case with no energy left to fight for survival. Ever since she can remember the period between Bonfire Night and Christmas has been her least favourite time of the year. But now she decides these hopeless, stop-start weeks of early spring are surely worse.

Glimpsing herself in the rear-view mirror, Alma stares at her reflection.

Her cheeks are lightly powdered, her eyes rimmed with blue, and with the lip gloss she has borrowed from Viola her face has a luminous glow. The world outside may be bleak but inside she feels hopeful – an indication of the extent to which her new life with Pete has dislocated her from the natural rhythms of her old one.

A passing shadow darkens her face as she remembers where they are going.

Will she pass muster?

Sunday lunch with Patsy in the tiny village just north of Gerrards Cross where she now lives is Pete's idea. Recently his mother has been unwell. But now that she's feeling better, he is eager to support her desire to reinstate the regular gatherings for family and friends that she once hosted in happier times, before becoming a reluctant divorcee.

Patsy was a one-time artist's model who'd married her childhood sweetheart, Bert – a compositor at a local print works in Clapton where Pete, their only son, was born. She met Phil when she was working double shifts as a waitress in a cafe on Rathbone Place during the difficult months after Bert was killed in a car accident. Pete was just five.

In her struggle to cope alone, Patsy was grateful for the small kindnesses dealt her by the kindly stranger who stopped at the cafe on his way to and from work each day. Cigarettes and stockings. A magazine he thought she'd like the look of. Some fresh fruit or maybe a few sausages for her and her small son's tea. Then gradually, as the months passed, her budding friendship with Phil Hamilton grew into something else. Casual talk turned more serious as he set about persuading Patsy how much better for her and her child it would be if she left the squalid flat she rented just north of Kings Cross. They could move north, together, Phil told her, into a small terraced town house he had his eye on in Newington Green.

By the time Pete turned ten, the string of pubs and rental properties Phil had assembled was generating enough cash for him and his adoptive family to move again – into a four bedroomed semi, complete with front and back gardens, close to his childhood home in

Colindale. And it was there that Patsy became known for the convivial lunchtime gatherings she hosted on the first Sunday of each month – until the breakdown she suffered after discovering her second husband's affair with a waitress ten years her junior. Phil's lover, Cynthia, was a young girl who worked at a French restaurant on Greek Street where he regularly dined with associates from work.

'How long ago did your mum move out of London?' Alma wonders out loud, intrigued why anyone would swap the bright lights and excitement of city living for a landscape so featureless and dull.

'Four years ago – about a year after she and Phil split, around the time I left school,' Pete answers. His eyes are fixed on the road ahead.

'So she came here alone, then?'

He nods.

'Goodness,' Alma continues. 'That must have been tough.'

'More so than you can imagine. She'd been in hospital, you see...'

'The breakdown.'

'Kind of...' Pete tightens his hold of the steering wheel. 'She took an overdose, Alma. After that she was in a private clinic for months to recuperate. Then, as a reward for getting straight and not making more of a fuss Phil set her up in the country house she'd always dreamed of.'

'Oh Pete, I'm sorry, I didn't—'

'Though they would separate, he'd not formally move out, Phil decided – shocked by her attempted suicide, I guess,' Pete presses on. 'He stays in London most weeks, free to do what the hell he wants, while Mum curates her small but growing menagerie. It began with one kitten but then became three, a pair of pedigree spaniels and

167

the horse Phil bought her soon after discovering he'd be a father for the third time. To soften the blow, he said. Despite the fact Patsy can't ride.'

Alma stares at Pete open-mouthed.

Why has he said nothing of any of this before?

'I'm sorry,' he concludes. 'I probably should have said something sooner, but having avoided it I realised I needed to tell you now, before we arrive, so you'll be prepared.'

'Prepared for what?'

'The unexpected. Usually she's fine but sometimes she's… less so.' Pete shrugs. 'You just don't know.'

Alma mulls over what's just been said before she continues. 'It's good Phil set her up, though, isn't it? I mean, in her own place.'

'Oh yes,' Pete replies, snappily. 'That's Phil, all right. He's all heart.'

–

At last, they turn off the country road onto an unmade track at the end of which is a large, tile-hung house. At the main entrance, Pete pulls to a halt then climbs out to open the white five-bar gate. Once inside, they park by an old stable block. Alma stares up at the building's black-framed windows and high-pitched roof. Though only an artful recreation of a period country pile, the house is far grander than she expected.

A dark-eyed figure with thick, waist-length hair appears at the front door before they can ring the bell. Alma guesses she is in her late twenties, with pink lips and a freckled face. The woman smiles, but not at Alma. As her plump mouth curves, it is clear that her attention is set on just one person. She tilts her head coquettishly towards Pete.

'Hey, little cousin,' the stranger murmurs, silkily. As she speaks her chest heaves beneath the close-fitting cashmere cardigan she wears buttoned-up over high-waisted jeans. 'Patsy's in the kitchen. Come on in.'

Alma holds back, waiting to be introduced, but before Pete can oblige, the woman has disappeared into a side room and he is striding in, towards the back of the house.

Alma gently closes the front door.

Looking around her, she registers the carpet with its meticulously vacuumed deep pile. The wide wooden staircase dominating the hall with its vaulted ceiling above. The sound of men's voices from behind the half-closed doorway of what must be a sitting room to her left. Guided by the distant sound of Pete's laughter, she heads down a short stone-flagged passageway past the dining room with its large oak table set for six then turns right into a large kitchen.

A slim woman with ivory, back-brushed hair scooped back from her face by a navy hair band is standing at the cooker basting a large shoulder of beef. Unable to see Pete, Alma is uncertain if or how best to introduce herself until he suddenly appears from behind a large cabinet at the far end of the room holding the bunch of flowers he has brought behind his back.

'Mum?' he calls. 'Meet Alma. Alma, Patsy.'

Pete's mother quickly slides the roasting tray back into the oven then turns towards Alma. An uncomfortable silence dominates the room as the older woman, her face heavily made up and glistening in the heat from the stove, carefully appraises her guest, while Alma juggles with the awkwardness of calling mothers by their Christian names.

Then instinct kicks in.

'Pleased to meet you, Mrs Hamilton.'

'Oh call me Patsy, for God's sake, everybody does,' the older woman chuckles, tossing her oven gloves onto the kitchen counter. Her voice is loud with a breathless edge from too much smoking. She rubs the palms of her hands on a tea towel, then grabs a half-drunk whisky and soda. 'Come in. Have a drink. What can I get you – sherry? You look the type.' She turns towards her son. 'Get her a glass will you, luv.'

As Patsy turns back to the hob, lifting a lid to inspect the contents of a boiling saucepan, Pete gets Alma a drink then fills a vase with water for the flowers.

'You didn't tell me Chrissie would be joining us,' he says.

'Didn't I?' his mother answers. 'She came with Brian. Now come on, don't look at me like that, Pete. What else could I do? They've been going out a while.'

'Brian from Number Nineteen?' Alma asks, remembering the helpful barman.

Patsy nods. 'And my niece. Pete doesn't approve but as I keep telling him—' She drops her voice. 'It's OK, they're not really cousins because Brian's a bastard.'

'Mum!' Pete objects, trying not to laugh.

'Oh you know what I mean,' Patsy exclaims. 'Just like you know I think he's a total dear. And a miracle, too.' She leans towards Alma. 'For years, you know, everyone thought Phil was a Jaffa,' she confides in an indiscreet whisper. 'Fired blanks? But Brian, well, he's living proof that Phil's all man!'

As Alma chokes on her drink, a figure appears in the kitchen doorway.

'What's so funny?'

'Nothing, Chrissie,' Pete soothes, turning towards his cousin who is watching with folded arms and a petulant frown. 'Come and meet Alma.'

'Hi,' says Alma, taking a step forward.

Chrissie's face twitches. 'Good to meet you,' she says without enthusiasm, then turns away.

'Don't mind her,' Patsy sighs, taking another large sip from her glass. 'She's just jealous, that's all. Your cousin's always had a soft spot for you, hasn't she,' she adds, turning towards her son.

'For goodness' sake, Mum,' Pete begs. 'Please don't start.'

A short while later, Patsy loads up Alma with cutlery and side plates to finish the laying of the dining room table while Pete helps make some gravy. The room is large, with French windows that open into the back garden and a large fireplace on the wall directly opposite. Along the mantelpiece, framed photos are arranged beneath a striking painting of an Asian woman with a blue-green face, scarlet lips and jet-black hair staring down from the wall.

Alma lays the table. When she is done, she turns towards the family portraits, the largest of which is in the centre in a silver frame. It is of Pete's mother and Phil on their wedding day, which strikes Alma as strange given how distraught Patsy was left by their split. To its left is an assortment of elderly relatives with some of the men dressed in military uniform. To its right is a photo of two young boys in school uniform one of whom, though only eleven or twelve, is surely Pete. The features of the other, perhaps a little older, seem familiar though she can't place why.

'Haven't changed much, have we?'

Flustered, Alma spins around to see Brian casually leaning against the door. Dressed in dark trousers and a white pressed shirt, he looks just as he did when she last saw him behind the bar of the club only this time he is cradling his own drink – a tumbler of whisky. Her eyes dart back towards the picture. 'Is that you?'

Brian nods. 'With Pete.'

'You were at school together.'

'Yes. We lived a few streets apart – me with my mum, Pete with his… and my dad.' Alma nods, unsure how best to respond without sounding rude. 'Don't worry. You're right. It was odd. But it worked, kind of, because Pete and I have always got on. Even though the two of us have always been very different. I lived and dreamed football while he was always reading and drawing.' He smiles. 'Do you need a hand?'

Alma shakes her head. 'Thanks, but I'm done.'

With a single gulp, Brian finishes his drink then gestures towards the French windows. In the shadows, a piece of furniture draped a decorative cloth. 'You should check out the piano – it's meant to be a good one.' His gaze drops to his glass. 'Time for a refill, I think. What's your poison?'

'Another sherry would be nice.'

As Brian's footsteps recede along the stone-flagged corridor that leads back to the kitchen, Alma monitors the jovial conversation from the room next door where Chrissie is speaking to a man dressed in chequered trousers and a yellow roll-neck jumper. This must be Derek, the final guest Pete told her about – a neighbour who has become Patsy's close friend and confidant since being widowed a few months ago. The man is trying to explain the rules of cricket but Pete's cousin is either too disinterested to care or pretending to be so to wind him up.

Making her way towards the French windows, Alma stares out into the garden onto an unkempt lawn pitted with holes half dug by Patsy's dogs. Turning towards the piano, she lifts the cover.

It is an upright Blüthner, the same make as the baby grand her parents have at home, and when she raises the lid and lightly presses a key the instrument doesn't sound too badly out of tune. She pulls out the stool and takes a seat. Carefully spreading her fingers, she lets the tip of her pads gently rest against the polished ivory.

Closing her eyes, she thinks back to the distant Christmas when her father had their piano delivered. How solemnly the three of them stood in silence, watching, as two delivery men in white overalls gently eased the instrument into place. How her father had opened the instrument's lid – reverentially, almost – as soon as they were alone. Then, beckoned forward, she'd been placed upon the stool.

When you play just play, they told her. *Never mind who listens to you.*

Years later she found out this was something Schumann said.

'You!' a sudden voice exclaims, chilling the room like a blast of icy air. Caught off guard, Alma's hands shake and as she spins around on her seat, the piano lid slams shut with an electric crack. 'Yes, you!' the voice repeats. Gravelly and low, it comes from the squat man now occupying the space between where she sits and the French windows, which now stand ajar. 'It's not a toy, you know.'

'Of course not,' Alma objects. The stranger takes a step towards her and as he does she finds herself overwhelmed by the sheer bulk of him. But at the same time she feels anger. 'It's the same as the one I learned to play on many years ago,' she continues. 'I study music.'

'You study music, do you?' the man echoes with a smile that reveals a chipped front tooth. He is bald and thick of neck, with grey, close-set eyes and the saddle nose of a one-time boxer. But as he bends close, the warmth of his breath makes Alma's head spin and for a heartbeat all she can think of is being in that hotel room with Leonard in Vienna.

No, a voice inside her cries as she ducks out of the stranger's reach and springs onto her feet. Do not let him intimidate you.

'Know any Ella Fitzgerald?' the man demands. 'Or Sinatra? You know, classy stuff.'

Sensing the threat has now passed, Alma tries not to smile her relief. Instead, she nods. She had taught herself the piano accompaniments from *Strangers In The Night*, one of her mother's favourite LPs, the Christmas before Vienna and had played a number of the songs at the New Year's Eve party her parents had hosted that year.

Christ, the voice inside her shudders, adjusting its aim. How biddable you used to be. Little better than a performing seal.

'Of course,' Alma retorts, tartly.

The stranger narrows his eyes. 'Summer Wind?'

She purses her lips. 'You're Driving Me Crazy.'

As he stares at her she wonders if she might have gone too far and offended Patsy's rude friend. But then with a single, staccato laugh his mood abruptly lightens.

'Please, play,' he urges.

Taking a deferential step back, the man motions towards a second figure Alma didn't see enter the room, who now sits perched on the edge of a spare dining chair by the old oak bureau the far side of the French windows. The woman, who looks barely old enough to be out of school, is wearing a knee-length fur coat. Her face is drawn, partially hidden beneath wet, dyed-blonde hair. And in her lap, she is cradling what looks like a sheepskin car coat in gloved hands.

Alma guesses this must be her inquisitor's daughter.

'Go on,' the man presses. 'Show us you're as light on the ivories as you are on the eye.'

Once more seated at the piano, Alma starts with the opening bars of 'Strangers In The Night' and is swiftly transported by the melody and Sinatra's familiar voice serenading her inside her head. Though she has played many times before in public, rarely if ever has it been like this – interpreting the music as she goes along; with no one standing on the sidelines grading her performance. No pursuit of perfection. Just music as it should be: a living, breathing thing.

Looking up every now and then, Alma sees her tiny audience watching, rapt.

Perhaps I can do it – make a career of this, she thinks. Not as a classical performer but playing other kinds of music, entertaining people live like this; recording, even. The thought has never even crossed her mind, though it has long been a dream of Viola's. For her roommate is determined to become a singer and is already regularly contributing vocals for Geoff's band – a prog rock group which is starting to gain some serious attention.

This must be how Viola feels, Alma realises. Special.

'Oh Alma, that's really lovely,' Patsy declares, suddenly appearing in the doorway. But as she steps into the room, the dish of roast potatoes she's holding out slips from her hand and falls to the floor. 'Oh now look what you made me do,' she exclaims, dropping to her knees. 'What are you doing here?' she mumbles without looking up as she stifles a sob. For a moment Alma fears Pete's mother is addressing her. 'Why have you come?'

Derek appears in the open doorway with oven gloves on. He is closely followed by Pete and Brian, who is carrying a carving plate on which sits a large shoulder of beef. 'Patsy, is everything—' Derek begins but then as he stares at the unexpected guests, the colour draining from his face, his head drops and his voice falters. 'Ah.'

'Here, let me,' says Alma, slipping to Patsy's side to help gather up the roast potatoes into the tea towel that, until seconds earlier, Pete's mother had held wrapped around the side of the dish to keep her hands from burning. 'They'll be fine, I'm sure. Let's put them in another serving dish.'

'What do you want?' Pete demands, stepping into the room. Only as he squares up to his stepfather a short distance away does Alma see the meat carving knife clutched in his right hand. Phil takes a step forwards and as his stepson's right arm tenses, Alma's insides lurch. 'I said,' Pete begins, determined to stand his ground, 'why are you here?'

'We came to see Patsy, didn't we, Cyn?' But the blonde woman still perching on the edge of the wooden chair is now searching for something in the car coat's inside pocket. Without looking up, she nods. 'To pay our respects.' As the woman finds what she is looking for and pulls free a packet of cigarettes, she nods again. 'And because we have something we wanted to tell her, isn't that right?'

'We do?' asks Cynthia. Her eyes jump between her audience's expectant faces as she puts a cigarette in her mouth.

'Go on, then,' Phil urges, proudly. As he offers his lighter, Chrissie slips into the room and takes up position by Brian's side.

Cyn inhales.

'Tell them,' Phil prompts, pointing to her hand.

For a moment Cyn looks baffled until something dawns on her. Pulling off her glove, she waggles her left hand. On the third finger is a silver ring with an emerald setting beside a thin gold band. 'Well,' the girl begins, self-consciously. 'We only just got married, that's all!'

'Married?' Patsy cries.

'You're kidding,' Brian exclaims, blindly reaching for Chrissie's hand.

Phil shakes his head. 'I can see why you'd hope that but no, Brian, it's true. Baby Tony – who, by the way, sends his apologies for not joining us today, only he's got a bad dose of colic, as Cyn's mother will surely vouch – he will be my heir, not you.'

Still holding the knife, Pete lowers his hand.

'Well now! This certainly looks like a fine feast, I must say,' Phil presses on, rubbing his hands together as he surveys the table then fixes his gaze on Patsy. 'Mind if we join you? Looks like there's more than enough to go round.'

To Alma's surprise, his ex-wife giggles. 'More than enough,' she echoes, brightly, waving for Cyn and Phil to pull up extra chairs. 'The more the merrier, if you know what I mean.' Again, Patsy laughs. 'As they say.'

'I'm not really hungry any more,' Brian mutters, grimly.

'You can have my place, too,' says Derek as he backs towards the door.

Chrissie, however, seems determined to stand her ground. 'Well, I'm so hungry I could eat a horse,' she declares. Phil laughs, loudly.

In search of a cue, Alma turns towards Pete, but he has his arm around Patsy's shoulders and is speaking to her in a low voice, so all she can do as Phil and Cyn take their seats at the table is hover, awkwardly, and wait. Until, at last, Patsy has made her intentions clear and the six of them sit down together to eat.

'Voila,' Phil declares from his self-appointed seat at the head of the table as, without being asked, he takes the carving knife. 'As the Frenchies say!'

Briskly, the man swipes the knife across a sharpening steel, the blade on the pad of his thumb, then tears into the roast. Damp-haired and flushed from the steam of it, he is repulsive and the look of that meat, pink around the outside and oozing blood at the centre, makes Alma feel sick. But as the others watch the knife part meat from bone, they do so in a reverential kind of silence.

'Help yourselves to vegetables, everyone,' Phil finally declares when the carving is done. 'Enjoy the meal my money has put on this table… And my ex-wife's exquisite preparations, of course.'

There is a pause once all the plates are full which Alma thinks, with a fleeting sense of hope, will be blessed by a grace. But instead, everyone waits for Phil to carefully prepare then consume his first mouthful. His final swallow is the signal for everyone else to commence.

Giddy with nerves – or, maybe, too much wine – Patsy lets slip a giggle. Turning to look at Pete, Alma sees the inner conflict between his loyalty to his fragile mother and his loathing for his oafish stepfather clearly etched into his face. Beneath the table, she feels for his hand. Why doesn't Patsy tell her ex and his new wife to leave, she wonders. Can the woman still have feelings for this ugly bully?

'Why don't you go and have a sit down?' Alma urges Patsy as soon as they have finished eating, shooting a smile at Chrissie in the hope of rallying her support.

'Go on, Pats,' Pete's cousin agrees, taking the hint. 'We've got this covered.'

As the two young women carry the debris from lunch into the kitchen and set about washing, tidying and wiping down it's soon clear how little they have in common. Chrissie dropped out of school at sixteen to work in a local beauty salon when her mother, Patsy's sister, died of cancer. Ten years on, her two aims in life are to marry and marry well, though despite a plan to move in soon with Brian, she is now unabashedly undecided about whether or not he'll end up the lucky man.

'Mum knew him and liked him which made her happier with the idea of us moving in together at some stage. But I guess with Phil and Cyn being married, and everything...' she starts to confide. 'Anyway, whoever I end up with has got to be my passport out of here.'

Alma smiles. Maybe they aren't that dissimilar, after all. A passport to London, yes, she can identify with that. But the other girl misinterprets her amusement and, an instant later, is flinging down the washing up brush and turning around to face her down.

'Are you laughing at me?' Chrissie demands.

Alma hesitates, for in truth the answer is yes and no.

'Do I amuse you?' the other girl hisses, poking Alma in the chest with her forefinger so hard it makes her gasp. 'You stuck up cow, with your posh voice and your airs and graces. Think you're too good for us, don't you? Well let me tell you something, you'd better make the most of your bit of rough on the side, darling, because trust me, it won't last. And I should know.'

'No,' Alma objects, struggling to see what the girl could mean. Too good for Pete? 'Honestly. I wasn't laughing – smiling, maybe, but no, not at you, at me. Look Chrissie, I'm really sorry but I think you've got the wrong end of the stick. It's what you said about needing a passport – you know, to London? It's just, well, I know just what you mean. I've got my music, you've got—'

'Don't put me down.'

'Sorry?'

'You heard me, bitch.'

'I think you've misunder—'

'Are you calling me stupid?'

'No, that's not what I—'

'All right, Chrissie?'

As both girls turn towards Phil, the thought of how much of their exchange he has heard makes Alma flinch. 'Fine, thanks,' the other girl beams, unabashed, as she peels off the rubber gloves she is wearing with a snap. 'Seen Brian on your travels?'

Phil shrugs.

'Not to worry,' Chrissie grins, stepping towards the doorway in which her one-time uncle stands – a position he must vacate in order to let her pass by. 'He'll be tinkering with the car by the garage, I expect,' she adds. Then, as she draws level with Phil, she pecks him lightly on the cheek. 'Good to see you again, Phil. As always.'

Without warning, Phil pulls her towards him, cupping her buttocks so firmly that she struggles to move away until, a second or two later, he sets her free. Flush-faced, she hastily straightens her hair.

Her one-time uncle smiles. 'Likewise, I'm sure.'

—

'She did what?' Pete exclaims. He is laughing so hard he slows the car to a halt in a muddy pull-in at the side of the single track road.

Alma giggles. The relief of leaving the awkward gathering at Patsy's has left both of them giddy. 'She kissed Phil.'

Pete shakes his head. 'Christ, Alma, if I'd known it would be like that I'd never have—'

'Stop apologising,' she smiles. 'Seriously, it's OK. You should meet my family. Though on second thoughts, please don't.'

'It's Mum, you see,' he presses on with a sigh. 'She's been through so much. I wanted to show some support, you know, now she's getting back on her feet. And, of course, I wanted the two of you to meet.'

'She's lovely,' Alma soothes. 'And Derek seems nice, too.'

'Nice.' Pete frowns. 'But she deserves better.'

'I'm not sure Chrissie liked me much, either.'

'Oh I wouldn't mind her,' he replies, checking the road in both directions before driving on. 'Chrissie's bark has always been worse than her bite. And besides, once she decides she likes you you've got a trusted ally for life.'

'Let's hope she's not made up her mind too quickly, then.'

Pete laughs. 'What shall we do next weekend, then – visit your parents, perhaps? Or are there any skeletons from your past you'd like to share?'

Alma stares at him for a moment, wondering if she'll ever dare invite him into the straitlaced world of the person she used to be, let alone tell him about what happened in Vienna. The risks feel too great. Who she is now is the person formed by breaking free from childhood constraints and guilty secrets. She should be thankful she escaped from her past unscathed. No good can come from looking back.

She laughs, tentatively. 'If only.'

Chapter 17

'We're back,' Sam calls from the hallway as Matty charges ahead and into the sitting room where Zeb is sitting on the sofa once more, staring into the shoe box.

'Hey champ,' she wearily smiles. 'Did you have fun?'

The child nods, looking at the box on her lap but saying nothing. He is distracted by the thought of something far more exciting. 'Can I use the laptop, Mummy? Please? I promise to be careful, only I want to show Auntie Sammy the Puffle Party on Club Penguin. Say yes, Mummy, please?'

'It's on the floor by my bed, charging,' Zeb says. 'Give her a few minutes, though – I need a word with her first, OK?'

'Is everything all right?' Sam frowns, sinking down onto the sofa. She is still wearing her coat. 'Only you look awful. Did you get the letters back OK?'

Zeb nods. 'The whole file. And this. It's a box of… stuff.'

Taking the shoe box from her Sam sorts through it for a moment then raises her head. 'Where's it from?'

'An old friend of Dad's who lives in Scotland.'

Sam looks thoughtful. 'Do you know what it is? What it looks like, at least?'

'Keepsakes.'

'A memory box. Sian, a friend of mine from school, she made one when she was diagnosed with breast cancer – for her kids.' Sam smiles. 'Though thankfully she's never had to use it as she's in remission now.'

Zeb shrugs. 'Well yes, I guess that's what this is.'

'So who's the old friend?'

'Anna someone, though the name means nothing to me,' she adds, pulling free a black, plastic jewellery box – the last item she's yet to examine. Lifting it up, she opens the lid but there is nothing inside other than an empty velvet mound marked with two holes and small indentation – perhaps where a pendant might sit. Fingering the chain at her throat, she thoughtfully traces the contours of the silver piano.

'Goodness, I almost forgot,' Sam exclaims, dipping into her coat pocket and pulling out a small padded envelope. 'As we were leaving, a delivery man was dropping off this – I said I'd take it for you.'

Tearing open the packet, Zeb pulls out a mocha-coloured Mulberry purse which she recognises instantly as the one Richard gave her the last Christmas before they split. The purse she'd used every day since until she'd lost it in Scotland, along with the handbag Dad gave her and all its contents. The accompanying letter from PC Heath, the constable she met while in hospital in Fort William, explains that the purse had been handed in at a local police station – though any cash and all the cards are, sadly, long gone.

Even so, Zeb opens the flap and checks inside. It is indeed empty, or almost, for buried in the back pocket is a small, handwritten card like the ones that come with floral arrangements.

Never forgotten, never forgiven, she reads, *A*.

'What is it? Who's it from?' Sam begins, peering over her friend's shoulder.

Zeb turns over the card. On the reverse is the circular sticker she'd saved from the tribute's cellophane wrapping bearing the logo of the shop that did the arrangement. Fleur's Flowers of 10, The Parade, Fort William. She puts the box and empty envelope on the floor then lays the card from the flowers beside the postcard from the music shop, side by side on her lap. Her attention flits between the two for a few seconds as she compares the handwriting, but there's no way they're the same. Then something strikes her: it would have been the florist rather than the sender who would probably have written the message. She stares at the initial, A, and thinks of the teenage sweetheart's letter she found at Dad's.

It only takes a moment to spot the papers she brought from her father's, left unsorted on the floor next to the coffee table. She extracts the handwritten note and places it beside the postcard and once more compares the scripts. This time there is no doubt. The two messages, though separated by decades, are almost a perfect match. The sender of the flowers from Fort William is not only someone who knew Dad many years ago but she also appears to have known – still knows, if Zeb is reading this correctly – her mother.

Zeb frowns, frustrated by how little she understands of her family – which, as Dad was an only child whose parents died when she was just a toddler, now amounts to just two people: her and Matty. The possibility of more is tantalising.

Impatiently, Sam tugs Zeb's sleeve. 'For Christ's sake, what is it? Tell me!'

Zeb wonders where best to begin.

'So you think this Anna, some old flame of your dad's, knows where your mum is?' Sam asks when she is done, doubtfully.

'I guess that's what I'm saying, yes.'

'But that would mean your dad—'

'Yes, I know. Lied.'

'But why?'

Zeb sighs. 'Now that, I don't know. And if I'm honest, I can't really believe it. He never lied to me, why would he? He shared so little about her – not even pictures of what she looked like – because of how cut up he was when she died.'

'Left.'

'Sorry?'

'Maybe she left. Walked out on him. Perhaps that's why he lied.'

'He wouldn't do that,' Zeb answers, stiffly.

'But you just don't know, do you, Zeb,' her friend murmurs. 'None of us do; about who our parents really are – what they are capable of, I mean. Because to us they are, well, just our parents. We never see those other sides of them, do we? Rebellious child. Or abusive lover.'

'Dad would never—'

'No, I wasn't saying that about your dad. But—'

Zeb springs to her feet. 'You're wrong. We didn't have secrets. Which is what I'm going to tell this Anna when I see her.' Her friend's eyes widen. 'Yes, Sam. I'm going to see her to put a stop to this. First she sent flowers, then she sent – this.' She waves at the shoe box. 'And she shouldn't have. Because what she's suggesting is a lie.'

'I hear you,' Sam soothes. 'Really, I do. But you don't have to go to Scotland again, do you? I mean look at all your dad's papers, the ones you've got right here.'

Zeb eyes the black metal filing box beneath the window.

When she was little, it always stood on the floor to one side of his desk, with the dent in its side from that time when Wendy dropped it. Though plain and unobtrusive, it had long held a treasure trove of grown-ups' secrets – their passports, Dad's driving license and insurance details, her school reports – all locked away safe from prying hands.

It was where he continued to store important documents long after she'd left home. Like her birth certificate, which for some reason he'd continued to look after. Even when she'd applied for her driving license, he'd been the one to send off the form. Zeb steps towards the box, crouches down by its side and opens the lid.

'Zeb, what is it?'

As soon as she scans the hanging files, each meticulously labelled, she realises her birth certificate is missing. Which is strange, she thinks, inspecting the folder marked 'Personal ID' which contains his own. Dad was always so meticulous.

Zeb opens the folder and scans the top sheet.

She is touched by the fragility of a life, book-ended by flimsy bits of paper. *Peter Philip, boy*, his birth certificate reads. *To Bert and Patricia. Born Mile End, October 1, 1952.* Her gaze switches to the A4 sheet which she must have slipped in beside it just a few weeks earlier. *Died Woodleigh, Wilts. January 26, 2016.* At the back of the folder Zeb finds a copy of his marriage certificate paper-clipped to another death certificate, but it is Wendy's.

'Zeb?'

But Zeb is no longer listening. Instead, she shuts her eyes as she tries to make sense of Dad's story.

What she knows is that Peter Philip Hamilton was born in Clapton, north London. That though he never revealed why, his relationship with his family was fraught. His sole passion was for photography, until he met a beautiful young woman. A talented musician, she too had a troubled relationship with her family and – like him – dreamed of escape. The pair became lovers but before they could marry, she fell pregnant. Though it all happened too fast they vowed to make it work – and would have, too, had she not died during a difficult labour.

Zeb opens her eyes to see her friend seated on the edge of the sofa opposite watching her, anxiously. 'I'm fine,' she sniffs. 'Honestly. But I could murder a coffee.' Sam busies herself in the kitchen. Because it strikes her, for the first time, that something about Dad's story doesn't sound quite right.

As a child, his explanation had seemed reasonable to Zeb. Its details were unquestionable; romantic, even. How many times had she imagined their first meeting? So many that she can still see the fictionalised version of it playing out in her mind. Now, though, it seems a stupid fairy tale.

How obviously Dad sugar-coated details, she thinks, trying not to give in to the creeping realisation that Peter Philip Hamilton is feeling more and more like a stranger.

Most awful, though, is the thought of what he left out. The truth – even more dreadful than a mother who died – a mother who'd lived and chosen to go away. How could he have continued to love her after that, Zeb marvels. For Dad's love for this woman is something she never questioned and still believes in, recalling the one and only time she ever saw him cry. It was the day he announced he and Wendy would marry.

Tears for what could have been, he'd told her, ruefully wiping them away.

But what if he'd been crying for a different reason? Like losing the woman he loved to something – or someone – other than death? Might that explain how he'd abandoned his old life; the many sacrifices he'd made? Turning down lucrative newspaper work that would have taken him away from home in favour of a so-called career as a small-town wedding photographer.

Why couldn't you tell me, Dad? a voice in her pleads. If I'd known the truth, nothing would have changed.

'I'm sorry. Really, I didn't mean to upset you.'

Zeb looks up and sees Sam holding out two mugs of coffee. 'I know,' she mumbles, taking the nearest. 'But I think maybe you should go.'

'If you're sure,' her friend frowns. 'Look, I'm sorry. I don't want us to fall out again—'

'We're not,' Zeb cuts in, forcing a smile. 'Honestly. It's just… I feel… After sleeping on the sofa, you know… Just tired.' And to underline her assurances, she walks Sam down the communal stairway to the front door where they hug warmly, before her friend steps out into the bright, late February morning.

'Tell Matty I meant it when I said he can show me those partying Puffles next time, won't you?'

Zeb nods. 'Don't worry, I will. Talk later, OK?'

Back upstairs, she sees the light flashing red on the answering machine as soon as she closes the door. She hesitates, distracted by the sound of electronic music as Matty – nestled on her bed, wrapped in the duvet – plays on the laptop. 'Won't be a minute, luv,' Zeb calls as she lifts the handset to her ear and presses Play.

'I got your message,' says a stranger's voice. A woman. 'And I'm glad you called. I know I missed you when you came to see me the other day but we really must speak. So do, please, try me again. At the shop. I'm there four days a week – Mondays, Tuesdays and Thursdays are always best, but not weekends I'm afraid, Elizabeth. Just let me know when.'

How soon can they go? Zeb wonders. She will take Matty – he's still little, school won't mind. It will be an adventure. Perhaps they can take a detour on the way home via Loch Ness.

But then she pauses. This is madness. She can't take her son away without Richard's say-so. And if she takes him out of school so soon after the trip to Spain she knows what her ex would call her – selfish and irresponsible, and she can't have that. Even if he could take Matty abroad during term when he wanted to, and for a whole week, too.

Today is Sunday, though. If she goes this afternoon she can see Anna tomorrow and be back tomorrow night. It would just be one night away. She searches online for a flight but finds no seats available. The only other option is the overnight train, which would mean she could be back to collect Matty from school on Tuesday. Not ideal, but do-able.

Reluctantly, she picks up her phone and calls Sam's mobile in the hope she can persuade her to exercise some of her godmotherly duties. Far better for Matty to have a couple of nights staying with her than to ask Richard, she thinks.

A short while later a tide of bodies carries Zeb across concrete slick with rain, and onto the bus heading south along Camden High Street to Euston Station.

Fighting her way towards the rear of the lower deck, she eases into an empty seat next to the window. A moment later, a man in a padded jacket takes the seat beside her, thrusting her up against the window. The bus accelerates to a crawl. Trying hard to ignore the stranger's encroaching thigh, Zeb uses her sleeve to wipe a porthole in the fogged-up window.

As the bus stops just before Mornington Crescent, a dozen people bump against each other in their scramble on board. At their rear, Zeb notices, is a figure swathed in a dark overcoat whose face is obscured by his upturned collar. Though he is standing with his back towards her, three seats in front, there is something about the shape of him, the spade-like dimensions of his gloved right hand, that makes Zeb shake.

Shrinking down into her seat, she wills her pursuer to stay facing the other way.

A woman carrying a tiny baby beneath her plastic mac appears on the stairwell, fighting her way downstairs to alight at the stop she's almost missed. Realising he will have to move to let the woman pass by, Zeb looks down and furiously fumbles in her bag as if searching for something she's lost.

'Dropped something, darling?'

The man next to her is loud and impossible to ignore. As he twists towards her, a thick trunk-like arm pushes downwards between them, crushing her even more tightly against the pane as he feels around, blindly, for whatever it is he thinks she must have dropped.

'No, honestly, it's fine,' Zeb begs, praying the exchange will pass unnoticed by her fellow travellers. 'I must have been mistaken. Really, it's OK.'

Turning away as if to stare out of the window, Zeb shields the side of her face with the palm of her hand. But she is watching the reflected image of the man in the overcoat as he pumps the call request button to force the driver to reopen the rear doors. The bus slows to a halt and when it is stationary, he steps to one side to let the woman and baby alight before quickly resuming his position, facing towards her this time.

Sweat beads Zeb's hairline and her neck feels hot and itchy, but when she touches it the skin is clammy and cold. A cloying smell of wet clothes now fills the bus. At the next stop, the man in the overcoat takes a few steps towards the driver to avoid a surge of people from the top deck. The bus starts to slow. With only a narrow window before the crowd clears, Zeb's eyes skitter towards the opening door as the stranger in the seat beside her gets up to leave. She has to get out. Grabbing her overnight bag from the floor, she makes a dash towards the exit just as the automatic doors start moving together with a weary shudder.

She shoves her bag through the narrowing gap like a nylon battering ram and pushes her way out – half-leaping, half-slipping onto the wet pavement. Only then does she look up. The doors are shut, but the man in the overcoat is looking her way. Staring at her, hard, as he pounds the call request button.

Zeb stands outside a brightly-illuminated coffee bar. Inside, counters are being wiped down, chairs stacked and the floor swept. Spinning around, desperately, she considers her options. Though she could make it by foot to the railway station from here, she'd need to follow the route which the bus has just taken. Turning back to face the way she's just come, she sees a minicab firm's neon sign and runs towards it.

The interior of Ace Cabs is little bigger than a walk-in cupboard with a shabby counter and enough floor space only for two wooden chairs. The air inside is thick with the smell of damp fabric, stale nicotine and mint tea.

'Any chance of a taxi to Euston?' Zeb calls from the open doorway.

'Fifteen minutes,' a youth with an Arab scarf tied round his neck replies. He doesn't bother to look up from the magazine he is reading.

Backing out onto the pavement Zeb nervously scans the busy high street in either direction. Two black cabs, both with orange lights, pass on the far side of the road going the wrong way. As she wonders whether it is better to stay the right side of the road for the station and wait or to run over towards the cabs, a car quickly approaches down the outside bus lane. The vehicle, a silver BMW, draws level then starts to slow until, with a last minute pumping of the brakes, it draws to a halt a few paces ahead.

Zeb struggles to decide whether or not she recognises the driver. Too scared to wait and see, she rushes out into the busy road. Weaving her way through four lanes of traffic, she makes the central reservation only to find a waist-high wall of metal railings. But there is a jagged hole in the divide to her left, so she clambers through it then crosses more lanes of slippery tarmac.

Once she has stumbled onto the pavement on the far side of the road, she pauses to catch her breath. To her left is a narrow alley, to her right a one-way street. But before she has to choose, her flailing attracts the attention of a rapidly approaching black cab.

'Where to, luv?' the driver asks once Zeb has clambered inside.

'Anywhere.' Zeb slides down in the seat as the taxi retraces her steps back along the High Street then arcs right towards the bus stop she's just run from. 'Please, just drive.'

'Boyfriend trouble?' The cabbie is a whey-faced woman dressed in a candy-pink Juicy Couture hoody which makes her look even paler. She has a pierced lip and closely-cropped, peroxide-blonde hair, and her grey eyes are watching Zeb intently through the rear-view mirror. 'Back streets preferred, right?'

'Something like that.'

With a jolt, the woman executes a tight U-turn then accelerates northwards towards Chalk Farm. 'Tell me where you're really going and I'll take the scenic route,' she says with a sly grin.

'Euston – the station.'

Zeb closes her eyes as they head north past Camden Lock and swing a left towards Swiss Cottage before cutting along the leafy avenues of St John's Wood towards Regents Park. Then they dart across Marylebone Road before slowing to a pace more appropriate for negotiating the narrow backstreets of Bloomsbury, criss-crossing the grid of streets around Russell Square until her pulse is calm. There's little chance he will have been able to follow them by car. Zeb now sits in the back seat, straight-backed, staring out through the rain-streaked windows but seeing nothing.

He must have been waiting for her on the street outside, she thinks. Followed her on foot. Why hadn't she ordered a taxi in the first place?

Biting her lip she tastes blood as the driver heads the wrong way between two bollards marking a cobbled cut-through just south of Somers Town. Then, at last, the driver slows at a darkened junction beside a sign for Phoenix Road. She gestures briefly towards the brick colossus before them, now visible through the rain.

'There's a rear entrance if you go across Eversholt Street and turn right,' the woman advises.

Raising her collar against the rain, Zeb makes her way towards the station's rear entrance. Once inside, she tells herself, she will be fine. All she needs is to get her ticket then find somewhere out of the way to wait until the train is ready to board.

She stops on one side of the main concourse to look up at the departures board. Glancing at her watch, Zeb sees she has almost an hour to wait for the train she has booked to Fort William. The overnight service is non-stop and will allow plenty of time once she gets there to find a hotel room before visiting Anna. Reminding herself of her plan makes her feel calmer.

When the train is ready to board, Zeb walks towards her platform. As she approaches the barriers, she inspects her ticket – flattening the bends to help it slide easily through the machine. But as she feeds the cardboard slip into the slot to open the electronic gate, a commotion from the far side of the concourse makes her look round.

Outside the flower stall next to the coffee shop Zeb's just left a stout, middle-aged woman is shouting angrily as she rights upended buckets and gathers up the long-stemmed flowers now littering the floor. Turning again to see the subject of her fury, Zeb sees a man of medium build with a squat neck and shaved head charging towards her; the tails of his overcoat flapping in his wake like wings.

Spinning back towards the gate at the blast of a guard's whistle, Zeb barges through the channel left open for suitcases and buggies. Then, a moment later, she is on the platform hurtling towards the closest carriage as from somewhere behind more angry shouting erupts. She sees the man is still running in her direction.

Who is he and what does he want? she wonders, desperately. *Why me?*

With sixty seconds before the train's scheduled departure and as the automatic doors are about to close, Zeb somehow manages to throw herself inside, landing heavily on her burned arm as she crashes to the floor. Pain and relief pulse through Zeb's body simultaneously as the doors shut with a mechanical wheeze. She pushes her head out of the window as the train starts to pull away.

Craning her neck, Zeb looks back along the receding platform. The ticket barrier she just plunged through is still within sight, as is the florist standing behind it watching two transport police officers struggle to restrain the running man. He is on the wrong side of the gates – still on the station concourse, she realises, as her aching body is overwhelmed by a sense of giddiness and an urge to laugh.

It's going to be all right, Zeb tells herself, as she searches her coat pocket for her seat reservation. The train picks up speed and as the world outside rolls away, the city centre quickly melts into the looming darkness.

Everything is going to be OK.

–

Zeb sleeps fitfully on the train as it journeys north towards Scotland and wakes, finally, into half-light. The world beyond her window has become a craggy landscape ruled by gathering waves of grey hills. A desolate environment, lashed by rain.

A fragile sense of hope kindles inside her as the train slows towards the imminent end of her journey. Zeb fingers the piano charm that still hangs from her neck, considering the one word that kept turning over in her mind, again and again, in the days following Dad's death. Orphan. Because that's what she became once he had gone. Unless what Anna said is true. And even if it's not, maybe this old friend of Dad's can answer some of the questions for which she's long craved answers.

As the train reaches the outskirts of Fort William, Zeb folds the street map she's torn from the in-train magazine and slips it into her pocket. Her first priority will be finding somewhere to stay. Then, if she's lucky, she will look for the shop where Anna works. With a final glance out of the window towards the hunched shoulder of what might be Ben Nevis, Zeb rises to her feet, slings her bag over one shoulder then makes her way towards the exit.

To the left of the main station concourse stands a line of minicab drivers, some holding make-shift signs on which they've written their passengers' names. Along the far wall to her right stretches a line of pay phones. Before she can make her way between either towards the world outside, however, a stooped woman steps in front of her, barring her way. She is of indeterminate age, cloaked in ill-coordinated layers, with strips of plastic secured around each shin. Bent almost double, she is holding out a mittened hand.

'Spare us a couple a' pound, 'hen,' she rasps. 'I'm short for m'ticket home.'

Reluctant to open her purse amidst the throng of strangers, Zeb checks for loose change but, finding none, shrugs apologetically. 'No, sorry, I haven't—' she begins as the woman springs forward and clamps a hand onto Zeb's arm. Surprised by her unexpected agility, Zeb wavers as she stares into the stranger's face for the first time.

Though hunched, the woman is young. In her late twenties, probably. Her hair is a dull blonde, scraped back in dreadlocks. Her nose is pierced. 'Haven't got what?' she mutters, thickly.

Zeb wonders if she is on something or maybe drunk, though she doesn't smell of alcohol. 'Change,' she stammers. 'I don't have any—'

'Time,' the woman shouts suddenly. 'That's what you really mean, isn't it? You just don't have the fucking time to care.'

Zeb tries to free her arm but the woman's grasp is too firm. 'No, honestly, that's not what I—'

Releasing her grip, the woman pushes Zeb hard, almost making her lose her balance. 'Watch the fuck out where you're fucking going, bitch!' she screeches, spinning around on her heels to direct her gaze at the small crowd of onlookers who have gathered at a safe distance to watch, as if challenging someone to intervene. 'Did you see that?' she presses on to her audience. 'Almost knocked me flying, she did, and me all done up in my finest because it's such a beautiful day.'

Someone to the woman's right, a youth dressed in a bomber jacket and torn jeans, starts to laugh. As her accuser sets her sights on him, Zeb melts into the crowd.

The station's main exit is ahead, blocked by a crowd of teenagers dressed in army fatigues spread out amidst a sea of discarded kit bags. Zeb struggles to find her bearings as, barely conscious of the idea forming or where it has come from, she turns back towards the toilets opposite the platform from which she's just come. Beside the entrance to the Ladies is an unmarked door which she pushes open.

At the end of a short corridor is an emergency exit leading directly into the station car park. Good luck for a change, Zeb thinks as she emerges into a world of daylight, rising wind and a marked chill which makes her zip up her jacket and pull a grey knitted hat from the inside pocket.

The outlook is gloomy. But as she checks the map to plan the shortest route to the town centre, Zeb has a renewed sense of purpose.

Chapter 18

Hampshire, July 1975

Stepping into the room like an intruder, Alma is dismayed at the transformation: the floral walls, the matching curtains in Laura Ashley pinks and greens. Her mother has removed all of her books bar the classics, and her collection of glass animals and other childish ornaments are in the large trunk beneath the bedroom window. A cardboard fruit box has been left open on the bed for her to sort.

It is the start of the long summer holidays and the first time Alma has visited her parents' house in weeks. The last time she came, just for lunch, she didn't venture upstairs: though she'd hoped for a few hours' respite from her studies, all her mother and father had done was nag. About her disappointing grades. The Monsoon dress she was wearing. How short Viola had trimmed her hair.

Alma can't help wishing she'd said something sooner – though she guesses her mother would have pressed ahead with the redecoration even if her daughter had tried to object.

Beside the box on the bed, her mother has left out a neatly folded bath towel, matching hand towel and flannel. Dropping all three onto the floor, she slumps into the space they have left. She bounces once then twice on the edge and the mattress beneath emits a familiar creak. At least some things don't change, she thinks.

Alma pushes the cardboard box to one side and stretches out on the bed. Not so long ago, her mother's meddling would have felt like an intrusion; she would have sulked, and an argument would have ensued. But now, as she sits in this tiny box room that she has long ago out-grown, she feels almost nothing. Just a hope that maybe this means her parents don't expect her to move back home after college, and with this comes relief.

Folding her arms beneath her head, Alma stares up at the ceiling. For as long as she can remember, it has felt like she has fallen short of their expectations. Never quite good enough or sufficiently committed, her achievements were shadowed by faint praise. Well, not any more. Others are better-positioned to judge her now. And rather than resenting her parents' ambitions for her, she will damn-well exceed them. She grins. London started out in her mind as a place of sanctuary, but by releasing her and inspiring her over the past nine months it has become so much more.

The Conservatoire has provided her with the foundation for a new beginning, and what she builds on that must be good. All she has to do is decide just who she should be. Alma the classical musician – a position for which, if she works hard and steps up her practice, she could just about pass master. Alma the session musician – a less predictable option but perhaps a more attractive one, with opportunities to meet a wider array of people and players.

If all else fails, she can teach. And by the end of her course, she's decided, should she still not know, then she will take some time out to travel.

Already, Viola is talking about visiting a place called Kovalam in southern India when her studies finish. The plan is to take a few months out to travel by bus overland. It has become quite an established rite of passage, her friend claims, with plenty of budget hotels, restaurants and cafes along the way catering for young adventurers just like them.

Assuming Viola still wants her to come along. Recently, since the start of the summer term, the two roommates have spent more time apart than together.

The thought of a conversation she had with her friend saddens Alma. It was before Viola's first live performance with Geoff's new band in a pub on Upper Street. The venue was in the cavernous basement of a four storey building with a red brick façade, decorative columns and tall, arched windows. The place seemed at once both grand and seedy.

They were drinking shandies in the ground floor bar at a table by the window through which they can hear a distant radio. A song was playing: 'Three Steps to Heaven' by Showaddywaddy.

Feeling nervous? I would be, Alma asked.

A bit, Viola agreed.

The group is now called Lovefox – renamed in Viola's honour, Geoff said. And securing the warm-up slot in the basement of the Hope & Anchor was little short of a coup. Later that evening Viola was to sing throughout the entire set for the very first time. Which would have been enough pressure on its own, only they'd just found out through a friend of a friend that someone had managed to persuade a reporter from *NME* to come.

Don't be, Alma grinned. *You're really good.*

I'd better be, Viola groaned. *Because there's a lot riding on this, and I don't just mean the review.* Dropping her voice, she leaned forward, confidentially. *I want it to be really, really good for him, you know? I mustn't – can't – cock up.*

You won't.

Viola's eyes clouded. *I might, and you know what? For the first time ever, the thought of getting up there and performing makes me scared. Because I don't want to let him down.*

Geoff, you mean? said Alma, understanding now. Her friend nodded. *You really care about him, don't you?*

The thing is, my friend, I think I'm falling in love – and that's not happened to me before, Viola admitted, awkwardly. *I've had plenty of fun, if you know what I mean, but none of it really mattered. And the even scarier thing is I think I want to tell him.*

Really?

I know it seems mad, but I couldn't bear it if he didn't give a shit about me. If this was just a bit of fun. I'm not saying I want to get heavy or anything, just that I'd like to know it means something, you know? That I'm more than just a bit on the side.

Alma couldn't help but laugh. *Christ, Viola, have you looked at yourself recently? I can't believe anyone would dismiss you as merely a bit on the side.* She took a long sip from her glass. *But I think I know what you mean. It's good to know you both want the same thing – that's important.*

Viola groaned.

No, seriously, Alma pressed on. Because she'd been thinking about this a lot – at least, about her and Pete. *I think it's important someone wants to get to know you for who you are, you know? And that you're straight with each other about what you want. You've got to know if it's just a bit of fun, a bit more than that, or something else – and then, knowing how you feel, you can decide whether or not that's OK.* Her voice faltered as she noticed Viola's expression. *I think it's about self-respect, really. What's the matter?*

Who have you been reading, lately? Viola grinned. *Claire Rayner?*

Alma sighed. *You know what I mean.*

I do. Viola nodded. *And though I might not have seen it that way before, with Geoff I think I agree. Not that I'm anywhere near wanting to get serious yet, or anything. But, Christ, I do want this to mean… something.*

You old romantic. You'll be wanting to settle down and have kids with him next. So much for women's lib! Alma exclaimed without thinking. Viola's face darkened. And then she remembered about Viola's abortion. *Sorry, I didn't mean anything.*

Christ, Alma, her friend snapped, draining the contents of her glass. *Since when did you become such a… child?*

Ashamed by the indigestible memory of it, Alma rolls onto her side and hugs her knees.

–

Downstairs a short while later, Alma waits in the sitting room, flicking through the latest copy of *Cosmopolitan* she bought to read on the train. Though hungry for distraction, she is wearied by the prospect of actually reading.

Rising to her feet, she takes up position once more by the window overlooking the vicarage's shingled driveway, the open gateway, and beyond that the empty road. Checking her watch for the umpteenth time she sees it is five to eleven. Which makes him almost late.

Turning away, Alma rolls the magazine she's still holding into a baton then jabs it into the weekend bag which she's left standing on the floor in the hall. She lets out a sigh.

At first, the prospect of the long summer break had hung heavy; some kind of holiday job, ideally in London, would seem be the only way to survive. She'd made little effort to stay in contact with any of her old classmates from Burford and a year since leaving seemed too late to rebuild bridges. Meanwhile her friends from the capital had quickly gone their separate ways.

Viola would already be at her parents' place in the south of France with Geoff. Trish and Judy, the two girls from their year who shared the room next door, had headed back up north. Pete, meanwhile, had left London for Southend-on-Sea for the last few days of term to take some pictures for a local magazine. And to make matters worse, the weather had turned dreadful.

Five days into the holidays, things started to look up. Her parents confirmed they would once more be running the annual young Christians' summer camp in Hertford-shire – this time without Alma's help.

A day later, Pete travelled south to meet her outside the Odeon in Southampton where, Alma assured her mother, she had arranged to meet some girl friends to see the latest Pink Panther film. He had a plan, to take her away for a few days while her parents were busy. Which made not exposing their relationship to her parents' scrutiny – for fear they might change their minds about leaving her alone – all the more pressing.

Finally, yesterday afternoon, her parents had set off, and this morning, Alma had woken to the kind of brassy summer day that makes the world feel unbreakable.

Now she turns her attention back to the sitting room. An antique coffee table stands at its centre on which thirty-six weekly instalments of a Cordon Bleu cookery partwork are diligently stacked. The empty basket in the open hearth is guarded by an intricate wrought-iron fire-guard. Her mother's prized cherry blossom three piece suite.

Alma stares at the Blüthner baby grand, recalling the Christmas her father bought the piano. The reverence with which he introduced her to it. The silence with which he would sit listening to her play. The weight of his expectation that she would commit herself to her music, exclusively. And then she grins. Because since meeting Pete, far from distracting her from her music, his presence had reignited her love of it. With him, maybe she really could be as good as everyone once said she'd be.

Noticing the arrangement of lilies on the windowsill with water clouding at its base, Alma despairs. With the bed and breakfast in Dymchurch booked for the next three nights, she can't leave it like this. It will give Mrs Douglas, her parents' next door neighbour, a tell-tale sign she isn't in if the woman pops round to see how Alma is doing while her parents are away.

She carries the arrangement into the kitchen and empties the vase, rinses it out then put it away. As she dries her hands, a car draws into the drive. It parks up and the door opens. She hears footsteps.

'What time do you call this, then?' she calls from the front porch.

'About time?' he grins, pulling her towards him for a kiss.

'Not outside,' begs Alma, shooting a nervous look over his shoulder towards the point where, beyond a stretch of lawn bordered by pink rose bushes, an old stone wall marks the boundary with the Douglas's place next door.

Pete gives her a squeeze before letting her go. 'Walls have eyes, do they?'

'I think it's ears, silly,' Alma grins, tugging him through the open front door.

A surge of excitement pulses through her as they step inside. Even at school she'd rarely had friends back to the house to play, let alone a boyfriend. Now here she is with Pete in her parents' house, alone. The novelty of it feels thrilling.

'I thought you'd never come,' she sighs, relishing the pressure of him against her hips.

'Don't you know by now?' he counters, cupping her chin in his hand and raising her face towards his. 'Don't you know by now I always keep my word?'

As they kiss if feels to Alma as if her whole life has been leading up to this moment. Gently, he slips his hand beneath the hem of her sundress and his fingers slowly make their way up her thigh. Overwhelmed by an unexpected sense of urgency, she sinks back against the wall. Grasping the buckle of his belt, she slips the leather free.

'What, here?' Pete whispers, stopping her hand by holding her wrist. 'Are you sure?'

'Sssh!' she giggles.

Afterwards they roll onto their backs on the hall floor and lie in silence, side by side, listening to the muffled sounds of the world outside as their bodies cool. A bird circles unseen above with a listless shriek. A tractor's steady rumble from a nearby field. The distant A-road with its steady traffic pulse. Then three sharp raps on the frosted glass of her parents' back door, shattering the moment.

'It must be Mrs Douglas,' Alma whispers, grabbing for her dress. 'Oh Christ,' she mutters, hotly. 'Dammit, have you seen my pants?'

Flattening her hair with her hands, she hurries into the kitchen. A moment later, she is smiling politely at the stout woman in her late fifties whose white hair makes her humourless face even more severe as she stands, impatient, on the vicarage's back door step.

'I saw the car,' Mrs Douglas barks, swinging an ancient pair of secateurs.

'Yes?' Alma replies, noting her inquisitor's beady demeanour. Her thick rubber Wellingtons and A-line skirt. The woman is wearing a long-sleeved blouse beneath her padded gilet. Just how many layers does the nosy old parker need on a warm summer's day?

'In the drive,' the other woman presses on, gesturing towards Pete's car with a calculated glance.

'Oh, it belongs to a friend from college.' Alma steps outside, hopeful she can sweet talk her parents' neighbour back towards the gap in the fence through which she's come. Trying not to think of her lack of underwear, she smooths the front of her dress. 'She just popped over for a cup of tea. Gillian—' she calls back over her shoulder. 'I won't be a minute.' Then she turns back to the neighbour. 'Would you like to join us?'

Mrs Douglas frowns. 'No, it's all right.'

'Yes,' says Alma, lightly. 'It is.'

'Only your father specifically asked me to keep an eye on things while you were here on your own,' the other woman presses on.

Viola-style, Alma beams. 'Which, as always, is very much appreciated.'

'Yes, well, if there's anything you need – anything – I'm always here.' Relaxing her grip on the secateurs, Mrs Douglas laughs: a brittle sound. 'Perhaps you'd like to come round for supper a little later?'

'Oh, well, that would be lovely but I've got some chores to do in town then I'm meeting some friends.

We're planning to see the new Pink Panther film – you know, with Peter Sellers?'

Mrs Douglas looks blank. 'As you wish,' she says, turning away.

Alma waits for the woman to disappear from view before retreating back into the house where she finds Pete sitting on the bottom stair. 'Forgotten these?' he grins, holding up her pants then gently lobbing them towards her.

'Stop it,' she protests, slipping them back on. 'Though I did forget something else.'

'What?'

'Cash. I meant to go to the bank.'

'It doesn't matter, I've—'

Alma shakes her head. 'No, it's fine, just wait.'

Hurrying back into the kitchen, she stops in front of the fridge. She opens the door of the cupboard above which contains assorted tins of biscuits, savoury and sweet. Squeezing her hand between the stack of boxes and the tea caddy by their side, she feels her way towards the back corner where her fingers close around a black and white plastic figure of a suited man.

'Come on, Fred,' she whispers, unscrewing the flour sifter's bowler hat. 'Good man!' Inside is stowed a roll of pound notes. Slipping the bundle out of its rubber band, she counts out twenty and puts back fifteen. 'Don't worry, I'll pay it back before they get home,' she adds, noticing Pete's surprise. 'I'm a good girl, honest!'

They take their time, relishing the drive down narrow country lanes pooled in shade from the interlacing foliage above their heads. They stop for a late lunch in a pub overlooking an immaculate village green, taking in a lazy game of cricket. Then they set off through parched fields once more.

Just past Winchester, Pete pulls in at the side of an elevated A-road section where metal barriers obscure what would once have been a panoramic view. 'Just for a minute,' he says, answering her as yet unasked question. 'You'll like this, trust me.'

Alma climbs from the car to stand by Pete's side, behind a temporary wall of broken rocks caked in earth. They are close to the top of one side of a tree-rimmed valley, though an area of vegetation the size of a small field below them has been cleared. Staring down through a gap in the bank, she sees a fleet of giant diggers with dusty caterpillar tracks preparing the ground for construction.

'It's the next new section of the M3 motorway to link Southampton with London,' he murmurs.

Uncertain why they have come, she turns towards him in search of further explanation. Then, registering the expression on his face, she knows there will be none. 'How old are you?' she laughs.

'Old enough to know better,' Pete shrugs. 'But come on, isn't it fantastic? I mean, look at what's happening. This is progress. Life moving on.'

Gazing back down onto the construction site where the bronzed bodies of the workers below are gleaming with grit and sweat, Alma sees what he means. That the people down below could be from any time, forcing their will onto nature. Without the toys, they could just as easily be carving out stone to build the pyramids.

'You should come back here,' she purrs. 'Take pictures.'

'I already have.' Turning towards her Pete kisses her cheek. 'I knew you'd see it like I do, you know. That you'd understand. Because we're soulmates, you and me.

Listen,' he adds. 'I've got something for you.' He tugs from his pocket a small cardboard box little bigger than a box of matches, wrapped in candy-striped paper that reminds Alma of the seaside. 'It's not much, but when I saw it... Well, I thought of you.'

'A token of your affection?' Alma jokes, squinting into the solar glare.

'If you'll accept it, yes.'

Taking the gift, she slides her forefinger beneath the paper to reveal a tiny jewellery box and peers inside. Buried within a nest of cotton wool is a slender, silver chain.

Hooking the necklace with her little finger, she raises it to the light. But as she stares at it she sees something else. That in this simple exchange is a kind of a turning point. Alma takes his hand in hers then drops the chain into the centre of his open palm.

'Oh Pete,' she murmurs, noticing the uncertainty now clouding his face. 'It's beautiful. Really, I love it. Can you help me put it on?'

Dipping her head, Alma relishes the dry touch of sun against the back of her neck as Pete secures the clasp. Then, as she closes her eyes, she experiences a curious sensation of completeness. This is it, isn't it? she asks the voice inside her. A coming together of two separate halves. A perfect submission to our fate.

Chapter 19

Zeb takes a seat on the bench outside the bookies then unfolds her map and plots a route to the shop where Anna works.

As it starts to rain, she pulls the hood of her jacket over her head. But as she tries to make sense of the scrap she tore from the magazine, sheltering it as well as she can, she realises the map is too imprecise. Of the alien fretwork of streets, only the largest are marked by name and the landmarks detailed are a handful of town centre pubs which stock the beer sold by the map's sponsor, a local brewery. What she can see, though, is that the town centre appears too small to get lost in.

Behind her, next to the bookies, is the tourist information office. *Closed 'til lunchtime for family service*, a handwritten note stuck to the inside of the window says.

Rather than wait and get drenched, Zeb sets off at pace towards a pedestrianised street lined by shops on either side, some of which contain staff getting ready for the start of business.

Without thinking to ask directions, she turns on what feels like a whim down a left-hand side street where, at the bottom, she finds an alley on her right. Scanning the blackened walls of the end buildings on either side for any hint of the street's name and finding none, she is about to retrace her steps to the shopping street when she spots a sign hanging from above the door of a small building at the far end. Three words that spell out the name The Bass Clef.

Barely able to believe her good fortune, Zeb rushes towards the building with three worn stone steps at the front, leading up to a glass-windowed front door that's been left ajar.

Pushing the wooden panel just above the old-fashioned knocker, Zeb feels the door give a little before any further movement is halted by the tautening of a heavy black security chain. She steps back, as her efforts have triggered a cacophony from a bunch of cowbells suspended from the ceiling. Noticing a neatly printed sign, Zeb sees the shop does indeed open each Sunday – but from 10am. Checking her watch, she finds it's five to nine. Only when she looks up again does she notice the figure moving around inside.

Could this be her? she wonders as the shop assistant starts moving her way. The woman is tall with short grey hair and dressed in a charola jumper and black velvet ankle-length skirt.

'Yes?' the assistant inquires. Her tone is brusque, but as she registers Zeb's matted hair, her air of awkward anticipation, her whole demeanour changes. 'Can I help?'

'I've come to see Anna,' Zeb begins as the rain abruptly thickens from persistent drizzle to steady pelt.

The woman cranes her neck to glance at the sky. 'Come in, just for a minute,' she says, standing to one side.

The shop is dark and cluttered. Ancient oak shelving crammed with music books and piles of stacked sheet music line each wall. In the centre of the room an assortment of classical instruments is displayed on two large wooden tables which have been pushed together. A selection of violins and associated stringed instruments sit upright on stands along the counter, where an ancient till dominates the rear.

Dropping her bag from her shoulder and placing it on the floor, Zeb scans the room with undisguised surprise, amazed that shops like this could still exist in the internet age. 'What an amazing shop,' she exclaims.

The woman nods, then scrutinises her visitor closely. 'What do you play?'

'Oh no,' Zeb laughs, shaking her head. 'At least not any more. Just at school, really – I played the piano. Though my mother was a talented musician.' Suddenly, she thinks of Matty. 'Maybe it's jumped a generation—'

'I'm afraid you're out of luck,' the woman interrupts. Perplexed, Zeb frowns. 'Anna's not here.'

Struggling to mask her disappointment Zeb exhales, slowly. 'Oh.'

'She's usually here on a Sunday but has today off for a piano recital in her local church. She'll be in later in the week, though, if you'd like to pop back then.'

Zeb bites her lip.

The thought of having to wait days feels unbearable. 'I've just come up from London and I was so hoping to see her this afternoon,' she blurts out. 'Anna is an old friend of my dad's, who died recently. I don't suppose you can give me her number, can you? I'm sure she won't mind.'

The woman prevaricates. 'I'm sorry for your loss, but I'm afraid that's just not possible. I am more than happy to pass on a message, however.' Zeb notices a line of slim boxes containing an assortment of local flyers neatly arranged along the sill. 'Wait while I find something to write on.'

Zeb isn't listening, though, but staring instead at the bundle of leaflets promoting a recital taking place that evening at a church, St Mary's, in a town called Beauloch. For some reason she can't quite recall the name seems familiar. 'Don't worry,' she calls out brightly. 'I'll pop back. Actually, I'm not staying far from here. In Beauloch?' She smarts at her clumsy pronunciation. 'Someone recommended the local B&B.'

By the time the older woman looks up Zeb has pocketed the flier, stepped away from the window and is examining a piece of sheet music. Something or other by Bach. 'Glen View?' Zeb nods. 'Why, that's just next to the chapel,' the women observes, putting down her pen and paper. 'You'll find Anna there a little later, I'm sure. That B&B is good but small and often fully-booked this time of year. In which case you should try the hotel on the far side of the village.

A place called McLellans.

–

The journey takes less than half an hour, though the town's one-way system and the winding B-road make it seem longer. But at last they pass the simple sign that marks the Beauloch boundary, and the cab pulls up outside a single-storey pre-fabricated village hall a few minutes later.

Zeb pays the driver and climbs out of the car. She stows her change. Glen View is indeed fully occupied, she can see from the wooden sign outside. She will have to try McLellans, she decides with a mounting sense of anticipation.

A cold blast of wind slaps her back, as she walks along the road towards the other side of the village, where she finds the hotel with little trouble. It is a bleak four-storey lodge with a shallow roof and net curtains at every window.

Close up, the hotel's wooden window frames are cracked and perished and pebble-dash is just visible beneath a thin veil of white paint. Screwed to the wall at eye level next to the main entrance is a pair of antlers. A plaque beneath details some indeterminate endorsement of the quality of service one can expect within.

The place looks traditional at best, Zeb decides as she opens the front door. But its anonymity is perfect.

The young woman behind reception is dressed in a dark suit and a cream silk shirt with matching cravat. On the desk, a striking arrangement of dried heathers sits self-consciously in an antique porcelain tureen. There is an open stone fireplace beyond flanked by leather sofas which, though aged, are meticulously buffed. Upmarket glossies fan across the oak coffee table. Walls tastefully hang with artistic black and white shots of the surrounding landscape.

Zeb adjusts her expectations. Despite its lacklustre façade McLellans is clearly an establishment with pretensions.

'Good morning,' the woman at the reception desk offers, brightly, as a burst of laughter erupts from the far side of the lobby. Turning to its source, Zeb sees a group of retirees decked out in top-of-the-range walking gear are making final adjustments to day packs, binoculars and shooting sticks. 'May I help you?'

'I'm looking for a room.'

The woman swivels towards a flickering computer screen on the desk behind her. The gesture strikes Zeb as odd, given that from the outside the building doesn't look as if it accommodates more than five or six bedrooms, but there must be some kind of extension at the rear.

'Well, I've the double with a full ensuite on the second floor. Or a generous single in the stable block at the rear – but it doesn't have a bath, just a shower.'

'I'll take the double, please,' Zeb replies, staring at the framed list of room tariffs on the wall. Though aspirational, the establishment is still affordable – by London standards, at least.

'I'm afraid it's a little early,' the receptionist apologises. 'But it should be ready within an hour: if you leave your bag here I can have someone take it to your room. We've a comfortable lounge where you could wait. Or we serve breakfast until twelve.'

Gratefully, Zeb hands over her bag. 'Actually, I could do with some fresh air,' she smiles. 'Do you have a local map?'

–

St Mary's is at the end of a row of terraced dark stone cottages, a few streets up the looming hill above the main road.

The church is set back from the road behind a rough stretch of ragged ground and uneven headstones, the larger of which provide sufficient shelter for leftover snow. It is a modest building – with grey stone walls, plain windows and a sombre wooden door – and an empty one, too, judging by its darkened interior.

Zeb tucks the map away then zips her jacket back up. Above her, dark clouds twist like fish and it looks like there is snow to come. Adjusting her beanie to cover her ears, she proceeds further up the shingled pathway lined on either side by grey piles of swept snow. At the door she twists the iron handle, willing it to provide fleeting shelter from the wind. But the heavy latch refuses to budge.

Anna is probably at home getting ready or rehearsing, that's all, she thinks, clapping her hands together for warmth. Though a quick glance around her confirms she is indeed completely alone.

Heading back to the churchyard gate, Zeb spots a small bench set against a stone retaining wall which separates a raised tier of family plots – reserved for the local gentry, perhaps – from the communal path on which she currently stands. Humbler headstones stretch out below.

Suddenly hungry she takes a seat, grateful for the natural cover from the damp cold provided by a broad-limbed cedar tree. Having forgotten both last night's supper and this morning's breakfast, she is ravenous. It's almost lunchtime, which might also explain where everyone has gone. Maybe she should wander back to the pub in the village centre, find something to eat then come back later – though the thought of sitting alone in a bar in a strange place is hardly appealing.

Perhaps it would be better to return to McLellans instead and call for room service. She hears voices. Zeb turns around in her seat and sees a man and child.

'Come on, Dad, let's go home – I'm hungry,' a girl about the same age as Matty pleads. The pair are walking across the raised bank behind where Zeb is sitting.

The child's blonde hair has been worked into two rough plaits, the ends of which are visible beneath a red crocheted tam o' shanter. The girl is wearing a navy duffel coat toggled to the throat and non-matching wellies – the right is black, the left is green. Watching her weave to and fro between the plots, bobbing in and out between the bushes, makes Zeb's heart skip.

'We've got shepherd's pie,' the young girl trills. 'And you know it's my favourite.'

'Okay, okay,' the man concedes. Rising to his feet from the graveside where he has just placed fresh flowers, he raises his hands in mock surrender. Tall and thin, the father is dressed in walking boots, jeans and an orange mountain rescue jacket. Unlike his daughter, his head is uncovered and wind and rain have tousled his thick blonde hair. 'Say bye to Nana and I'll drive you back to your mam's.'

'Bye Nana,' the girl dutifully repeats. Without warning, she jumps down from the bank and lands on all fours by Zeb's feet.

'Hello,' Zeb smiles.

The little girl frowns. 'Hello,' she replies, cautiously.

'Evie?' the man's voice calls from behind some bushes. 'Over here, Dad.'

A moment later, he jumps down onto the path beside his child. 'Ta-daaa!' he declares, reaching down to scoop her up onto his shoulders. Only then does he notice Zeb. He nods. 'All right?'

Zeb smiles. 'You?'

'Sound, eh.' He sniffs, reaching out his hand to the child who grabs it fast as he pulls her up. 'Just visiting?' he says, nodding towards the locked church door. 'It's one of this area's oldest, though the village now has to share the priest, so there are only services here alternate weekends.'

'Kind of,' Zeb replies. 'I'm staying at the hotel down the road. I came up here for a musical performance that was due to take place, but I think I must have made a mistake.'

'The recital?'

'Yes.'

'It's been cancelled, hasn't it, Evie?' The man looks down at the child who nods her head, glumly. 'She and a couple of her school friends were due to take part, but the organ broke so it'll have to be another time.' A crestfallen smirk is the only response Zeb can muster. The stranger smiles. 'Goodness, you look even more disappointed than this one did when we got the call yesterday.'

'Sorry,' Zeb mumbles. 'It's just I've come a long way to see an old family friend and now it looks like I may miss her.' She struggles for a moment to remember the surname she'd seen on the flier in The Bass Clef. 'Anna Dee?'

The stranger blows on his hands then tugs a pair of gloves from his jacket pocket. 'The piano teacher who lives up at the Duffys'? Yeah, I know her. I've got to drop off my daughter at my ex's place back near the village centre. But if you like, I can show you – if we take the back road down, it's on the way.'

Zeb barely dares to believe her luck.

'Fraser.' He holds out his hand.

'Zeb,' she replies, self-conscious as she sees his eyes make a quick sweep of her from feet up. Her running shoes. Jeans. Her shower-proof jacket.

Fraser sniffs the air. 'The weather is closing in. And it is a little way up the hill on the outskirts of the village.' He winks. 'But don't worry about those shoes – I've got a car.'

Wondering what's wrong with her trainers, Zeb glances up at the lowering sky. But then she remembers the last time she was in Scotland. The snow-clad morning when she was picked up by Jean, coatless; her feet sodden.

How easy it is to underestimate how much colder it is up here; how changeable the conditions, too. 'That would be great, Fraser,' she smiles. 'Thank you.'

He is also a visitor – of sorts – to Beauloch, he tells her, as they climb the stony footpath to the top of the churchyard. On the other side of the back gate sits Fraser's four-by-four, a tank-like vehicle of indeterminate colour, thanks to a coating of dried mud and salt residue from snow-covered winter roads. For though he grew up here and returned, briefly, with his childhood sweetheart to raise Evie, the marriage was over almost before it began.

Fraser describes himself as a born outdoorsman. Even so, after university he turned down an offer of a job with the local mountain rescue team in favour of making a fast buck in the City as a graduate trainee. Which he did for a while until, tiring of London, he returned to Scotland and hooked up with his girlfriend Jeanette, who'd known him since school.

But once Evie came along the dynamics of their relationship which had worked so well before no longer made sense. Frustrated by the hours Fraser had to put in setting up his new adventure activities business, Jeanette moved back to her mother's place in Beauloch from their house in Aviemore, and never went back. Now, the pair live apart and Evie is with him alternate weekends. Though he has been off work in Beauloch for the past fortnight following the death of his mother, once the village primary school's head teacher.

'I'm sorry,' Zeb says, eyes fixed on the pitted road ahead. 'Really, I am. As if it isn't bad enough coming to terms with what's happened, there's all the administration, the paperwork, the arrangements to be made. I don't think I've ever felt quite so overwhelmed, or alone. Because though everyone has been so kind, it's something we all end up having to deal with in our own particular way on our own. Goodness,' she exclaims, her line of thought broken as one of the front wheels catches in a jagged pothole. 'It's just my dad… he died, too. A month ago. And, well, it was – still is – such a shock.'

'It's tough,' Fraser answers. 'The not knowing, I mean. We had a little warning as we knew Mum had cancer, but still, nothing ever prepares you for your first parent dying.'

Zeb prickles with sympathy. 'I guess not,' is all she can say as the track on which they are driving steepens and the car slows to little more than a walking pace. For a moment there seems to be nothing more to say. Until the silence is broken by a burst of fairground music from the back seat where Evie sits, playing on Fraser's mobile phone. The short sequence of notes stops then repeats, again and then again, producing a refrain which is at once saccharine and sinister. *Candy Crush Saga*, Zeb notes, thinking how much Matty loves that game. She will call him as soon as she gets back to the hotel, she decides.

Fraser pulls into a tight passing space and kills the engine. Zeb is overcome for a moment by the smell of him – soft notes of heather, soap and tobacco – it takes her a moment to process what she can see. The slope above must rise at an angle of at least thirty degrees. At its peak is a house with an unkempt front garden staring out across patches of lowland too rugged to farm. Iron Age circles of ragged conifers. Pied hilltops. The building is stone-roofed, austere; its façade, pitted with tiny windows set deep into the rain-lashed stone. It seems impenetrable.

But Zeb's attention is drawn back to just one feature. A few feet above the front door a circular window peers out from the stone like a Cyclops' eye. The echo of Billy's picture makes her left hand tense around the door handle. For this is the place where she came before. The house where she was invited in for tea. Where she was asked to wait while her host popped out for milk. And where something unspeakable happened while she was waiting.

'Looks to me like there's no one in,' Fraser observes. 'She converted the place into flats when her husband died, you see. But neither of the cars that are usually there are parked out front and none of the windows are open, see?'

Stunned, Zeb answers automatically. 'They have them open in winter?'

'You southern types with your City shoes and central heating,' he teases. 'Yes, in winter, too – though I think some might count this as early spring.' Fraser looks at his watch. 'Mrs Duffy will most likely be out at the shops. Davy will be out setting his traps. And Miss Dee will be music tutoring, I'd expect. Right, it's later than I thought and I really should be dropping Evie off. Sorry, I should have thought this through.'

The temperature is falling as Zeb makes her way to McLellans by foot from the crossroads in the village centre where Fraser drops her off. The weather is indeed closing in, which gives the hotel lobby a certain womb-like allure. Though grateful for the temporary excuse not to investigate further, she knows she will have to return. As Zeb approaches the reception desk to pick up her room key she sees a new receptionist. This one has a heavily lacquered helmet of silver hair and makes no effort to end her phone call.

Taking a seat in the leather armchair by the side of the desk, Zeb spots a large, leather-bound visitors' book and pulls it towards her. Opening the cover, she flicks through its heavy, gold-trimmed pages to pass the time. Despite the inhospitable time of year, dozens of visitors have stayed at the hotel in recent weeks from places as far afield as Hong Kong, New York and Ontario. As she waits for the woman to finish her call, a mobile phone rings. It is a tone Zeb does not recognise, so it takes her a moment or two to extract it from her coat pocket.

'Zeb?'

'Yes?' she answers, straightening up instinctively at the sound of Richard's voice.

'That was lucky, I was just about to hang up.'

'How did you get this number?'

'You left it with my parents, remember?' Her ex's response is punctuated by an impatient sigh. 'Yesterday afternoon when you dropped off Matty. Where are you?'

Finally, the receptionist has finished her call. She points at the visitors' book with a freshly manicured forefinger. 'Could you fill in your details, including your home address?' she mouths.

'A place called Beauloch near Fort William.'

'Why?'

Zeb scowls. Why not, she thinks, crossly, balancing her phone against her cheek as she fills in her details. What right do you have to judge? But no, she must rein it in, she knows; try not to be so defensive. It's important for him to believe in her efforts – her determination – to get things back on an even keel.

'I'm just up here for a night for… work. There's a collector Kirsty wanted me to meet,' she ad-libs, wildly. Did she tell him she quit her job? She can't be sure. 'He's thinking of making a donation of some early daguerreo-types to the gallery. I'll be back Tuesday in time to collect Matty from school, as I've a meeting first to see Dad's solicitor.' But that meeting is tomorrow, she now realises, angrily. How the hell could I forget? As soon as she gets into her room she will call to express her sincerest apologies. 'How's Matty? Can I have a word?'

'Of course not,' Richard grumbles. 'I'm at work and he's at school.'

Slumping against the reception desk, Zeb struggles to swallow back the disappointment. Barely seeing her son in the days following Dad's death was a trial, but one she dealt with by keeping busy. Then when Richard suggested that he take Matty away around the time of the funeral because he was too young to attend, she'd been too emotional to disagree. But after no contact for two weeks then only the briefest of reunions, her need to hear his voice is a desperate craving.

'I'll call later then.'

With a glance at her screen, the receptionist reaches towards a bank of hooks on the wall, in search of Zeb's room key. She slides it along the counter.

'Try after six but before bedtime – so no later than half seven.'

'I know when bedtime is,' she answers, tartly.

'Just to be clear.'

Zeb winces. 'Thank you Richard,' she tries, more gently this time. 'For being so supportive at what's been such a... difficult... time. And please do pass on my thanks to Hugh and Jennifer, too. They've been a great comfort.'

Her ex's voice warms. 'You know my parents dote on Matty.'

As the line goes dead Zeb waits for her nerves to subside. She is relieved Richard didn't challenge her lie about being here on business. Yet his pompous tone makes it hard to feel anything but resentful.

The hotel lobby with its distant clatter of lunchtime service, its damp dog and woodsmoke smells slip in and then out of focus. Fearful she might faint, Zeb's knuckles whiten as she grasps the counter's edge. She stares at the oil painting of a Highland landscape on the wall opposite, then at the ornate silver dagger displayed in the glass-fronted box beneath.

Then a chilling memory. *Angel!* the man child had cried, hugging the creature to his chest. Inert now, its spume-flecked mouth was clotted. It was a lumpen, crimson, broken thing. *My Angel!*

She remembers how the dog had leapt towards her. The dull weight of the kitchen knife. The rage in the creature's eye. The taste of whisky from that miniature she'd downed for Dutch courage before leaving the hotel. The shock that even as the blade slid hilt-deep there was no blood, not at first. But then, as the knife withdrew, the rapid release of scarlet. Blood on her face, her hands; the heat of it. Then, worse: the stranger – a man yet a man with a wet-lipped boy's face – dropping to his knees. And finally, the awful truth.

I killed it, she acknowledges, horrified. Davy's dog, Angel. I stabbed it, through the heart.

'Is there anything else I can help you with?' The receptionist is peering at her over a pair of half-moon spectacles balanced on the end of her nose. 'A table for lunch, perhaps?'

'No, nothing – thanks,' Zeb says, startled. All she wants now is to retreat. 'Really. Thank you. Everything… really… it's all… OK.'

The woman nods. 'Through the far door then right past the breakfast room, up the stairs to the first floor, then third along the corridor to your left,' she instructs. Then her face twitches into a faint smile. 'And Miss Hamilton?'

'Yes?'

'Welcome back.'

Chapter 20

Mornington Crescent, September 1975

Alma is woken by a distant rumble, like furniture being moved. She grasps the corner of the eiderdown which has fallen to the floor her side of the bed. She is naked. But though the flat was hot and airless when they lay down on the bed a short while earlier, now the open bedroom window is shaking in a gathering wind.

Curious to know if Pete heard the sounds that have just woken her, Alma rolls onto her back. But he is fast asleep, snoring. As she tucks the eiderdown around her, occasional shafts of feathers poke her skin.

Tilting her face up towards the window, Alma stares at the darkening sky. Jostling rain clouds are all she can see, which makes her uneasy. Like the way she felt as a child when, returning from a wet Sunday afternoon outing, it looked like darkness would fall before they could make it back home. Though this is early September. And it's only mid-afternoon.

Must be one hell of a late summer storm, she thinks, flinching as the first drops of rain break against the pane.

Closing her eyes, Alma imagines the weekend shoppers in the West End for the day cramming the streets below now hurrying, ant-like, towards Kings Cross and Euston for their trains home. The stallholders at the new market by Camden Lock deciding whether to shut up early. Morecambe & Wise and a TV dinner for the keepers working late at the nearby zoo.

She slips her feet onto the floor. The carpet's deep pile is a delicious contrast to the stripped wooden floors of Pete's old place on Rivington Street, which Phil had lost – pub and all – to a business debt.

With just forty-eight hours' notice, Patsy had insisted her ex find her son somewhere else, however temporary. And for perhaps the first time in his life, the man was as good as his word. For a peppercorn rent, Pete now has use of this two-bedroom flat on the tenth floor of a high rise built in the mid-Sixties behind Mornington Crescent.

With its panoramic views across Victorian rooftops westwards, and the valleys of railway tracks pointing to the tree-lined fringes of Regent's Park, the place has quickly become a welcome refuge. Secret and secure, this eyrie has provided the perfect antidote to her return to The Conservatoire for the autumn term. For despite talk last year of renting a flat with Viola, Alma's parents have forced her to return, instead, for a second year in halls.

Alma can now see it was inevitable her parents would find out about Pete.

Watching from her upstairs window, Mrs Douglas had spotted the sitting room table lamp which Alma left on, and the upstairs bedroom window curtains left undrawn. She had wasted no time telling the Reverend and his wife about Alma and the male companion she had seen. And she knew for a fact they'd gone away together, on their own, for almost a week.

It was all somewhat suspicious, the woman had said.

As was the timing of Alma's return four days later when Pete had dropped her off just an hour before her parents' arrival. Most damning, however, was the length and intensity of their parting kiss. It was an intimate moment which given the care Pete had taken to shield her out of view beneath the leylandii, Alma calculated the old cow could only have witnessed through a crack in the fence.

Punishment was inevitable, and all about teaching Alma a lesson.

She would return to London, and be grateful for it, on significantly reduced living expenses until Christmas, her father decreed. She would live in a single room to guard against an inappropriate roommate who might lead her further astray. And she would end her friendship with her boyfriend, too – something that he planned to work in close contact with college authorities to ensure. Which is why – for anything other than official, supervised course-related activities – Alma must now adhere to a 6pm nightly curfew.

It was a high price to pay, but one in line with the severity of her transgression, her father said. And standing before him, with her fingers crossed behind her back, she had agreed.

Buoyed by the memory of those four glorious days with Pete in Dymchurch, spent mainly in a four-poster bed in the front-facing bedroom with its barely noticed sea views, she knows she will somehow bear it. Evenings out with friends may now be banned, but in her father's naivety he has failed to limit her from spending daytime hours with Pete.

Alma's wings may have been clipped, she thinks, but she is far from beaten.

All she needs now is Viola.

Within hours of her return, Alma had been thrilled to discover that her old roommate had been allocated the only other single room in hall on the same floor as her, just two rooms down. But she must wait another day or two more to learn precisely why – and, indeed, what are the *family reasons* that have delayed her friend's return to London.

Knowing Viola, however, she is sure that this is just a manufactured excuse and that really everything is OK.

On the mattress by her side, Pete rolls over without opening his eyes.

Careful not to disturb him, Alma gets out of bed then creeps out of the master bedroom, along the corridor and into the bathroom then closes the door behind her. What would her parents think of it all, she wonders, pulling a face at her reflection in the mirror as she brushes her teeth before stepping into the shower.

They would be horrified by the speed with which Pete and she became intimate, of course. By the fact they are still together, too. The spontaneous rough cut of him. His mother's open-hearted giddiness and the roulette-wheel unpredictability of his stepfather's late night world. They would be bemused, too, by how effortlessly wealthy bankers like Viola's dad rub shoulders with upstart market traders and West End theatre types. A place where cash talks louder than class.

But this is a world as legitimate as her parents' cloistered rural fiefdom. A world of possibility that certainly feels more vibrant and alive; somehow, more real.

Wrapped in Pete's dressing down, Alma pats her hair with a towel but as she tries to comb it through finds it knotted and tangled. She spots a bottle of hair conditioner standing on the shelf, between bottles of shower gel, shampoo and Pete's shaving products, and reaches for it.

The treatment is for coloured hair; an expensive brand. Alma sniffs the contents. Squeezing a small amount into the palm of her hand, she slowly rubs the conditioner into her scalp. Once more she runs the comb through her hair but this time meets no resistance. She stares at the bottle for a moment, wondering if she could take it, but has second thoughts.

Tightening the lid, she drops the conditioner into the plastic carrier bag propped against the wall next to the bin, into which Pete has placed assorted items left in the flat by the previous tenant. There is a half-used bottle of baby oil. Three silk stockings. A large canister of heavy-duty, professional hair lacquer. Vaseline. A pair of eyelash curlers. A black silk sleeping mask.

Alma is intrigued. Without these clues, she'd simply have assumed from the flat's taupe-coloured carpets, khaki walls and dark grey curtains that its previous occupant was male; perhaps, even, Phil. Someone who stayed over a few times a week when he was too late to get home to his wife, or too drunk. Maybe just to get laid.

Thank goodness Pete's plan is to lighten the decor to make the most of the rooftop views and natural light, just as soon as he has a free weekend.

As she makes her way back towards the bedroom, a clatter from the kitchen makes Alma jump. Assuming Pete has woken, she turns back along the corridor to follow the sound to its source. But as she steps into the sitting room, an unexpected figure standing at the kitchen counter, filling a teapot with boiling water, stops her in her tracks.

'Excuse me—' Alma calls out.

The figure, an auburn-haired woman wearing a long-sleeved denim dress, spins towards her, abruptly. 'What?' she counters, defiantly.

'What do you think you're doing?'

The woman frowns and folds her arms. 'A question I might just as well ask you.' Alma's eyes widen, for the woman is familiar. Though it's been a while since they met – and, even if she is right, she can't imagine why Pete's cousin would be here, unannounced. The other woman reaches for something on the countertop then holds it up, pointedly. 'I have a key,' she presses on. 'Where's yours?'

'None of your business,' Alma retorts. 'Who said you could let yourself in?'

Chrissie smiles. 'Pete did.'

'Rubbish. Pete's asleep.'

'Not just now, earlier in the week. He let me have the spare key so I could come and go if I needed, when things get tricky with Brian.'

Alma takes a step forward. 'That's very—'

'—generous. Yes, it is. But that's Pete for you. He's all heart.'

'I was going to say, unlikely.'

Now Chrissie takes a step towards Alma. 'Really, how so?' she glowers.

'Because he would have told me.'

The other woman laughs. 'Tells you everything, does he?'

Alma nods, firmly. 'In the main.'

'Told you about us then, did he?' she sneers.

'I'm sorry?'

'Us. Pete and me. We used to go out.'

Alma snorts. 'Don't be ridiculous, you're cousins. Besides, he would have said.'

Chrissie shakes her head. 'Not unless he had to. So I guess he hasn't had to, not until now. But the thing is, Little Miss Perfect, blood's thicker than water, see? And when it comes to the crunch, family trumps all. We were each other's first kiss. Our first something else, too—' She interrupts herself with a laugh. 'But let's not go into that. Just think of us as kissing cousins.'

Alma narrows her eyes. 'Well that's your thing, I guess.'

Chrissie takes another step forward. 'Are you suggesting I'm a—'

'What's going on?' Both women turn towards Pete who has appeared in the sitting room doorway dressed only in a pair of crumpled jeans. 'Chrissie, what are you doing here?'

'She let herself in,' says Alma, affronted.

'Because you gave me a key.'

'For an emergency,' Pete interjects.

'Which this is?' His cousin shrugs.

'Sorry,' he adds. 'I didn't quite hear you. What happened?'

'Brian and I… we had a row,' she mumbles.

'A row. But not an emergency. Look, Chrissie, I meant what I said about being here to help as and when you need it. But until you do, please—' he holds out his hands then lets them fall '—just don't take the piss. And while you're at it, you can set the record straight about what you just said to Alma about you and me being kissing cousins. Go on.'

But Chrissie says nothing.

'How old were we…? I said—'

'Oh all right, then.' She scowls. 'Ten and twelve.'

'And what happened, exactly? Other than a misguided peck and a grope, I mean.' His cousin mumbles something. 'I'm sorry, I don't think Alma and I quite caught that.'

'I said, nothing,' snaps Chrissie, reaching for her bag and coat.

Pete accompanies his cousin into the hall. Closing the front door behind her, he secures the chain before coming back into the room and taking a seat beside Alma.

He smiles, tentatively. 'Are you OK?'

'I guess. Is there anyone else who might drop in?'

Pete shakes his head. 'I'll change the locks. You can have the spare key.'

'Thanks.'

'Hey, are you sure you're OK?' Pete says, reaching his arm around her shoulders. 'I'm sorry if that gave you a fright.'

Though the exchange with Chrissie has unnerved Alma, it isn't that that plays on her mind. It's the same idea she had after that Sunday lunch at Patsy's. The sudden hope, buoyed by a growing understanding of some of the family dynamics in Pete's life, that maybe the time will soon be right for her to open up fully to him; to come clean about the conflict of emotions that muddy and magnify the feelings she has for her own family. Anger and resentment. Pity. Guilt. Regret. The lingering belief that only by admitting what happened in Vienna can she ensure the love they feel for each other will take root on solid ground.

But, as ever, her chance has passed.

Pete walks to the kitchen counter and takes out two mugs from the cupboard. 'Fancy a cuppa now it's brewed?'

Bending down, he takes a bottle of silver top from the fridge.

'OK. But no milk for me,' she mumbles, suddenly feeling queasy.

Chapter 21

Beauloch, February 2016

The bedside table vibrates as the phone, a retro Bakelite replica with an old-fashioned rotary dial, lets out a tinny ring. More asleep than awake, Zeb struggles at first to remember where she is. Wrapped in a soft white towel, she is lying adrift on a sea of tartan that covers a large double bed.

Her eyes quickly scan the unfamiliar contours of a spacious bedroom. In the corner is an oak wardrobe tall enough to almost brush the ceiling. To its left there is a broad bay window, with a seat built into the base, upholstered in tartan. On the other side, a leather armchair and matching footstool beside a large chest of drawers, on which rests the crumb-covered plate from the club sandwich she ordered earlier. Her black holdall sits on a collapsible case stand.

Scotland, she remembers, reaching for the phone.

'Hello?'

'Zeb?' It is a Scottish voice, male, which she cannot place.

'Yes?'

'It's me, Fraser. I'm in reception downstairs.'

'Fraser? Sorry, I must have dozed off—'

'No, I'm sorry – to wake you, I mean. I'll come back later.'

'No, don't do that,' she says. 'Wait. I'll only be a minute.'

For she has had an idea. The thought of returning to the Duffys' place, later, in search of Anna Dee has been playing on her mind. She's come too far to give up, yet is fearful of meeting the landlady's son; terrified, too, of being invited inside. But maybe Fraser can help her. By accompanying her back, perhaps he could take a message to the door. News that she has come, and a suggestion they meet somewhere neutral.

'Fraser, I need your help,' she begins a short while later, as they sit at the McLellans bar. She is eating a lunch so late it's almost high tea – a toasted sandwich with a glass of sparkling water. He has just ordered a beer.

I believe I can trust you, her instinct says.

'Shoot,' he says, topping up her ice-filled glass from a bottle of carbonated Highland Spring.

'I need to see Anna. But there's someone else who lives in the house I'd rather not see – not Mrs Duffy, but her son.'

'Davy Duffy?' Fraser looks thoughtful. 'Oh he's all right, really. Though I can see your point – he doesn't usually venture very far.'

'What do you mean?' Zeb asks, wiping mayonnaise from her lips with a paper napkin.

'He's not quite right in the head, you know? It's sad, really. I mean he never seemed that screwed up as a kid, just a bit slow. Always preferred being off on his own in the woods rather than hanging out with other kids. Then in his teens he got into a bit of trouble, nothing serious at first – peeping Tom stuff, petty theft – until he ended up with a conviction for burglary. He tried to kill himself in prison—'

Zeb says nothing.

'When he came out he went back to live with his mother and after that was rarely seen at all,' Fraser continues. 'It seemed kind of strange when Mrs Duffy took in a lodger, but as it turned out the piano teacher had a real way with him – even taught him music. He didn't get very far with that, of course, but his mother once told me it made him calmer and brought him out of himself. Finally, he seemed to be getting his head back together – at least until a couple of weeks ago.'

A gobbet of something leaden has lodged in Zeb's throat and though she swallows hard, she fails to shift it. 'What do you mean?'

'He just flipped all of a sudden, apparently. Killed his dog first – left it in a pool of blood on the kitchen floor – then slashed his wrists.'

Zeb closes her eyes but this only makes her feel worse for now the room feels as if it's spinning. Worse, in her mind's eye she can see the man clearly crouched beside his dog, staring up at her in fury while on the stone tiles the blood pooled in the shape of a full-blown rose.

His mother had begged him to stop, but it was as if he couldn't hear or wouldn't listen. And then, by the time he sprang towards her, it was as if he'd lost all reason.

Hurtling out of the kitchen, she turned a sharp left into the woman's downstairs bathroom and slammed the door. She cowered in the corner, her imagination supplementing what her ears struggled to decode. The approach of footsteps. Fists pounding the door. Then his mother's outdoor boots clattering across the flag stones. Her attempts to pull him away.

No. Please God no, Davy! Then, as the pair retreated into the kitchen, a more soothing tone. *Give me your hands, there's a good boy. Now let me bind them.*

Zeb opened the bathroom door and poked out her head. The dimly lit hallway was empty; the front door at its end just open. With head down and feet pounding she ran, propelled by the knowledge there was just one chance; determined not to slow her pace – even to grab her coat. Until she burst outside into the darkness, an iron world encased in snow. The cold made her body brace.

'Zeb?'

'I'm all right, really.'

'No you're not,' he counters, gently. 'How can I help?'

'It's hard to know where to start,' she mumbles.

'At the beginning?'

But where is that, exactly? Zeb wonders. The break-in at the flat? Her last trip to Scotland? The funeral, or before? She shrugs. 'I guess it all begins with Dad.'

'Doesn't it always?' Fraser smiles. 'Sorry, go on.'

'He brought me up after my mum died. And we were really close, you know? But then when I left university... well, he and I had different ideas about what I should do. I moved to London, a place he'd hated and left long ago. And it was fun. I had lots of different jobs. Travelled a lot, with friends. We didn't grow apart exactly – he was always there for me, helped me buy my first flat... But I guess looking back I always knew deep down, I suppose, that he disapproved of the choices I made...'

'That's tough,' Fraser concurs when, reaching the part about balancing caring for Matty with working at the gallery – the job Dad found her – she pauses for breath. 'Raising a kid on your own.'

'Not really alone. We share custody, and Dad was always happy to help…' Zeb presses on, defensively. He doesn't understand, that's all. Now is her chance to explain.

'Anyway, earlier this year when Dad died a woman got in touch with me claiming to be an old family friend. She sent me this box of bits and pieces from when I was little, and other stuff I didn't recognise, along with a letter in which she told me my mum is still alive.' She falters as the thought of the letter she found at Dad's place, what this could mean, and the implicit suggestion of a side of life Dad might have tried to conceal, makes her eyes well. 'The point being that all my life Dad lied.'

Fraser nods. 'So can't you ask the woman – the one who sent you the letter – to explain what she means?'

'That's the thing,' Zeb sighs. 'I'd like to and that's why I came.'

He nods. 'Anna Dee?'

'Yes.'

'Well that's easily enough sorted,' Fraser smiles.

'Actually, it's complicated.'

'Try me, I'm an expert at puzzles.'

Zeb juggles with what excuse will sound most convincing. 'It's Davy.'

'Ah, well I'll grant you he looks pretty intimidating, but really he's—'

'Would you speak to Anna for me?' Zeb says suddenly. 'Arrange a place other than Mrs Duffy's where she and I can meet?'

'Is that all? Sure, of course.'

'That would be great. Really. Thank you.'

Fraser drains the last of his beer. 'Then what?' he asks. 'I mean, once you've seen Anna. Will you track down your mum?'

'I guess I just want to find out… why she left me.' Zeb bites her lip, for this is something she's yet to fully think through. What will she do if she discovers from Anna her mum really is alive? How will she feel? 'It's important – to me, at least. More important than ever now Dad's gone, I guess. It's about where I came from, who I am.' She rubs her nose with the back of her hand. 'Does that make sense?'

When at last Fraser speaks his voice is quiet. 'It does, though I can't say I'd do the same—'

Zeb starts to interrupt but pauses as he holds up his hand.

'I never knew either of my parents,' he says, ignoring the change in her from surprise to contrition. 'We were adopted, me and my sister, when we were babies. By a couple who couldn't have kids of their own. We were loved and happy, too – even when they eventually told us the truth. Because by then I knew it didn't matter. I was who I was – and still am – because of the life I had led rather than some hand-me-down genetic blueprint. So when the law changed and I had the chance to find out about my real parents I knew what I had to do – or, rather, not do. I did nothing. They didn't want me and I didn't need them. Trust me, Zeb, you're better off not knowing. Because knowing is, well, irrelevant.'

Anger burns away the tears that have been welling in Zeb's eyes. He is so wrong, she thinks, but she lacks the words to structure a coherent defence.

'No,' she insists. What does Fraser know about her life, Dad, their family? How dare he. 'It is important. It does matter.' She sniffs. 'Well, it matters to me.'

'Don't be cross,' he soothes. 'I'm not judging, honest. Look, of course I'll help.'

She turns towards him. Thank you, she wants to say but before she can he touches her hand. Her skin tingles. His face creases into a smile as the gulf between them closes.

–

They emerge from the hotel a short while later to find the wind has dropped and patchwork clouds are hanging high against a limpid sky. It is cold, though, and as they cross the car park at the hotel's rear Zeb buries her hands deep into the fleecy lining of her jacket pockets.

They have decided to walk back up to the Duffys' place and as they traverse the village centre past the empty pub, Fraser loops his arm through hers. The moment seems charged. On the far side of the road, he tells her, they will take the right-hand track that leads up the hill to the north of the village where the Round House will be visible through a wall of ragged trees. But the incline seems steeper than it did driving in Fraser's van, and soon after starting their ascent Zeb is hot-cheeked and short of breath.

'Tell me about Matty,' he prompts, as she frees her arm from his and slips into step slightly behind. 'Short for Matthew, right?'

Out of breath already, all Zeb can do is nod.

'How old is he?'

'Seven.'

'Same as Evie! It's a fun age.'

Zeb grins. 'He had an imaginary pet rabbit for a while which he had to take with him everywhere, even in the bath. But that was before *Star Wars*.'

'*Star Wars?*'

'Now it's Finn and BB-8.'

'On the way to school? In the park?'

'Everywhere,' she smiles. 'The boy's obsessed!'

'Evie, too. And not just with Rey. She's got five lightsabers.'

As they draw level with the Round House's garden, Fraser pauses by the rough stone wall, moss-veined and shoulder height, which marks the boundary with the public right of way.

'Wait here,' he says as Zeb draws level.

Peering over the wall at the front of the house, Zeb spots a broad figure standing in the open doorway of an outhouse to the left of the main building. Quickly she ducks down and out of view.

'Are you OK?' Fraser asks.

'All good,' she answers, lightly, hoping he does not notice her clenched fists.

Cautiously peeking over the wall Zeb watches as Fraser passes through the gate then climbs the drive to the three stone steps leading to the front door. The clouds twist and turn like wringing hands. The morning has turned even colder and the occasional fleck of rain feels more like snow. Adjusting her hat, she shakes her arms and stamps her feet to get the blood circulating.

Looking towards the outhouse, Zeb sees that Davy has disappeared from view. Refocusing on Fraser, she watches as he pauses at the bottom step before reaching out to grasp the ancient metal knocker. A moment later, the front door opens just enough for Mrs Duffy and him to exchange pleasantries.

An engine burst signals the ascent of a car from the valley below as the driver changes gear. Please, God, let Anna be there, Zeb wills, as she scrutinises their body language for any clue. But then, almost as if in answer, the woman is shaking her head and stepping back into the darkness. As the car rounds the bend to her left, she realises the road merges to a single track just before the point at which she is standing.

There is ample room for the vehicle to pass and sufficient time for anyone to see her and brake, she figures, yet the driver does neither. Without slowing, a four-by-four screams past her with just inches to spare, forcing Zeb to flatten herself against the wall. It is a silver BMW, like the one she saw at Dad's and outside the flat in London. But, the driver's apparent lack of interest in her means it cannot be the same one, she decides.

She brushes shards of stone and fragments of lichen from the sleeves of her jacket. She is shaken but unharmed. Mystified, too, by what kind of an emergency could make someone drive so recklessly. But the car is gone, leaving the road empty, the morning silent. And it is only then that Zeb raises her head and sees, with a surge of excitement, that Fraser has not moved. He is waiting, and the Duffy's front door still stands wide.

Zeb crosses her fingers as a slender woman appears in the doorway. Though she is too far away to see properly, Zeb is sure this is Anna, and words from her letter begin to soar and dive inside her head.

She thinks of Wendy and the morning Dad told her they were to be married. The way his dark eyes that never missed a trick had been incapable of meeting hers. How the tension in his jaw had made his lips as taut as wire. She'd noticed how his thick, dark hair was fading to grey at each temple. It was the first time in her life he'd seemed vulnerable to the passing of time.

Back then, Zeb had assumed this was all about how Dad feared his daughter would take the news of Wendy finally, formally, becoming her stepmother. Now she is not so sure. Wendy had been a part of their lives for almost five years by then and she and Zeb had grown close. But now, looking back on it, it strikes her as strange to think that Dad could have had any doubts about his daughter's reaction to his putting their relationship on a more formal footing, unless he felt guilty in some way for betraying his first love.

'All sorted.'

Zeb's eyes snap open.

Tomorrow at midday – not long to wait, Fraser explains, pausing briefly to blow into his hands. She's suggested meeting somewhere discreet – a tea room a short drive away at a Forestry Commission-run place. Then he thrusts his hands deep inside his jacket pockets, leaving his left one elbow kinked enough for Zeb to slip her own arm through.

'I don't know about you, but I could murder a drink,' he grins. 'Coming?'

–

Beauloch's stone-clad pub, The Crofter, sits on the far side of the crossroads opposite the village post office which doubles up as a convenience store. On its far side is a modern extension with floor-to-ceiling windows – to sustain a promise of every table having a panoramic view, perhaps. Not this evening, though. It's dark, and the low cloud has brought with it flurries of snow.

Zeb thinks of a painting she once saw of a late-night American diner – though the scene now before her is like an inverted pastiche of it.

This bar may also stand out from the inky blackness, but rather than providing sanctuary to a couple of loners, its interior is alive with the buzz of animated chatter. Dozens of customers – locals and outsiders alike – stand shoulder to shoulder, talking and drinking, as they must have since daylight faded. *Who are all these people and where have they come from?* she wonders.

Fraser opens the door with a dramatic flourish as he ushers her inside.

'So, what's a nice girl like you doing in a place like this?' he asks a few minutes later, placing a pint of Guinness and an orange juice and lemonade on the table.

Zeb grins. There is something about this soft drink that will mark the start of the next beginning, she has decided, determined to prove to the world – Richard, especially – that she is OK. She raises her glass in thanks, though toasts in silence.

To the new me.

They are in the Garden Room at the far end of the bar where drafts from the windows make the tealights flicker. The cramped annex is filled with glass-topped tables and wicker chairs, with each cluster of seats carefully positioned to look out at the view. However, this early evening, the only thing visible is the outline of a nearby clump of conifers. Prime position for an approaching storm, Zeb notes as a gust of wind rattles the window by her side.

Fraser is now wearing faded jeans and a thick plaid shirt which he's rolled to the elbows, revealing a white long-sleeved T-shirt beneath. Without his padded coat, Zeb can see his body is slim but muscular – from mountain running, he has explained. With his high cheekbones and sculpted jawline he has a strong face. Though the fact she's noticed all this now makes Zeb awkward.

'How do you know Anna?' she asks.

'She teaches Evie piano.'

'Local?'

'No, a southerner, like you.'

'But after the referendum, isn't Scotland—'

He smiles. 'You know what I mean.'

'So she didn't grow up here?'

'I think from what Jeanette said she moved here ten, maybe fifteen years ago. I was living in London at the time, so I'm not sure. What I do know is that she's always lodged where she lives now, though – Aileen Duffy is an old family friend.'

A roar of laughter from the far end of the bar distracts for a moment as they turn towards a group of men in padded shirts and waterproof trousers sitting around a table crammed with a dozen or more empty pint glasses. They are exchanging jokes as they wait for the sixth member of their party to return from the bar with yet another round of drinks. Fraser rolls his eyes at Zeb.

'Friends of yours?'

'Contemporaries, I guess,' he winces. 'We all went to the same school, though I managed to get away.'

'A lucky escape?'

'For a while, I guess.' He shifts in his seat. Leaning across the table he reaches out to touch her hand. Staring at his fingers, she is too surprised to move her hand away.

'You're very pretty, you know.' His forefinger draws a fleeting circle on the inside of her wrist. 'Sorry, you don't mind me saying that, do you?'

'No, I don't mind at all,' she exclaims.

Raised voices once more interrupt them, though this time from the opposite side of the room where another group of men are standing by the side exit leading to the Gents. It is the sound of heckling as their target – a long-limbed figure in a navy boiler suit – sways clumsily into view. He must be at least six foot tall, she reckons. And as he makes his way through the throng of people, a number of drinkers jeer until he disappears from view.

'Sorry,' Fraser smiles, sheepishly. The hand on hers has gone.

'Me too,' she mouths, before she can stop herself.

But Fraser is once more watching the lumbering giant who is now stumbling back into the room. His lips are butcher's pink from constant wetting by the tip of his tongue. And now that he's unbuttoned his boiler suit and tied the sleeves around the waist, padded bandages are clearly visible around each wrist.

Though she's not seen him since, apart from in her waking dreams, Zeb recognises him immediately. And she is struck by the curious contradiction of her feelings. First relief – her temples ache with it. The realisation that, thank God, he hadn't... wasn't... that he is OK. And then a surge of fear.

It was me. I did it.

By killing his dog, she was the one who drove him to howl like an animal. To shake the creature's lifeless body as if convinced he could force the life back into it. To sob like a baby into its fur. It was her actions which made him grab the knife from the kitchen floor then draw it once, twice, three times and more across the inside of his wrists. Like he was punishing himself for letting it happen; carving himself an escape route to follow.

He was deranged, of course. Why else would anyone do what he did, she thinks, staring miserably at his bandaged wrists. Which is when it strikes her. All he has to do is look up and he'll see me, she thinks. And when he does, remember…

She wants to leave, right now, but dares not risk it. He's not seen her. Getting up will only draw his attention. So instead she hides low, warily observing his reflection in the windowpane.

Fraser looks anxious as the hulking figure barges like a trapped bear through the throng of drinkers, impervious to the cries of those whose drinks he's spilled. Then, sensing Zeb's fear, he slides his chair towards hers, obscuring her from potential view.

'Hey,' he whispers. 'Is everything OK?'

Burying her face in his shoulder, Zeb finds momentary comfort in the musky smell of him. Woodsmoke and recently-laundered brushed cotton; his body heat. But then, as she twists her head to peer over his shoulder, she finds her face being turned back into the light. Her body tugged closer against his. His mouth tightly locking with hers. No, she tries to say. Zeb pulls away from Fraser and breaks free. This is not what this is about. Not here. Not like this.

A few paces away, a couple of the men Davy's knocked into are man-handling him towards the rear door. It's her only chance, she thinks, striding towards the bar with such haste she only just manages to avoid colliding with one of Fraser's schoolmates, returning to his friends with yet another tray of pints.

'Watch yourself,' the man barks as a tall figure in a donkey jacket roughly shoves Davy into the car park.

'Zeb—' It's Fraser.

She presses on, desperate to be outside – away from the clamour of voices, the bass line pulse of the place, the company of strangers. But he won't take the hint, and is closing the distance between them, pushing his way across the room. She's nearly at the main door, just another few paces should do it. But suddenly someone is holding onto her arm. Trying to hold her back. Dragging her back into the light – the piercing, searching, unforgiving light which leaves no room for shadows; no place to hide.

'Hey,' he pants. 'Wait a minute!'

'Please,' she cries out. Her body is shaking, her forehead is damp with sweat. It wasn't her fault, but self-defence. She killed the dog, yes, but not its owner. The wounds on Davy Duffy's wrists were self-inflicted. Which is awful and shocking. But. Not. Her. Fault. 'Let go of me!'

Oblivious to the faces turning their way, Zeb shakes her arm free then shoves Fraser with such force he almost loses his footing. She runs, out through the front door of the bar into the darkness beyond. Down towards the crossroads. Back towards McLellans, where, a few minutes later, outside her room, she is fumbling with the key when a figure appears beside her.

'Here, let me try,' Fraser offers, and a warm hand enfolds hers.

'Really, I can manage—' Zeb retorts, indignant that he has followed her not just back to the hotel, but inside. After two turns the door opens.

Taking care to remain in the corridor outside the open bedroom doorway, Fraser reaches inside to turn on the light. Which is when she sees a folded piece of paper on the floor – someone must have slipped it beneath the door while she was out. Scooping it up, Fraser passes it to her unopened.

'I'm sorry,' he says, taking a conciliatory step backwards. 'Whatever is going on, I've obviously made things worse. I just wanted to make sure you got back to your room OK. And now you have, well, I think I should say goodbye.'

'No, wait!' Zeb cries, her attention split between what he is saying and the message she now holds in her hand. The neatly printed note on McLellans-headed paper is from one of the receptionists – to let her know that someone called for her, earlier, with a London accent.

No message, it reads. Just left his name, Brian, and said that he'll be back tomorrow.

Zeb's legs buckle as she thinks of the man who broke into her flat. The same man, she fears, she's seen parked in her street and who chased her across the concourse at Euston Station. Can he really be here?

'You've got to help me,' she sobs, holding Fraser's arm to stop herself from falling; praying she can trust him. 'Please don't leave.'

Chapter 22

Kensington, October 1975

Fists of rain drum the pane of the window then splash inside the cubicle, wetting Alma's head. Opening her eyes, she looks up and considers whether if she stands on the toilet seat she'll be able to reach the catch. No, she decides. With her arms clasped tightly around her knees, waiting for the dizziness to subside, she does not have the strength.

'Hey, are you in there?'

Viola's voice is accompanied by a soft tap-tapping. Mr Steadman must have sent her out of their tutorial to see if everything is OK. Maybe if Alma says nothing, just sits there, quiet and still, she'll go away. It will pass in a few minutes. All she needs is some quiet. A drink of water, perhaps.

'Alma?' Viola knocks twice this time. 'Come on. I know you're in there. Open the door.'

'I'm fine,' Alma croaks. 'Really.'

'Like hell you are. What's up? Come on, tell me.'

Though insistent, her friend sounds weary. Just as she has since she arrived back at The Conservatoire a few days earlier, with little explanation of what has made her miss the first two weeks of term. All Alma has been able to deduce is that she has split with Geoff and now prefers to stay in her room every evening reading *Valley of the Dolls*.

But she has not yet had the courage to talk to her friend directly, given how distant and offhand Viola has grown since she last saw her earlier in the summer.

Alma feels jaded, as if teetering on the brink of flu. Even the memory of the long, summer days she shared with Pete can't rally her as, with tears welling, she flinches at another slap from Viola's palm against the cubicle door. Biting her lip, she tastes blood then sees traces of red on her skin.

'Well hello,' Viola declares, stepping backwards to let Alma pass when she finally opens the door. 'So, are you OK?'

Pressing her hand to her mouth, Alma counts to ten before she replies to check she's staunched the flow. What a fool she's been to skip breakfast, she decides. Running the cold tap for a moment, she splashes her face with water.

'Here.' Viola holds out a handful of paper towels.

'Thanks,' Alma replies, scrutinising her reflection.

'Mr Steadman wonders how you're doing.' Viola is leaning against the wall by her side, watching her in the mirror. 'What shall I tell him, or are you going to come back in and tell him yourself?'

'Coming.' Alma dries her face then tosses the paper towels into the bin. 'How do I look?'

'Peachy,' Viola lies. Turning to stare at her own face in the mirror, she rubs her eyes which, Alma notices, are surrounded by dark rings. Her skin is grey, too, and it looks as if she's lost weight.

'Thanks.' Alma hesitates. 'Though I can't say the same for you. Is everything OK?'

Viola pulls a packet of cigarettes from her pocket, offers one to Alma which she refuses, then lights up. 'I'll survive,' she observes. 'It's just… it's been a difficult few weeks.'

Alma turns away, sickened by the smell of smoke. She knows just what her friend means. In the wake of another terrorist bomb going off just a few days earlier, this time in the lobby of the London Hilton, the whole city now feels on edge. 'Look, I'm sorry I've not been around much,' she begins. 'And being grounded after six each evening is a real pain. But maybe we could go out together, just the two of us, one lunchtime.'

Viola's face brightens. 'Saturday?'

'Ah, well, no, not tomorrow, I'm sorry,' Alma flounders, for she has already arranged to spend the day with Pete. 'But maybe after we could go to the student union bar?'

Viola groans – the bar, which doubles up as a communal TV room in The Conservatoire's main building next door, is usually empty and sells only pints of warm lager. 'It's OK you know,' she snaps. 'To have a life. But you'd better watch out, Alma Dean, if you and lover boy are getting serious. You need to be careful. Take precautions, if you know what I mean.'

'Sorry?' How dare Viola think she could be so naive? Alma wonders, crossly. What does she take me for, a fool?

'Don't be angry,' her former roommate blurts. 'That's not what I meant. I'm sure you know what you're doing, it's just… be careful, that's all.'

'Like you are, you mean?'

'No,' Viola replies, firmly. 'Not like me. I mean—' she drops her voice '—learn from my mistakes, that's all.'

Alma turns away, unconvinced.

'No, wait,' Viola insists, reaching for Alma's arm. 'Over the summer I got pregnant. It was his. I didn't want to keep it; that was never an option. But I told him, and when I did he didn't want to know – not about me, not about what I'd do, how I'd cope. That was it. He dumped me. It was over. Finished. Just like that.'

'Oh Viola, I'm so—'

'So I sorted it out. Got another abortion.' Viola's laugh is hollow. 'It was all quite simple, really. The same private clinic. I got it done a week before coming back to college. Look, I'm sorry… it's just, it all still feels a bit raw, you know?'

'Losing it, you mean?' Alma offers, gently.

'No,' her roommate exclaims, recoiling. Incredulous. 'I mean splitting with Geoff.'

Alma runs a hand through her hair in a vain attempt to relieve the dampness now pricking the back of her neck. *What's her point?* she wonders, vaguely, at once hot and short of breath.

'So, Alma Dean,' Viola presses on, though her tone has cooled, 'I wanted you to know that just because life starts to get serious doesn't mean things can't go wrong, OK? And that if you ever need anything, just let me know.'

'Sorry?'

'I've got some of those new home pregnancy kits – you know, so you don't have to go to the doctor? Well, not to find out, at least.' Though she throws her cigarette butt onto the floor, Viola doesn't bother stubbing it out as she turns towards the door. 'I just thought you might want to know, that's all.'

Alma stares at her, unsure what to say. Because she isn't pregnant. Just hungry, that's all. Skipping breakfast always makes her feel queasy.

Alma rings the bell then steps back from the communal front door.

It is Bonfire Night and the air tastes of cordite, giving the streets through which she's just raced an incendiary feel. With a shiver, she begins counting backwards from one hundred. As she hits seventy-five it starts to sleet. *Where is he?* she wonders, as she presses the bell for his flat again. Will she have to stand here, alone and in the cold, waiting for long? *Come on*, she wills him. *Be there, Pete.* Please. Come. Now.

'Christ, Alma, is everything OK?'

He is standing behind her and must have seen her hunched in the half-light, wet and bedraggled, as he made his way from Mornington Crescent. But he is here now, which was why she has come. To see him. Tell him. Beg for his help. Though the enormity of the situation she now finds herself feels too great to articulate; too frightening to say.

As she dithers, the void is filled by Viola's voice.

I told him and he didn't want to know. Didn't want to know – not about me, or what I'd do.

As the church on the corner chimes quarter past the hour, the wind brings with it the smell of woodsmoke. A distant memory forms: the thought of simpler times and the excitement of raking leaves with her father to burn on the bonfire.

Pete scoops her in his arms as soon as they are inside.

'Come on, tell me – whatever it is,' he whispers, rubbing the warmth back into her hands. 'Nothing can be that bad.'

Though it is, of course. Viola was right. And her roommate's words now threaten to eclipse reason. Though

Alma had guessed a while before, she's only known for sure these past three long miserable days – seventy-two hours, during which she's never felt as miserable. Fearful, too, of Viola's I-told-you-so's. So she's kept it to herself, to wrestle alone with the likely outcomes of the stark choices that lie ahead.

'Trust me,' she mumbles, dully. 'It is, and worse.'

With Viola's support, Alma knows she could have sorted it without telling anyone else. But she was frightened. Guilty, too.

Then, as the hours passed, she came to realise something else. That telling Pete isn't just something she wants, but needs to do. Because despite what her parents would say and what she was brought up to believe, confronted by the blunt reality of the thing she cannot keep it. Admitting this, to anyone let alone him, is the ultimate challenge. But she must test him, too. Because after what Viola said about Geoff, she has to know how Pete will react.

'Ah,' is what he says at first, repeating it a few times as he buys time to think. 'Only I'm not quite sure what to say. How do you feel about it? How do you want me to feel about it? What do you want us to do?'

Us. A simple word but one that says it all. Not you, us. The relief of hearing it makes Alma cry.

'I don't think I can—' she stammers. Tell her parents. Explain to them that, contrary to everything they'd raised her to believe, she will choose to have a termination. Because it is the wrong time; too soon. And she is the wrong person; too immature. 'You know, go through with it.'

'The abortion?'

'No, no. Not having an abortion.'

Doesn't everyone need to live a little first if they are going to be a good mother? She can't help wondering if that's maybe where her own mother went wrong. And she does want to be a good mother, very much; but one day, not now. Which doesn't make her an evil person. Her parents won't understand, but God will. Because this is about doing the right thing. And it is the wrong thing to bring a child unwanted into this world. If she did that she'd be a bad mother, surely.

Alma gulps. 'I don't think I can keep, it, I mean...'

'I'm not sure I'm ready for that, either,' Pete says. 'In fact I know I'm not, not yet. But that doesn't mean never. We could always wait for the right time and try again.'

He makes her soup, assembling whatever he has left in his fridge with results that are unexpectedly rich and comforting. Then they sit on the sofa underneath a tartan rug, until she is warm again. She drifts off for a while into a dreamless sleep, until he tries to squeeze out from beneath her and wakes her in an instant. It is past seven and through the window fireworks pepper the city skyline with smudges of colour.

'Open your hand,' Pete whispers, placing a small, brown paper packet into her palm. 'I was going to wrap it and give it to you for Christmas but I think it would be best if you have it now. To wear it, and by wearing it to know that I am – we are – serious.'

Alma opens the packet carefully to discover a slip of tissue paper folded over, twice. Inside this she finds a tiny silver charm in the perfect, detailed shape of a miniature grand piano. 'It's for the necklace,' he smiles, reaching out to release the chain from around her neck. 'It should be a perfect match.'

'Oh Pete,' says Alma, trying not to dampen the moment with tears. 'It's beautiful.'

As he refastens the necklace around her neck he positions the piano to hang just beneath the soft dip at the base of her throat which he then leans forward to kiss, just once.

'I want it to remind you whenever you look at it that we're in this together, you and me. We don't have to decide right here and now, do we? We can sleep on it, just for a bit. And whatever we decide and whatever happens next, Alma, remember: you can always trust me.'

Chapter 23

Beauloch, February 2016

Zeb wakes early the next morning, before daylight. Lying on her back. Half covered by the duvet. Her head pounding.

Staring up at the ceiling rose, she wonders where she is as other details creep into focus. The room is lit by silver threads which spill through the cracks around the bathroom door. Empty whisky miniatures decorate the floor. And beside her in bed, a sprawled figure breathing quietly.

My God, a voice inside her chides as she tries pulling herself upright without disturbing the cover. *What have you done?*

Balancing awkwardly on the edge of the mattress, her naked body cool and spent, Zeb gazes miserably at the empty minibar bottles on the bedside table. Her head seems surprisingly clear – thanks to Dad's old tip about not mixing grape and grain, perhaps, but her conscience hangs heavy. For breaking her so recently-made resolution not to drink so as to prove to the world – Richard in particular, but also herself – that she is in control. And for Fraser, the stranger whom she met only yesterday, whose presence right here, right now seems the ultimate proof of folly.

What was I thinking? I'm not in my twenties any more – I've important stuff to deal with; responsibilities. Dad's affairs to sort out. Matty, for Christ's sake.

But as she turns towards the man beside her, her pulse quickens. At his tousled hair and the kiss-curl at the nape of his neck. Scrutinising the outline of him, she marvels at the symmetrical muscularity of his back, his lean physique; wonders how old he is. Younger than me, she thinks, though not by much. She resists the urge to kiss the smooth skin at the base of his spine, remembering with a blush that she had kissed him there earlier.

Christ! Zeb thinks, though now she is thrilled; overwhelmed, too, by a sense of release. Maybe this isn't a mistake. He has freed her from the events of these past few weeks. Made her feel truly alive, happy even, for the very first time since Dad—

'Didn't anyone tell you it's rude to stare?'

'Oh!' she exclaims.

Fraser rolls over to face her. 'Been awake long?'

'No, you?'

'A while. I was watching you, actually,' he admits, ruefully. 'Until I realised how early it was. Then I was trying my hardest to get back to sleep.'

Zeb resists the temptation to cover herself. Daring him to drop his gaze from her face.

'So here we are, then,' Fraser smiles. 'Both awake.' He reaches out and strokes the side of her thigh then runs his forefinger up and onto her hip bone, which makes her shiver. 'Come back to bed.'

Slipping back beneath the covers, Zeb rolls into his embrace. But as his hand slips onto her breast, she gently halts it. *Can I trust him?* she wonders. Though as she lies in his arms, naked and exposed, she knows this question has landed too late.

—

'Mummy!'

'Are you OK, darling?' Zeb exclaims, her heart surging at the sound of her son's voice. While Fraser showers, she has called Sam to check on Matty. But there's been some kind of a rush at work – an unexpected deadline from an important sponsor that the team are struggling to hit without Zeb's help. And before she can call her ex, Matty has rung her from Richard's parents' number. It's almost eleven. Why is he there and not at school?

'I'm a Jedi,' he declares, proudly.

'Good for you,' she laughs. 'But why aren't you at West Heath, you're not poorly, are you?'

'Nah, it's an upset day. That's why I'm at Grandad and Nana's until Sam's finished work,' her son replies. 'So we've been to the park and after lunch Daddy's taking me to the cinema. I just cycled without putting my feet down, Mummy. Helene says I won't need trainer wheels at all very soon.'

A teacher training day, how stupid of her to forget. Zeb grimaces. 'Clever you.'

'Like Action Man, Grandad said. We ate squid, too – did I tell you? In Portugal. When are you coming, Mummy – today?'

'Oh darling, I'd love to – really – but I'm in Scotland—'

'Scotland?'

'I'll be back the day after tomorrow, though, so not long.'

'I want to be back in my own room.'

'I know, champ, I want you back there too. But there's something important I've got to do first,' Zeb answers. 'I'm taking some time off work soon, though, so when you come home we can do a bunch of stuff together, you and me,' she presses on, brightly. 'Would you like that?'

'Lots—'

'Now wait a minute, Zeb,' Richard unexpectedly cuts in. 'Best not to promise what you might not be able to deliver.'

'I beg your pardon?' she asks, trying to remain polite though the realisation he has been eavesdropping on their conversation makes her tone chill.

'Well you need to make sure you can get the holiday, first, don't you? What are you doing in Scotland? I thought you said you'd used up this year's allocation with the leave of absence you took before your father's funeral.'

Ever the accountant – always keeping track, she thinks, bitterly. Of course he is right. Though he doesn't know that since then she has walked out of her job, of course. 'It will be fine, Matty,' she says, emphatically. 'It's all sorted out.'

'What's in Scotland?' her son echoes.

Fraser emerges from the bathroom with a bright red bath towel knotted round his waist. 'Men in kilts,' she smiles, trying not to laugh as he raises his arms and performs a surprisingly dainty pirouette that seems more Lord of the Dance than Highland jig. She looks away, coyly. 'The Loch Ness monster. And an old friend of Granddad Pete's.'

'Say hello from me.'

'To a man in a kilt or the old friend?' she teases.

'Of course not! To the monster, silly.'

264

'I'll do my very best,' she laughs. 'If the monster doesn't get me first.'

'No!' Matty shouts, excitedly. 'If it tries to get you you must run away and find a place to hide. But if the monster turns out to be nice will you invite him to stay?'

'I'll see,' she promises, troubled by the inadvertent echo in his words. 'And Matty?'

'Mmm?'

'I love you lots and miss you madly.'

'Miss you madly Mummy, too!'

'Keep us posted, Zeb,' Richard urges. 'And see you—'

'Tomorrow, I hope. If not, definitely the day after,' Zeb replies, firmly. 'As I said. There's just one last thing I need to sort before I can come back to London. It's to do with Dad.'

Outplayed – for now, at least, her ex grunts.

Keep us posted, she thinks as she hangs up the phone. Us. Does that mean Richard and Matty? Matty, Richard and his parents, more like. Why, then, does she suspect he also meant Helene? Though younger than her, her ex's fiancée is desperate for a child – any child – having recently been diagnosed with unspecified infertility.

My child, even. Catching sight of last night's minibar detritus, Zeb winces. Well she can't have him. Because I'm his mum and more than capable, they'll see.

–

How far up is the cafe? Zeb asks, squinting up towards the summit, where the trees are at their thinnest.

The car park she stands in is a barren expanse of quartz-like stone chips, neatly corralled on each side by lines of rough-hewn logs. In its furthest corner a Forestry

Commission information board displays a map and a detailed list of safety restrictions. Beside the sign is a painted post marking the official start of the public footpath and a sign for the cafe. The arrow points along the track which stretches away in a straight line for fifty metres or so before disappearing into a wall of trees that fringes the hill like a receding hairline. The footpath comes into sight again as it winds across heather-scored terrain to the top, where there are picnic tables and a small viewing platform.

Not all the way up there, surely, she thinks. Can this really be the right place?

Leaning her arm on the car's roof, Zeb dips her head to speak to Fraser through the passenger window. 'What time is it?' she asks.

'Quarter to,' he replies, reaching forward to turn on the car's stereo, which punctures the silence with a shrill burst of rap. He tweaks the dial with the concentration of a safe-cracker, sifting through the static until he finds something more appropriate. On a local news station, two men are discussing some disagreement or other with the Norwegians about territorial fishing rights.

'I should probably head on up…' The statement of intent ends up sounding more like a question as Zeb's free hand hovers over the car door handle.

'You'd better – it's at least a ten minute walk to the cafe. Don't worry, it's not as far as it looks,' he smiles, reassuringly. 'The views up top are stunning, by the way. And I'll be waiting for you here.'

Zeb crosses the empty car park, then goes through the gate, between two densely planted plots of young conifers which mark where the footpath begins. The rain has held off but the temperature has fallen further – a sure sign, according to Fraser, that snow is not far behind. Adjusting her scarf across her mouth and nose, she hurries on.

Zeb briskly follows the track. Not far, he'd said. And for at least half of her ascent, she calculates, she will be in full view. The thought sustains her as after cutting through open land the path traverses a sudden and sheer ravine.

The trees are packed so tightly that within just a few metres the space between their trunks is filled by darkness. Every sound she makes now seems muffled. Unnerved by the gloom, Zeb fixes her sights instead on the sullen strip of sky above her head. Only a few minutes, she tells herself mechanically. Not long now before you'll see the cafe. She imagines an alpine cabin made with rough-hewn logs – its windows fogged with steam, its interior bright and warm. By the time she gets there she'll have more than earned a steaming hot coffee.

At last, the path widens and the trees begin to thin. Zeb checks her watch. She slows as the path curves once more across open terrain carpeted with heather and gorse. She calculates the path must circumnavigate the mound twice more before she'll reach the summit. She waves towards Fraser's car.

Which way will Anna come from, she wonders, surprised that his is still the only car in view. If not by car, would she come by foot? Zeb falters, at the thought – registered then quickly tossed aside – that maybe Dad's friend won't come. Or else Fraser has got the details for their rendezvous wrong. Her chest tightens. But then, gazing down the hill once more she experiences a jolt of relief as a grey four wheel drive pulls into the car park below.

Emboldened, she strides on.

Though the morning has grown windy and overcast the view from the top is indeed stunning, she decides. To her left runs a snow-scored backbone of rock, the incline of which gradually tapers down to the water-filled socket of a loch. A patchwork of low, undulating hills in the foreground to the right makes her think of a winter sea. It is a barren landscape, yet crouching beneath the February sky, it is beautiful, too.

Zeb scans the terrain for the cafe but the only building she can see is the roof of a squat Portakabin, partially obscured by a clump of trees.

Making her way towards the cabin, she can soon see its door is padlocked and the interior empty, with tables and chairs piled floor to ceiling in one corner. It's five past, she sees, once more checking her watch. But Anna is surely just running a bit late, that's all. The ragged picnic area is just wooden tables and benches beside a green plastic recycling bin in the shape of a smiling cartoon frog. This is the right place, just as Fraser described it, even down to the grey viewing platform a short distance beyond.

Zeb heads towards the telescope mounted on a large concrete block. Squinting through the viewfinder, she swings the instrument across the horizon. Adjusts the focus. Pans in on closer points of interest. The steeple of the church where Anna was due to perform her recital, just visible through the trees. The winding ribbon of road from the village below. The car park, which is now home to two cars.

Zooming in on the second vehicle now parked below, Zeb sees it is a silver BMW. The vehicle is empty. As is Fraser's car, though the driver's door stands wide open. She experiences a surge of panic.

Anxiously, Zeb surveys the car park and its hinterland for any sign of where Fraser has gone but can find no evidence – aside from his car – that he was ever there. Uneasy now, she scans what's visible of the road but again sees nothing. No vehicle, nor movement. Or any sign of life. Maybe the tank was running low so he's walked to the petrol station back in the village, she thinks hopefully – though she knows this is unlikely and besides, why would he leave the car like that?

A dull throb presses on Zeb's temple. *What should I do?* Stay put or retrace my steps down the hill through the woods to the road below and somehow make my way back to the village? A nearby sound makes her jump and turn towards the furthest picnic table, where a figure now stands just a few paces away.

Zeb takes a step back, keeping her eyes fixed on the stranger, every sense primed to detect even the merest hint of movement. The figure's face is covered by a woollen scarf and the raised hood of a dark green canvas jacket. Yet it is watching her, intently. For an age they just stare at one another, until the person lowers their scarf to reveal a heart-shaped face framed with the ivory-coloured hair of a once-natural blonde.

Though heavily lined, the woman's face is lightened by the humorous slant of her light grey eyes. Her full lips and refined cheeks are devoid of any make-up. She is attractive, might once have been stunning, but the life she has led over intervening years has taken its toll.

'Hello.' Just a single word, but enough for Zeb to tell the woman's voice is tentative. And her accent is English, not Scottish.

'Anna?'

The stranger nods. 'I hope you've not been waiting long but I had trouble getting away.'

Zeb takes a few steps forwards, uncertain what to say or where to put herself until, thankfully, the other woman takes the initiative and sits down on the far side of the wooden bench then motions for Zeb to join her. The unlikeliness of the setting for such parlour politeness makes both women smile.

'You came,' the woman says.

'Of course I came,' Zeb asserts, not noticing how Anna's face has hardened. 'You mentioned you have something to tell me about my... mother?' Just one word, but enough to push a powerful heat through every fibre of Zeb's being. 'Mother', 'Mummy', 'Mum' were all alien words which lodged stubbornly in her throat. 'I'm Zeb – Elizabeth? Pete Hamilton's daughter.'

The woman says nothing for some seconds. Her fingers are long and delicately tapered, with unpolished nails that are rounded and buffed like shells. At close quarters the contrast with the coarser skin of her face seems stark: this woman has built a protective shield around herself, Zeb senses. At last, her face starts to move.

Zeb can't tell, but the woman's eyes look glassy. Is she fighting back tears?

'So,' Anna begins, swallowing hard. Her voice is unsteady. 'It's you.'

'Yes.'

'You got my letter.'

'Letter?' The only personal letter she got – or, rather didn't get – was the one she found at her neighbours'. From Cynthia, the woman who'd come to Dad's funeral.

'The box, then.'

Zeb nods.

Then, without warning, the older woman's hand reaches for Zeb's. Skin brushes skin, then she gives it a squeeze. 'I had to—' her voice falters '—get in touch, you know? After I heard about Pete's death.' She swallows and gathers her composure. But then, before she can continue, they are interrupted. Zeb's is drawn immediately to movement, to the steady clenching and unclenching of a man's fists.

He is standing between where they are sitting and the mounted telescope. His grey-flecked hair is cut into a close crop, military-style. A black leather coat firmly belted at the waist reaches down to his knees. Beneath this are dark combat trousers and scuffed lace-up boots. He is appraising the scene, his arms loose by his sides.

'Elizabeth?' As Zeb makes the connection between this stranger and the burglar who broke into her flat, a shot of panic powers her to her feet. The man smiles. 'It must be,' he exclaims. 'The elusive daughter.'

Anna frowns. 'Brian, wait—' she begins. She holds out her hand as if to placate him, then, seeing Zeb stumble to her feet, grabs at her sleeve. 'Wait a minute. Please,' she adds. 'It's important we speak – about your mother. About me.'

A distant whistle, high and shrill, makes all three of them turn in its direction. Down along the footpath leading back to the car park then away to its right, in a ragged field left fallow is the moving black cursor of a dog, running free. Its owner, a lone figure, waits by a gate in the furthest corner of the field. The creature turns on its heels and is heading excitedly back towards its master; in response to a second whistle, perhaps.

'Please,' Anna tries once more as Brian takes a step forward. Frightened – by the advancing physicality of him, by the strangeness of this woman's pleading – Zeb looks to the middle distance for a suitable escape route. The woman tries again. 'Zeb' she calls. 'You've got to listen—'

But Zeb is turning away. Whatever binds them to each other and this moment is their business, not hers. It was a mistake coming. She does not have to listen. And a moment later she is flying. Running, full pelt, as the voice behind her cries out, desperately. Cascading straight down the hillside – the shortest and most direct route, though the going is treacherous and the uneven ground makes her slip and stagger.

'Elizabeth, please!' she shouts. 'It's me. I'm—'

But all it takes is a gust of wind to carry whatever Anna is saying away.

Chapter 24

Staring across Marylebone Road towards The Globe pub, Alma tries to remember the directions he gave her. They have arranged to meet at eleven o'clock outside Abbey House. It's on the left-hand side of the road, only a short distance away; heading in the direction they will be travelling together, north.

Clutching the handles of her weekend bag, Alma steps out onto the pavement into a gauze of early winter rain. She makes her way past the newspaper stands and then across the uneven paving stones that line the busy junction, determined to fulfil her mission. But then, as she rounds the corner, she is startled by a pulse of nausea.

Alma stops beneath a shallow awning, abandoning her bag to the gathering rain. Unbuttoning her coat, she runs her finger around the rim of her collar. As she feels the chain of the silver necklace, warm against her skin, her pulse starts to calm.

It will be all right, he told her. *We'll get through this together. Everything will be OK, you'll see.*

Alma catches sight of herself in a shop window. Her waxen face framed by a helmet of lank hair. And then a second face – not hers, a man's. Pinch-eyed and scant-haired in a garish tank top, he is tutting at her through

273

the window display of hats, gloves and umbrellas. As Alma steps away she spots the empty wooden bench facing the road at the point the pavement widens. This is where Pete will pick her up in the second-hand Audi he has bought to celebrate his first professional commission, from the *Sunday Times*.

It began as an exploration of childhood memories. But after Pete revisited the terraced streets where he and Brian played as boys, the picture editor had been so impressed with the resulting images that he'd offered a good price for them to be used in a forthcoming special report.

One image particularly struck her. It was of a girl of about twelve, scruffy and coatless, standing on the street beside a tiny boy with a vacant stare. Between them stood an ancient pram in which they'd propped up a man's suit stuffed with crumpled paper and topped with an outsized trilby. *Pennies for the guy*, their handmade sign read.

Pete had taken this only two weeks earlier, but there was something so unremitting about it – the blankness of the boy's face, the defiance in his sister's eyes – that it could be a scene from any time over the past two hundred years. The picture will be the central image accompanying story about the great British economic decline. *Cruel Britannia* is the headline.

Alma's heart sinks as a clock strikes for the half hour. Though she is in the right place, in her eagerness not to be late she has arrived half an hour too early. She sinks down onto the bench then quickly springs to her feet. The seat is sodden by repeated splashes from the passing traffic. Seeking shelter, she sizes up a cafe a short distance ahead. The place has a warm, inviting glow.

Inside, the hectic cafe proves anything but the anonymous sanctuary she craves, but the smell of yeasty dough is soothing. A flickering light on the ceiling emits a nicotine glow which she barely notices. Nor does she see that the brown Formica table tops are still waiting to be wiped down. Or the tramp-like man muttering incoherently, seated by the window.

As Alma picks a table away from the door by the retro jukebox any lingering doubts quickly fade. She peels off her mac and hangs it over the chair opposite then stows her bag, upended, on the floor against the wall by her side.

'What'll it be, luv?' A bottle-blonde waitress in her late fifties has appeared at Alma's side.

She would prefer to eat but knows from bitter experience accumulated over the preceding few weeks how bad consuming anything before midday will make her feel. Recurring nausea has become a clockwork reminder of the tiny life now unfurling inside her.

That, after all, is the reason she's here, waiting for Pete to drive her north to the clinic he has found just outside Scarborough. In just a few days, they will return to London to pick up where they left off and everything will be fine. She prays Viola is right when she says the pain and discomfort will be only short-lived.

What Alma dreads most of all is the awful possibility that once it is done she might regret it; that somehow the course on which she's decided will prove too awful to live with. A mistake, or something worse: a sin. Alma tries to swallow but the lump in her throat is stubborn and when at last she speaks her voice is hoarse.

'Tea for one, please. And don't worry about the milk.'

The waitress nods, her face impassive as she heads back towards the counter where a young man with a shaven head stands by the till watching. He is wearing a stained apron tied tight enough to emphasise the bony contours of his narrow hips. The youth is not much younger than she is, Alma decides, but a broken nose and tattoos roughly scored across his knuckles suggest they have led rather different lives.

The young man steps out from behind the counter and walks towards the jukebox.

Oblivious to Alma's presence, he now stands by her side reviewing the playlist. Having made his selection, he pulls a coin from his back pocket, thrusts it into the slot and turns back towards the counter. The waitress, watching, shows a mixture of curiosity and disdain.

As the mechanism lifts the record into position, the youth places one hand across his heart and with the other blows his colleague a kiss. His words are overwhelmed by a sudden shiny wave of trumpets. *Dream-boat*, trills the familiar voice. *You loveable dream-boat. Say that you'll b-e mine. For-ever-more.*

Alma closes her eyes, and tries to moderate her breathing as she listens. For as long as she can remember, the song has been her mother's favourite. Alma bloody Cogan, she thinks, battling in vain to wipe from her mind a lifetime's references, associations and allusions to this plastic promise of perfect love. It is a golden world that did not, could not and would never exist.

Yet she is unable to leave the cafe, because the music is familiar and comforting, even as those swinging trumpets hammer intrusively.

I would sail the seven seas-with-you. That voice, again. A powerhouse, that's what the papers called her. With talent that came from nowhere like a natural spring. *I-love-you-so dear-ly.* Alma screws her eyes shut but now she can see old black and white footage of the woman. *I'd-follow-you*

276

dar-ling. To any sho-re. A satin cocktail dress with matching shoes encasing tiny feet.

A sob suddenly bubbles. She curses the singer who, two decades earlier, her mother had chosen to name her daughter after. The woman whose singing would always mean home.

A beautiful name for a beautiful girl, her father had told her. *The A in Alma*, he'd once said, stood for *A Wonderful Promise To Be Fulfilled*.

Alma's eyes snap open.

Well, she'd certainly shown them, hadn't she? By immersing herself in music. Studying piano. Singing solo in the cathedral choir. Winning a music scholarship to The Conservatoire. Fulfilling her parents' dreams, then throwing them all away. Though she can fix it, she tells herself defiantly; she can make things right again.

The track ends and Alma senses something odd has happened. While she's been lost, alone in her own nightmare, people at different tables have exchanged glances. Strangers have started talking to one another. Smiling. Even the waitress has relaxed, she notices, as she sets down Alma's tea.

'Can't beat the girl with the laugh in her voice, can you?' the woman smiles.

'No,' Alma replies. 'I don't suppose you can.'

It has stopped raining by the time she makes it back out onto the street. But as she takes up position a few paces from the still-wet bench, the dull sky shows no sign of clearing. *Where is he?* she wonders, though she is confident he'd not let her down. Because once the initial shock subsided, he'd asked her to marry him. And he didn't have to do that, did he? It's a way of proving how serious he is about sticking by her, he has told her, repeatedly, because they are both in this together.

Again, Alma checks her watch. What can be holding him up?

At ten past, as a number 13 bus pulls up at the stop to her left, the driver stares at her, blankly. His only two passengers disembark and he switches off the engine, leans back in his seat and pulls out a Sunday paper. At quarter past, an elderly man in an old jacket shuffles past dragging a tiny terrier on a lead. At half past, the bus driver refolds his paper, restarts the engine then pulls away.

Finally, at twenty-five to, a brown BMW draws to a standstill by her side.

'Alma!'

Looking up she sees not Pete but Brian, rolling down the driver's window. The car is otherwise empty.

'Hi,' she acknowledges, cautiously.

'Pete sent me,' he calls. 'He asked me to give you this.' Confused, she stares for a moment at the brown padded envelope he's holding out towards her. 'It's for you,' Brian nods, encouragingly. 'It's the keys. To his flat?' Alma accepts the envelope without a word. 'He asked me to tell you to wait for him there and he'll pick you up a little later.'

'Later,' she echoes. All she wants is to get going and get it over with.

Brian's face softens. 'Yes, not long. It's Patsy,' he adds. 'She's in University College hospital – they think it was an overdose.' He scrutinises Alma's reaction to what he says next. 'That's where I was just now, with Pete and Derek. I just popped out because he begged me to come and find you to let you know.'

'Why?' Alma mumbles. 'I mean, Patsy – why would she do a thing like that?'

'I would have thought that was pretty obvious.' Then, clocking Alma's bemusement, Brian's eyes widen. 'So you don't know about Phil?'

'What about him?'

'Lung cancer. A few days ago the doctors told him it's terminal. My guess is Patsy's only just heard.' He shakes his head. 'Poor cow,' he murmurs. 'Christ alone knows why she's never managed to get over him.'

'Sorry?'

'She swallowed a bottle of sleeping tablets. Derek found her just in time. They're probably pumping her stomach as I speak. She's fragile, see – always has been – only it's got worse recently what with Cynthia and now the baby.'

Alma stares at the brown envelope which Pete has folded in half, in half again and sealed with Sellotape. Through the padding she can make out the familiar shape of his leather key ring fob. She shakes her head at the thought that these are the only keys they have between them: he never got round to giving her the spare set.

Of course Pete will want to be with his mother, she decides, bravely. Just as long as it takes to make sure she's going to be all right.

'Tell him thanks,' Alma mumbles. 'I'll see him there. And I hope Patsy is OK.'

'Will do.' Brian's looks at Alma's bag. He smiles. 'And I hope wherever it is you two are sneaking off to together will be worth the wait.'

As Brian disappears from view it starts to rain again, but this time Alma doesn't move. Instead, she watches the surface of the envelope darken with every droplet. Until, when the ink on the A of her name starts to run, she breaks the seal. Inside is a slip of paper wrapped around a key.

I need to stay with Mum a little longer, Pete has written in a rushed hand. *The car's parked close by on Mornington Crescent. Wait for me in the flat. I'll be there as soon as I can. Px*

How can he do this? Alma wonders, bleakly. Leave me standing in the street like this. Not ask Brian to take me back to the hospital with him. Though perhaps that is for the best, considering what is happening on Monday morning. His flat will be warm and dry, at least. And according to Brian, Pete won't be long.

This is a family crisis; an emergency, she tells herself, firmly. And at time likes this, well, you've just got to muck in.

Refolding the note around the key, Alma slips both into her coat pocket and reaches for her bag. Then, with head bowed, she starts to trace her steps back towards the Underground. He'll be coming, soon, she reassures herself. Even so, she can't help remembering what Chrissie said that afternoon she let herself into Pete's flat, unannounced: about Hamilton blood being thicker than water.

Chapter 25

Zeb charges downwards, numb to the cuts on her hands from flailing limbs of gorse as thick as hawsers; oblivious to the clatter of dislodged scree. With her eyes fixed on the flat, she twists her back into the slope to stop herself from falling. With each step, the pressure of absorbing every jolt and jar makes her knees scream.

At last, when the slope starts to even, she dares to draw breath.

The hill above her is empty. There is no sign of the man who chased her to Euston, the same man who broke into her flat – for it is him, she is sure. She turns back down the hill towards the car park and the road that connects it to the world beyond. The path gradually flattens out towards the clump of trees she remembers walking through earlier. *Not much further*, she thinks, though she can't be sure how far as the car park is out of view.

I should never have come, the voice inside her cries. *What was I thinking?*

Where the hell is Fraser?

A distant sound makes her stiffen. She strains to hear, and then she is sure: she can hear someone behind her. With legs pounding and shoulders hunched, Alma gallops forward. Any second now, she fears, the man will grab her from behind.

Ahead, through a gap between the tall banks of maturing conifers that flank the path, she spots the wooden gate that will lead her back into the car park – and full view of anyone further up the hill. For now she has the advantage, but only a small one. So she must act quickly to make the most of it. Get off the path. Cut through the wood and find a way out onto the road back towards the village and then, a bit further along, hitch a lift.

Three strides on, Zeb dives into the densely-packed trees.

It takes a few seconds for her eyes to adjust to the darkness, a delay which disorientates her. Scared she might allow her pursuer a chance to reach her, she keeps running. But it's difficult to stay in a straight line despite the apparent regularity of the rows of trunks. The ground is uneven, littered with hollows and broken branches hidden beneath a carpet of pine needles and dead bracken. As she twists and turns within seconds all sense of direction is lost.

After a few paces more, Zeb stops.

Leaning an arm against a nearby tree for support, she bends double. Her lungs ache. She pinches at the stitch in her side. But when Zeb straightens up she is dizzy, and it takes another minute for the snowstorm in her head to subside. Glancing back, Zeb half expects to see the man lunging towards her from the shadows. But there is no sign of him, not yet.

What she does see, though, is almost worse.

Darkness.

Without any trace of sky or the outer fringes of the copse in any direction, she notes with a plummeting heart that the clump of trees is far larger than she expected. That she has run too far into the heart of it, too fast. And that the trunks among which she sought shelter now enclose her like the bars of a cage.

Rubbing her eyes, she tries to think. If she can't see, then maybe she can hear. Yet now there is no sound whatsoever from the hill above, the road, the car park. There is nothing. Just silence. And the harder she tries to listen, the more she concentrates, the more it clangs inside her head like the heartbeat of a dreadful living thing.

Zeb forces herself to keep scanning the trees encircling her. There's no evidence of any life. Even rain, it seems, struggles to reach this part of the forest, she thinks as she sees the ground at her feet is tinder dry. As she gazes up at the impenetrable canopy above her head, she tries to feel grateful that she is safe, for now at least.

Zeb tries to visualise how the wood looked from the top of the hill. It is lozenge-shaped, she recalls. If she walks long enough in any direction it shouldn't take her too long to find her way out, and then she can make her way around the outside until she finds the road.

Choosing a point in the middle distance where a tree trunk displays a jagged vertical gash, she starts to walk, making sure not to lose sight of this fixed point as she zig-zags around obstacles. Then, when she reaches the trunk, she squints into the darkness beyond, finds another suitable landmark and does the same again. Until, some minutes later, she senses a perceptible lightening of the gloom ahead.

It's only a small gap in the trees, not worthy of being called a clearing. But as Zeb gets nearer she can make out the shadowy outline of a low construction no bigger than a two-man tent, made from a collection of branches neatly aligned then meticulously interwoven. A lean-to shelter of some kind, just big enough for an adult. Built as a den, probably, by local kids. On the ground a few feet from the shelter's side are the charred remnants of a fire.

Careful not to get too close, Zeb draws level with the den's opening and bends down. Inside, the ground is covered by an old tarpaulin weighted down with an old toolbox. Eager to arm herself, she stumbles towards the shelter's entrance then drops to her knees. She crawls inside the shelter and reaches out to grab the box and drag it towards her.

There is no padlock, just two metal flaps that when lifted reveal the upper tray. On the top is a magazine which is dog-eared and stained. Zeb stares for a moment at the uppermost page from which a doe-eyed girl with straw-blonde hair stares up open-mouthed as she pushes a large black dildo between her legs.

Tossing the magazine towards the back of the shelter, Zeb scans the tray beneath, which contains an assortment of rusty DIY tools and kitchen equipment. There's a collection of barbecue skewers. Plastic straws. Some string. A fruit knife with a serrated edge, which she quickly pockets.

Sitting back on her haunches, Zeb hears the sound of branches moving.

Folds of tarpaulin twist around Zeb's legs in her haste to scramble back outside. Kicking her shoes free at last, she pulls herself to her feet and stumbles out of the gloom into the tiny clearing. Something is caught around her ankle, and when she looks down she sees it is the handle of a leather shoulder bag.

Her shoulder bag. The one Dad bought her for Christmas.

Hurriedly, she yanks it open, but it is empty.

She kicks it away impatiently.

With no time to lose, Zeb thrashes over to the far side of the shelter then plunges through the trees in the direction she's been heading. Running, careless of the snapping of twigs, her panting breath, her mind fixed only on escape.

What does he want? How can any of this have anything to do with me?

Quickly picking a direction, she presses on until she is close enough to the outer line of trees to listen for any sound of life from the world beyond. Is she on the car park side – the way she came in – or the edge closest to the road leading back to the village? With no desire to go back into the woods, there's only one way to tell.

Creeping from tree to tree towards the light, Zeb pauses behind each trunk to check for signs of Brian before moving a few metres further forward until, at last, she sees the grey expanse of empty car park. With a surge of relief, she realises that the BMW has gone. And with a stab of disappointment, that Fraser has still not returned. But there's no time for that now. Instead, she must press on.

With the coast clear, she staggers towards the road.

Beyond the protection of the trees, the wind is gathering once more.

As she reaches the point where rough track meets tarmac, Zeb notices for the first time how the banks are raised either side of the road, which is the only route back down to the village. She stops. Once she starts walking she will be committed to continuing along the same way until either side of the road flattens. There will be no place to hide should she encounter the man along the way. But she has little choice, and the sooner she starts the sooner she'll be out the other side.

Zeb breaks into a slow run.

The road is straight for the first half kilometre, so she reduces her speed only as she nears the point at which the road curves out of sight to the left. Walking, she rounds the bend and sees a shorter strip before it kinks once more, this time to the right. She starts to run again; her sights fixed on a spot a couple of paces before the bend.

The road begins to narrow and then she recalls how on the way up the width had shrunk at a couple of points to a single lane. She takes her time, peering around the corner cautiously then ducking back at the sight of a silver estate car tightly wedged into a passing place on the left-hand side just a dozen or so paces ahead.

Zeb sinks back against the grassy verge, desperately considering her options. She must pass the car if she is to get back down to the village – there really is no other option, but how?

A gap has been cut into the bank opposite: there is an overgrown path leading up and through it, into what must be the field beyond. It might be possible to make her way down towards then past the car, shielded by the verge.

Crossing the road to investigate, she almost loses her balance as she stumbles through the gap, catching her foot on something solid, half-buried in the ground. It is a piece of discarded agricultural equipment. A bit like a lawnmower blade. She stares at it for a moment.

Wary of staying still, Zeb steps over the metal and presses on.

The cleft in the bank leads her not into a farmer's field but a desolate, almost lunar landscape. It is some kind of abandoned industrial site, with a piece of bare ground on the far side on which squat a cluster of prefabricated outhouses. She hesitates, perturbed by how perilously exposed she is, even though the buildings appear deserted.

A rough track leads away from the closest outhouse, towards what looks like a gate at the furthest end of the plot – well beyond where the silver car is parked on the road, she calculates. But the terrain between where she is standing and the distant exit is scored by a series of empty drainage ditches. She will have to stay close to the road but concealed below the bank if she's to make it, she decides.

Crouching low, Zeb makes her way along the side of the road, praying the man will not think to scale the uneven banks either side of the road to get a better view. Passing what must be the halfway point, she catches sight of a dark shape lying on the ground a dozen or so paces ahead – a pile of discarded clothes, perhaps. But as she draws closer, she breaks into a desperate run.

'Fraser?' she calls out, as loudly as she dares. A beat later she is on her knees by his side.

Lying on his back with his head against a large clod of earth, he is barely conscious. It's not his ashen face or incoherent mumbling that claims her attention, however, but his right foot. It is trapped between the rusted jaws of an old-fashioned poacher's snare.

'Fraser,' she says again, frantically scanning the ground around them for anything she might be able to use as a lever to wedge the trap open. 'Help me, here,' she implores. 'Tell me what I should do.'

'Nothing,' he rasps, his eyes sharpening as they come into focus. 'Don't try anything. Don't touch it – it's one of Davy Duffy's, so God only knows what might happen if you do.' His eyes roll for a moment. 'Just get help,' he groans.

'But your foot—' Zeb objects, noticing for the first time the ugly, chewed-up mess of it. The depth of flesh into which the metal teeth have sunk. The glimpse of white from bone now visible between the blackened fabric of his ripped trouser leg. How much blood has spilled out into the surrounding grass. She can't leave him, not like this. She fumbles in her jacket pocket for her phone but finds there is no signal, then pats Fraser's jacket to see if he's brought his, but all he can do is shake his head.

'There's never any signal up here. Just tighten my belt if you can,' he pants, motioning towards the makeshift tourniquet he has somehow managed to fashion around his injured leg, just above the knee. 'Then get help. Please. As fast as you can.'

Zeb adjusts the belt then takes off her scarf and gently knots it around his neck. She slips her hat over his head, too, but it refuses to sit snugly over his curly hair. 'Don't go anywhere,' she whispers, her stomach tripping as he stares back at her, bleakly.

It takes just a couple of minutes to reach the gate which, as Zeb hoped, brings her out onto the road a short distance below – and out of view – of the pull-in where the silver BMW had stopped. Her ears strain for the distant sound of life, but she hears nothing.

Struggling to think against the swell of blood now pushing at her temples, Zeb works out that the road she's on is a minor one – a single lane that snakes with little enthusiasm in either direction through a kind of no man's land: silent, empty, abandoned. But it shouldn't take long to get back down to the village once she gets onto a busier road, where she will surely be able to hitch a lift.

Fraser, the voice inside her chants, blotting out any lingering thought she might have of her meaningless exchange with Anna, the appearance of her pursuer, how foolish she'd been to retrace her steps to Scotland, what Richard will think, how she should never, ever, have left Matty.

As her breath shortens, her chest grows tighter.

You've got to get help. For Fraser.

A short while later, just ahead, is a junction where the track must join the road back to Beauloch. Zeb bursts out onto the road amidst the unexpected grind and squeal of brakes. She is struck heavily from the blind spot on her left and for a second she is flying, then she is sent crumpling downwards onto the tarmac where the side of her head meets the ground with a sharp crack.

The world darkens, briefly, and she smells the burn of overheated rubber.

'Christ, girl, what were you thinking?' It is a man's voice, and as he bends towards her she notices his breath smells like fish. 'No, focus on me – that's it. Keep looking, good girl. Are you OK?'

Though her shoulder is screaming and her head is pounding, Zeb senses that otherwise she is unhurt. She turns her head delicately, and as she does her eyes widen at the sight of the car that's just hit her. A silver BMW. Its driver side door yawns open. A figure is slumped on the back seat. It's the woman she met earlier, Anna. Has she fallen asleep?

As the man offers to help her to her feet, Zeb groggily pushes his arm away. 'I'm fine,' she declares.

'Can I give you a ride back into town?' he presses.

Zeb peers into the car at Anna who seems to be panting heavily. 'Is she OK?'

'It's happened before,' he replies. 'A panic attack. Though this one's bad, which is a worry given her asthma. That's where we were heading, to get her checked out. Let me give you a lift – we can drop you off en route.' He opens the nearest rear passenger door.

Zeb thinks of Fraser and the blood from his mangled leg clotting the grass. She has seen no other traffic pass since they had set out from McLellans this morning.

How long would it take by foot? she asks herself, noticing the spots of rain now starting to streak the car's windscreen.

Too long, surely, for him to stand a chance.

'Well if you could drop me at the hotel—'

'Climb in, then,' the man says. 'I'll drop you at the crossroads – you can walk from there, if you prefer.'

'OK, thanks,' she mumbles. As she clambers onto the seat next to Anna, she almost sits on something blue and plastic. 'Yours?' she offers, passing the reliever inhaler to the woman. But Anna is so short of breath, all she can do is close her fingers around it and nod.

'Hold tight.' The driver's foot pumps the accelerator. 'Breathe long, breathe slow, Alma, all right?'

Zeb turns to stare at the woman beside her whose gasps now slow as she battles to regain her breath. Alma? Perhaps she's misheard him. Maybe it's the ache now pulsing in her head. Too much to think of. So much going on. 'Shouldn't she breathe into a paper bag or something, if she's having a panic attack?' she calls out, suddenly struck by the greyness of Anna's face. The stickiness of her hair. The drops of sweat freckling her skin.

The driver shakes his head. 'The opposite, if you're an asthmatic,' he replies. 'A paper bag is for when you hyperventilate, but when you have an asthma attack the problem is you don't get enough air.'

The woman beside begins to mumble. 'Anna…' she gasps. 'It's Anna, not Alma… Anna Dee—'

'Enough, Alma,' he interrupts, gently. 'Please, I mean it. You've found her. She's here. Now tell her.'

'Alma?' Zeb exclaims, turning towards the woman by her side. 'But you said you were—'

'No,' Alma gasps, tightening her grip around the door handle with a shaking hand. 'Not… like this… Brian. Not… now.'

Not like what? Zeb thinks, reaching for her own door handle as the car slows to a halt at another blind junction. It can't be far from here back to the hotel.

'Sorry, love, faulty child locks,' he says without turning around. 'But you don't want to be getting out now, surely?' He waves with a dismissive hand towards the bleak, wind-swept landscape, now dashed with slants of sleet. 'There's water in the back footwell if you're thirsty, by the way,' he adds, almost kindly.

Zeb sees a bottle of water at her feet. It looks full; its seal unbroken. But she doesn't move.

'Two peas in a pod,' he mutters.

An odd couple, Zeb thinks, as the car rides over a bump in the road. What past do the two of them share? They must be around the same age, she guesses, though that's as far as any similarity goes.

The man, Brian, has a physical intensity that makes her think maybe he's served time in the forces. He speaks with a flat, anonymous accent peppered with the occasional East End intonation. Alma, though, seems to have come from another world – an artist, her birdlike frame and slender hands suggest – though she, too, speaks in a flattened, neutral tone that gives little hint of where she might have been raised. England, certainly; southern probably.

Is this the same woman whose plaintive love letter she found at Dad's, what now seems like weeks ago?

The driver sighs. 'Like mother, like child.'

The cry this elicits from the woman sitting beside Zeb is more like a yelp of pain; desperate and uncontrollable. Involuntary. And it is this – more than anything that has been said so far – that feels most shocking. Makes her realise the seriousness of the situation. Forces her to admit that she, like Anna – Alma – is completely at their driver's mercy.

The car, which has turned onto an A-road to bypass the village she noticed a little earlier, is circumnavigating a large, inland expanse of gunmetal-coloured water. But with no signposts visible, it's impossible to tell if they came this way before, and nor can she see which direction they are driving. *If he won't stop...* she thinks, remembering Fraser with a dread that verges on hysteria. *How. Can. I. Get. Out?*

'Look, I should explain,' she gushes. 'I've a friend who's been hurt and he needs my help. So perhaps if you let me out here?' Another car will come along soon enough, surely? But before she can continue, Alma reaches out a hand as if to reassure, then quickly lets it drop.

'I'm so... sorry,' the older woman gasps.

What's wrong with her? Zeb wonders, regarding the stoic toughness in her fellow passenger's face. This woman seems like the sole survivor of some catastrophe, the wreckage of which she has dragged herself through against all odds by sheer strength of will. But then Zeb is struck by something else. The unexpected memory of the photo she found in that memory box of a younger, smiling Dad beside a pretty young woman. It was taken in a pub garden somewhere. They were standing hand in hand. 'You know, Elizabeth…' Alma begins.

Zeb turns towards her, sharply. Is this the same woman in that old snapshot, thirty years on? she wonders. *It can't be.* There is a hardness about Alma that makes her seem at once both broken and resilient; passive yet, in a curious way, threatening. The woman next to her is surely some kind of chancer. Zeb narrows her eyes.

Alma watches her companion as she struggles to regulate her breath. 'Pete would have… so… hated this,' she wheezes eventually.

Floored in an instant by this unexpected reference to Dad, Zeb's spirit folds in on itself then crumples as she turns away.

Outside, the air is filled with snow. Inside, the car windows have begun to mist. Her face feels damp and hot. Her coat is still twisted around her – she should take it off; but to do so would be like admitting she knows she's going nowhere, and that would be like an admission of defeat.

Closing her eyes, Zeb reluctantly finds herself back in a tree-lined cemetery.

The morning of Dad's funeral had dawned unnaturally bright. So bright that as she left the chapel the white light wrought in her a curious sensation, like being reborn. She remembers, too, the flowers laid across the stone flags just outside the main door. How overwhelming they were in their textures, scents and colours. How different was the stranger's tribute, so simple and plain. How she read then reread the card with its cryptic message and no name.

Straightening up, she'd stared across the sea of granite and stone towards the solitary figure in the ragged shadow of what in a few months' time would reveal itself as a maple, staring back at her. Thick-set. Square-shouldered. Dressed in black.

With a gasp, Zeb's eyes open.

'It was you,' she exclaims, fixing her gaze on the rear-view mirror. 'At his funeral. In the graveyard after. You were there.'

Alma groans. 'I... asked him to because... I couldn't.'

Zeb stares at the woman, hoping to find some sort of reassurance, but Alma has slumped back against the headrest. Though her eyes are still open it is as if she is shutting down, somehow – closing in on herself. Zeb's head is throbbing and she's becoming increasingly uncertain whether this is her imagination or for real.

Until, suddenly, she sees the outskirts of Beauloch.

'Just here would be lovely, thanks,' Zeb cries out. But as the crossroads comes into view Brian shows no intention of slowing down: they overshoot the turning up to the Round House, then speed right past McLellans.

Zeb prods Alma's arm to get her attention but now her head is lolling. 'Wait a minute, you said—' she begs. The thought of Fraser pinioned by the mantrap, broken and bloody, is dizzying and for a second or two Zeb fears she will be sick. But when nothing happens she moves her hand to the inside catch on the passenger door. Weighs up the speed at which the vehicle must now be travelling. Assesses the potential risks of barrelling out. Remembers the faulty child locks.

What the hell does Brian think he's...?

Her consternation quickly fades, to be replaced by something else. Fear. For as she stares into the rear-view mirror, willing Brian to meet her gaze, Zeb sees his sights are set; his attention is elsewhere. He is fixed on the unfolding road and with hope of finding help for Fraser fading fast, Zeb's grasp on the present – her sense of self and desire for escape – melt away, to leave only despair.

Succumbing to fatigue, her body is all out of fight. Her eyes close and the world fades into darkness.

Chapter 26

As soon as Alma pushes open the door to Pete's flat she is struck by its fetid smell. Feeling her way down the inside wall, she finds the light switch. She steps inside and shuts the door, then dashes along the corridor into the sitting room to throw open both windows.

Leaning with arms crossed against the sill, she stares out at the cityscape below. Allowing her eyes to trace the railway tracks, she starts to calm. Mapping the roads like concrete threads, she ponders the legions of nameless towns and faceless cities that lie beyond the uncertain horizon with their promise of anonymous sanctuary.

A sharp breeze makes her step back from the window. She turns to survey the room: the collection of dirty plates on the side table; hand-washed stockings on the fireguard with the suspender belt still attached; a plastic bucket containing a soiled terry nappy.

Alma gags. Hurrying into the kitchen, she stumbles towards the sink and gulps handfuls of cold, running water. After a few minutes she takes rubber gloves, a roll of dustbin bags and a bottle of bleach from the cupboard beneath. Holding her breath, she flushes the liquid mess from the bucket down the toilet and seals the nappy in a knotted polythene bag.

Only once she has liberally sprayed both sitting room and kitchen with cologne she's found in the bathroom does she check the rest of the place, opening every window. Until, finally, she steps into the spare bedroom and sees the wooden cot.

Nappies stiff as boards hang from the radiator beneath the window, though these ones are clean and dry. Someone has left a pin hairbrush on the windowsill; its spikes are clogged with long bottle-blonde hairs. A plastic make-up pouch as big as a granny's handbag lies on its side on the bed. On the bedside table someone has left a diamond and emerald ring.

Alma sinks onto the edge of the candlewick bedspread and shakes her head. The place feels transformed since she was last here, only a week ago. And when she'd seen Pete for lunch earlier that week, he'd made no mention of having guests. She stares at the array of lotions and cosmetics. More hair lacquer. Expensive conditioner. Baby oil.

Is this Cyn's stuff? Is it possible the woman used to stay here before marrying Phil and still has a key?

Sweat runs down one side of Alma's face. Wiping it away, she takes off her coat then shrugs herself free of her jumper. She must leave, she half-decides, impulsively rising to her feet. But where else can she go?

A child's cry just outside the front door makes her brace.

'Are you here yet?' a woman calls, unlocking the front door then stepping into the flat. At the sound of the child's whimpering, someone moving around the sitting room, windows being roughly closed, Alma freezes. 'Come on – show yourself. I know you're here because I'm in the hallway looking at your bag. I need you to keep an eye on this one while I get some stuff to take back to the hospital. Pete told me to tell you he won't be long.'

Chrissie's voice is getting closer, louder, so with nowhere else to go Alma steps into the hallway.

'There you are, though what you were up to in there God only knows. No matter, now you can make yourself useful.'

The two women stand and stare at each other – long enough for Alma to register Pete's cousin's smudged make-up and messy hair and the toddler in her arms. Damp hair plasters his crown, while his mouth is a tight pinch, sucking furiously on a plastic dummy.

'How's Patsy?' Alma offers.

'Who cares?' Chrissie snaps.

'Only I thought you said you needed to take something to the hospital,' Alma stammers, taking a step back.

'Not for her, for Phil,' the woman repeats. 'He's having some tests. I'm taking him some bits and bobs as Cyn is out of action. I work for him now, see? It's all official. I'm Phil's personal assistant, or didn't you hear? Pete knows. He even sent me a congratulations card. I am surprised he didn't share that with you.'

Alma digs the nail of her right forefinger into the palm of her left hand. Don't rise to it, she tells herself.

'I mean, what do you do when your ex-husband gets cancer?' Chrissie presses on. 'Bleeding obvious, isn't it? Overdose on antidepressants, of course.' Without warning, Pete's cousin thrusts baby Tony into Alma's arms then barges past into the bathroom to take a pee. 'Because if you're Patsy, everything always has to be about you,' she calls out through the open door. 'Poor old Phil, it's the fucking story of his life.'

Alma stares in shock at the baby she is holding. He seems remarkably placid, if not limp, as if he's diverted all his energy into maintaining his scowl. *What is he doing here*, she wonders. *Where is his mum?*

'Where's Cyn?'

'In bed with flu,' Chrissie chuckles. As she reappears by Alma's side she gives her wet hands a final rub on her trousers. 'That's how come I ended up holding the baby. But Phil needs me and I won't let him down. So now it's over to you. Talk about perfect timing.'

Alma is lost for words. How could Pete do this to her? Though of course this can't be his idea. He would be livid, surely, if only he knew. But for now he isn't here. Which leaves her feeling unexpectedly powerless. She is unsure how to object. She recalls how readily Chrissie ended her relationship with Brian, the bastard son, following the birth of Tony – Phil's only legitimate heir. She suspects the woman's opportunism is as boundless as it is brazen.

'Tony, sweetheart, be good for Auntie Alma,' Chrissie chirps. 'Everything you'll need is in that bag over there,' she adds, gesturing towards an occasional table beside the front door, beneath which another holdall brim-full of baby things is stowed. Then she opens the front door.

'Hang on a minute—' But by the time Alma has carefully placed Tony on the floor then stumbled out onto the communal landing, Chrissie is stepping into the lift. 'Wait, please! What should I do if Pete gets back first?'

The lift doors close.

Alma stares at the row of doors for the other flats, praying for someone to pop their head out to see how they can help. But though she knocks on each, no one answers – not even the owner of the flat from which, when she puts her ear against the wood, she can just make out the second concerto from Vivaldi's 'Four Seasons'.

Reluctantly, she steps back inside Pete's flat and shuts the door.

'Don't you worry,' Alma ventures, staring at the child still seated on the floor. 'Mummy's coming later.'

Inside Tony's bag of things she finds an assortment of clothes, a bottle of milk, a selection of baby food in jars, and a cuddly elephant. She reaches for the bottle. She moves to lift him. But the child suddenly arches his back, making his entire body go rigid, just as Alma is about to take his weight.

'Now come on, don't be like that,' she soothes, sitting back. They stare at each other for a moment in silence then, lifting him up once more, she sits him on her hip. 'Can't we be friends?' The child lets slip a half-smile. She doesn't see the door key he's picked up and clutches in his closed fist which the next moment he pokes into her left eye.

Reeling backwards, Alma cups the side of her face with her free hand, as instinct makes her hold Tony close against her with the other. Tears run down her face and her left eye feels ripe enough to burst but she won't, can't, let him fall.

As the shock starts to subside, Alma sinks to her knees then gently sits the child by her side. Tentatively, she feels her face. The skin is all sticky and wet but when she checks her fingers thank God there is no sign of blood. The pain starts to ease. She walks unsteadily towards the bathroom where she douses her face in cold water then pats it dry.

How on earth will she occupy the child until Pete comes home in a couple of hours?

Back in the hall, Alma takes care this time to make sure Tony's hands are empty before picking him up. Holding him close, she walks him into the bedroom and places him in the travel cot. Gripping the headboard, he quickly pulls himself to his feet. He spits out his dummy then lets out a fierce scream as it tumbles to the floor.

Alma stares helplessly as his face puckers into a purple knot. Perhaps he is hungry or, worse, needs changing. But the thought of battling to remove his clothes makes her head spin. She tries to think. He felt dry when she held him against her just now, which surely means it is more likely he needs food and sleep. So she fetches a teaspoon from the kitchen. And then, as the child watches her pull a jar of food from the bag, his wails subside to a whimper.

Alma begins to feel pity for the child left alone with a stranger. Wiping her eyes on her sleeve, she twists open the jar's lid then smarts at the cloying smell of sweetened apple.

'How about lunch?' she offers, brightly. 'Something to eat, then a little nap?'

Alma holds out a spoonful then laughs in relief as he opens his mouth. Unsure how much of the food to give him, she feeds him until he begins to lose interest, then takes the bottle of milk from the bag. When he extends his hand towards it, she holds it up for him to drink.

'Slowly, slowly,' she urges, pulling away the bottle. But it is too late. Tony is crying again – more urgently this time.

Alma holds him tight against her as he pulls away with all his might. She raises him slightly so his head lolls on her shoulder then rubs his back, but his bellows only get louder.

With tears now running down her own cheeks, she paces the room.

Round and around she walks, jiggling the child gently, one arm around his waist; desperately working his back with her free hand – until, after minutes that feel like days, he emits a loud belch. As she marvels for a moment at her nascent maternal instinct, something warm trickles down her neck.

Swapping hands, she feels her palm is damp.

'There, there,' Alma tells him – firmly this time, making no effort now to round the edge from her voice as she walks him to the bathroom and lowers him back onto the floor. 'Better out than in.'

Holding him down with one hand, Alma unbuttons Tony's suit with the other then gently bounces him over the bath until the dirty nappy flops onto the porcelain. She stares for a moment at a string of tiny purple bruises arcing from the child's waist to halfway down his left hip. Like fingerprints, she thinks. But softly touching the largest makes him lash out and kick her squarely in the belly.

Caught off guard, Alma cries out in pain then fear as Tony slithers from her grip. It isn't a high fall, just a few inches. Still, it's awful to watch as he falls back onto the porcelain. Lies there for a moment, silent. Widen his eyes. Puckers his mouth into an affronted 'o'. Then his body starts to shake with silent sobs.

'Sssh, Tony, it's OK,' she soothes, reaching forward to pick him up then cradling him towards her. 'I'm so sorry, darling, silly, silly me, but you're all right, really, you're all right. Everything's going to be OK.'

Thank Christ, thinks Alma, stroking the silken skin of his neck just below his hairline. Not a high fall, just a few inches. A foot at most, certainly no more. Carrying him back to the cot, she lays him down on his back and draws the curtains. Reassured by the gentle sound of a thumb being sucked, she creeps towards the door.

Back in the sitting room, she changes her shirt and slips off her boots then lies down on the sofa. But as she tries to get comfortable, a sudden realisation makes her tremble.

The abortion is a grim reality she's all but forgotten during the past hour with Tony. But now, at the thought of the tiny, stubborn human sleeping in the room next door, she can't help but wonder if there might be some other way. Perhaps she could lay low for the last few months and have the baby adopted. Or maybe she could keep it and drop out of college, get a job in a bookshop, teach music or something. It is, she knows, a ridiculous plan, which she and Pete have already discussed and dismissed. Yet despite this, in recent weeks it has become a familiar motif.

Alma thinks of her parents. How disappointed they'd be if they knew. How she let them down and is now poised to do something far worse, because in their eyes going ahead and having the baby would be the Christian thing to do. She imagines them standing by her as it was the right thing to do. The three of them shouldering the inevitable scandal. The burden being the lighter through the sharing. Guilt would make her grateful. And though she'd be obliged to stay, a prisoner, that would be a fitting penance.

Tony is silent now, yet her head still jangles from the intensity of his earlier cries. Her neck feels stiff and her nerves frayed, but now something else is bothering her. A vague, butterfly twitch deep inside below her ribs. Her eyes snap open. Staring at the dome of her belly in disbelief, Alma waits for some further indication. But there is

303

none. It can't have been – not this soon. More likely a muscle spasm triggered by getting upset. Or indigestion… though, as usual, she's skipped breakfast. A hunger pang, then. Straightening her top, she creeps into the kitchen but finds nothing to eat.

From somewhere nearby comes the wail of a police siren.

Back in the sitting room, Alma walks towards the window. She can see traffic is at a standstill, gridlocked in every direction. The thought of how this will impede their escape makes her spirits drop further. Resuming her position on the sofa, Alma closes her eyes. He won't be long, she tells herself. Everything will be OK.

–

The room is dark when Alma wakes some time later. She peers at her watch but it seems to have stopped. She turns on the radio. The sudden blare of 'Bohemian Rhapsody' makes her flinch. Unnerved by the clash of rock guitars and grand piano, she hastily retunes the stereo and finds instead a concerto: something by Brahms. Settling back against the cushions, Alma gives into the music as the notes wash over her.

Come Monday afternoon it will all be over, she tells herself.

And life will carry on.

She thinks of how rubbish she's been with Tony. Of his solid warmth when she picked him up. She's never held a baby before – has never had the chance, let alone wanted to – but the experience has moved her; awed her, too. How dependent and vulnerable he is. How, in the steadfast anger etched in his face, she glimpsed the man he would become. Will she see that in her own baby's face, too – if it lives? Rolling onto her side, Alma hugs her knees.

Don't give in to this, she urges herself. It is too soon for what's inside her to be either girl or boy. A foetus is just a foetus until it's born.

She switches off the radio and turns on the TV. Wrestling on one channel; Elvis Presley in a Hawaiian shirt on another. Leaving the set on mute, she heads for the bathroom. But as she approaches the room where she left Tony, something makes her pause. How soundly he sleeps, she marvels from the bedroom doorway.

The room is peaceful. The cot is silent.

Almost as if he isn't there.

Alma steps into the room and creeps towards the cot. Looking down on the baby, she stares hard at the stillness of his face. Struggles at first to decode his waxen cheeks. His limp hands with fingers uncurled. Unmoving. So peaceful he barely looks…

Her glare drops to the baby's chest, waiting for it to rise and fall, then back to the empty face; willing a lip to quiver.

But something seems wrong.

'Hey,' she whispers, leaning over the side of the cot and reaching out to lift him. 'Tony?'

His skin is cold and as she lifts him up the weight feels awkward against her hands. Without warning, his head lolls to one side. She keeps quiet for fear of making him cry. A voice inside her starts to jeer. *What have you done?* But he is sleeping, that's all, she decides, wiping her mouth clean of blood. How can a child be fine one minute and not the next?

Grabbing the cellular blanket from the far end of the cot, Alma fumbles as she wraps it around the child then realises too late that she has obscured his face. She desperately tries to loosen the fabric and let him breathe.

Alma? the voice says. *Put him down.*

What should I do? she panics, desperately. *Ring for an ambulance?*

Do it, comes the reply. *Tell someone – someone in authority who'll know what to do. Even though it's too late.*

Alma places the bundle on the bed and walks into the sitting room in search of a phone. But as she tries to lift the handset halfway to her ear, her hand refuses to move. *A child I've been looking after is dead,* she rehearses inside her head. But that makes no sense because there's been no accident. *I didn't hurt him, or anything.* Which is when she remembers how, while changing his nappy, he slipped from her grasp. Not a high fall, just a few inches.

Alma, what have you done?

A foot perhaps, certainly no more.

Call them and you'll be the one they blame.

She stares at the phone.

Leave him and go, now, before it's too late.

If I put him back in his cot – just the way I found him, then leave, will anyone know? Apart from Chrissie. Unless I hide him.

Alma stares at the bag of baby things the woman left her. She could use it to take him outside. Leave him somewhere. But the thought of this is just too awful. Through the window she can see it is raining and though not yet five, it's getting dark. He'll be frightened; cold, too. To leave him outside in the darkness would be too cruel.

A noise from the communal hallway makes Alma sprint towards the front door. Finally, he's come. But as she reaches for the catch, a woman's voice makes her hand freeze.

'Alma! Open up – I can't find my key.'

Alma casts a glance back down the corridor towards the bedroom.

No, they mustn't find us like this.

Back in the bedroom Alma lunges towards the cot, snatches the sheet and wads it into a tight ball. Spotting an empty laundry bag beneath the window, she quickly gathers up the rest of Tony's things then stuffs everything inside. The room looks clear, she decides. Which leaves just one thing. Staring at the shrouded body, Alma weighs up the space still left in the bag.

Yes, there is room, she reasons, calmly, picking him up just as Cyn hurries in.

'Here, you don't want to be doing that, he won't be able to—' Cyn reaches for her son before Alma can react. Grabbing the bundle, her hands fumble to free the blanket covering his face. 'What's wrong with him? Why's he not moving?'

Time stops as the mother leans over the baby. Unwraps his body. Picks him up then hastily puts him back down. Looks at Alma in mute shock. Spots the bag almost packed. Guesses what she was about to do. Accused stares at accuser. Sees the shadow that now clouds the mother's eyes. Acknowledges not just her shock and horror, but hatred. Rage.

Someone sobs as Alma slips to the floor; it could be her. Then finally the other woman speaks.

'What. Have. You. Done?'

Some time later somewhere close by, strangers talk in low tones.

No, pleads the voice in Alma's head. *You've got this wrong. I did nothing. It was an accident. Not deliberate or intentional. Why would it be anything else? I don't even know you. Please, I meant no harm, you've got to believe me.* She shakes her head at the sound of sirens. Are they from outside or on the TV?

Hands grip her, pushing roughly.

Please, it wasn't me.

Someone guides her along a hallway. She is dazzled by strip lights. They walk past where a sofa should be. She hears sirens. Walkie talkies. The blare of breaking news from a TV. She is made to sit on a hard, wooden chair. Eventually, a man speaks.

'What's your name?'

Though she answers, he does not hear.

'Alma,' another woman says.

'After that singer?' asks the questioner, gently. He is a policeman. His voice is kind. He'll understand. Won't he?

Somewhere close by there is weeping. A voice on TV talks about a man being shot. Ross McWhirter was there, too. Stood on the doorstep of his family home. More sirens. Whatever it was happened in Enfield. Too loud. So confusing.

'Turn that ruddy thing down.'

'So wicked,' says the neighbour.

'I said—'

'Why did you do it?'

'Sorry, Sarge.'

'Shot in the head at close range.'

'How could you kill my baby?'

'Make her a cup of tea, would you? Lots of sugar.'

The room slips in and out of focus.

Did I do it already? But no, I can't have – not without Pete.

'You were supposed to mind him, just for an hour or so.'

I didn't do it, not me.

'Please, take her to the kitchen.'

It's Saturday, not Monday.

'What went wrong?'

It was me. I went wrong. Lied to my family. Let bad things happen. With Leonard, Pete. Took money, though I meant to give it back. Because it was all about me. Not the baby. Us. Just me. Listen. Please, understand.

'Were you jealous?'

Me.

'Did he slip?'

All about me.

'She's evil, that's what she is.'

Me and my word—

'You know what you should do with someone like her, don't you?'

—my word, against hers.

'Lock her up, that's what.'

Not a bad person. Just a bad mother.

'Lock her up and throw away the key.'

Chapter 27

'Miss Hamilton?'

Her eyes open onto a world without colour. Just blankness. An expanse of white. Clean and true. Until she moves her head. Away from the bulb that blinds. Refocuses onto the lines between the pale ceiling tiles. Tilts her head to face the man who now stands by the side of her bed.

'Yes.' She replies without doubt.

He smiles. 'Well, I must say, this is starting to become a habit.'

'Sorry?'

The man has a white coat and silver-fox quiff. He holds out a hand. 'Dr Prentiss.'

'Yes, of course. I'm sorry, I just—'

'No need to apologise,' he beams.

Zeb is in a curtained cubicle this time rather than her own room, in a side bay on a busy A&E ward – she can tell by the sounds, though the patterned fabric obscures the view.

'No need to ask where I am.'

'Indeed not,' he demurs.

And then, she remembers. 'What's the time?'

310

Dr Prentiss glances at his watch; it looks reassuringly expensive, with an azure face. 'Just gone five.'

Zeb frowns. 'Wednesday?' He nods. 'Thank God,' she exclaims. 'It's my friend, I was trying to get help when… he's in a field a mile or so outside Beauloch with his leg caught in a trap, someone needs to—'

'It's OK. He's fine – or will be. I saw him a short while ago,' the doctor says, checking his notes. 'Fraser… Kiernan?'

'That's him.' Zeb sinks back against the pillow. 'Yes,' she sighs.

'He lost a lot of blood and needed quite a few stitches but, otherwise, the leg will mend. As for you, how's the head and shoulder?'

Zeb sees for the first time her left arm is in a sling.

'A temporary measure to hold it at the right angle after the dislocation,' Dr Prentiss explains before she can ask. 'We've X-rayed everything we need to and apart from that you're in the clear. Although I'd like to keep you in for observation for tonight given it's your second head bang in as many weeks, just as a precaution.'

Gingerly, she nods in acquiescence. Her head still hurts, yet the tension in her body has already been eased by the reassurance of knowing Fraser is not just OK, but also close by.

'Now all we've got to do is find a bed for you for the night,' the doctor concludes. 'Don't go anywhere, I won't be long.'

Zeb thinks of the back seat of Brian's car where she must have passed out beside Anna. Or, rather, Alma. Alma Dean. Their exchange replays in her head. *You've found her, now tell her*, the man, Brian, had said. And something else.

Like mother, like daughter.

Can it be true?

Zeb thinks of how Alma looked when she last saw her – in a bad way. She wonders how she could find out what happened to her and, if indeed there is a way, whether she should try. Alma is a stranger to her, after all. A mother who turned her back on her child. A woman whose reappearance in her life has triggered no flicker of recognition and with whom she feels no affiliation or bond.

What's passed is past, finished. Done.

I don't have to know her to know who I am or where I'm going, Zeb tells herself, though as she does, her resolve starts to quaver. Because inside her there is a twist of doubt. A niggling realisation fed by the reluctant knowledge that as a result of recent events – the split with Richard, her struggle to cope, Dad's death and now her mother's return – her life seems to spinning her round and around. That without acceptance and resolution she will continue to struggle to move in any direction at all, let alone forward.

Another patient is wheeled by and a voice just beyond the curtain catches her attention.

'A little girl, called Evie,' a man says. The voice is familiar.

'Why, I've a boy the same age, at the same school,' a woman replies. 'His name is Billy. Is Evie in Mrs Mitchell's or Miss Halligan's class?'

Fraser – it has to be Fraser, Zeb thinks.

She lowers her feet onto the floor. Though she is fully clothed, someone has removed her shoes which are now neatly stowed beneath her trolley. She sways, then her head quickly settles. Cautiously, she parts the curtain.

To her right, a nurse is supporting a teenage youth on crutches as he hops along the central aisle towards a sign marked X-Ray. In the opposite direction, a nurse is pushing a patient on a trolley out of the A&E area through a pair of double doors.

Without stopping to find her shoes, Zeb chases after them. But by the time she reaches the corridor, she finds it is empty. She reads the departments and directions listed on the wall opposite. Which way might Fraser have been taken? Following the signs, she makes her way towards the nearest set of lifts. But there is no sign of Fraser nor any hospital staff to ask, so Zeb has little choice but to head back towards A&E. She tries to open the swing doors, but instead they are parted from the inside by a porter pushing a wheelchair.

'Elizabeth? Thank God. We wanted to make sure you were OK,' his patient cries.

Zeb stares at Alma in bewilderment. She struggles to find the right words – any words – to respond as, a second later, Brian appears behind the porter in the open doorway. Horrified, Zeb lets slip a gasp and backs away.

'I'll take it from here,' Brian declares, taking control of Alma's wheelchair from the porter. He turns to Zeb, his eyes noting her bare feet. 'No more running, for either of you. You and Alma – your mother, here – have got to talk.'

–

They sit opposite each other in the hospital's ground-floor cafe, a cluster of tables and chairs in the main atrium. Juvenile clusters of silver birch grow in pine-clad troughs. Brian has made some excuse about needing to check the car. Ambushed into this reunion, there's no place left for either of them to hide; nowhere left to run.

'There's no point in saying sorry,' the mother begins. 'But please, please let me try to explain—'

With a shake of her head, Zeb dismisses these words. The enormity of the chasm that this woman has created (and now seeks to fill) feels unbridgeable. But then, as Alma's hands start to shake, Zeb finds her hostility start to diminish.

What choice do I have? *I need to know*, she thinks.

'OK,' she murmurs softly.

'We loved each other very much,' her mother begins. 'When I fell pregnant with you I won't pretend it wasn't awkward. We were young, it happened too early. We both had our doubts, considered other options. But I couldn't... and then when you were born... you can't imagine how awful that time was. The only thing that made it almost bearable was knowing Pete would always be there for you.' Her voice cracks. 'Just like he said he'd always be there for me.'

Only it hadn't quite worked out like that. As she reaches for her cup her hand shakes, spilling some coffee. For they had to be apart, she explains. They had written to each other – week in, week out. But then, as time passed, Pete's responses had slowed. Until she had to move further north and his visits tailed off altogether. This was some time after he met Wendy.

Zeb shakes her head. What her mother is saying makes little sense. First she talks of *other options*, now she's blaming Dad. Why did they have to write? What possessed her to move away? 'I'm trying – I really am, but I'm sorry, I... I don't understand.'

'You're right,' Alma says, faintly. 'I'm not being clear. I think I need to start again.' She breathes in then exhales, slowly. 'Look, Alma. Soon after you were born... I went to prison.'

'OK,' Zeb answers, slowly, as her mind races. A criminal, though she hardly looks it. What was it: drugs, theft, fraud? 'But that still doesn't explain—'

'For a long time. Years.'

'Years?'

Alma nods. 'It was to do with... the death of a baby.'

Zeb opens her mouth to say something but no words come. Instead, all she can do is stare at Alma as she works to decipher precisely what the woman is saying. 'You've got to believe me, it's not how you think,' her mother continues. Her words tumble out now, fast. 'I didn't do it.'

A baby killer. Though she pleaded innocent, the woman is a convicted baby killer, Zeb thinks. That's what she's saying, isn't it? The words conjure an alien, tabloid world of deadly viruses, drunk drivers, neglectful mothers and careless social workers who fail to spot abuse. Women responsible for their babies' deaths.

'I didn't do it,' Alma repeats, forcefully. 'But it was my fault.'

Zeb shuts her eyes, but Alma carries on, undaunted.

About how she fell pregnant too soon and considered an abortion. But then, rather than go through with it, someone else's baby died instead. A terrible accident. Even so, soon after her own baby was born, Alma was sent to prison. But by now Zeb is struggling to listen. She is thinking of her father. No wonder Dad chose to leave this woman; to lie. Because she knows him – knew him – and there is no way he would ever have seriously considered an abortion; that must have been Alma's idea.

Help me, says a voice. *Please, Dad, tell me what to do.*

Zeb reaches into her memories in search of a gentler place and she finds herself outside an ice cream parlour with Dad and Wendy overlooking a tiny Mediterranean harbour.

Dozens of yachts are moored round an ancient stone jetty. Tanned crew members sat in waterside bars chatting loudly over beers and cigarettes while mysterious young women in chic swimwear baked themselves on the boats' scrubbed decks. All she could hear was the hearty collision of French, Italian and German voices as she, Dad and Wendy sat eating ice cream beneath a giant parasol with stripes of custard cream and toy-box blue.

It was 1993. The summer after she sat her A levels. In Corsica, she recalls, as her eyes snap open. Why the hell am I remembering this now?

Alma is watching her daughter, attentively. And as Zeb stares back into her mother's eyes she sees not anguish, anger or regret, but passive acceptance. A dead-eyed expectation that she will be judged badly. Resignation to her fate.

Who are you? Instigator or victim of the disaster that broke you? then, before Zeb can soften it, the question is out: 'Whose baby was it?'

Alma shakes her head. 'It's complicated.'

'And what do you mean it was your fault?'

'I mean, he died. But I didn't kill him. Back then it didn't have a name but they call it shaken baby syndrome these days.'

'You shook him?'

'No, but he fell – not far, but it winded him.' Alma wipes her eyes. 'It was my word against the pathologist – there were no such thing as expert witnesses back then. Severe brain haemorrhage was the official cause of death. They found damage inside the skull. Even though it was too much to have happened just that one time. In more recent cases, the same kind of injuries have been found to have been inflicted weeks before death.'

Zeb shrugs. 'So why, if that's true, did they find you—'

Her mother laughs, a bitter sound. 'What's that saying about the past being a different country? They did things differently in the Seventies.'

'And no one believed you.'

'No. And I guess I wouldn't have believed me either. I was in such a state I didn't know what I was doing.' Alma's eyes cloud. 'The prosecution said I did it in a "frustrated, unhappy and resentful rage".'

'And did you?'

'I don't think so, no.'

'You don't think so.'

'Oh Elizabeth, listen. Did I mean to hurt him? No. But I was guilty... in other ways.'

'Because you wanted to get rid of me.'

Alma lets loose a wail. 'No. Not like that.'

'Like how, then?'

'We thought about it, yes. But then it was—'

'—too late.'

Zeb watches a tear slide down Alma's face. Is she being unfair? Her mother had been little more than a child. Maybe it was some kind of accident. And whatever Alma considered doing while she was pregnant, Zeb had been born fit and healthy; had been well cared for and deeply loved.

A vibration in Zeb's pocket makes her go for her phone. It is a text from Matty, she sees – quickly scanning her son's mistyped request for her to come home soon, and bring him a likeness, ideally soft and cuddly, of the Loch Ness Monster. She breaks into an indulgent smile, which swiftly fades when she sees how curious Alma is, how she views the close-up of Matty which serves as wallpaper on her mobile phone. No, Zeb thinks. I will not comment or explain. You'll have to earn it.

'How long were you in prison?' she asks.

'I was released in 1990.'

My God, thinks Zeb. She was in prison for the first fourteen years of my life.

'That must have been… hard.'

Alma nods again.

'But you never stayed in touch.'

'I did, for a while.'

'And then what?'

'Pete, he—'

Zeb frowns. What's this woman suggesting, that her father somehow kept them apart? But no, none of this was his fault.

'Dad what?'

Once more she has a sudden image in her mind's eye of Corsica.

Dad's there and Wendy, too, laughing as they hunch over a large bowl-shaped glass piled high with ice cream. There were five different flavours – vanilla, chocolate, coffee, pistachio and something else. And cascading down from the peak was a sugary avalanche of coulis, nuts and whipped cream. It was a real adventure – no one she knew had ever been there. And a surprise, too, for usually they holidayed closer to home: a couple of weeks in Cornwall,

Wales and, once, ten days in a borrowed tent in rain-lashed Normandy.

But this year will be different, he said, mysteriously. *Something special.*

'After all this time, does it really matter?' sighs Alma. 'I wasn't there for you. And then, when I was finally released, it was too late.'

'No it wasn't – I would have understood.'

'Trust me, it was too late.'

Zeb's eyes fill with tears. 'So you gave up on me?'

'No,' begs Alma, reaching for her daughter's hand. 'Never.'

'Why didn't you write?'

'I did.'

Zeb shakes her head. 'How can I believe that when—' And then she remembers the memory box she found in Christine Allitt's flat. 'How did you get those things in the box you sent me?'

'You father sent them to me. I kept them all that time. But then, when I heard he'd died—' Alma pauses, to wipe her eyes. 'I thought you should have them. They belonged to you, after all.'

'Because you wanted to see me.'

Her mother nods. 'I did. But then I got cold feet. There was so much going on – not just with you, but an old friend whose son slashed his wrists. I wasn't thinking straight. And that's when Brian offered to help me get them back.'

'Get them back?'

'It was a mistake. I'm so sorry if he scared you – that was never my intention.'

Zeb is unconvinced. 'He was too early,' she mutters dryly. 'Mrs Allitt, the old woman in the flat next door, had been taking my post. It was all in her flat until I got it back.'

Alma's face pales. 'Allitt?'

'Christine Allitt.'

'An old friend of your father's?' the older woman asks, weakly.

'I don't think so, but she has lived in the place for years so maybe they did know each other once, a long time ago, when he lived there.'

Alma slumps back in her chair. 'After Tony.'

'Sorry?'

'Pete bought the flat... after Tony.'

'Really, I don't think—'

'It doesn't matter.' Alma exhales, as if regathering her strength. 'Look, I'm very sorry,' she continues, when at last she speaks again. 'I was selfish. Always have been. You're entitled to your own life. Peace of mind. I should never have got in touch. I don't deserve—' she waves her hand, vaguely '—this.'

Turning towards the cafe counter, the older woman beckons Brian who, unnoticed by Zeb, has taken a seat at the table closest to the cash desk. A moment later, he is by her side.

'Can you help me to the car?'

'What, now?' The man looks crestfallen.

'I think it would be best,' Alma says.

'You're wrong, you know,' says Brian, turning to Zeb. 'Alma is a good person. And if she'd had a chance she would have been a good mother, if it wasn't for Pete. Who are you to judge? Without knowing what really happened, you can't know what he was really like.'

Zeb's jaw clenches. Dad wasn't in the wrong, she knows. He was a straight man who led a decent, honest life. A good father. Her rock. That's what the name stood for in Greek, he told her once. She had trusted him and always would. Suddenly, she hears his voice.

\-

The end of her last year at school deserved marking, that's all, he told Wendy.

It was late on their final night in Corsica and they were sitting on the balcony beneath a starlit sky. Zeb was supposedly sleeping inside. The recent death of a distant relative Zeb had never heard of meant they could afford to treat themselves, just this once. The funeral had taken place at a crematorium just outside London, while Zeb was at school. There'd been no mention of him before, which was strange, as for some reason the old cove had remembered his estranged nephew in his will. Or maybe Dad was a second cousin, once removed. Either way, his secretiveness had infuriated Wendy.

I thought you trusted me, Pete, Wendy had snapped back. It was the only time Zeb remembers ever hearing her stepmother and father row. *First you refuse to discuss what happened with Zeb's mother, and now this. Who was he, Pete, this Uncle Phil?*

You've always said you had no family.

\-

'What do you mean?' Zeb demands, turning angrily towards Brian, for she is sure now that both of them are lying.

Dad was a good man. Alma, her mother, is a convicted criminal and, at best, naive. And this oaf before her, Brian, is a liar. How dare he suggest she doesn't know what her own father was really like? She thinks of Matty. Fraser was right, she now understands. *They didn't want me and I didn't need them*, he'd said of the parents who'd had him and his sister adopted. *Life makes us who we are. Trust me, you're better off not knowing.*

Zeb stares at Brian. 'What do you want? Why are you lying to me?'

'Stop it!' cries Alma, grasping the wheels of the chair as she struggles to remove herself from the table unaided. 'Nothing. He means nothing,' she insists. 'I'm sorry. For this. All of it. Everything. It was a mistake. I should never have got in contact. Please, let's just leave it at that.'

Chapter 28

'This isn't goodbye,' Pete smiles, squeezing Alma's hand. 'We'll be with you every step of the way, whatever happens next.'

They are seated on a wooden bench in the narrow strip of shade cast by the pebble-dashed side of the two-storey visitors' block. With their backs to the wall they sit rigidly, without touching. Elizabeth is finally sleeping, in the pram which is parked by their side, beyond the sun's reach. The warden who so grudgingly allowed them their brief escape in order to settle their fractious baby stands a short distance away. He is pretending not to listen as she smokes her cigarette.

Alma wipes sweat from the side of her face. The hot spell began in mid-June. Now officially designated a heatwave, the newspapers are predicting this summer will be the hottest in more than 350 years. Too hot for the other remand prisoners and their visitors to venture out. But with Elizabeth so restless, they had no choice.

'I know that,' she nods. 'It's just that with the trial about to start, it seems so close – you know, me being sent even further away.'

Pete frowns. 'If you're found guilty.'

'If. Yes. Of course.'

'And even if the worst does happen, it might not be North Yorkshire, you know.'

'Yes,' says Alma monotonously. 'I know.'

'Listen,' he presses on, once more squeezing her hand. 'Whatever happens, we'll deal with it, OK? You, me and Elizabeth. We've come so far unscathed, haven't we? She's doing well. I'm coping. You've been so strong. If it comes to it, we'll move to be close to wherever you are.'

'But your work—'

'My work will be just fine.'

Alma shakes her head. 'I know, but if only we had family, you know? I mean, I wouldn't want my parents to raise Elizabeth or anything, but if they took an interest – that would be something, at least.'

'It's still early days, Alma. Maybe they will come around.'

'Or if your mum…'

Pete releases her hand. 'I know, but she's dead.'

'Sorry.'

He nods. 'Me too.'

The warden clears her throat. Having caught the pair's attention, the woman mimes tapping her watch then holds up five fingers. Alma nods. 'Any news from anyone, then?' she asks. At Christmas, her former roommate had got back together with Geoff. By Easter she'd dropped out of The Conservatoire and gone travelling with him. They could be back any day now.

'Viola?'

'Damn,' Pete exclaims, reaching for his jacket and pulling a postcard from the inside pocket. 'Sorry, I nearly forgot. She sent this.'

Alma stares for a moment at the picture. It is a photograph of a Keralan houseboat with a cabin made from woven reeds. The craft is pictured floating in a drowsy backwater lined with coconut palms. *Greetings from the Malabar Coast*, is the caption. Scrawled on the back are the words *Wish you were here*.

How easily people move on, Alma thinks.

'Thanks. I'll add it to my collection.'

'Brian sends his regards.' She nods. 'He and Chrissie have officially split up, too, though I guess we could see that coming.'

'She still thinks I did it, then?'

'It wasn't just because of that. She's been seeing someone else – an older man.'

'I can't say I'm surprised, she always was a—'

'I know. But she's also my cousin.'

Though Alma says nothing, Pete's stubborn loyalty irritates her.

Family first, she thinks. As always.

From the pram, a flutter of coughs breaks the silence opening up between them as Elizabeth stirs. Though they rise as one, Alma gets to the baby's side first. The child is lying on her back, dressed in a short pink gingham dress over a plump terry nappy. The child stares up at Alma and smiles.

'Go on, pick her up,' Pete urges.

With both hands, Alma gently lifts Elizabeth to her shoulder. Her heart skips as she soaks in the baby's living, breathing mass. Her intimate smell. But then, as a tiny hand reaches towards the chain around her throat with its dangling silver piano, Alma has a sudden memory of Tony. She stumbles back.

'No,' she gasps, fumbling against the tiny fingers, trying to loosen their grip on her necklace. 'I can't. Take her, Pete. Please.'

Within seconds, Elizabeth is safely enclosed in Pete's arms and eyeing her mother cautiously.

'It's OK, Alma,' Pete murmurs, bobbing the child in his arms until she starts to giggle. 'Just take it one step at a time.'

–

'Who's the kiddy?' asks Aileen Duffy, squinting. She leans across the bed to get a better view of the picture Alma has just stuck on the wall, above the bedhead.

'My daughter, Elizabeth.'

Aileen chuckles, indulgently. 'She's a pretty wee thing, isn't she?'

Alma smiles. 'I know.'

'What's the special occasion?'

'Her birthday – last weekend she turned seven. Have you got kids?'

Her new cellmate's face clouds. 'No. At least, not yet. But I will. Not a prissy little girl, though – it has to be a boy for me.' She laughs. 'Though I mean no disrespect.'

Alma sits down on the edge of her bed beside Pete's letter which is still folded inside the envelope. The letter is late and she can see he has written on just one sheet this time, not three, and is disappointed, given it was Elizabeth's birthday ten days ago, so she is savouring the moment and taking her time. There'll be a reason for this delay, she knows. Just like there was for the last one. But she can't help thinking that Pete's dedication to a regular, open and all-embracing dialogue – albeit paper-based – is beginning to wane.

'Have you got anyone?' she asks. 'You know, back home?'

'Back in Scotland? No, not now,' the other woman sighs. 'Which is why I'm here at all, though let's not get into that.' Noticing Alma's expression, she quickly presses on. 'Don't worry, he's still with us, if you get my drift. Let's just say, I gave him what for when I caught him with his pants down making out with my best friend.'

'Your best friend? That's tough.'

Aileen shrugs. 'That's their nature, though, isn't it? Men.'

Alma turns back to the wall and the latest picture of her daughter. She is standing on a chair at the dining room table, blowing out the candles on a three-tiered chocolate birthday cake. She is flanked by four or five other girls of a similar age. Each has long, wet hair. Either they've overheated through excitement or they've just got back from swimming, Alma guesses.

Standing behind Zeb is Pete, casually dressed in jeans and a tie-dyed T-shirt, and a slim, dark-eyed woman she does not recognise, with a wide, open smile and a sleek chestnut bob. The pair stand close but Alma's daughter obscures whether or not their hands touch.

You're being stupid, she tells herself. *Overly suspicious. Paranoid.* Yet it would be difficult for anyone, surely? Fifteen years is such a very, very long time. Maybe she could ask Brian. He is her only other visitor, after all. And he was there, of course. At Elizabeth's party. It would have been him who took the picture.

She squeezes Pete's letter out from the envelope.

The first thing she notices is that the writing seems bigger, too, with a stilted feel that slows its flow. She skim-reads for any obvious cause for concern. But there is nothing that immediately stands out.

Elizabeth has lost another baby tooth. The party went well. All's good at school. And the photographic studio Pete set up has just had its best year. Meanwhile he will be taking the pictures at Chrissie's wedding next month. After seven long years Bernard Allitt, the older man Pete's cousin has been dating, will finally make an honest woman of her.

Alma wonders if Elizabeth will be going to the wedding but guesses not. Which is just as well. Of course, Cyn has had no contact with any of them since Tony's death and then, two years ago, Phil's death following the return of his cancer. Even so, it is important Elizabeth learns nothing of this side of her so-called family, and of what happened, until she is old enough to understand. And that won't be until Alma and Pete can tell her, together.

We've got to put Elizabeth first, always, Pete had said.

So, reluctantly, she'd agreed that Pete should stop bringing Elizabeth to the prison so regularly. When she was younger and they lived only an hour's drive away it worked fine. But when Alma was moved to a prison north of Birmingham, it was just too big an upheaval for them to move house again, given Elizabeth had settled in so well at the local primary school.

The most important thing, he said, *is that she knows she is loved and cherished by the people who matter.*

So Pete would record their child's every milestone for her, and send pictures, too. And while he worked at home to keep Alma alive in their daughter's hopes and dreams, she would write regular letters to Elizabeth that the three of them would open, together, when she was free.

All that matters now is us.

Alma had believed Pete because she wanted and needed to.

Soon after her trial her own father, with his reputation indelibly tarnished by the publicity, had resigned his parish post and accepted a non-public-facing administrative role working for a neighbouring diocese where he was less well-known. The lighter duties enabled him to care for Alma's mother when, five years later, she was diagnosed with cancer. Then, soon after Angela Dean's death in November, Reverend Dean suffered a fatal stroke.

With Pete now Alma's only family, and parole becoming possible after serving her minimum term, their focus has to be not on the day-to-day difficulties of weathering their separation but what will come next. And whatever it is could come sooner than she'd dared hope, as her solicitor is now advising that a review of her sentence might be possible within just a couple of months.

'Cheer up, it might never happen!'

Alma looks up to see Aileen, now seated on her own bed, watching her intently. 'Seriously, girl,' her cellmate cautions. 'You'll do yourself no good if you give in to the black dog and start to brood.'

Alma lets the letter drop onto the mattress. After the lies she told, the mistakes she made, the woman is right. She considered depriving her own child of life. She ruined two people's lives – three, when you consider Tony. She bore a daughter she is scared of hurting. She mucked up everything for Pete. She must be punished. She does not deserve the luxury of hope, given everything she did.

As for looking to the future, well, all she can do is take things as they come.

–

'Did you see her leaving Number Ten last night on TV? She almost had tears in her eyes, Alma.' Brian shakes his head. 'I mean, really! Did you ever think you'd see the day?' He chuckles. 'No more Iron Lady.'

Alma, who has been listening to music for the first part of their journey to London, looks up. Of course she had heard about Margaret Thatcher's resignation, the day before. As she sat in the canteen, slowly eating her final breakfast before returning to her cell to pack, all the wardens were talking about it. But no, she had not watched it on the dayroom's communal TV.

'It's on every front page this morning, of course,' Brian carries on, regardless. 'Here,' he offers, stretching his arm back to the rear seat without taking his eyes from the road. 'Look at the *Daily Express*.'

Alma stares at the front page, a picture taken through the open window of a limousine in which the former prime minister leans forward with glistening, bloodshot eyes. It seems strange to think that the time this woman has been in power almost exactly matches the duration of her stay in prison, powerless.

On the radio, music resumes as the news bulletin ends. The Righteous Brothers sing 'Unchained Melody'. The original recording had been one of Alma's mother's favourites.

Tapping his fingers against the steering wheel in time to the music, Brian laughs at a sudden irony. 'You know, everyone might think this is from *Ghost*, but back in the Fifties there was this prison film called *Unchained* and it was originally written for that—'

'I know.'

'Look, I'm sorry.' Brian says. 'I don't mean to say the wrong thing. It's just... Well, ever since I picked you up this morning, it's been like dancing on eggshells, you know?'

'Sorry. And thank you. For collecting me and for driving me to London.'

'Well, someone had to!' As Alma grimaces, Brian's mood turns thoughtful. 'So you're really going through with this plan to move to Scotland, then?'

'Yes.'

'And she'll be meeting you at the other end, will she, this friend?'

'Aileen Duffy, yes.'

'And you'd really rather get the train from London. Because I'd drive you all the way, if you wanted, you know.'

'I know.'

He would, she is sure. Only she relishes the freedom and the anonymity of simply buying herself a ticket then boarding the train of her choice from Euston. Perhaps she'll catch the first one, perhaps she'll eat a coffee and a sandwich first at a station cafe. But either way, she will be in control.

'Scotland is a long way away, you know.'

'It is,' Alma smiles.

That's why she's chosen it. Because she can't go back to London after so much has happened. The last thing she wants to do is try to salvage what fragments, if any, remain of her old self. London was a lifetime ago. What she needs is a clean slate to start again. Maybe a new name.

To be someone simple and forgettable.

An Anna, perhaps.

The plan is to move in with Aileen who, since her release two years earlier, has settled in a small village not far from Fort William.

Soon after leaving prison, her friend began a regular weekly correspondence with Alma that continued uninterrupted despite the upheaval and heartache she suffered over the next few years. At first, everything seemed to be going so well for Aileen, Alma remembers. Through a new job as a cleaner at a local hotel, she met and got engaged to a gamekeeper who worked on a local laird's estate.

But then, when she was eight months pregnant, everything went wrong. First, the man died in a car accident. Then, a premature and protracted labour brought on by the upset culminated in Aileen's son being starved of oxygen during birth. Though the child survived, her friend confided that only time will tell if poor little Davy is *all there.*

Alma's hope is she can help her friend while she sets about finding paid work to cover the cost of her lodging.

'A long way from Somerset, I mean.'

He means where Elizabeth now lives, of course. She nods again. 'Yes.'

Brian frets. 'You know I didn't know about Pete and Wendy, don't you? Not at first.'

Alma forces a smile. 'You don't need to worry.'

'When I think of it now.' The man shakes his head. 'I mean, falling for someone's one thing. But telling Elizabeth her mother is—'

'Dead, yes, I know. That was wrong.'

Totally and utterly wrong, she knows. Who gave him the right to issue her a double sentence?

While Alma had long-suspected he might eventually find someone else and settle down, even marry, she had grown increasingly resigned to this lurking dread. What he did next, however, had been far crueller than anything

she could have imagined. His lie to their daughter was –
still is – the ultimate betrayal. And it left her bereft, her
resilience weakened.

'What I don't understand, though, is this,' says Brian,
turning towards her. 'Why aren't you angry?'

Alma shrugs.

'What's done is done,' she says. 'Besides, what would
be the point? You can't force someone to love you again
when they've stopped. The more I thought about it, after,
the more I began to wonder if maybe it wasn't so bad an
idea for Elizabeth not to know me. I mean, she's done
fine so far without me. From what you say she's confident
and bright. She's doing well at school, isn't she? She has
plenty of friends. She's happy. And in four years' time
she'll leave home. Meanwhile, Pete sends me her news
and pictures—'

'But only at Christmas and on her birthday—'

'You keep me posted.'

'When I can. Though it's been tricky since I burned
my bridges with Pete. I shouldn't have said what I said,
but I was so cross when I found out what had been going
on behind your back. By the way,' he says, changing the
subject abruptly at a sudden memory. 'I ran into Chrissie
when I was in Camden at the weekend. She's bought a
flat now she and Bernard have finally got divorced.'

'Another reason to move to Scotland, then.'

'You're not wrong.' Brian laughs. 'She mentioned Pete
helped her find it and was so taken with the place he might
buy one in the same block, if another one came up – for
Elizabeth, as an investment.'

'That's Pete,' Alma replies, dryly. 'The perfect father.'

Chapter 29

Holborn, May 2016

Zeb stares at the envelope. It isn't the expensive grade of the paper that holds her attention. Or its creamy richness. It is the embossed lettering neatly centred across the flap on its reverse. Michael Jenkins & Partners LLP. A name she's never heard of, and can't remember Dad mentioning, ever. Yet it turns out this firm has been her family's solicitor for years.

It is Mr Jenkins himself who has just handed her the envelope. An elderly man whose half-moon specs teeter precariously on the brink of his Grecian nose. The guardian of Dad's secrets. Protector of the smokescreen to Alma's disappearance and the events leading up to her own birth. What's the word he used a few moments earlier? *Fabrication.*

The man was so coy, she can't help but be impressed that he managed to say it without even a hint of irony.

'Thank you,' Zeb answers, vaguely, her gaze drawn from the interior of this airless, top-floor garret in a Georgian terrace to the window, through which she can see the upper portion of a blossoming cherry tree.

The sudden knowledge that their time is nearly up – that she will soon be able to leave this dreary, fusty building – is reassuring. She glances towards her glass but she's drunk all the water. Either that or it's evaporated. When – if ever – would Mr Jenkins, or more likely his secretary, get round to adjusting the radiators to a spring setting?

Zeb reaches for her bag.

'Actually, before you go, Ms Hamilton, there is one last thing.'

Dutifully, she straightens up.

'This.'

Zeb reaches for a second sealed envelope being passed across the desktop. On the front, the address, which is handwritten, is Dad's. Before her fingers get close enough to take it, the solicitor's hand stops.

'It is a letter your father received last year. It was sent by the mother of the child who died while in your mother's care, Alma.'

'She's still alive?' Zeb gasps.

'The woman, Cynthia, married Phil Hamilton, your father's stepfather. Phil married your late grandmother, Patsy, when Pete was very little and raised him, which is why he – and you – share that name. But around the time your father left school, Phil left Patsy for Cynthia. They had a baby, Tony – the child who died.'

Cynthia. Zeb thinks for a moment but struggles to recall why the name seems familiar. 'OK. But I don't see—'

'Cynthia wrote to your father last year when she was diagnosed with terminal cancer. The letter is here, for you to read at your leisure. Your father was very specific that I should keep it safe and, when the time came, pass it on to you.'

'Thank you,' Zeb mutters, before dropping this letter and the larger envelope of Dad's papers into her handbag. She reaches for her coat.

Rising from his desk, the solicitor accompanies her to the landing to bid her farewell. 'Good luck,' he declares, shaking her hand in a grandfatherly sort of way, though his grip is formal; his palm cool. 'Go through everything in your own time. There's no rush.'

The spring sun blinds Zeb as she steps out onto the paving stones. Doughty Street – a road now inextricably linked to the story of her real father: the Pete Hamilton she didn't know.

At the thought of her dad here, standing where she is now, Zeb's anger starts to ebb.

She sees another text from Fraser – his third that morning. Still off work, recovering, he's been in London a fortnight teeing up prospective business for his outward bound courses. And as Zeb has struggled to come to terms with everything that's happened, which she knows she must do before her life can move forward, his presence has been a welcome distraction.

Having finally managed to persuade Richard that she had not taken leave of her senses by going back to Scotland, she's only just got Matty back and finding a way of looking after her son full-time is her top priority. Kirsty, her boss at the gallery, has refused to accept her resignation and she's been granted compassionate leave. Apart from this, she wants to delay any other important decisions or firm conclusions – for now, at least.

After the will's been read has been her personal mantra for weeks.

Zeb clicks on the text.

See you in the cafe by the sandpit, she reads. *PS Matty's hungry (again!). And Evie, as usual, needs little persuading.*

Zeb turns to her right and starts to walk.

The wide street, which has cars parked nose-to-tail along either side, is unusually still despite the steady buzz of engines from Gray's Inn Road just a block away. With a shake of her head, she loosens her hair, relishing the fledgling sun as it warms her face. And as she savours the vague sweetness of nearby blossom she experiences a curious sensation, like being roused from a deep sleep.

Heading north towards Camden and home, Zeb walks briskly. It's way too warm to wear her coat, which she has wrapped through the handles of her shoulder bag, and as she turns onto Guildford Street her shoulder aches beneath its weight.

At the first traffic lights she crosses into the shade.

A few minutes later she passes some railings beyond which, through the bushes, spring flowers are just visible along the far side of a flat expanse of grass. As she stops at an iron gate, she looks up at a vapour trail, hanging in the sky like a gleaming question mark.

A nerve twitches in her neck. What is it about staring up at a narrow strip of blue like this that seems so familiar? How many times have I done this before?

Her thoughts turn to a spring long, long ago. She was lying on her back in a garden. The world was so much bigger then, as she stared up through trees, their wadded branches thick with leaves, towards a distant silver dart. A plane, though she was too young to know. Captivated, she'd stared upwards, rapt, as an adult's face had eclipsed her view. A woman with light hair and pale eyes who hummed a tune as she lifted her from her pram. And from her throat dangled a silver chain.

Your mother, Dad told her when she was little and used to ask if he remembered, too. *It was her, yes.*

Where did this memory come from? Wishful thinking, perhaps. Or a film she'd watched on TV. Either way, she now knows it is false. When she was seven she was told her mother was dead. Then, three decades later, she discovered that was untrue. Either way, though, Alma couldn't have been with her because she'd been in prison – which made the memory of that morning just another lie.

Until not so long ago, memories were something Zeb simply took for granted. Like faded snaps in old photo albums kept under the bed. Why wouldn't you trust them? But it isn't just Dad's lies that have changed all that; it's the thought that in some way she is equally culpable. If her memory of that morning was always just wishful thinking, how could Dad be to blame for colouring it in?

Her thoughts turn to the weeks between his funeral and her first journey to Scotland. She remembers most of it now, though she still has eight hours or so unaccounted for – between the time she fled the Round House and when she was picked up by Jean. A conscious act of editing, perhaps. A protective shutter to help her deal with having provoked Davy's attempted suicide. Maybe she will never remember it all. But even if she does, it won't matter, because nothing will change.

'You going in, or what?'

Zeb looks down at a skinny boy of nine or ten who is standing in front of her with a football under one arm. He is dressed in a spotless Chelsea kit at least two sizes too big, with his thick white socks double-rolled at each knee. The lace of his left trainer is undone.

'Sorry?'

The face morphs to an impatient scowl. 'In there. Chorus Field.'

The child points behind her into the park where the large patch of grass stretches away beneath tall trees, towards an under-5s play area. To the right of this, through a wall of bushes that are still winter-thin, she can make out a number of half-size football pitches. An articulated lorry thunders along the road just a couple of yards from where they stand. As it draws near, it belches diesel fumes.

'Yes, sorry. Here you go.'

Zeb holds open the gate for the child, then follows him inside. They walk together for a minute or two along a gravel track. He wipes his nose on the back of his hand.

'I'm late. See ya.'

'Bye,' she calls as the child runs off towards the sports pitch. He slows just once, to hitch up his shorts.

Zeb turns towards the play area, locates the sandpit and the cafe which overlooks it, then walks in that direction. Coram's Fields. A children's park built on the site of the old foundling hospital. Though she's read about the place, she's not been here before.

Fraser waves through the cafe window. Beside him sit Evie and Matty. They appear to be eating sandwiches out of decorated cardboard boxes. Zeb waves back, then tugs the larger envelope from her bag and holds it up to show him. She heads towards an empty bench, intent on reading while the children are occupied. She sees Fraser smile and nod.

Zeb tugs free a handful of papers. The first to fall into her lap is a bundle of photocopied newspaper cuttings, to which a handwritten letter is attached with a large, silver bulldog clip. There is the copy of her birth certificate, which she was unable to find a few weeks earlier. And yes, it gives Alma's name. There is a smaller sealed envelope, too – also addressed to her – written in a familiar hand.

Zeb opens it quickly.

Her father's message is written in the grey-blue ink of the Mont Blanc pen she had bought for his last birthday. As she starts to read, she remembers with a stab of guilt the way he always wrote the date numerically, month before day then year, American-style. Only once she's logged every distinctive quirk does she start to read.

> *Dearest Zeb,*
>> *Can you remember the Easter of your last year at junior school, and the week we spent in north Wales at that bed and breakfast in Portmeirion? You made friends with two girls, I forget their names but they were the daughters of the couple who ran the place...*

Susan and Kate, flame-haired sisters who looked like twins, though really they were three years apart and loathed each other with a preternatural intensity.

>> *...I've thought many times about what happened that week, not how you could have done what you did, but how brave you were owning up to it...*

Tears begin to fall. Her face feels hot.

The letter was Susan's idea. *Just a joke on Kate*, she'd said, handing Zeb the kitchen scissors and a pile of Sunday supplements. *All you've got to do is cut up the words*, the girl urged, slyly. *And I'll do the rest.*

As soon as Zeb read the anonymous message the other girl had written she'd known it was wrong. Nevertheless, she'd done nothing. Just stood by as Susan sealed the

340

message inside then addressed the envelope in anonymous block print. Allowed herself to be frog-marched to the post box where she was made to post it, too. Susan had laughed as they did it, though Zeb had felt only regret at the realisation there was no taking it back as soon as it was gone.

When the letter arrived the next day, the girls' mother rang the police. It was the latest – though most upsetting and extreme – in an offensive series of anonymous letters sent to local residents, it turned out. Luckily their mother had snatched it away before her younger daughter had a chance to read it properly. *Only a pervert could have sent something so nasty*, the woman said.

On the last evening of their stay, Zeb was invited to eat supper with the girls in the farmhouse kitchen, which was usually out of bounds to guests. All these years later, she can still see Susan seated opposite, pinning her to her seat with a cold, unblinking stare as the girls' mother spotted the newspaper remnants Zeb had placed in her coat pocket.

Honestly, love, Dad confided, sadly, on the long drive home. *I'd never have thought it of you.*

Zeb turns back to the letter.

…What you did was wrong, of course, he continues. *But it took great courage to own up to it when you could have passed the blame. I only wish I'd been as brave and not taken quite so long to come clean…*

Here it comes, she thinks, quickly scanning the paragraph that follows outlining Dad's lie.

…You asked why she went away, when you could see her. Didn't she love us any more? he writes. *You were crying. I was conflicted. Guilty. Upset. Saying she was dead simply fell out. But I was the adult and I should have known better…*

Tears well in Zeb's eyes. Yes, it was true it had just slipped out. As young as she had been, she had seen his shock and anguish at her response.

Was it me? she'd begged him, feverish and quaking, again and again before she'd fled upstairs to hide beneath the blankets. Because if you died when you gave birth to someone, surely that meant whoever you gave birth to was to blame. If she'd not arrived when she had, maybe Mum would have been OK.

Daddy, please, she'd cried, over and over. *Did Mum die because of me?*

Zeb turns her attention back to the letter.

…There was an important reason why we felt it best for you not to know what really happened, Dad writes. *And now I'm gone, my lovely girl, it's more important than ever that you know the truth. But first you have a choice to make…*

There is a second, separate letter containing her mother's contact details which Zeb now takes outs.

…Before you decide what to do, think long and hard, he counsels *And while you do, remember that your mother was – still is, above all else – a good person caught up in a situation beyond her control. Think of a photograph, Zeb…*

Immediately, she thinks of the photo Alma sent of her and Pete in London, taken some time during the early Seventies. How young they both looked, and how in love.

> *…is an image trustworthy because it is of something that looks real, or because someone we trust made it? Or a news report. A good reporter, however honest, decent and truthful, will highlight some things over others. I wasn't perfect, but I did my best. As Alma did, too.*

*You must understand she came from a good
family and led a very sheltered life until she came
to London.*

*But she had spirit, a passion for life — and
courage, too, when I think of what she had to go
through, and how strong she was once she came
out the other side. I still think of the day I told
you that Wendy and I planned to marry. I cried
that day, remember? Tears of shame. Because it
was hard, us being without her for all that time —
harder than I ever imagined. And eventually I had
to decide, for both our sakes, it was time to move
on.*

*Remember, Zeb, if nothing else, your mother
deserves the second chance she never had from
me…*

'Excuse me, but are you here alone?'

A thick-set woman with blonde hair scraped back into
a ponytail is standing a few paces away peering at her
suspiciously through wire-framed glasses. Zeb puts down
the letter.

'Sorry?'

'Did you come in on your own?'

'Just now? Yes.' The woman folds her arms. Like a
bouncer, Zeb thinks. If you're name's not down, you're
not coming in. 'Well, I'm sorry, but you're going to have
to leave.'

'Sorry?'

'Adults are only allowed in when accompanied by a
child,' she repeats, impatiently. 'Didn't you read the sign
outside? It's the rule.'

'No I didn't, sorry,' Zeb replies. 'But when I said I came
alone I meant I'm meeting my son – he's eating lunch

with my friend in the cafe, inside.' She waves towards the window where Fraser is still sitting. He waves back.

'All right then,' the woman concedes. 'But as I hope you understand, these days we have to check.'

Zeb rereads the letter.

There isn't much else, really. She mustn't judge Alma too harshly. Nor should she trust the way the papers painted it. How Alma's decision not to be a part of her life was proof of her love for her daughter, not lack of it. How he wished he could tell her all this in person but that, of course, was now impossible. He mentions his various bank accounts – Michael has all the details – half of the contents of which are for her and Matty.

> *...As I don't know how you will be fixed when you read this, I'm going to leave how you deal with it up to you. But what I want to make known is that the other half should rightfully be Alma's. After everything she's been through, it's the least we can do. When you've thought it through, let Michael know.*
>
> *I know you'll make the right decision.*
> *Be strong, girl.*
> *All my love,*
> *Dad*

Zeb refolds the letter then turns her attention to the second envelope containing the letter Cynthia sent a year ago. Only as she rips it open does she recall why the name seems familiar. And in an instant she is back in Christine Allitt's flat having tea, gazing at the letter her neighbour had stolen from the stranger who turned up, uninvited, at Dad's funeral: Cynthia Purnell.

Quickly scanning the letter's opening lines, Zeb reads how this old acquaintance of Dad's is reaching out, as there is something on her mind.

…I've now been told that I am dying, Pete, though at times the twenty years since Phil's passing were not much better than a living death, Cynthia writes.

> *Often, I dream about how different life could have been – if he'd died sooner, or if my precious little Tony had lived. But life's not fair, Pete, as you know better than most.*
>
> *Phil seemed generous to those he cared for but at his heart he was a bully, only doing what he did to please himself. I know you and he never saw eye to eye, but you don't know the half of it. Which is why, in the light of present circumstances, I felt that at last I should get in touch. It was Phil who killed Tony, not Alma. I am sure of it.*
>
> *I lost count of the times he lost his rag with Tony in the weeks before my baby passed. It was the crying that got to Phil, especially late at night. He told me Tony would only learn if I was strong enough to let him be and cry himself to sleep. Then, when that didn't work, he'd go into Tony's room to tell him to quieten down. There was only one time I can recall actually seeing Phil throw Tony into his cot. But there were often bruises. I'm ashamed to admit, Pete, that I always knew it happened more than once.*
>
> *To be blunt, though our solicitor said otherwise, I never believed Alma was to blame. Obviously I never dared mention this to anyone, especially Phil. But then, when Phil died a long time after,*

I wished I had. Because I believe that leaving you and your daughter that money was his way of offsetting his lingering guilt.

Putting down the letter, Zeb flicks through the newspaper cuttings. The top ones are the oldest and cover Alma's trial. The ones at the back are more recent and outline other cases of shaken baby syndrome where convictions were quashed or appeals upheld. Struggling to make sense of it, Zeb picks the last item from the envelope – a cream-coloured postcard. On one side is printed Michael Jenkins' contact details, on the other is Alma's address and phone number.

First Dad, Zeb thinks, now Phil and Cynthia. None of them should have lied for so long. But then, who has any right to judge? I'm hardly blameless, either. Who is? How awful to have lived with so much for so long.

Raising a hand to her throat, she feels for the silver chain beneath the collar of her shirt. She wishes her dad were still here. Then her thoughts turn to Alma and how conflicted she feels towards her. Though it's hardly surprising, given how undeserving the woman appears – a result, no doubt, of the needless burden she's carried for so long.

What a waste of life, she thinks, as she takes her mobile from her bag.

'Mummy!'

Looking up, Zeb sees Matty aeroplaning towards her with arms spread wide. The wind is lifting his hair, and his expression is joyous. She closes her eyes, determined to imprint the moment in her mind. She can do this; be the best mum she can be. Work with Richard, too, in the best interests of their son. They may be a small family –

and fractured, too – but they are all she's got. The clarity of this thought, she senses, marks a coming of age.

As her son hurtles towards her, Zeb scrolls through her mobile's address book, quickly finding the entry she is looking for. She presses call.

It is the moment she's held off from for weeks, ever since she reluctantly accepted the woman's number. A step she's given more thought to than Dad could ever have expected. But now, at last, the mist has lifted and she can see. That there is no black or white any more, no right or wrong; just shades of grey. Dad could only ever do what he thought was best – the only thing any parent can do. He was merely mortal, after all. Like Alma.

Matty is by her side now staring up at her, expectantly. His mouth is stained with ketchup and there's a morsel of chip in his hair. Crouching down by her son's side, Zeb tugs him towards her.

'Who you calling?' he asks in a conspiratorial whisper.

Zeb lowers her finger. 'You'll see.'

The world around her becomes a distant hum as Zeb presses the phone closer to her ear. Once, twice, three times she hears it ring.

As she rehearses what she is about to say, she savours the unfamiliarity of the words. Considers the conclusion she has come to that Fraser is wrong: not knowing who you come from is not best. Recalls how she'd never been asked to speak of or to Wendy by anything other than her first name. Stares at the slender hands of the child before her.

Piano-playing fingers, the midwife who delivered him said.

At last she hears Alma's voice as the answerphone kicks in.

Zeb hangs up quickly, without leaving a message.

Chapter 30

Beauloch, June 2016

Alma prises the plastic cover from her paper cup and pokes the teabag with the wooden stick she's been given in lieu of a spoon. Because it's biodegradable, the woman behind the counter has just explained.

She scoops out the bag and drops it onto the side of the paper plate she used for the flapjack she's just eaten. Taking a sip of her drink, which she always has black, she relishes the brackish taste of it even though the water is still scalding. She replaces the cup on the wooden picnic table. Then, moving along the bench, she stares out from the hilltop viewing point.

A web of dry-stone walls divide the patchwork fields below. Ribbons of grey mark the tracks and roads leading back to Beauloch. Somewhere in the distance, hidden behind rolling hump-backed mountains, is Fort William.

This is the first time she has returned here, to the spot where she met Elizabeth on a brighter, warmer day. That was over two months ago, just before Easter – the weekend that traditionally heralds the reopening of the cafe. But now, with the landscape finally unfurling beneath a softening sky, the time is right to gather herself and face down her demons; the final – and now, absolute – loss of her daughter and the need, despite this, to carry on.

At the memory of their dreadful encounter, her eyes prick.

Though the yearned-for moment had come, Alma had found herself numbed by fear. For years she had lived as if her mind were cauterised – as if its neurons and synapses had been burned to prevent any spread of her infection. Yet rather than wipe the pain from her memory, all Alma had been able to think of as she moved towards her daughter was the sadness of an encounter long ago.

Shiny-eyed and defiant, Elizabeth had been just shy of five.

They were sitting either side of one of the tables in the visitors' room while Pete tried to juggle their daughter, a soft toy and a dog-eared book. Though she'd tried to calm her, Elizabeth was fractious and tired. Pete, with the cumulative strain of managing everything, had not been much better.

The child had cried out as soon as Alma had tried to hug and kiss her. To read her something. To make conversation with her via the cuddly tiger whose tail was held firmly in her right hand.

Don't want to be here, Elizabeth mumbled, sucking on her thumb. Don't want to be talked to. To be kissed, or held – she'd tried once more to wriggle free, more vigorously this time. Roughly enough to knock the table with a flailing leg and spill a plastic tumbler full of water. *Don't. Want.*

Exasperated, Pete had taken her to the far corner of the room which once a week was turned into a makeshift play area with an old rubber gym mat, a few cushions and two boxes full of second-hand toys. *This can't go on*, he'd said as their daughter sat cross-legged on the floor a few feet away, upending a duffel bag of Galt block-wood building bricks. *We've got to rethink this.*

Alma rubs each eye socket with the heel of her palm. She can still hear his voice.

There must be a better way for all of us to get through the next ten years.

Alma zips up her fleece. She digs in her bag for a tissue as her eyes start to water. As she fumbles, blindly, her fingers brush against the solicitor's letter she received in the post that morning. The envelope beside it – from Pete, personally addressed to her – is still sealed.

Whether or not there is some kind of apology, she expects a heartfelt explanation of how difficult it had been for him. How he had tried to keep the faith – and succeeded, too, for a number of years… But then, he would insist, who wouldn't have struggled with raising a daughter without any family support, while trying to maintain a business? It would have tested the resolve of anyone, even a saint.

Which, clearly, he was not.

Pete had left her a small annuity, the covering letter noted. And he ensured her daughter and grandson would be provided for with what was left. Which is what Alma would have asked him to do, if she'd ever had the chance. But now, as she sits on the hilltop, wondering for the umpteenth time this morning whether her decision not to read Pete's letter is the right one, she feels misused.

What happened with Tony wasn't Pete's fault. But nor was it hers.

Yet it was she who'd been forced to pay – with a quarter of her life. All these years later, she has just about come to terms with that. And yet, despite this, she still feels unfairly blamed. Tainted by the knowledge that, had it not been for Tony's death, another child would have died: her own. Infuriated by the fact that had that happened it would have been a joint responsibility – not just hers.

As she carefully places Pete's unopened letter on the wooden picnic table, Alma can't help but wonder what Viola would advise her to do.

They had exchanged letters a few times over the first few years of Alma's sentence. During that time, on returning from her travels with Geoff, her friend's singing career had stalled and she had switched to acting. But around the time Elizabeth turned three, the letters stopped.

She only found out what happened next by chance when, thumbing through an old edition of *Hello!* a few years later, she discovered Viola was dating an up-and-coming film producer, having recently relocated to New York. A few years later – by which time her old friend had married, borne three sons and proudly declared herself, this time in *Cosmopolitan*, to be a *soccer mom* – Viola was living on the West Coast administering some charitable foundation or other set up by her husband, by then a major player in Hollywood.

Two figures appear in a gap between the trees. Aileen and Davy are plodding up the hill towards her.

Glancing back at the letter, Alma makes her decision. She tears it in two, lines up each half and then tears them in half again and again until the message is confetti, scattered by the wind. She then whistles sharply to attract her friends' attention.

Davy, who clutches the empty dog collar, does not respond. He looks dejected, which is a shame considering the progress he's made in the fortnight since adopting the new puppy. The recent change of his prescription drugs has helped too. But as Aileen waves, something small and furry hurtles out of a clump of bushes and heads for the picnic table. With no time to think, Alma drops to her knees and opens her arms.

'Angel!' she exclaims, urging the bounding creature towards her. 'Come on, now.' Alma finds a bone-shaped dog biscuit in her fleece, which she offers up in the palm of her hand. 'Here you go, then,' she coaxes, gently. Then, grabbing hold of the puppy, she cradles her tightly. 'There's a good girl.'

Straightening up, Alma holds up the baby Alsatian to show the approaching walkers. Warm and solid, the dog crouches in her arms with one ear cocked; the other is down.

With a whoop of joy, Davy breaks into a run.

–

Alma's phone rings as the three of them are finishing their sandwiches. As she wipes her hands on her trousers, Aileen kicks the tennis ball they have brought for Angel. Davy laughs as the puppy stumbles in its scramble to chase it.

'Hello?'

'Alma?'

'Yes.'

'Goodness, I've been trying you for days.'

Alma's throat tightens. They have not spoken, even by phone, since they last saw each other in the hospital in Fort William. Though Alma has thought of her daughter often, she has struggled to find enough courage to get in contact with her via Fraser, and a letter she began writing remains unfinished beneath a pile of paperbacks on her bedside table. Because it is pointless. Existence is a brutal struggle for survival, rather than a rose-tinted happy-ever-after. Not everything in life can be resolved.

'Eliza— Zeb, is that you?'

'It is. Listen, there's something I need to talk to you about.'

'It's all right, I know.'

'You do?'

'I got the letter this morning, from the solicitors.'

'Oh. Well that's great, isn't it?'

'The annuity? Yes. It will be a big help.'

'What? No, not that. Dad's letter. He wrote me one too.'

Alma hesitates, her attention snagged by a fragment of ripped paper lodged between the slats of the wooden table. Idly, she places her nail into the gap and pokes it through.

'The letter.'

'Yes, you have read it, haven't you?' Zeb replies, quickly.

'Not yet, no…'

'Well, you must. It's important.'

'Actually, that might be a bit—'

'It's about Cynthia. Did you know she contacted Dad last year about, you know, what happened?'

Alma's chest tightens. 'No.'

'Well, you need to know she's been trying to contact you.'

'Oh no,' the older woman gasps. 'Really, I can't—'

Taking a seat at Alma's side, Aileen gives her friend's hand a squeeze. 'Are you all right?' she mouths. 'Is everything OK?'

'Listen, it's a good thing,' Zeb continues. 'Kind of. Cynthia wrote that she never thought what happened was your fault. Phil had such a temper he'd hurt Tony a number of times before. She said she felt terrible about what happened to you, but that she'd been so upset by Tony's death she had some kind of breakdown. She was on drugs but also drinking for many years. Anyway the thing is, she wanted you to know that she is sorry, and that she knows it wasn't your fault.'

'Not my fault,' Alma echoes.

Aileen watches her, expectantly.

'Yes,' says Zeb.

Alma struggles to comprehend the meaning of this moment – what her daughter is saying and, more importantly, why she has rung. Because she is guilty and always has been, in the broader sense; tainted, too, by what happened with Leonard and the subsequent decisions she made. A liar and a cheat. A naïve fantasist who dreamed her salvation lay not in her own sense of self and right and wrong, but with Pete. She was selfish and undeserving. Not a good person. Certainly a bad mother.

'Hello?'

Finally, she knows for sure that what happened to Tony wasn't her fault. But rather than relief, all she can feel is curiosity at the void in her emotions. The truth is numbing. It changes nothing. Her punishment had been unfair, yet she had chosen to embrace it.

What's left? Who is she now that Cyn's taken that away?

'Are you still there?'

What she endured was no more than she'd deserved.

'Mum? Is everything OK?'

Mum. She called me Mum.

'Say something, please, you're beginning to worry me—'

Alma gasps. 'I'm still here.'

354

'Can I see you?'

'Come here? I'm not sure that's a good…'

Aileen's vigorous head-nodding makes Alma pause. 'For God's sake,' her friend is whispering, emphatically. 'Yes. Say yes, you fool!'

'I'll think about it. Some time soon, perhaps. If you give me your number, maybe I can—'

'No, Mum. Today! I'm here already, in Beauloch for a few days, with Fraser.'

Without warning Alma thinks of Jean-Claude and what he said when they met in Vienna, about the importance of dealing with what happens in life and not letting it define you. Her hands start to shake.

'What's a good time? We'd love to see you.'

'I'm out at the moment, I'm not sure—'

'Hang on a minute.' Zeb's voice becomes muffled. 'What is it?… Oh, right. OK… Mum? There's someone else here who'd like to talk to you.'

'Really?' Alma mumbles, tightening her grip on the phone.

This isn't happening. Can't happen, she thinks. She mustn't risk her sanity by building her hopes up, then having them dashed when things go wrong once again. They've lived apart for so long; have coped without each other and will surely continue to do so, quietly. Each of them must protect themselves by turning their backs on the past and moving on.

As Alma thinks this, however, she knows it is untrue. To move forward, you need to know where you are going. But how can you know where you want to go if you're still fighting against where you are now? And that's what she's doing, surely: fighting against a present she's never wanted and – worse – actively hates.

355

Finally, she knows she must accept everything that's happened. It's the only thing to do if she is to be healed.

'Hello?' It is a child's voice.

Confused, Alma looks at Davy, who is squatting on his knees. He is cooing at Angel as he rubs her tummy, and as she squirms joyfully on her back the puppy offers a playful yap.

'Ooh,' the voice on the phone exclaims. 'Is that a dog?'

'It is. My godson has a puppy. Who's that?'

'It's me, silly! Matty. Can we come? Mum bought cake. Only I'd love to see the—' The child is paused for a moment by muffled whispers on the far side of the phone before speaking once more. 'Puppies are my favourite thing, ever,' he exclaims. 'But more important, Mum says, is we'd love to come and see you, too. We're really close by. Say yes, Granny, please do.'

Alma stares into space. She is oblivious to her companions. The puppy at her feet. Her family, holding their breath as they wait for her to speak. Until she finally starts to understand what's just happened. Who she's been talking to.

Her lips curve into a smile as the years between her past, present and future fall away.

Acknowledgements

Heartfelt thanks to Sallyanne Sweeney – for her unerring support, encouragement and sage editorial advice – and also to the rest of the team at MMB Creative. Thanks, too, to the wonderful people at Canelo – Iain Millar, especially, and also Louise Cullen and Emily Bedford. My dear friends Helen Meller, Helen Jones, Sophie McKenzie and Lesley Hannaford-Hill, whose support and love have carried me along the way. Lindsay McMurdo, Caroline Marshall, Philly Makepeace and Penny Kiernan for the same reason. And to Martin and Tom, always.